Friends and ~~Enemies~~

Best Wishes

Steven Turner-Bone

Steven Turner-Bone

Published by Turner-Bone Editions.
© Copyright Steven Charles Southcoat
All rights reserved

This book is a work of fiction. Names, characters, places, and incidents either are
products of the author's imagination or are used fictitiously. Any resemblance to
actual persons, living or dead, events or locales is entirely coincidental.

Also by Steven Turner-Bone

Friends and Enemies

The Enemy Within

Farewell to a friend

ISBN: 9780993548734

Printed by Book Printing UK
Remus House, Coltsfoot Drive, Peterborough, PE2 9BF

Acknowledgements

To people I owe much and without whom, I could not have written this book.

My wife Sue: for her help, understanding and patience, and putting up with me while creating this work.

The Fairfax Battalia of The English Civil War Society

De Bergsche Battery, Geertruidenberg

My editor, Geoffrey West

Dedicated to my Granddaughter
Isabelle Southcoat

Author's Note

This story is part one in the trilogy about Surgeon Mathew Fletcher, and is set at the beginning of the English Civil Wars. The background event to this story really happened. Many of the characters are based on real people, though Mathew Fletcher and his family did not exist.

One thing has become very apparent in the telling of this story, and that is, history repeats itself. The English Civil Wars came about because a King lost touch with his people and Parliament, and brought about a set of civil wars that changed this country's politics forever. Today, it's our Parliament that has lost touch with its people and the country is divided once again. As always, it will be the person on the street who suffers the most for the mismanagement of the country, just as they did nearly four hundred years ago.

The medicines and surgical procedures I describe in this book have been taken from original 17c medical and apothecary books which I have collected. Under no circumstances, do I recommend the use of these procedures today or any attempt to make any of the medicines; most of them are very toxic and very dangerous.

I have tried to preserve the historical accuracy of the events as they happened, but I have had to adjust events and timings to fit the flow of the plot line.

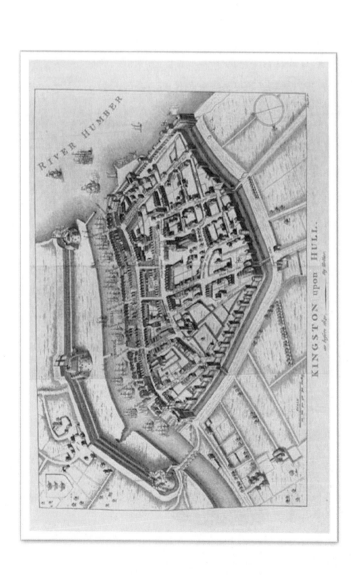

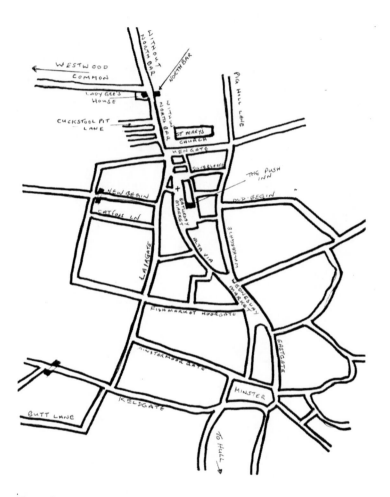

Beverley

Chapter One

This year was to be Mathew's year, or so he thought, in the same way, that all young men confront the future, he faced his with optimism and zeal. He would soon graduate from apprentice surgeon to a Journeyman Surgeon. He would be free to set up his own business and take on his own apprentices.

Daydreaming as he walked the streets of Hull on this cold January day, his thoughts jumped to Elizabeth, the apothecary's daughter. Free from the ties and conditions of his apprenticeship contract, he would be able to ask for her hand in marriage, if, he could pluck up the courage to ask her that is, and if she would take him. However, before that, he would have to ask her father's permission to walk out with her. Yes, he would find the courage to ask her, he knew he would, why wouldn't he? This year was going to be the year his life's dreams would all come true.

1642 was going to see him flourish in Hull. This busy trading port and town, exporting lead from Derbyshire, wool from the Yorkshire Dales, with grain and vegetables grown in the local fertile soils of East Yorkshire. Hull also boasted a fishing fleet and a whaling fleet. Dutch merchant vessels sailed the German Sea bringing goods from all across Europe: Coal Luggers came from Northumberland to unload their black gold, and a small garrison of soldiers was rebuilding the town's defensive wall. Hull also housed the second most significant arsenal in the country; only the City of London had a more substantial store of arms and black powder. The town was becoming prosperous and growing beyond its walls on the eastern banks of the River Hull. He would make his fortune here, he was sure of it.

After completing the errand for his master, Mathew Fletcher was on his way back to his employer's shop and home. The premises where he worked and lived belonged to Master Surgeon Adams and his wife. The surgery was situated just off the High Street, the main thoroughfare of Hull. It ran from north to south through the town, a mixture of wealthy merchants' houses, shops and warehouses. Today was Friday and Mathew had been trusted to buy linen from the market to turn into bandages. It wasn't a difficult job to buy the right linen, but it was an important one. He had to get the right quality of material: too thin and light and it would fall apart when cut into strips to make rollers, while if it were too thick, it would be of clothing weight and thus too expensive to use as bandages.

Making the linen into roller bandages of different sizes was the job of the younger apprentices, as Surgeon Adams liked to say; *if you cannot put the correct dressing on the wound, what's the point in treating the wound in the first place*. The giving of this errand to Mathew showed that Surgeon Adams trusted him, not only with his judgement but with his money. He had been apprenticed to Surgeon Adams for nearly seven years and was now his senior apprentice. Being trusted with money to purchase the correct medical supplies was as much a part of his training as the surgery itself.

2

He enjoyed these trips to the market, but today the weather was cold and damp, the wind blowing in from the German Sea. He pulled his hat down over his ears and tugged his coat more tightly about him. As he turned the corner from the market square back onto the High Street, he heard a commotion up ahead. It was the sound of horses in distress, dogs barking and people shouting, but as yet, he was too far away to see what was going on. However, sounds like this were not unusual in this busy town, so he didn't make much of it at the time.

As he drew closer to where the disruption was coming from, his step instinctively quickened. He could see two dogs lying dead in the street and a soldier cleaning blood from his sword. People were gathering around the rear of a wagon. A man he recognised as a neighbour to Surgeon Adams was lying on the ground. It was the baker who was crying out in pain, while a crowd gathered and pointed at him. As Mathew approached the scene, he overheard someone say, 'He's hurt awful bad!' Mathew grew more concerned and pushed his way to the front of the crowd to find the baker lying behind the wagon with blood pouring from a wound in his leg. The baker's wife knelt beside her husband, clearly overwhelmed by her husband's plight. His two grown-up sons tried to help their father get to his feet, but he was in too much pain.

Taking charge of the situation, Mathew examined the baker's leg. Finding it badly broken he ordered the bakers two sons to get a length of board on which to carry their father and directed them to Surgeon Adams, whose shop was just around the corner.

As Mathew had suspected' the baker's leg had been so severely crushed and broken when the wagon rolled back

3

over it, Surgeon Adams would have no choice but to remove the baker's leg from just below his knee.

Later that night, Mathew crept downstairs to the room in which Surgeon Adams performed surgery on his patients. Sat at the table Mathew looked down at what remained of the baker's amputated leg. It was very late; everyone else in the house was in their bed. The night air was cold; the embers in the fireplace had died back to a dull glow, and only thin wisps of grey smoke rose in tight ringlets up the chimney. On the table, alongside the severed leg, stood two good beeswax candle, but it was still hard to see the limb clearly in the artificial light. Mathew couldn't risk adding another candle, too much light or making any noise might disturb Surgeon Adams or his wife. So he made do with the dim flickering candles to light his investigation of the limb. As he worked, the candles cast his shadow on the plain plaster wall behind him. The draught from below the door causing the flames to gutter and dance, making his shadow on the wall prance about like a demon trying to escape the underworld. He worked as quietly as possible. If he were found with the remains of the leg, Mathew would not only be in a great deal of trouble for not discarding the leg as directed, but for keeping it to examine later, which by church law, was regarded as a sacrilegious offence, yet Mathew couldn't help himself. His thirst for medical knowledge was all-consuming.

He needed to know how the human body worked; he was driven by a compulsion to try and understand the mystery of life and death. Whenever the chance arose, Mathew would carry out his macabre research on body parts he should have disposed of after surgery. Earlier that day, Surgeon Adams had told him to throw the leg in the river with the rest of the daily waste, but Mathew had hidden it in a cupboard; he was going to learn more about the structure of the leg, how the muscles were connected together and to the bones and where the nerves ran to, and why?

Mathew was a man driven by an unseen devil of obsession brought about by the death of his mother when he was a boy. He wanted to understand why she had died and if, with better medical knowledge, it would have been possible to save her. So now Mathew did his research in secret, learning how the muscles, sinews, veins, arteries worked together, how they fitted around the bones and how they made the body move. There was so much he didn't understand, so much that was unclear to him, he wanted to know more, and not just become another butcher of human flesh, like Surgeon Adams, whose motto was, *if in doubt cut it out.*

The baker had been unloading sacks of flour from a wagon when a couple of dogs had startled the wagon's two horses. The horses shied away from the dogs and backed up, pushing the wagon over the baker. He had fallen awkwardly, the vehicle rolling over his lower leg, breaking the tibia and fibula, pushing the fibula through the skin and creating a compound fracture. Had the leg not been amputated the baker would surely have died of gangrene or shock from blood loss. As it was his chances of survival were still slim, for the infection that would inevitably set in after the surgery and the fever that would follow, would prove to be a more significant threat to the baker's life than the amputation.

Mathew examined the leg on the table before running his scalpel down the left side of the amputated limb and then turning the limb over he ran the blade down the right side, allowing him to draw back the skin and let it hang back over the heel and foot. Doing this revealed the *Soleus Muscle* and the *Gastrocnemius Muscles*, or what was left of the calf muscles after the damage caused by the fracture and surgery. The amputated limb showed the baker's muscles to big and powerful. Mathew guessed this was from the long hours the baker spent on his feet and from carrying heavy sacks of flour.

Pulling the muscle away from the shattered bones Mathew saw the torn *Periosteum*, the milk-white membrane which wrapped around the bones. He didn't know what its function was, or if it had one at all, it was one of the bodies' mysteries he would have to discover.

The top of the bones were splintered causing cracks to run down the remains of the tibia and fibula, only the membrane surrounding them preventing bone splinters from coming away from the rest of the shattered shafts. Mathew wondered if that was the function of the membrane, or if in some way it helped repair broken bones. He found the *Great Saphenous Vein* running over the calf muscles, sending out its many tendrils through the tissues of the severed limb. He could see, the *Calcaneal and Flexor Digitorum Sinews* which ran down from the muscles and attached themselves to the bones of the heel.

He had seen these things before, but he was looking for something that would give him a clue as to how God's magnificent creation worked. There were so many questions and so very few answers. He had been taught by Surgeon Adams, that if the blood were removed from the body, it would die; he also knew that if the lungs were prevented from filling with air, the body would die. His medical books and his teachings from Surgeon Adams told him that the blood nourished and warmed the body, and the air was the 'vital spirit', which cooled the body, the two working together keeping it at an even temperature. However, he wondered, did they do more than he had been taught? What was so special about the air we breathe and the blood that causes through our veins?

Over the years Mathew had proved to be an excellent apprentice, quick and keen to learn. Watching his mother's slow painful death from a kidney stone when he was ten years old had given him the desire to learn medicine. The physician who had attended his mother could do nothing for her; the condition was inoperable. The medical man had prescribed *Antimony*, *Sal Nitre*, *Crocus Metallorum* and *Saxifrage*, to be taken six times a day, expensive medicines his father could ill afford. The physician had given her laudanum for the pain, which had helped at first, but later, as the stone grew in size, had become ineffective. Eventually, her kidney had ruptured, and she had bled to death screaming in pain in front of him and since that day he had known what he had wanted to do once he had grown up. However, his father William could not afford to send him to university for medical training. So he had set him as an apprentice to Surgeon Adams in Hull. As a wheelwright, William Fletcher had hoped his son would follow in his footsteps, but it was not for Mathew. However, Mathew's older brothers Charles and Henry had continued in the family business and entered the wheelwright's trade. The best he could do for Mathew was to give him a chance at becoming a surgeon. He was proud of his sons and knew that if Mathew put his mind to it, he would make an excellent surgeon. The monetary cost of the apprenticeship had been high, but he knew Mathew would not let him down. Now Mathew's learning was nearly over, he would soon be a journeyman, but only if he could prove to the Guild of Barber Surgeons that he had gained sufficient knowledge to be accepted into their profession.

It was getting late, and though Mathew had made notes on the internal structure of the amputated leg, he frustratingly hadn't furthered his understanding of what made the leg move. He had been told that the fluid in the nerves carried messages from the brain, but when he had cut through the nerves, no fluid had drained out: it was just one of the many puzzles he didn't understand. He couldn't stay up much longer he would need to be up early in the morning. It was time to get rid of the leg. So he wrapped the leg in a length of linen and placed it inside a large bag to take it to the refuse tip beyond the gate that opened onto the Humber River. To be thrown where all the rest of the town's rubbish was dumped, and wait to be washed away by the tide. Mathew would have to be careful not to be seen with the leg in his possession. If he were stopped by a constable, he would have difficulty explaining why he was out so late and why he was carrying the remains of a human leg. However, if he avoided the High Street and the taverns that most of the constables frequented, by keeping to the dark lanes, all should be well. As a last resort, he could always fall back on the pretence that he'd been called to a patient who could not afford to pay the full price of a fully trained surgeon, and he was just disposing of their limb before morning. The trainee surgeon blew out the candles on the table.

Leaving the shop, he closed the door quietly behind him. Making his way down Lowgate, he turned left and crossed the western part of town towards Hull's defensive wall alongside the River Humber. A penny to the night guard and the gate was opened for him to throw the leg onto the mudflat for the next tide to wash it away.

Then he turned back and began to retrace his steps home to Surgeon Adams's shop. He'd not gone far before a dark shape crossed the street ahead of him and stopped in a shadowy doorway. Hull was not a town to be caught out and about while on your own, and in the dark. It was a busy port, with all the vices that such a place was associated with. He waited a moment. There was no more movement, so he continued on his way.

He had reached the bottom of Lowgate when the shadow jumped out in front of him: a tall, broad man with a long pointed knife. Mathew stepped back, pressing his spine against the wall of a house. His knees were shaking, and his blood was pounding in his ears making his head buzz. His focus narrowed to block out everything but the man with the knife up ahead of him. The man had unexpectedly hesitated a few feet away from where Mathew stood.

Mathew was unaware of it, but he was in deep shadow from the overhang of the house, the man opposite him could not be sure if Mathew were armed or not. The hesitation gave Mathew the few seconds he needed to gather his thoughts. Putting his hand in his purse, he drew out a few copper coins and threw them on the ground. The shadowy figure turned towards the sound of the coins as they hit the cobbles giving Mathew the chance to turn and run.

He ran all the way back to the shop, fear giving strength and speed to his legs. He paused at the front door, his hands trembling as he fumbled with the handle. Once inside he leant on the table gasping for breath and tried to regain control of his shaking limbs. He felt ashamed; he should have stood up for himself as his father would have done and had tried to teach him when he was a boy. He had only been accosted by one man, who had probably been drunk and had proved to be no real threat to Mathew. However, he had run away like a child, and he had lost money that he could ill afford to lose. However, what hurt most was his loss of self-respect. His only comfort was that no one else had been there to witness his cowardice.

Chapter Two

Two months earlier Sir John Hotham, MP for Beverley and councillor for Hull, received a letter at his family home in Scorborough…It read.

'Attend on me at the home of the Belasyse family,
Newburgh Priory, near the village of Coxwold, South of
Thirsk, on the 1st November 1641.
  I have asked Sir John to make you comfortable until
my arrival.
  Lord Newcastle.

Sir John Hotham had known the Earl of Newcastle for many years. But, strangely the letter gave nothing away as to why he should meet with the earl, though go he must, for the Earl of Newcastle had the ear of the king, and was useful to a man with ambitions, such as Hotham.

Turning to his clerk, Hotham started to make plans. 'Bottomley,' he began, 'we are going to Newburgh Priory—you are to accompany me, so start making preparations for the journey. This letter does not state why the Earl wants to see me or why the meeting is to be so far away from Hull. I suspect my Lord Newcastle has secret business he wants to share. When we arrive, I want you to note down everything that happens and everything that is said. When dealing with men like the Earl of Newcastle, it pays to be cautious.'

Bottomley nodded, 'Yes, sir.' He turned to leave the room, stopped and turned back to his master.

'Forgive me, sir. Do I understand you correctly, you do not trust the Earl? Only, I thought you were friends.'

'We are friends, Bottomley, but if this letter were from a true friend, he would have mentioned why he wants to meet me, and why we are meeting in such a remote location. I believe My Lord Newcastle is plotting something.'

The location which the Earl of Newcastle had chosen was a wise meeting place: isolated enough to be private, and owned by not only a loyal follower of the King, but one of the King's spymasters, Sir John Belasyse.

Hotham instructed his clerk to hire a plain-looking coach for the journey. If anyone should ask about Hotham's sudden departure from Hull, he'd left instructions to say that Sir John was visiting an old friend who had been taken ill in York and he had taken his clerk Bottomley to act as his servant while he was away. Were it known to members of the Hull Council that Sir John was going to a secret meeting with the Earl of Newcastle, one of the king's closest confidants, as a Member of Parliament it may have raised suspicions about his loyalties to Parliament? But, the simple ruse of the sick friend would suffice to cover his temporary absence. This opportunity of making himself useful to one such as the Earl of Newcastle could undoubtedly help his career prospects and was not an opportunity to be missed.

Hotham and his clerk set out for Newburgh Priory two days before the meeting was due to take place. The journey was long, cold and tedious in November. Frost covered the ground and the further away from Scorborough they went the thicker the snow covered the ground. The snow was beginning to drift, blown by the wind into the bottoms of hedgerows and the frozen field drainage dykes either side of the road. Heavy grey clouds skidded by overhead, threatening to deliver more snow soon; Sir John hoped they would reach York without incident. The freezing conditions were keeping the roads open for now; the unmetalled roads frozen solid. The carriage made rapid but bumpy headway over the iron-hard ground.

Sir John Hotham sat wrapped in a heavy woollen cloak with a thick blanket across his legs, wishing that the next stop at a tavern would soon arrive so that he could warm himself. Bottomley was driving the coach, fully exposed to the bite of the wind; he cursed Hotham for taking him along as he shivered in the biting cold.

At York, they broke their journey to stay overnight at one of the town's many inns before they carried on to Newburgh Priory the following day. In the tavern, Bottomley parked himself closest to the inn's fire, a hot bowl of pottage in his hand, and a plate with a large pie on the table by his elbow. He didn't want to think about facing the journey tomorrow, for now, the hunger in his belly and the pain in his frozen hands and feet were all consuming. Sir John Hotham had decided to eat in his room, sat by his own fire, and with a bottle of fine wine to help him sleep.

After an early start the following morning, the coach entered the grounds of Newburgh Priory before midday. Had they arrived during the summer they would have been greeted by four acres of Elizabethan formally laid-out garden. The Box Hedge sections of garden contained flowers depicting every colour of the rainbow during the warm summer days. Today they were covered with snow, with just the geometric outline of the formal designs emerging above the white surface.

Bottomley gladly left the coach in the care of the stable hands that ran across the gravel drive to meet them. Driving his master around the freezing countryside of Yorkshire was not what he was used to or cared to do again. He preferred to be at his desk with his books in the draughty guildhall office, with its fireplace, warmth and protection from the weather or at the sumptuous home of his master at Scorborough. Bottomley's limbs had become painful and stiff from the cold, and his back ached from being bent against the wind while driving the coach for the past two days. The unhappy clerk's hands were so numb he wondered if he would ever be able to hold a pen again. His only thoughts were for a bed and warmth. He gave a silent prayer *if only Sir John would leave me in peace for the rest of the day so that I could recover the lost feeling in my hands and feet.*

Sir John Belasyse and his son Thomas greeted Hotham at the door as the coach was taken away. 'Sir John, it is good to meet you at last. Lord Newcastle informed me that you would be arriving sometime soon.' As Lord Belasyse spoke his breath hung in the still, frosty air like a small white cloud. The frozen crystals of moisture glinting in the weak northern sunlight that failed to add any warmth to the day.

The temperatures had been very low over the past few days, and the bare twigs and branches of trees were covered in a hoar frost, making them appear as though they had been sugar-coated.

'I have rooms for you and your servant.' Sir John Belasyse led his guest into the house, leaving his son to deal with Bottomley and the luggage. As Hotham had stepped through the front door he was met with a narrow hall which ran the length of the central part of the house, its wood-panelled walls intricately carved with scrolls and stylised plant designs. To the right, through an open door, he caught sight of the dining room as it was being set for dinner by servants. Sir John led Hotham into a sitting-room to the left of the front door, the blazing fire in the grate and comfortable chairs, a welcome sight to any traveller arriving at this time of year.

During the afternoon the Earl of Newcastle arrived with Captain Legge. They too were warmly greeted by Sir John and his son. Before going to see Hotham, they were shown to their rooms, where Fisher, their host's steward, busied himself running between the two men fetching and carrying and tending to their needs. Lord Newcastle had decided to stay in his rooms, but Captain Legge came down to find Hotham sitting by the fire, a half-empty glass and a silver jug containing wine at his side while he read a book of verse by Francis Beaumont. Legge joined him, glancing at the author's name.

'A little scurrilous, wouldn't you say?' said Legge with a high tone of disapproval. Hotham closed the book, laying it carefully on the table.

'Care for some wine?' Hotham replied, ignoring Legge's jibe at his reading choice.

Legge poured a glass of wine. 'I have little time for poetry,' confessed, Legge as he sat in the chair facing Hotham.

'The book belongs to Sir John,' Hotham volunteered, referring to their host. Legge gave Hotham a sideways look and fell silent, staring at the red and amber flames in the grate as they licked at the logs stacked in the fire.

After the Earl of Newcastle had spent the afternoon resting, Fisher showed him into the room where Legge and Hotham maintained a stony stand-off. Hotham had gone back to reading the book of poetry and ignored the captain, but as Lord Newcastle entered he made a show of welcoming his friend. Captain Legge ignored the display of over familiarisation. Sir John Belasyse announced that a meal was being prepared in their honour, confessing that it wasn't often he entertained guests at this time of year and hoped the meal would be satisfactory.

As the evening meal drew to a close, the Earl of Newcastle announced, 'I have a special treat for you, gentlemen. I have acquired a taste for a drink they call 'coffee'. It is gaining favour among the more refined people in London, and I have brought some for you to try.' He signalled to a servant to bring it through. 'I understand a family of merchants by the name of Harvey import it from the land of the Turks and that their eldest son is a physician to the King. They tell me the drink is very beneficial to one's health. It is said that it strengthens a weak stomach, aids digestion, cure's tumours, and obstructions of the liver and spleen. Though I must warn you, gentlemen, its bitterness is an acquired taste, but there again so is tobacco, and we have all acquired a taste for the weed. I'm sure gentlemen such as your good selves will enjoy the experience of my new drink. My servant is preparing it for us. Shall we talk and enjoy a game of cards while we wait for it to arrive?'

While Sir John Belasyse's son Thomas, dealt cards around the table, the earl's servant arrived, carrying a tray on which stood a large silver jug with an ornately decorated lid and five small glasses set in beautiful silver basket frames with handles. Hotham had heard of coffee but had never been able to afford to buy such a luxury, so he was keen to try it. He was determined that, regardless of whether he liked it or loathed it, giving the Earl of Newcastle the right impression of oneself, was all important.

The following day, Sir John Belasyse arranged for a private room for his guests to hold their meeting.

'Hotham—get rid of your man,' the Earl of Newcastle ordered. 'What I have to say is not for servants to gossip about in corridors and behind closed doors.' Newcastle looked at Captain Legge then at Hotham, a severe expression on his face. Bottomley left the room.

Thomas Belasyse sat at the back of the room, impassively listening to their conversation.

'Gentlemen, the King needs our help,' began Newcastle. 'As you know he is having difficulties with his Parliament, so we are going to help His Majesty gain support around the country, and force Parliament to become sympathetic to the King's desires. To this end, I propose that you, Hotham, go to Westminster. You are to plant the idea in the minds of your fellow M.Ps that it would be in Parliament's best interest for them to appoint you to a position of influence within the council of Kingston upon Hull. The arsenal there and the location of the port will be useful to the King. The port is well situated for bringing the King's allies from Europe into the north of the country.

'While you are in London, Captain Legge will visit Hull and access its defences, after which, he will visit men of influence in the northern shires to raise money and military support for the King, should it be needed. You will tell them to make them ready to aid the King. I will attend on His Majesty, to advise him with the difficult decisions of state that are to come.'

Hotham rubbed his hands together, his mind racing through all the possibilities that could arise from aiding the King, and at the same time being in control of an important town like Hull.

'You are all aware, gentlemen,' Newcastle continued, 'that the King looks very favourably on those who prove their loyalty. Securing Hull for the crown could make you all very wealthy men.'

Lord Newcastle thought it prudent to sweeten the trap he was setting for Sir John Hotham and would stop him from thinking too deeply about whether or not he was being used.

Some weeks later at St James Palace, London

The double doors opened into the Royal State Rooms. A gentleman in a suit made of red silk, and carrying a jewel-encrusted sword entered. He bowed low, with his hat in his right hand, his left hand controlling the pommel of the sword at his side, as he waited to be recognised.

'My Lord Newcastle, it pleases us that you have made good time in attending on your king. The weather is foul, is it not?' said King Charles.

Lord Newcastle rose and replaced his hat as he drew closer to his sovereign.

'Your Majesty, I am, as ever, always at your service,' he responded. 'The weather is unimportant to me; whatever I can do to assist Your Majesty, you have only to command.'

The sycophantic manner of the Earl of Newcastle masked an intelligent mind and a shrewd head for business.

'Come, my Lord Newcastle, take a seat, we have need of your counsel.'

Lord Newcastle sat at a small table close to the fire while a servant poured him a glass of fine Spanish wine. The King paced the room, preparing his thoughts for what he was about to say. He had recently been rebuffed by Parliament when he had tried to arrest five troublesome members of the House of Commons. The men he wanted to capture had been forewarned and escaped.

'Parliament is rebelling against us—they are getting above themselves,' declared the king. 'They forget that I am the K-King of England, Scotland and Ireland, and rule by d-divine right and they need to be reminded of that.' He spoke slowly, trying to mask the slight stammer that crept into his speech when he became stressed. 'To that end, it is our intention to compel P-Parliament to bend to our will. Our plans require that we start from a position of strength in that the crown obtains the arsenal stored in K-Kingston upon Hull. It is our wish that you, my Lord Newcastle, secure the town and its arsenal for your king. With that in mind, and as our trusted servant, we are appointing you Governor of Hull.'

King Charles stopped pacing the room and looked out of the window at some distraction in the courtyard below. He turned back to look at the expression on Lord Newcastle's face. The latter had been taken by surprise at the news the King had given him; it had not been what Lord Newcastle had wanted to hear. The earl had to regain the initiative and stop the King from doing anything too hastily. Lord Newcastle had plans of his own that involved the King but wanted to choose his own time and place to disclose them to his sovereign and being governor of Hull would get in his way. The King smiled; he mistakenly took the shocked expression on Newcastle's face for one of a pleasant surprise.

'Sire, I thank you for this great honour,' Newcastle began then faltered. 'If you will forgive my presumption, Your Majesty, I have put plans in place that may better suit Your Majesty's wishes.'

The Earl of Newcastle, ever mindful of his own ambitions, and his unceasing desire for power and influence recognised how his wealth and status put him in a unique position to align himself with a King in need of money and friends. However, he still needed to ensure that the King felt that he was in control of his own decision making and that he was not being manipulated by those around him.

'Your Majesty, I have taken it upon myself to make use of a man by the name of Sir John Hotham. I have known him many years; he is the Member of Parliament for Beverley and a councillor in Hull. He is an ambitious man, whose political loyalties change as rapidly as the mind of a woman if he perceives a profit for his pocket or career. I have therefore suggested to him that by making use of his friends and connections in Parliament, he should persuade them to make him Governor of Hull. This would enable Sir John to secretly secure the town for Your Majesty's pleasure, and in doing so, it might endear Your Majesty to reward him in some fashion in the future. By this means it would allow Your Majesty to take possession of the town and its arsenal without any direct involvement. I believe from the reports I have received; the town is loyal to the Crown, so I expect little resistance from the populace. Hotham, of course, is disposable. His ambition and greed will get the better of him one day. John Hotham is a man that cannot be trusted. His greed will eventually cause him to betray one side or the other. If he sides with Parliament, Your Majesty can declare him a traitor and execute him. He will not be able to implicate Your Majesty in any plot because he will be the person who has bribed and cajoled to become Governor of Hull. If he betrays Parliament, any excuse he gives will be seen as a feeble attempt to save his own life for siding with the King, and he will have no proof to support his accusations against Your Majesty. Therefore it will be Parliament who will have his head. He is a pawn we can use because he cannot be trusted by either side.'

King Charles pondered on Lord Newcastle's words. To have a strategically significant town like Kingston upon Hull presented to him, without force or deception contrived by the King directly, would be a blow to the growing confidence of Parliament and its desire to stand up to their king.

'My Lord Newcastle,' he answered at last, 'your ideas please us. You have our blessing to proceed with your plans.'

The following day, Lord Newcastle dispatched his spies to Hull to gather information on the strength of its defences, the movement of its troops and the cargos on the ships in its port. In the meantime Sir John Hotham had spent his time at Parliament fruitfully, spreading rumours that a foreign power was preparing to land near Hull, take the town and its arsenal, and join up with a Scottish army to march on London. He took the opportunity to voice his loyalty to the elite within Parliament, and announce his willingness to use his influence as Colonel of the East Yorkshire Trained Bands to defend Hull against any invader, no matter their origin.

Having spent a great deal of his time and money entertaining members of the House of Commons and building allegiances with influential people within Parliament. Sir John Hotham wrote to the Earl of Newcastle indicating that he felt confident that it was only a matter of time before Parliament announced his appointment as mayor or some other such position of authority within the administration of Hull. This, he explained, would allow him to carry out his mission to aid the king; more importantly it would give him access to the extensive armaments stored in Hull, which were so desired by the king. He would secure the town under his command, as the main Royalist stronghold in the North of England.

Over the previous weeks and months, Captain Legge had been working hard spreading misinformation about Parliament across the northern shires for the Earl of Newcastle. Speaking with the great landowners, telling them of the generosity of the King and the favours he would bestow on those that aided him in his overthrow of this rebellious Parliament. At thirty-four years of age, the captain had been with the King on his ill-fated attempt to convince the Scots to accept the King James Version of the Bible in 1639. He was Master of the King's armouries and as loyal to his King as any man could be.

On the eleventh of January 1642 by a strange quirk of fate. Lord Newcastle explained his plans for Hull and Hotham to the King. Sir John Hotham received his letter from Parliament declaring him Military Governor of Hull, and apprentice surgeon Mathew Fletcher found the injured baker in the street. After that day, though they did not know it at the time, their futures would intertwine and influence the fate of a nation.

Chapter Three

The Parliamentary warrant Sir John Hotham received gave him authority to secure Hull and its arsenal at once, with orders to prepare the arsenal for shipment to the Tower of London for safekeeping.

Lord Newcastle's plans were beginning to fall into place, but not everything was going his way.

Shortly after Hotham received his warrant, Parliamentary spies intercepted a letter addressed to Sir John Hotham from Lord Digby, a close friend and confidant of the King. In this letter, he foolishly revealed that the King had mentioned his desire to capture the arms stored in Hull and implicated Sir John Hotham in the plot. In response to the letter, Parliament sent Peregrine Pelham with reinforcements to Hull and a message for Captain Overton, apprising him of the situation between Hotham and the King. Captain Robert Overton was a close friend of Sir Thomas Fairfax an influential and loyal supporter of Parliament. Fairfax had convinced Parliament that they should put their trust in Captain Overton in ensnaring Sir John Hotham and keeping Hull safe from the King.

Sir Peregrine Pelham instructed Overton, 'I am ordering you to allow Sir John Hotham to continue as governor of Hull, but he must remain unaware of his unmasking. You are to watch him, and under no circumstances allow him to surrender Hull or its arms to the king. We need to know who else may be involved in this plot.

As a captain commanding a company within one of the five East Yorkshire Trained Bands based in Hull, Colonel Sir John Hotham was Captain Overton's commanding officer. The orders Captain Overton had received from Pelham put him in a perilous situation. He had to spy on the commander of Hull, disobey any order that placed the town in danger of capture by the King and still carry on as though he was a loyal officer to his commander.

Captain Overton, believed that Parliament ruled by the will of the people, for the benefit of the people. Allowing the surrender of the town to a tyrannical King was anathema to his values of equality for all men. However, Sir John Hotham *was his commanding officer and as such was due his loyalty.* Captain Overton had a decision to make that would set him on a path, which before long, many others would also have to decide upon, breaking friendships and dividing families alike. Sir John Hotham was going to betray Hull, its people and his military command, to a corrupt and foolish monarch with only Captain Robert Overton to stop him.

'Sir, I have long believed in liberty and freedom for all men, and that no one should be master over the will of another. I will have to share this information with the others I trust, but I am sure I can convince them to remain loyal to Parliament and not their corrupted commanding officer,' Overton informed Pelham.

'Do as you see fit, Overton,' replied Pelham, 'but remember, these are troubled times. What we do now and how we act, may set us on a road from which there is no turning back.'

Peregrine Pelham took his leave of Overton and returned to London, satisfied that the town was in safe hands. But, he left behind, under Overton's direct command, the five hundred cavalry he had brought with him from London. Captain Overton, after secret talks and some persuasion, received the assurances from his fellow captains of their loyalty to Parliament and of his leadership until Parliament resolved its differences with Sir John Hotham and the King.

The Earl of Newcastle's plans were taking shape. He would not only be the richest man in England but the power behind the throne and an infelicitous King.

On Thursday the sixteenth of January 1642 the King left London, to make his way to York to raise the army he needed in the northern shire's and to meet up with his trusted confidant, the Earl of Newcastle. From York, it was an easy two-day march to Hull and the town he expected to be handed to him in a grand ceremony.

On the twenty-first of January of that year, Sir John Hotham received a letter from the Earl of Newcastle informing him that the King was on his way to York. When ready, he would march on Hull would arrive with a large contingent of men within the next couple of months. Colonel Hotham and his son Captain John Hotham were instructed to be ready to secure Hull, when notified, in preparation for the king's triumphal march into the town. Sir John Hotham ordered his son to bring his company of soldiers into Hull to keep order in anticipation of the King arrival, just in case of any unrest. Father and son both fully aware of the tortuous game they were playing. If Parliament found out about their plans to turn over the town to the King, they would both lose their heads.

Henry Barnard may have been usurped by Sir John Hotham as Mayor of Hull, but he was still an alderman of the town. With friends and informers from within the town council, watching Sir John Hotham and waiting for any snippet of information that could be used against the usurper. He would make him pay for taking away his role as leader of the Hull Council. The letter Hotham had received from the Earl of Newcastle, warning of the King's arrival in York, had found its way into Barnard's hands via one of his tame clerks.

This was the chance Henry Barnard had been waiting for to get back at Hotham. Barnard sent a fast rider with a note to the King stating that Sir John Hotham knew of His Majesty's imminent arrival at York, and his plans to acquire Hull and its arsenal. The letter went on to say that Hotham would refuse His Majesty entry to Hull, on the grounds that Parliament had promised to bestow on him the title of Lord Mayor and Governor of Hull for his lifetime. Barnard, also knowing of Captain Overton's loyalty to Parliament, requested an interview with him, suggesting that in the interest of saving civilian lives, when the King arrived at Hull, a curfew should be imposed, restricting all civilians to their homes, in case of civil unrest.

Barnard, by chance, was informing Overton of what he already knew, but for Henry Barnard, the vital part of the trap had been set. So long as all went to plan, the days of Sir John Hotham acting as Military Governor and Mayor of Hull were numbered.

On the twenty-second of January, Captain Overton received the ex-mayor in his rooms. Barnard could hardly contain himself, at the prospect of informing against Sir John Hotham.

'What can be so urgent that you insist on speaking to me here, Alderman Barnard?' asked Captain Overton. He would normally have been happy to attend on the alderman at the Guildhall, but his message had insisted that the meeting must take place in Overton's rooms for security reasons. Barnard leaned forward as he sat in the chair, rubbing his hands together, more from glee at the news he was about to divulge than from the cold winters day outside.

'Captain, I have grave and disturbing news to impart. It is important that I bring it to your attention, without the risk of being overheard, or it being intercepted by others,' Barnard spoke with gravity. He was going to enjoy this moment of triumph over Hotham. Captain Overton offered Barnard a cup of warm spiced wine before he continued his story.

'It pains me to be the bearer of bad news, Captain, but it has come to my attention that Sir John Hotham means to betray the town of Hull, and the trust put in him by Parliament. I have here a copy of a letter from the Earl of Newcastle to Sir John Hotham requesting him to secure the town ready for the King's arrival. It offers him the governorship of Hull for life, and in return, requests that he turn over the garrison, its armoury, and the town to His Majesty when he arrives later this year. In the meantime, he must carry out the duties that Parliament has tasked him with, so as to reassure them of his loyalty and efficiency. I have now been informed that the King is on his way to visit York, which is only two or three days' march away.'

Captain Overton waited a moment before he replied to Barnard. Captain Overton not only found it distasteful that

Barnard was stabbing a fellow official of the town in the back, but that he was doing it with such relish. 'Is that all you can provide me with as evidence, Mr Barnard?' Overton asked, 'A single copied letter and a rumour? That's very weak evidence on which to accuse a man of a crime.' Captain Overton was suspicious of Barnard. He knew the man had lost his position of authority and with it, the opportunity to control the taxes levied on ships entering the port, from which, a lucrative fee went to the mayor. At first, Barnard was surprised by Captain Overton's lack of outrage and interest in his tale, but undaunted, Henry Barnard continued, 'He is going to betray Parliament and the town. You cannot ignore my warning! If you want further proof, I will find it. I have a man working in Hotham's office at the Guildhall; he will find the evidence you need.' Barnard slammed down his empty cup on the table as he stormed from the room.

Captain Overton sat back in his chair in front of the fire and pondered the news he had just been given. He couldn't accuse a man of treachery on such flimsy evidence, but he couldn't ignore Barnard's warning either. The problem for Overton was that news of the king's plans for Hull were becoming too widely known. Barnard was also well-known to be a loyal Royalist, so it could only be for reasons of petty revenge that he had denounced John Hotham. What would Barnard have to gain from betraying Hotham to Parliament, but revenge? If Hotham was removed from office, Barnard was the most senior alderman on the council and the logical person to take over his job.

The dilemma now faced by Captain Overton was he now had two members of the town council who would probably hand over Hull to the King. Overton decided that he would wait until Henry Barnard provided him with firm evidence of his treachery before taking action against him. In the meantime, the captain would have to be cautious as to what information he passed on to Sir John Hotham. Captain Overton didn't want to give Hotham any indication that Barnard had been to see him. The best he could do for now was to appraise Parliament of this news and await further orders.

Chapter Four

The following morning Mathew awoke tired after his late night flirtation with danger but remembered it was Saturday. Saturday was the day that Surgeon Adams did his stock take of all the herbs and minerals he used to make the different ointments, plasters, salves, unguents and creams for his patients. Mathew's job was to write the list as Surgeon Adams called out the names of items he was running low on.

As his top apprentice, Mathew was his trusted and senior aide, and it was another of his duties to go to the apothecary on the corner of Chapel Lane and the High Street to buy the supplies his master needed replacing. This was one of Mathew's more pleasurable tasks, for he would get to see Elizabeth Moor, the apothecary's daughter. When Mathew was free of his apprenticeship, he planned to speak to her and declare his feelings to her in the hope that she might feel the same way about him. But, for now, each time he visited the shop, all he could do was try and find excuses to speak to her, to say 'hello', and 'may I have such and such', enjoying the occasional touch of her hand as she handed him an item. He delighted in the way she moved around the shop, her slight frame dressed in a dark grey woollen dress which brushed the floor with its hem, the way her bodice enclosed her trim, slim figure up to her long slender neck. As well as her small round perfectly formed face, her blue-grey eyes, and her chestnut hair which would keep escaping from beneath her coif. She would always speak to him politely, but would never look him in the eye. She was shy and unable to speak more than simple sentences, but she was always there when he arrived, helping her father with customers or sweeping the floor, little tasks to keep her busy in the shop, rather than helping her mother with domestic chores in the living space behind the store.

The shop wasn't a big one, it didn't need to be, but every space within it was filled with herbs, plants and spices. The wall behind the counter was a wall of drawers, and each drawer contained a different spice, powder or seed. From the ceiling herbs hung in bunches tied together with cords, on the walls to the left and right were shelves of jars and bottles containing oils, tinctures and distilled waters, of different colours. On the floor, to either side of the door stood baskets of roots of all types. But the thing you noticed first when you walked through the door was the smell: a pungent, exotic aroma that filled the nose with spices from the Indies and scents from the Orient—cumin, coriander, mace, ginger, aniseed and many more.

Elizabeth watched the young man entering the shop; he was tall, just over six feet, around twenty years old, slim, and with brown hair down to his shoulders. She liked his hair most of all; it was unusually sleek for a man, not straight, but not curly, with a natural waviness to it. He made her heart flutter. She enjoyed the times their hands would sometime touch and when he spoke to her, but she was far too embarrassed to talk to him when her father was watching.

Elizabeth's one desire was to speak to Mathew, but she couldn't, not without the permission of her strict father, and he wouldn't approve of such contact without Mathew making the proper introductions to him first. She dreamt of being taken away from this dreary existence, in a dull shop, in a town smelling of fish, to have a life with lots of friends, to be able to wear beautiful clothes and maybe own some jewels. She knew that Mathew would be a surgeon one day, a trade that just perhaps could introduce them both to new and different places and people with exciting lives, wealthy people who would pay him well to cure their ailments.

But she didn't dare speak to him unless he spoke first. So how was she to make him notice her? Just for him to say 'hello' was enough to make her heart beat faster and bring colour to her cheeks. She couldn't help but glance into those dark brown eyes and not dream of what her life with him could be. At seventeen she'd had no experience of men other than her father and the strict religious doctrine he maintained over the family, but something inside her wanted more, *needed* more than the life she was living now. Did Mathew think of her in the way she thought of him? She burned to stop and talk to him but knew that if she tried to her father would ban her from helping in the shop, and she would never be able to see Mathew again.

After leaving an order with the apothecary and informing Mr Moor that he would return later to collect his supplies, Mathew left the shop with a last glance at, and a smile for, Elizabeth. Returning to the surgery of Mr Adams, he found his master sitting at the table examining his ledgers. Mrs Adams busied herself stirring a pot over the fire—from the smell something good was cooking for tonight's dinner. A large fruit bag pudding already stood cooling on a brown-and-cream coloured slipware dish close by. Mathew was very partial to Mrs Adams's bag puddings with fresh cream and a sprinkle of ground ginger.

'Ah, Mathew,' Surgeon Adams welcomed him, distracting his attention from the bag pudding. 'I've just been reviewing my books. It seems it's about time you were making your own way in the world.' The older man looked up from his ledger. 'Your apprenticeship with me is complete at the end of next week. I am going to sign your father's contract with me, releasing you from my service. You've been a good apprentice and have learnt as much as I can teach you. Your father will be as proud of you as I am.'

Mathew had known the time was coming when his apprenticeship would be over but had not realised it was so soon; the news came as a bit of a shock. He had enjoyed his time with Surgeon Adams, and being allowed to live with Mr and Mrs Adams in their family home. It had given him the opportunity to assist the surgeon when he had been called out at night and act as his assistant. Mathew's real home was in Beverley, eight miles away. His father had brought him to Hull for an apprenticeship because he couldn't find a place for him with a surgeon in his hometown of Beverley.

'Thank you, sir,' Mathew replied, not knowing exactly what else to say.

The realisation that he was going to have to make his own way in the world came as a shock. Mathew had made minimal provision for this day's arrival, even though he knew it was coming. He had put off making plans for the event, almost as though if he ignored it, it wouldn't happen. But now, somehow, hearing the words spoken aloud by someone else, telling him he was to be released from his apprenticeship, made him feel unsure of himself.

He had lived and worked with Andrew Adams and his wife for the past seven years. They had been kind to him, almost adoptive parents, and now in a roundabout way, it felt as if they were throwing him out. Mathew had managed to save some money for when this time had to come, but it was far from enough to set up in practice on his own. He would have enough money to enable him to rent a small place for a while, but he also needed to buy equipment and medicines. He also knew that he needed patients of his own if he was to make a living as a surgeon.

Mathew arranged a meeting with the head of the Barber-Surgeons Guild at the Guildhall for the Monday after he released from his apprenticeship. He was keen to become licensed as a surgeon in his own right, even though he had no money and made no preparation for how he was going to set up in practice. The comfort and security of living with Surgeon Adams and his wife had made him procrastinate and now the time had come for him to leave their employment and set up on his own. His final examination would be in front of a panel of four prominent surgeons, at the Guildhall. They would test him on the knowledge of his craft. If he passed the test, he would have to request and pay to become a member of the Guild of Surgeons to gain a licence to work in Hull or any other town.

The examination was a formal but small affair, lasting two hours with questions from the panel on how he would deal with various illnesses and surgical procedures. On the day of his examination, Mathew was shown into a wood-panelled room in which stood a long table. Four elderly men in black robes awaited him. They were seated with their backs to the windows through which the sun shone. In the centre of the room was a single chair, for Mathew. He sat down with the sun shining in his face, making him squint. Mathew began to sweat, and his knees shake as his four examiners talked amongst themselves. When they finally stopped talking, and introductions concluded, Mathew began to relax a little. He soon learned Surgeon Adams had given him a good reference as Mathew's old Master was well-known and liked within the guild, which Mathew took, to be a good sign.

As the examination proceeded, Mathew was able to provide the correct answers to the questions asked, despite them requiring varied and in-depth responses. Thankfully Mathew hadn't found the questions as difficult as he had expected. At the end of two hours, the examination panel departed leaving Mathew to await their verdict.

A clerk who had been recording a written account of the proceedings, he was required to pay ten pounds to join the guild. For Mathew, this was the hard part. The charge used up most of his savings from the past seven years, and he was left with just thirty-five shillings, which would not last him very long, now he had his own lodgings to find and pay for. The clerk returned and congratulated Mathew presenting him with a document on which Mathew's name had been written. He had done it! He was now a qualified surgeon and a member of the Guild of Surgeons. The future was he hoped, and with a bit of luck, going to be one of his own making.

Mathew decided to visit his father and brothers in Beverley to give them the news of his success. Then he would return to find a shop of his own. It would have to be away from the premises of Surgeon Adams, perhaps on the west side of town, as it would be cheaper than somewhere on the High Street. If he could find a place on one of the main streets which ran to the town gates, he reckoned that he might be able to catch passing trade from the merchants as they entered and left Hull.

The next day, after saying his farewells to Mr and Mrs Adams, Mathew went to the White Meat Market in the centre of Hull. Mathew planned to buy a ride to Beverley with one of the merchants leaving Hull. It would cost him a shilling of his hard-earned and dwindling savings, but the road would be hard to travel on foot at this time of year, as well as being extremely cold in February.

After asking a couple of wagon drivers, he found one going north who was willing to take him and his large wooden surgeon's box. With luck, Mathew would be in Beverley before nightfall, though the merchant had told him he would be making stops at the small hamlets of Dunswell and Woodmansey.

Luckily the weather was dry for the time of year. There was no rain or snow, but there was a bitterly cold damp wind blowing across the flat farmland of East Yorkshire. It carried cold, moist air inland from the German Sea. It was the kind of wind that penetrated your clothing and chilling your flesh down to your bones and set your body shivering.

Mathew pulled his thick woollen cassock around him, turning up its collar and pulling down his felt broad-brimmed hat. The versatile army coat he'd taken as payment for services to an injured soldier with no money was now showing its real worth against the bitter wind.

Mathew didn't feel like indulging in conversation with the driver, he was too cold, and the large collar on his cassock covered the lower half of his face, making anything he would want to say inaudible. The road to Beverley was a busy one, even at this time of year and they passed plenty of traffic going in both directions, as people made the most of a dry cold day.

The day's journey was uneventful and allowed Mathew the pleasure of breathing cold, fresh country air, instead of the stench and filth on the streets of Hull. But he knew that Beverley wouldn't smell much better than Hull, with its streets often swimming in animal waste from the cattle market.

The wagon driver took a leisurely pace, stopping twice to enjoy a beer in taverns along the road. It was at these stops that Mathew learned of the wagon's cargo. The merchant carried imported goods from Holland across the German Sea, Delft Ware and Jenever, to be sold in Beverley and York. On the return journey, the merchant would carry wool from York and tanned leather from Beverley to the villages and finally back into Hull.

The slow trip gave Mathew time to reflect on the time he had spent away from home. He'd been unable to return to his family as often as he would have liked because his apprenticeship contract tied him for seven years to the service of Surgeon Adams.

In that time his elder brother had married, but he had been unable to attend the marriage ceremony. He missed his brothers and his father. Mathew's thoughts inevitably turned to his mother and how he wished that she was still here to see him now, fully grown, and for her to know that she was the reason he became a surgeon.

Entering Beverley from the south, they passed Beverley Minster, with its magnificent twin towers and steeple visible for many miles around across the flat farming countryside. Passing the rear of Beverley Minster, they entered East Gate and onto Wednesday Market, a large triangle of cobbled street amidst the shops surrounding it. Then up Alta Via and onto Saturday Market, full of stock pens and water troughs, with a large covered well in the centre of the rectangular marketplace. Then they went on towards Within North Bar, the street from which Cuckstool Pit Lane ran and his home. Mathew would surprise his father as he turned up unannounced, but still, no doubt be welcomed warmly after so much time away from home. Mathew wondered how much his family would have changed over the years. His brothers would be strong men now, skilled in making wheels; his father would be older, but still as strong as an ox, just as he always had been.

Leaving the cattle market, they pushed their way through the streets crammed with people, dodging past the cattle and sheep being driven down the street of Within North Bar. The wagon driver found it difficult to make headway through the crowds and was getting frustrated with the people who continually blocked their path. After much shouting and abuse, the wagon finally stopped at the end of the Cuckstool Pit Lane.

Mathew unloaded his heavy surgeon's chest and thanked the driver as he drove away. From the end of the lane Mathew could see the wood-and-plaster building that was his old family home and, struggling to carry his massive chest, he began to make his way down the narrow lane. Entering the wide gate that led into the yard and workshop which fronted onto the lane, he put down the chest and watched two men working there. They were busily fitting a new section of felloes (outer rims) to the spokes of what was to be a cartwheel. One of them glanced away from his work towards Mathew.

'Be with you shortly, sir,' he called politely, then, turned back to his work.

Mathew sat down on his surgeon's chest to rest and to watch the two men working. One man held a section of felloes in place over the spokes, while the other tapped another part into position. While the wheelwrights finished their task, Mathew looked around the yard. Lots of completed wheels stood in rows according to their size. All kept off the ground by standing them on lines of stone blocks, which prevented them from absorbing ground moisture before the wheels were sold or fitted to wagons once more.

Having completed his task, one of the men turned to speak to Mathew. 'Now, sir,' said the smallest of the pair. 'How can we help?' A stunned silence fell between them as he looked closer at the new arrival. 'Mathew? It's Mathew!' he called out in excitement.

'Charles,' Mathew replied, smiling, 'And, Henry, you look well. Where's Father? I've missed you all so much. I've so much to tell you.'

Charles and Henry took it in turns to hug their brother, shaking his hand, both talking over each other, wanting to know all the news concerning the youngest member of the family.

'Where's your horse?' asked Charles. He was the elder of the two, but shorter than his brother Henry.

'I don't have one,' replied Mathew. 'I bought a ride on a merchant's wagon travelling from Hull to York.'

'Bugger me!' said Henry. 'Wait till Father sees you. Why didn't you send word you were coming?'

'It was just as quick to come myself, and I wanted to see you after all this time. Now where is Father and how is he?' Mathew was anxious to see the man to whom he owed so much.

'He's delivering a set of wheels to Baker's Farm over at Cherry Burton,' replied Henry. 'He'll be back before dark.'

The three brothers went into the house. A black and white Border Collie puppy lay near the fire; it looked up and wagged its tail as the brothers burst through the door. Charles introduced the young woman who was standing at a pot, held by a hook over the fire within the large fireplace. The aroma of baking dough from the bread oven next to the fire filled the room with its homely smell.

'This is Mary, my wife,' Charles said proudly. 'I wrote to you about her just before we married.'

Mathew stared at his new sister-in-law. She was taller than most women, not slim, but not fat, dressed in a blue woollen bodice laced up the back and with a matching woollen skirt, her blonde hair just showing below her ear. She stepped away from the pot and came to greet Mathew.

'Welcome, brother,' she said in a soft, warm voice, giving a short curtsy. Her cheeks were not yet wrinkled or showing signs of age and worry; they were still smooth with youth and only the smallest hint of a smallpox scar here and there. With her hazel eyes, perfect nose and pink lips, Mathew could see why his brother had fallen for her.

Mary sat next to Charles at the table, leaning against him, wanting to be close to the man she loved, in the way newly married couples often do. She drank ale and ate bread and cheese with them, listening to the brother's exchange stories. The collie pup sniffed around under the table looking for scraps that had fallen to the floor, brushing past Mathew's leg. Mathew bent down and picked up the dog, asking, 'Who's this little bundle of fluff then?'

'That's Bess,' Mary declared with a smile. 'Isn't she lovely?' Mary took Bess and fed her a bit of cheese from the table and put her back on the rag rug near the fire. A horse and cart pulled into the yard; their father had returned.

'Charles? Henry? Where are you?' The big booming voice could have carried clear across the market. The door opened, and in burst, a tall man built of muscle and sinew and having to duck under the door lintel to enter the room.

'You two finished that wheel yet?' he bellowed.

Standing up, Mathew turned to look at his father. The two men stared at each other.

'Mathew!' his father said in almost a whisper. 'How I wish your mother were here to see you now, my son,' the shock of the sudden meeting making him hoarse with emotion. William Fletcher crossed the room from the door to the table in two strides and clasped his arms around his son, holding him close as only a father could. The bear-like grip around his upper arms was not what Mathew was used to after being away from his family for so long.

'It's good to see you, lad,' his father said in an unsteady voice. 'How's it been in Hull? You must have finished your apprenticeship by now, tell me what you've been doing?' The words ran one after another without a pause.

They all sat at the oak table in the centre of the room, while Mary brought more jugs of ale and pewter plates full of bread, meat, cheese and butter.

Mary built up the fire then settled next to Charles, listening to the stranger that had been made so welcome into her home. She liked the look of him: he resembled his brothers, but he was different in his manner, which she put down to the time they had all spent apart. Mary decided she could grow to like her brother-in-law.

The family talked and laughed late into the night, beyond Mary's bedtime, so she left the men to their tales of missed times together and of all the events that had passed during the seven years they had barely seen each other. Mathew explained that this could only be a short visit, for he needed to get back to Hull and set up his own surgeon's practice and justify his father's faith in him by becoming a success.

After much talking and drinking, the four men, too drunk to undress, took to their beds. Mathew found that a palliasse, (a mattress stuffed with straw), and blanket had been put on the floor for him in Henry's room above the workshop. Mary had laid it out ready for him before she had gone to her own bed. Crashing down to his knees at the foot of his makeshift bed, he slumped forwards, falling into a deep sleep within seconds.

The next morning Mathew awoke with a head which felt like it was being crushed and a mouth tasting bitter and dry, he woke his brother, Henry 'time to be up'. They splashed their faces with water from a jug on a stand in the corner of the room and went down to a breakfast of bread and rough cider. While eating his breakfast, his lack of funds played on his mind, until the thought occurred to him, that he could ask his father if he could stay with the family until he had earned enough money to set up his own surgeon's practice. He would ask him later, when he had thought the idea through properly, and his head had stopped aching.

A couple of days later, Mathew had made up his mind. 'Father,' he began. 'I know I said this was going to be a short visit, but having to pay the Surgeons Guild a fee to become a member of their society has left me short of funds. Don't worry; I'm not asking you to give me money—but if I could stay here a while longer, it would give me time to earn enough money to take back to Hull and set up my own business.' Mathew outlined his plan to do his medical work from the house and to give a share of what he earned to his father to pay for his keep.

William Fletcher looked at his son with pride. 'You know there is, and always will be a home for you here, lad. I'm glad you've done well, but I'm even happier to have you home again. All my sons under one roof, what more could I ask—except maybe a grandson, eh, Mary?'

Mary turned to glare at her father-in-law, her face red. 'In God's good time,' she retorted. 'Shouldn't you be finding something useful to do instead of talking all day?'

William Fletcher let out a loud laugh.

'Come on, you three—we've got work to do,' broke in Henry. The family had been busy of late, carts and wagons had been coming from far and wide to have wheels made or repaired. The unusual amount of work that was being offered to the Fletchers had turned their fortunes around. Where all this work was coming from was not something they wanted to think about, they were just grateful to be busy.

Mathew hung the surgeon's pole he had painted above the front door of the house to advertise his trade. It was painted white, with a blue band spiralling up the pole to the top.

On the first Saturday of Mathew's return to Beverley, it was the day of the weekly cattle market. Mathew's father and brothers were busy with customers needing repairs done to their wagons wheels, so Mathew paid the cattle market a visit. His sign outside the house had been up for four days, but no one had called to ask for his medical help. He was not surprised: it took time to build a reputation and earn respect as a newcomer, but he was optimistic that his fortunes would pick up soon.

In the cattle market, the stock pens were full of sheep, pigs, cattle and horses, waiting to be sold. Traders selling pies, ale, baskets and leather goods had stalls around the market. While farmers haggled over the price of their livestock, the farmer's wives bought what they needed from the stallholders. The streets were crowded, and stank of raw animal waste and the unwashed bodies of people jammed together on the busiest day of the week.

As Mathew entered the market and wandered amongst the street vendors, listening to their calls advertising what they had for sale. Mathew's hand guarding the few coins he carried in his purse. Even in a small town like Beverley cutpurses were everywhere. This was no longer the quiet market town of the day before but a cacophony of sounds ranging from people laughing and talking to the loud calls of the street vendors and the frightened bellows of animals crammed together in small pens.

One of the street vendors aroused his interest. He had seen this particular display many times before while he was apprenticed in Hull. The vendor was drawing a crowd, telling everyone who was watching of his prowess as a remover of cataracts from the blind, enabling them to see once again. He was famous across the land for his speed, his skill, he boasted, his delicate hands and pain-free surgery were a marvel to behold. For two shillings he would restore the sight of the blind as if by a miracle medical science.

A man in his late thirties stepped forward, one of his eyes all milky white. From his clothing, he looked like a farmhand. He stood around five feet six inches in height and was of muscular build, wearing worn latchet shoes, woollen socks that disappeared into the bottom of his breeches, and a thick grey woollen jacket with linen ties holding it closed over a dirty linen shirt. His shoulder-length greasy hair hung down in knots under a knitted woollen hat.

This type of 'medical' market trader was common across the country, the surgery on offer was cheap, relatively quick and easy to perform, *and* just as easy to get horribly wrong. But people needed to be able to see to do their work and earn a living. The farmhand who had stepped forward was no exception. Mathew knew of many a poor family which had been forced to turn out a blind family member who could not work and earn their keep. In those cases, the person had to rely on the charity from the parish commissioners to take care of them. This was a legal obligation laid down in law during the reign of Elizabeth I, but Mathew knew it was rarely enforced by local justices of the peace, because of the expense it put on the parish church community.

Consequently, if the poor became blind and could not afford to seek proper medical treatment, they would be forced to turn to these opportunist street vendors and trust to luck that they would be cured and putting their faith in God, that all would go well.

Chapter Five

Mathew was intrigued to learn how the quack surgeon would proceed with removing the cataract. *He* had been trained correctly in the procedure, but many one-day market practitioners just preyed on the poor and the vulnerable. Although he wanted to call the unsuspecting man back and warn him of the dangers involved in what he was about to have done, the derision he would have received from the rest of crowd, who liked to watch the gruesome work made his stay silent. As it was, Mathew was saved from his dilemma by shouts and cries coming from across the market.

Everyone around him turned towards the kerfuffle, trying to see what was going on. A bellowing animal could be heard above the noise of the crowd, very quickly followed by the sound of men shouting and women's screams. As Mathew made his way through the crowded market towards the noise, it soon became clear that a bull had taken fright and had gored the stockman who'd been handling it. The young surgeon pushed his way through the farmers and between the stock pens to find the stockman still trapped inside the enclosure with the bull. The Bull had him pinned to the pen side for a moment then with a flick of its massive head, tossed the stockman up and aside as it tried to make its escape. The stockman landed heavily, barely conscious, blood streaming from a limp right arm, as he lay insensible on the ground. The bull, looking for an escape route, stomped around the pen wanting to take out its frustration on the noisy crowd. The injured stockman began to moan and move, catching the eye of the bull. As the animal ran in to attack, hands reached under the bars of the pen to pull the stockman clear.

'Stand aside, let me through!' Mathew shouted. He pushed his way to the front of the crowd, repeatedly having to say that he was a surgeon before the crowd would let him pass and get to the injured man. When Mathew finally got to the stockman, who had lapsed into unconsciousness, he was lying on his side, blood pouring from his wounded arm. The blood covered his shirt, staining it bright red, giving the impression that his body had been torn open by the bull's horns. Kneeling down beside his patient, Mathew tore open his shirt thankful it revealed no obvious wound; he just had the torn arm to deal with. Mathew established that the young man's breathing was shallow but steady, so he instructed four men standing nearby to carry the patient up to Fletchers, the wheelwrights' yard, where he would be able to treat the man's wounds.

'What's the point?' asked a wrinkled old man dressed in a farmer's smock. 'He's a goner,' he continued callously, 'I've seen men 'urt like that afore, chests all staved in, bleeding to death, 'e'll be dead afore the day's out, you mark me words.' He spat a gobbet of tobacco onto the ground. From the *oohs* and *aahs* of the crowd, many seemed to agree with him. Mathew knew he was taking a big risk: if the man died, it would ruin his reputation in the town before he had even got started as a surgeon. Such a thing might even harm his family's business, but if he could save the man, it could be the start of building him the reputation he needed to be a successful surgeon.

The injured fellow was quickly carried away from the Saturday Market to the wheelwrights' yard. A makeshift table was constructed for him in the yard made some planks of wood laid across upturned barrels. Mathew's father with Charles and Henry cleared the crowd from the yard, who'd accompanied Mathew and the injured man from the market.

Mathew's patient appeared to be not yet in his twenties, but he was already lean and muscular. He was still breathing, though his respiration had become raspy and shallow, and a trickle of blood ran from the corner of his mouth. The young surgeon's first examined the torn and bloodied arm. Cutting away the remains of the man's shirt sleeve, he exposed a large wound where one of the bull's horns had passed right through the limb. It had torn the skin open on the inside of the man's arm, from just above the wrist to below the elbow. The outside of the arm showed a smaller puncture wound where the tip of the bull's horn had merely broken through the skin, leaving little damage.

William Fletcher and Mathew's brothers looked on speechless, the shock of seeing so much blood making Mathew's brothers feel unwell; the brother's face's becoming deathly pale. Charles's wife, Mary broke their fixation on all the blood by opening the door to their house and telling them to bring the injured man inside. Before moving the patient, Mathew tied a short length of rope around the man's upper arm to staunch the bleeding before he was carried inside.

Once the man was in the house and lying on the kitchen table, Mathew had to gather his thoughts as his family stared at him in expectation of what he was about to do. He knew what to be done, but this was the first patient of his own without the supervision of Surgeon Adams. Whether the man lived or died, this time, the patient was in his hands. Mathew took a small bellarmine (stoneware) jar from his surgeon's box and poured out half a cup of brown liquid. The laudanum would help quiet the man as Mathew did his work, but the drug was not powerful enough to relieve all the pain the patient would experience, so he asked his family for help in holding the patient still when he started to work on him.

Mathew examined the arm. The Radius Bone was broken, but the Ulna was undamaged, the Brachial Artery hadn't been punctured and was still intact, but there was a lot of damage to the arm's tissue. His first instinct was to remove the injured arm from below the elbow, as Surgeon Adams would have done, but Mathew wanted to do better than that, he knew he could do better than his old master had taught him. Mathew got his brothers to hold the man down, Charles, by lying across the patient's legs and Henry by holding the man's shoulders down. He asked his father to grip the top of the injured arm just below the shoulder joint, telling him to apply as much pressure as he could in order to staunch the blood loss coming from the forearm when Mathew removed the dirty length of rope he'd used as a tourniquet.

Mathew's was now ready to show what he could do. He carefully washed the wound clean with hot water which Mary had brought from the fire in a large earthenware bowl. Dropping the bloodied cleaning cloth on the table, he carefully positioned the broken ends of the Radius Bone into line, and then pulled the two torn sides of the arm together. He got his father to move from the young man's shoulder to pinching the two sides of the ruptured skin and muscle together, keeping the wound closed. Taking a large suture needle from his surgeon's box. Mathew double-threaded the eye of the needle with silk thread, then, starting at the wrist, he began to sew the flesh together, using large stitches, one finger-width apart, leaving a larger gap in the middle and at each end to allow the puss to escape from the wound as it healed. He cauterised the smaller wound on the top of the arm and sprinkled both sides of the limb with *powdered sulphur* to try and reduce the chances of infection. He dressed the wounds with strips of linen soaked in *comfrey and rosewater*, to help the bones to knit together again; after that, he wrapped the arm in clean linen rollers and splinted it.

There was not much he could do now, but wait and see if the man came around. When he did, *if he did*, Mathew knew his patient would develop a high fever which would last for four days. Mathew would keep his patient cool with wet cloths to help lower his temperature, as well bleed and purge him to remove harmful humours that would be infecting the wound and to restore his patients natural 'humoural balance.' If by God's grace he survived the fever, he might still lose the arm to gangrene, but Mathew was confident he had done a good job in cleaning and restoring the injured arm. What mattered now was keeping the wound clean until it healed. 'Mary, would you like to assist me in caring for my patient?'

'Yes, of course, anything you wish,'

For three days the man lay unconscious and sweating, sometimes mumbling, sometimes writhing around, as the fever fought to take him. It was as though he was struggling with some unseen demon in his dreams. Each day Mary washed his face in cold water and fed him sips of broth from a spoon. Mathew checked and cleaned his wounds, wiping away the puss and cleaning around the stitches with a mixture of *rosewater and white wine*. On the fourth day, the fever broke, and the man slept peacefully for several hours. When he awoke, Mary saw him try to lift his head and went over to him. She carefully wiped his face with a damp cloth and gave him a sip of small beer.

'It's all right, you're safe,' she reassured him. 'You were attacked by a bull in the market—do you remember?'

The man nodded and took another sip of the beer.

'What is your name?' Mary asked.

'Peter Barns, Miss.'

No one had been to the house to ask after him once the initial excitement of his arrival had died down, so Mary continued to ask questions to find out more about him. Peter explained that he was from the village of Faxfleet close to the River Humber and that he had arrived in Beverley shortly after Christmas and was looking for work.

'By sleeping rough I have managed to save enough money to buy food,' he told her. 'And, as the weather improves and the markets and farmers get busier, I hope to find someone to give me a more permanent job.'

Mary smiled reassuringly. Peter, unable to find work in his home village of Faxfleet had travelled from town to town trying to earn money to take back to his family. But Beverley was not the town it once was. The clothes-making industry that had once been the backbone of the town's prosperity had gone elsewhere.

Peter stayed with the Fletchers for a couple more days to ensure that his arm was not infected and was on the mend; then he had to be off back home to his family. Mathew told him it would be some time before he would be able to use his arm for farm work. Peter had been unable to pay for his treatment, but Mathew's father had insisted that business had been very profitable of late, and playing the Good Samaritan from time to time was the godly thing to do.

William explained to his son that people had been coming from far and wide, to bring their wagons to have wheels repaired or buying new wheels for old carts. He had even heard a rumour that a new merchant in York was buying all the wagons he could get. Mathew father reminded Mathew that to start any business, a good reputation was worth more than the odd shilling or two. Peter being unable to pay for his medical treatment wasn't important—all that mattered was that the Fletcher family was doing well.

'We have received so much work, we haven't stopped for months,' William went on cheerfully. 'The business even provided the money for your brother to marry Mary. It's a pity the wedding went ahead so quickly and that you couldn't be here to join the festivities but we had so much work to do that we only stopped work for the day of the wedding.

A couple of days later Mrs Judith Beckwith knocked on the door. She had made a decision and was determined to go through with it regardless of the complaints from her daughter. 'Stop crying, girl, this is for your own good!' Mrs Beckwith admonished her only daughter. 'I explained to you last night it will be over quickly and in a couple of years from now you will thank me for what I am doing for you.' Mrs Beckwith was disappointment with her daughter. Why her girl couldn't be more forthright, just as she was, she couldn't understand.

Mary opened the front door to the two women, assessing the elder one as the kind of person you crossed at your peril and was used to getting her own way. Her daughter, however, seemed like a shadow of her mother. The girl stood there with tears running down her face, head slightly bowed, and her whole demeanour being that of someone who lacked spirit and confidence, and indeed, seemed utterly browbeaten.

'We are here to see the surgeon,' Mrs Beckwith informed Mary as she pushed past her, dragging her unhappy daughter by the hand. Mary, feeling very aggrieved at the woman's arrogant behaviour, shut the door without a word and left Mrs Beckwith and her daughter standing in the kitchen without being invited to sit down. Mary stormed out of the back door to the yard, where she found Mathew helping his father and brothers with a repair to a cartwheel.

'Mathew, you have a customer!' she called. Spitting out the words out as if they were poison on her tongue. Mary stood in the kitchen doorway with her fists clenched at her sides, and with a face like thunder.

'Err, thank you, Mary,' said Mathew. 'I'll come and see what they want.' He made haste going into the house curious to see who it was that had upset Mary so much. Meanwhile, Charles, Henry and their father went back to repairing the wheel in silence, aware that Mary was best left alone when she was in a bad mood.

Inside the house, Mathew approached Mrs and Miss Beckwith, a greeting on his tongue, but Mrs Beckwith beat him to it.

'I understand you are the new surgeon who healed that young man in the market the other day,' she declared. Mathew didn't know if that statement was meant as an accusation or as a request for more information. 'Yes, ma'am—that was me,' replied Mathew.

'Well, I'm Mrs Judith Beckwith, and I'm here to see what you can do for my daughter Sarah.' Making a half turn, she gestured with her hand towards the snivelling girl in the doorway.

Mathew began to suspect that the obnoxious woman had chosen him because she had tried all the other local surgeons, who had probably refused to deal with the woman and her arrogant attitude. Mathew, on the other hand, wasn't in a position to turn down patients and so, taking a deep breath, he asked the two ladies to be seated at the kitchen table.

'So, Mrs Beckwith,' Mathew enquired in his most patient voice. 'What exactly can I do for your daughter?'

'First, let me explain that we are very important people in this town, we are friends of Sir John Hotham, he's Beverley's Member of Parliament. We are also friends with the Warton family, from the Old Priory, the richest family in the county. We are hosting a grand dinner for some of our influential guests and friends. This dinner will be the first time my daughter will be allowed to join us on such an occasion, but she is not fit to be seen in such good company.' Mrs Beckwith turned to look at her daughter. 'Show him, girl!'

Poor Sarah Beckwith lifted her head for the first time, removing her kerchief from her face to wipe her nose on and to dry her tears. At first, Mathew was taken in by the intelligent grey eyes and small face with high cheekbones. It should have been an enchanting face; one that any young man could only dream about, but there, in plain view on her chin was a 'wen'—an unsightly swelling, like a wart. It was a big ugly looking wen, with tufts of wiry hair growing from the centre. Mathew asked Mrs Beckwith if he could examine Sarah more closely. Then, fetching a lantern and setting it on the table between them, Mathew made a closer examination of Sarah's disfigurement.

'You would like me to remove it, I take it, Mrs Beckwith?' said Mathew, asking the obvious question more from wanting to break the embarrassing silence and give himself time to think about how best to treat the girl.

Mrs Beckwith didn't bother to reply, she sniffed indignantly.

After a moment Mathew turned to Mrs Beckwith.

'It is a simple operation,' he told her. 'Would you like me to do it now, or visit you at your home? The charge will be five shillings.'

'Five Shillings!' she exclaimed aloud. 'Gracious me, just to remove that little thing? Do you take me for a fool?'

Mrs Beckwith was incensed at what even Mathew knew to be a substantial fee for such a simple operation.

'Mrs Beckwith, you must understand that it is delicate and skilled work to remove a wen of this size correctly, so as not to risk leaving your daughter's beautiful face disfigured for the rest of her life.'

'I will pay you three shillings if you do it now,' snapped Mrs Beckwith.

While Mrs Beckwith and Mathew bartered over the price of the operation, Sarah began to cry once again and hid her face in her hands. Mathew felt sorry for the girl, for suffering from such a disfigurement and for having a mother like this. But Mathew needed the money, and reluctantly agreed to three shillings, knowing it was still a reasonable price for such a simple operation.

The decision facing him now was what method he should use to remove the wen?

Turning to Sarah and taking her hands in his, Mathew looked into her eyes. 'I have to tell you that there are two ways to remove the wen so that it will not return, and that you can choose the one you wish me to perform. The first way is to burn it off with a cauterising iron. This will be the more painful of the two methods, but over with the quickest. The second way is to burn it off with acid. This will take longer but will prove less painful in the long run. Before I start the surgery, I will give you something to drink that will help relieve the worst of your pain. You will have to choose between these two ways of removing the wen.'

Sarah turned her head to look at her mother. 'I can't do it, Mother. I'm frightened. It is going to hurt. I won't go to the dinner —I don't want to meet those people anyway.' The girl began to sob again.

However, due to a combination of reassurances from Mathew and threats from her mother, Sarah finally gave in. Mathew poured out a cup of wine, and added some honey, mixing it with a dose of laudanum, and then giving it to Sarah to drink. She sipped it slowly at first but soon finished off the cup as the calming effects of the poppy juice and alcohol started to take effect in easing her fears. Sarah fell into a deep sleep. With the help of her mother and Mary: Mathew laid the girl on the table.

'I will burn the wen off with acid; it is easier to control the wens removal and will leave less of a scar. But first I will have to tie her down,' Mathew explained to Mrs Beckwith. 'The laudanum has relaxed her and allowed her to fall asleep, but as soon as she starts to feel any pain, she will begin to wake up and to writhe about.'

Beginning with her head, Mathew passed a two-inch-wide roller bandage over her forehead and under the table, so that she could not lift her head from the table top. He then tied her hands to her sides and bound her legs together at the knees and ankles. After that, he held her mouth closed using a roller bandage fastened around the top of her head and under her chin.

'Now, Mrs Beckwith,' he explained, 'as I drip acid onto the wen, you must hold your daughter as still as possible so that I don't drip acid onto other parts of her face. I will leave the chemical to do its work for a minute or two and then I'll wash off the acid, blood and fragments of wen tissue. I will have to repeat this process until the wen has been entirely removed. Hopefully, when I have finished, and the wound has healed, she will only be left with a small scar which can be covered with make-up.'

Mrs Beckwith had taken on a more conciliatory demeanour and seemed to care for her daughter as she helped Mathew prepare Sarah for the operation. Mathew asked Mary if she would assist Mrs Beckwith in holding Sarah still. Mary glared at Mrs Beckwith, moved to the opposite side of the table, and leaned across Sarah's midriff, keeping her eyes on Mathew, not wanting to look at Mrs Beckwith.

Mathew started the procedure, taking a glass bottle from his surgeon's chest marked '*oil of vitriol*', as well as a glass rod with which to deliver the acid. He stood beside Sarah's head. By using the glass rod as a dipper, he inserted it into the *oil of vitriol* and allowed the drops of acid to fall on Sarah's wen.

At first, Sarah didn't respond to the acid's effects, but as it burned deeper into her tissue, she started to fight the restraints. Incoherent sounds emanated from her closed and bound mouth. Mathew cupped her chin with his hand as she tried to shake her head, wanting to break free of her bonds. She made a half screaming, half gurgling sound, due to the delirium caused by the laudanum and the pain of the acid, but Mathew and Mrs Beckwith carried on with the procedure. The smell of the acid stung their nostrils as the fumes of the liquid began to fill the room.

Eventually, Mathew decided that he had done enough and washed away the last of the acid, fragments of wen and blood. He covered the wound with an *'emplaster'* (a plaster) containing a concoction made from fresh *egg albumin and the teasel from a Fullers-Thistle* (a medicinal herb), then released Sarah from her bonds. For the first time, Mrs Beckwith looked shocked. Against her daughter's will, she had put the girl through an ordeal for the sake of nothing more than vanity. Having to hold the girl still during her time of pain and suffering had clearly affected Mrs Beckwith. She was no longer the stern dictatorial woman who had entered the house less than an hour before. Mathew hoped the change was permanent.

Sarah sat on a chair, with her left hand held against the emplaster that had been applied to her face, and with her right arm, she rested on the table for support. Tears ran down her cheeks, her body swaying to and fro slightly, the poppy juice still affecting her senses. Mrs Beckwith, having quickly regained her composure, stood aloof next to her daughter. Her face now showed no sign of remorse for what she had put the girl through.

'I would like you to bring Sarah back tomorrow so that I can change the dressing and every day after that until a scab has formed on the wound. After that, the wound will heal itself.'

Mathew showed the two ladies to the door, with Mrs Beckwith steadying her daughter as they walked away.

'What a woman!' exclaimed Mary as Mathew shut the door, 'do you meet many people with attitudes like that?'

'As I see it, those who are better than us can do as they please,' Mathew replied, happy to have earned some money from his first paying customer. 'It's just the way things are. When we go to meet our maker, God decides who will be saved and go to heaven, and who will not.'

'It's not right,' Mary replied. 'Just because her husband has money it doesn't make her a better person than us.' Still feeling aggrieved and frustrated by Mrs Beckwith's attitude, Mary looked around, picked up a cloth and began to vigorously clean the table on which Sarah had been laid. Then went to the pot cooking over the fire, stirring it more vigorously than necessary, as she worked off her frustrations with the wooden spoon.

The following morning Mrs Beckwith returned with her daughter. Mary opened the door to her, and once again, she pushed past the lady of the house, leaving her daughter standing on the step. Sarah just looked at Mary apologetically. 'You'd better come in,' said Mary, incensed at Mrs Beckwith's rudeness. She summoned Mathew in from the yard, where he had been helping his father and brothers.

'Mrs Beckwith and her daughter are here to see you, Mathew,' she called across the yard. Mary had three tankards of beer in her hands for William and two of his sons. 'I'm not going back in there until she's gone; otherwise, I may say something that I shouldn't,' she told them as they accepted the drinks.

Mathew lit a couple of candles and stood them on the table. He asked Sarah to sit on a stool while he removed the emplaster from the day before. The wound was still weeping, but there were no signs of infection. He cleaned her chin with a new cloth soaked in *rosewater.* Sarah flinched at the pain.

'Don't worry,' Mathew said reassuringly, 'this is going to heal well. I'll try not to hurt you, but I need to put another dressing on it.' He separated the white from a fresh egg and spread it thickly onto a plegit (a small wad of soft material), applying this to the wound on Sarah's chin, using a new emplaster to hold it in place.

'You should notice a big change when you come tomorrow,' Mathew reassured her. 'The swelling and the redness will be almost gone by then, but it will still need a few days to heal completely.'

The treatments went on for two more days, and each time there was a noticeable improvement in Sarah's recovery. On the fourth day, Mathew decided to leave the wound uncovered, to allow the flesh to dry and for new skin to begin to form freely.

'Remember,' he said, 'do not scratch it. Clean it each day with a little *rosewater* and all will be well.'

The day after the Beckwith's final visit, a messenger arrived with a note for Mathew. The boy who brought it waited at the door for an answer. After reading the note, the young surgeon took it to Mary. 'Well, what do you think?' he said, with a smile on his face. Mary read the note.

'So the old hag must have a heart after all,' Mary said with a huff. 'Or a conscience and is feeling guilty about the way she spoke to you and how she treated her daughter.'

The boy stood in the open doorway, sniggering at Mary's words. 'Tell your mistress I would be pleased to accept her invitation,' said Mathew. The boy turned and ran off.

'Wait 'till your father and brothers hear that you're mixing with your betters!' Mary said as she laughed, her anger of the previous days was forgotten. 'When does she want you to attend?'

'The day after tomorrow,' Mathew replied. 'I have to go, don't I?'

Mary was quick to show the letter to Mathew's father and brothers, who took great delight in teasing him over the invitation.

Wearing clothes borrowed from his father and brothers, Mathew had done his best to dress as well as he could. He had a blue jacket and breeches from his brother, Charles (that had been specially made for his marriage to Mary), his father's best black broad-brimmed felt hat with a silver band, and his brother, Henry's boots. Dressed in such finery, he would easily pass as a young gentleman of Beverly.

Mathew had been instructed to arrive at seven of the clock, and he ensured he arrived on time at the grand house.

The Beckwith House was on Newbegin Lane and was a three-storey building, the ground floor being made of brick and the upper parts having a façade of timber and pargetting.

The front door was opened by the steward, an elderly man with a bald head, dressed in a black wool suit, black stockings and shoes. Mathew showed him the invitation; the steward looked Mathew up and down, then, stood aside to allow him to enter. Mathew followed the steward through to a large room to the right of the entrance hall; at least he was not the first to arrive, which was something to be grateful for. Mathew looked at the other guests dressed in all their finery and felt instantly out of place. How should he conduct himself in such a formal gathering?

To Mathew's great relief as soon as she saw him, Sarah Beckwith came over and curtsied, saying, 'Surgeon

Fletcher, you are most welcome. I was so pleased when mother said she wanted to invite you. Look, can you see? With just a little makeup there is no sign at all of that horrible disfigurement I once had.'

Sarah was now clearly excited at the prospect of the evening ahead. She was to be introduced to Michael Warton, a very eligible young man who was home from his studies at Cambridge University. She led Mathew to her mother, to whom he gave a low bow.

'Good evening, Mrs Beckwith,' Mathew said graciously. 'Thank you for your invitation.'

After just a cursory glance the older lady at first seemed to be ignoring Mathew, but then she turned to the man at her side.

'Mayor Mambie,' she announced, 'may I introduce the family surgeon, Mr Fletcher.' The imperious lady's voice carried around the room, evidently wanting to impress her guests. The immodest introduction did little to put Mathew at his ease.

'Welcome, Mr Fletcher,' Mayor Mambie said warmly. 'Sarah seems very happy with your work; indeed she is a changed girl since your cure.'

Sarah led Mathew on to meet another guest, Lady Gee, widow of the Hull alderman and merchant William Gee. She sat on a cushion, in a straight-backed chair, looking frail, but her bright blue eyes scanned him from head to foot, then, she looked deep into his eyes before speaking. 'You have a kind face, young man; you will do well as a medical man.' Mathew thanked her for her kind words.

More people were arriving so Sarah had to say, 'Excuse me,' to Mathew, the pained look on her face indicating she was evidently sorry that she had to leave him on his own, while she went to meet the new guests. Mathew gave Lady

Gee a slight bow and went to find a space out of the way, feeling somewhat out of his depth in such wealthy company. A glass of wine taken from a tray held by a young man, dressed in the same smart but serviceable way as the steward, helped take his mind off his awkwardness. Mr Beckwith came over and introduced himself to Mathew.

'Mr Fletcher,' he began in a friendly tone, 'I cannot thank you enough for what you have done for our Sarah— as you can see she is a changed girl. I insisted that my wife included you as a guest tonight by way of thanks and also as a way of introducing you to some of the influential people of Beverley who may help you to become established in your work.'

Mathew thanked Mr Beckwith for his generosity but refrained from informing his host that he planned to return to Hull. Mr Beckwith kept Mathew in conversation until the steward announced the food was ready, ushering everyone through to the main hall. In the centre of the main hall stood a long table around which chairs had been placed. The table was set with plates, cutlery and drinking vessels of various types. Mathew was escorted to a place in the centre of the table. 'Sit here,' instructed Mr Beckwith. 'You'll be able to hear conversation from both ends of the table.'

Grace was spoken by James Burney, Reverend at Beverley Minster. No sooner had he taken his seat than servants brought through plates of pea soup. At first, Mathew was taken aback: all these wealthy people were sitting at this grand table, and all they had been served with was pea soup and bread!

However, very quickly the servants returned with dishes of buttered eggs with anchovies along with plates of bacon tarts, leaving them on the table within easy reach of the diners. Mathew watched as everyone picked at their food seeming to eat little of it. But he was hungry, and tore a large handful of bread from a loaf and started to eat it with his soup. By the time he was finishing the bread and soup the servants returned. They brought platters of boiled leg of pork cooked in cider and mustard, steak pie with raisins, stewed venison in claret, potted pigeon, baked cod with mussels, chicken lemon salad, a salad of sorrel, beetroot and watercress, buttered spinach and mushrooms with garlic.

There was more food on the table in front of him than Mathew had ever seen in one place before. *So this is how the rich eat their meals*, he thought to himself. He watched as food was moved around the table by servants so that guests could help themselves from the different choices. A servant came to stand at his shoulder with a tiny dish containing a coarsely ground black powder. Mathew looked at the powder, then at the servant. The expression on his face must have told the servant everything he needed to know, for the sympathetic man bent lower and whispered in Mathew's ear, 'Its pepper, sir—very expensive; you sprinkle a little on your food to enhance its flavour.'

Mathew's face reddened, out of embarrassment and ignorance about the spice. He declined the offer of the pepper, and the servant moved on to the next guest.

A man named Nicholas Pearson sat on Mathew's left, he initiated the conversation by saying, 'So, sir, I deduce you must be the surgeon that treated young Miss Sarah.' The abruptness of his words startled Mathew.

'Good evening sir, my name is Mathew Fletcher,' he replied. 'And yes, I am the surgeon. Forgive me for not introducing myself first, only I am not used to being in such fine company, and I am unaccustomed as to how I should conduct myself.'

'Fear not, lad. I am clerk to Nicholas Osgodby, the vicar at St May's. Mr Beckwith is an up and coming herald for the king, and his wife revels in the association. Mrs Beckwith likes to show off her acquisitions. This dinner is for the benefit of her daughter, who she is trying to marry off to Michael Warton, grandson of the richest man in Beverley.'

The likeable clerk made small talk for the rest of the meal. In fact, to Mathew's relief, the only time he stopped talking was when more food was brought to the table. Mathew listened intently to the stories the clerk told him about himself and his work. The meal finished with a choice of rice pudding, sultana pudding, John Knott's Biscuits or praline cream. Mathew had been grateful for his new friend's conversation.

As the evening proceeded, the pair talked of their plans for the future. After they had finished eating Mrs Beckwith announced that she had arranged for 'Hot Waters' to be served. This was a new kind of drink from the Low Countries called Jenever. Mathew found it hard to drink—it had a bitter taste and burned his throat, deciding one glass was more than enough. Nicholas Pearson, however, liked his drink and was soon speaking very freely.

'You know, Mathew,' he continued, 'I may be in a lowly position, but as clerk to the Reverend Osgodby, I learn many things. People talk to the reverend, and I like to keep my ears open. You don't know what you might learn in these times of trouble.' He went on bragging about what he had overheard from various people. Mathew didn't know whether to believe him or not, but he reckoned most of what he said was probably a drunken exaggeration. As the evening wore on Mathew became bored with the drunken clerk, and began looking for an excuse to go home. As Nicholas Pearson fell asleep in his chair, Mathew went to find Sarah Beckwith, thanked her for her hospitality, and went home to the life he understood and was familiar with. As he walked home, he hoped that maybe one day, he would be ready for that kind of life with his betters. Mathew's family had waited up for his return and enjoyed listening to his description of the grand house, the fine foods and interesting people he had met.

The invitation to Mrs Beckwith's house seemed to have had some beneficial consequences for him. It wasn't long before people were visiting him with minor ailments and complaints for him to treat, and Mary was always there willing to give him a helping hand when dealing with the ladies, to which, many commented on, wishing other physicians and surgeons would do the same. Mathew wondered if this might be a useful arrangement to offer when he set up his own practice in Hull but using Elizabeth as his assistant. With the new customers Mathew was now getting, it didn't take long for him to replace the ten pounds he had spent to attain membership of the surgeon's guild. The more patients Mathew treated, the more his confidence grew.

The time passed quickly, and he began to think of his future in Hull with Elizabeth.

'Father,' he said one morning over breakfast. 'I am returning to Hull tomorrow. It is time to make preparations for making my own way in the world.'

The suddenness of Mathew's statement took his father and brothers by surprise.

'Do you really have to go, Mathew?' asked his father.

'Yes, I think so, father. Hull is a bigger town. There will be more work for me there. You have Charles and Henry to help you run the things here. Now I am my own master; I will be able to return and see you whenever I wish.'

Mathew had yet to tell his father of the other reason he wanted to return to Hull and now was as good a time as any. 'Father, there is also a girl in Hull I have taken a fancy to, and hope to marry if she'll have me. Her family own an apothecary shop. I sure you will all like her. With your permission, I would like you to meet her and her family. I was hoping I could bring them here to Beverley to meet you all.' If his father was going to object to his plans it was just as well he found out on the cusp of leaving home so he knew if he would be welcomed back.

William Fletcher's laughter filled the room. 'So that's what the rush to return to Hull is all about! Our Mathew's got a girl!'

Charles and Henry joined their father in poking fun at the youngest member of the family having fallen for a girl. Only Mary didn't join in with their teasing of Mathew.

'Tell us about her,' his father insisted.

'No,' said Mathew. 'You'll only make fun of me. You can judge her for yourselves when I bring her here to meet you.'

Chapter Six

Captain Legge rode into Hull alone, passing through the Myton Gate after his long journey from Newburg Priory. He was tired, cold, and regardless of the importance of his mission, his first priority was to call at the home of his friend Henry Barnard, with whom he would be staying. The Barnard house was on the High Street. It would give him the privacy and security he needed as Master of the Kings Armoury and Lieutenant of the Ordinance to meet his contacts, and his friendship with the ex-mayor would be a good enough reason for being in Hull if he was questioned about why he was there. It would also be convenient for entertaining Sir John Hotham, to discuss the progress on his plans to secure the town for the Kings arrival.

Legge was also carrying an important document, signed by many of the nobles in the north of England, who had pledged their loyalty to the King. If conflict between the King and Parliament were to become inevitable, it would be vital for the King to know whom he could trust.

Pleased to be back in Hull, Mathew had a number of things he wanted to do. Looking for premises to rent was just one of them. Being eager to see her again, visiting Elizabeth Moor was to be first.

Elizabeth was Mathew's first love, and he'd so far kept his feelings secret from her. Now he was free to call on her and make his intentions known if her father would let him. But, he still had to discover if she felt the same way about him? He would visit the apothecary shop tomorrow and speak to her father about calling on Elizabeth. Now that he had money to rent a house and to set up his surgeon's business, Mathew was feeling more confident Mr Moor would allow him to walk out with Elizabeth. He would explain to Mr Moor that, in due time, with some luck and hard work, he would soon have enough money put aside to ask Elizabeth to marry him.

But before he could do any of this, he needed somewhere to stay. He arrived at the Drunken Monk Inn on Lowgate and left his horse and mule in the stable at the rear of the premises. Inside the hostelry was much like many inns and taverns of its type in Hull. There was a stone floor, with a number of small tables and stools, around the wood-panelled walls were high backed settles, while in the far wall of the taproom was a large fireplace, over which was a long wooden mantelshelf. From the ceiling close to the serving hatch hung duck and geese ready for plucking and preparing for the pot. There were also legs of ham and sides of bacon all hanging from the ceiling beams, keeping dry and away from the rats, and bunches of herbs hung from hooks on the chimney breast. A large basket of dried lavender hung from the centre of the ceiling, sweetening the smell of the taproom and unwashed bodies of customers. Men and women sat at tables drinking and eating while their children played happily with a ball and skittles on the dirty rush-strewn floor.

A large woman wearing a two-piece woollen dress approached Mathew. Her shoulders were covered with a white linen scarf, its two points pinned to the bodice, and long curly brown hair dropped below her coif and over her shoulders.

'What can I do for you, my love?' she asked in her broad East Yorkshire accent.

Mathew explained that he needed a room, food and somewhere to stable his horse and mule for a few days. He gave the woman two shillings in advance, and she rewarded him with a smile and led him up the stairs located in the corner of the taproom.

She let Mathew go up the stairs first, pointing the direction he was to go, but on reaching the top of the stairs, she had to squeeze past him in the corridor in order to show him to his room. In this unexpectedly intimate moment, as she trapped his body against the wall, she pressed herself against him suggestively. 'We don't get many good-looking young men staying here,' she confided, leaning closer. 'If there's anything you need, *anything at all*, you just let me know.' So saying, she pressed her hips firmly against his, staring up into his face, then led him on to the room at the end of the passage.

'Er, yes, thank you. I will be sure to let you know if I need anything.'

The woman laughed and opened the door to his room. It was small and clean, with a single rope bed, straw mattress and a couple of blankets with a clean sheet. The bedding looked fresh enough, with not too many stains on it. A stool and small table stood against the wall, and a 'piss pot' with a lid stood at the foot of the bed.

The room was at the front of the inn, and the window looked out onto the street. Mathew dropped his saddlebag on the bed and thanked the landlady for the room. Mathew's saddlebag contained all his worldly possessions, apart from his surgeon's chest, which was still on the back of the mule, and his small box surgeon's instruments, which he placed on the table. The landlord's wife had offered him one meal a day which was included in the price of the room. Through the occasional crack in the floorboards, he could see the taproom below. Putting up with the noise from the inn's customers on the ground floor would only be a temporary discomfort, acceptable for the short period before he found a permanent home.

Mathew went back to his mule in the stable and unloaded his surgeon's chest. It took him half an hour to carry, drag and shove the heavy chest from the yard up to his quarters for safe keeping. After having a pie and a tankard of ale, he returned to his room and made up his bed. Giving in to the temptation to lie back on it and listen to the sounds of the taproom below, his envisaged short nap turned into a full night's sleep.

After a breakfast of bread, cheese and honey Mathew set off to the see Elizabeth and her father. Mathew was surprised the streets were not only busy with people going about their daily business but soldiers as well, far more than there had been when he left Hull for Beverley. The soldiers marched four abreast and eight deep with a sergeant keeping them in order. They were heading for the newly refurbished blockhouses that backed onto the River Hull.

Mathew was puzzled as to why the town needed so much martial protection, and why the town walls had undergone recent refurbishment. Yet, as far as he knew, there had been no rumours of a Scottish invasion and no notice declaring that England was at war with anyone else.

The distraction passed, and he continued on, finally arriving at the apothecary shop. He walked the street outside, nervously thinking about how he would bring up the subject of his feelings towards Elizabeth. He stepped to the shop door, gathering his courage before going in, but before he could enter the shop—before he had even thought of what he was going to say in fact—the door opened and there stood Elizabeth.

Face to face, they stood speechless. Mathew's mouth opened and closed, but he was lost for words. Moments later, seemingly from nowhere, came a distant voice, saying, 'Elizabeth—I love you!'

Elizabeth stepped backwards, red-faced, her hands trying to cover her burning cheeks. In an instant, the embarrassment became too much, and she ran back into the shop, and through to a room at the rear. Mathew entered, cursing himself for blurting the words out as he had, and wondered what kind of fool he had made of himself. Mr Moor stood in the middle of the shop; he had apparently seen and heard everything.

'Well, Mathew Fletcher, I think you need to explain yourself,' said Mr Moor, looking bemused. Mathew explained the feelings he held for Elizabeth, and that he had come specifically to ask for Mr Moor's permission to walk out with Elizabeth, and also discover the most critical question of all, did Elizabeth reciprocate his feelings?

Mr Moor laughed. 'Mathew, for the past year and a bit, you have come to my shop every Saturday for supplies for Surgeon Adams. Did you think I wouldn't notice the way you look at my daughter? The way you would fall over your tongue every time she spoke to you? You fool of a boy!' A broad smile stretched across Mr Moor's face. 'I've even overheard Elizabeth saying her prayers on a night time and at the church on a Sunday, wishing for your safe return from Beverley and for her to see you again. I knew you would come round one day when you had plucked up enough courage, so I've already spoken to Surgeon Adams about you. He has great praise for your abilities as a surgeon. He says you should become a successful young man. So yes, lad—you have my blessing to walk out with Elizabeth. This Sunday you may accompany us to church.'

Elizabeth's head appeared for a moment around the door into the shop; she giggled before popping out of sight again. Then she reappeared and stood with her back to the door, looking at her feet. Lifting her head, she gave Mathew a big smile and shuffled towards him. She kept her head low, staring at her hands, her fingers knotting and twisting. She stopped in front of Mathew and finally looked up at him. 'I always hoped that you would come back for me,' she said in an almost inaudible whisper, not wanting her father to overhear her.

'Go on, get out and go for a walk,' said Mr Moor, still grinning from ear to ear. 'I won't get any work out of Elizabeth while she's cooing like a lovesick dove.' He looked across at the couple, shaking his head in delight. Just wait till I tell Mrs Moor!'

Mathew took Elizabeth by the hand as the two of them left the shop. The young woman's father still smiling as the door closed behind them. He remembered the day when he had approached his wife's father with the very same awkwardness that Mathew had shown just now. He wondered if his father-in-law had then felt the same way as he did today. He was filled with pride at the way his daughter had grown up. It seemed such a short time since he had looked his new-born child in the face, and now she was a fully grown woman. He knew that his wife, Martha, would be happy with the match, for they had talked about it often, knowing that one day it would come about. He looked around his shop: it felt empty and very quiet all of a sudden. A heaviness fell on his heart, as he realised that his little girl had grown up and would one day leave to start a new life of her own.

Walking away from the High Street the young couple found themselves walking past the old monastery gardens. All that was left now of the old buildings were the occasional sandstone blocks, showing where the monks' cloisters had once been. The cleared land now contained trees and gardens, which made the south-western part of Hull a pleasant escape from the narrow streets and the overpowering smells of the town centre's open sewers.

Captain Legge pulled his horse to a halt outside a large house on the High Street. His body ached as he stepped out of the saddle and onto the cobbled road. He arched his back to release the tension in his muscles and brushed the dust from his clothes. A small boy ran up the garden path towards the gate at the same time as the front door opened and a man stepped through.

'Welcome, sir, I will take your horse,' said the barefooted boy. He took the reins and led the horse away, calling over his shoulder, 'I'll see your saddlebags are taken to your room, sir.'

The man at the front door of the house came down the path to greet the weary traveller.

'Good day to you, sir,' he welcomed his visitor. 'My name is Miller, steward of the house. I am afraid Alderman Barnard is not at home at the moment, but he has given instructions for you to be shown every courtesy. I have had a light meal made ready for you, but since I did not know when you would arrive, it is only a herring tart, cheese, and bread, will that be agreeable, sir?'

Legge nodded. 'Yes, fine. I am thirsty more than hungry. Have a jug of beer brought up to my room while I remove my riding clothes.'

Passing through the front door of the brick-built, double-fronted house with its large mullioned windows, Captain Legge stepped into a large wood-panelled hall. Along the right-hand wall, stairs led to the first floor. In the centre of the hall, on the orange-and-white tiled floor stood a large round table displaying a model of a fully rigged two-masted ship. Ladder-back chairs with embroidered upholstery stood against the left-hand wall and portraits of whom he assumed to be family members were prominently displayed along the length of the hall.

Miller led him up the stairs to his room. The room was spacious with an ornate canopied bed with heavily decorated drapes. Against one wall stood a wardrobe and chairs, in the opposite wall was a leaded-light window that overlooked the front garden and the High Street. Legge unhooked his sword and scabbard and threw them onto the bed.

'I will leave you for a moment, sir, while I fetch you something to drink.' So saying, Miller gave a slight bow and left.

Captain Legge slumped into a chair and removed his spurs and boots, relieved to have his feet free of their hot prison. Miller quickly returned with a tray containing a jug of beer and a blue-and-white tankard. Over his shoulder, he carried Legge's saddlebags.

'Put the saddlebags on the bed,' Legge told him. 'I want a fresh shirt.'

The house steward set the tray down on the table and poured the beer. 'If you leave your shirt on the chair, sir, I will have it cleaned for you. I will wait for you in the hall, and when you are ready to come down, I will fetch your food.' He left Captain Legge to change his shirt and put on a more comfortable pair of shoes.

Mathew took Elizabeth's hand and led her into the old garden that had once been part of the Blackfriars monastery. Finding the remains of a sandstone wall, they sat in the sunshine, while bees hovered over the clover flowers in the grass.

'Did you know that I liked you?' asked Mathew.

'I wasn't sure. I knew you used to watch me while I worked in the shop, but you never said more than a few words to me, so I couldn't be sure,' Elizabeth replied. 'All I could do was hope.'

They sat close, shoulder to shoulder, their hands entwined.

'Most of the people that come into Father's shop are older people,' she continued. 'You know most of the surgeons and physicians in this town—they're old, not like you. Otherwise, the customers are mostly old women who buy potions for their aches and pains. It's rare indeed for us to get a good-looking boy coming into the shop.' Elizabeth smiled cheekily.

Mathew blushed, stood and turned to face Elizabeth, a pained expression on his face. 'I'm not a boy; I'm a man. I'm twenty-one, I'll have you know!'

Elizabeth laughed at Mathew's hurt feelings.

'Little girls should mind their betters!' Mathew retaliated at her ridicule.

'That's not fair,' said Elizabeth. 'I can't help being younger than you.'

The young surgeon took her hand. 'Let us not fight like children. I will have to take you back to your father soon.

'What made you want to become a surgeon?' She asked pulling him back to sit beside her.

'I saw my mother die when I was a boy, the vision of it sometimes haunts me at night. It's why I'm so driven to find out what makes the body work and how to cure it when it becomes sick. I think back to that day when with my two older brothers we waited outside her room for news of our mother. I was about ten years old. I knew mother was seriously ill, but on that day we'd been summoned to stand outside our parents' bedchamber, I could feel my heart beating as we waited, and knew, as did my brothers, that we were not going to be given good news when we entered. Eventually, the door opened, and we were beckoned inside. The room was in near darkness; just a single small tallow candle burned in the corner of the room, fixed by a hook to the wall. The only window had its shutters closed, and I remember a stagnant smell dominating the air. Up against the wall opposite the door was the bed that father had built and standing by the bed was a man in black robes and skullcap. His wrinkled face looked solemn and dour. He glanced up as we entered and then stepped back from the bed, shaking his head. I ran to mother's side, while Charles and Henry, waited together at the foot of the bed with our father. I grasped mother's hand as she laid there, it felt thin and frail; her skin looked orangey-yellow in that dim candlelight. She opened her eyes and mustering what little strength she could; she turned her head to look at me.

She smiled at seeing me, and said, 'Don't be sad, my suffering will soon be over. I am going to miss you, all of you.' Then she gave a weak cough, the smell of her breath was sour and bitter. I remember starting to cry as tears ran freely down my face. I didn't understand why my mother was dying; she had taken ill and slowly deteriorated, the pains growing ever greater until she could neither stand nor walk from the pain in her back. The physician had bled and purged mother time and again, but nothing seemed to help. She took many strange and foul-smelling potions, but there was never any sign of any improvement in her. Then one day the physician said it was 'the stone' and that there was no hope. Now she lay on her deathbed, holding my hand. With tears in her eyes, she summoned up the last of her strength and gave her final instructions to the three of us.

'Be good for your father; you are all to help him whenever you can. God willing I will be watching over you.' She closed her eyes, her mouth pulling taut with pain, her body contorted unnaturally, and a scream broke from her lips as she convulsed on the bed. Eventually, she fell back, a sigh passing from her lips, and then her hand slipped from my grip. I stood there shaking at what he had seen. I looked up at father and could only think of one thing, bring her back! One word came from my lips: 'Father?'

It away, it was more than a question; it was a cry for help, understanding, compassion and comprehension, but I don't think father understood. I looked at my mother, she was still there, but she was gone. The mother who would hug me close when I was frightened, healed my wounds when I was hurt, comforted me when I was sad or kiss me when I had done well. I couldn't grasp where she had gone; or that at one moment she had been speaking to me and now she would never speak again. And, my father, the man who could make anything, fix anything, had an answer for any problem that my brothers at I had to face, stood there helpless. At the time I thought if father had really loved my mother as profoundly as he said he did, why didn't father bring her back, fix her, like he did everything else. As I grew up, I understood, but the thought of her that day never leaves me. Mathew fell silent for a moment. You know; you are the first person I have spoken to about my mother's death since it happened.'

Elizabeth drew him close, 'I'll never leave you, Mathew. Come, shall we go to the market? There are sure to be some peddlers there selling their fake medicines and quack surgeons offering cures for a few pennies. You'll be able to show me how clever you are and tell me all about the mistakes they are making.'

They made their way back to the High Street, where many markets were held along its western side. Most days, one or more of the markets would have a few traders selling their wares, but the true market days were Tuesdays and Fridays. As they entered Market Street, they soon spied 'Happy Pete', a peddler who was always to be found hanging around the traders; he was one of the regular peddlers. From a satchel he carried, he sold small bottles of potions that he claimed could cure everything.

Peter's trick was to watch people in the market and discern any affliction they might have, then, waylay them with a promise of a cure. Everyone knew Peter's remedies didn't work, but he always greeted people with a friendly smile and told a good story of how he had discovered the secret of the potion he was trying to sell them. Even if they didn't buy his medicine, he always wished them a good day.

The young lovers dodged around a pie seller who had set up his stall outside the Fishermans Rest Inn and continued to walk across the market. A tooth puller who had set up a chair between a stall holder selling wooden plates and tankards, and stall holder who was selling chickens.

The tooth puller, dressed in a jacket and breeches of fine brown wool with a matching coat, cut in the Dutch style and wearing a fashionable black felt hat that was tall with a narrow brim. His shirt sported small ruffs to the collar and cuffs, and with the gold coloured medallion hanging from a chain around his neck, he cut quite a dash. His goatee beard and moustache lent his lean, tanned face an air of knowledge and education.

To his left-hand side stood an upturned barrel, on which he had placed a board to lay-out and displayed his instruments, bottles and cups. A teenage boy accompanied by his mother stood in front of him. The boy appeared to be in pain, cupping the side of his face in one hand. The crowd was building, waiting for the entertainment to start. As the boy sat in the tooth puller's chair, the spectators pushed closer. Elizabeth stood in front of Mathew so that she could see the proceedings unfold.

As the unfortunate lad opened his mouth to allow the dentist to see inside, his many black and rotten teeth were put on view to all. Detecting the one that was hurting amongst so many possible contenders was going to take time and be painful. The dentist used the thumb of his left hand to press down on the boy's chin while he inserted the needle probe into his mouth. The boy was brave and kept his back straight. Suddenly he screamed, and the dentist jumped back. The boy leaned forward and spat a gobbet of blood and saliva on the ground. His mother looked on, fear for her child etched across her face. A murmur of approval rippled through the crowd at the first sight of blood. With his mother's encouragement, the boy once again leaned back in the chair. The dentist fumbled with his tools on top the barrel, eventually selecting a screw-adjustable clamp. Inserting it into the boy's mouth, he turned the screw that opened the jaws of the clamp which would force the lad's mouth open, so as to allow the dentist free access, precluding the possibility of being bitten. The boy gripped the chair seat again in preparation for what was to come, while his mother stood behind, pushing down on his shoulders.

The dentist selected his claw pliers, as the crowd saw the instrument they gave a simultaneous *oooh!* Quickly, the dentist inserted the pliers and, with a couple of twists of his wrist, extracted the tooth in one piece. A gargled scream came from the boy, who broke free from his mother's grasp and jumped out of the chair, struggling to remove the clamp from his mouth. The crowd went wild with laughter as the boy danced about in pain and the dentist tried to grab him and settle him down to retrieve the clamp still fixed in his mouth.

His mother fainted, the crowd cheered again. The dentist wrestled the boy to the ground and removed the clamp. With his mouth free of the obstruction, the youngster calmed down and went to the aid of his mother, blood still drooling from his mouth and dripping down his shirt. The dentist proudly held the tooth aloft, and the crowd gave a final cheer of approval, before moving off to continue their daily business.

Elizabeth turned to Mathew. 'That was horrible,' she declared. 'In future, I will always make sure I clean my teeth.' She gave a little shiver and stepped away, pulling Mathew by the hand.

'Let me see your teeth,' said Mathew.

She opened her mouth wide.

'You have beautiful white teeth,' complimented Mathew. 'Your mother clearly doesn't overindulge you in sweetmeats.'

The love-smitten girl looked up into Mathew's eyes and smiled.

'It's time to go back,' Mathew told her. 'Your father was good enough to let you come with me, but he may not be so generous the next time if I keep you longer without a chaperone.'

They headed back to the shop hand in hand.

'Elizabeth,' he began warily, 'you do know I want to marry you, don't you?' Mathew stumbled over the words. He stopped and turned to face Elizabeth. 'You do, don't you?'

Elizabeth pulled her hand from his. 'And how am I supposed to know that?' she asked scornfully. 'Have you asked me? No! I'm not a mind reader you know! For goodness' sake, you're supposed to *ask*, not just suppose a girl *knows* these things! For all, I knew you might just have wanted to have your wicked way with me so that you could then leave me as a fallen woman.' She pouted, feigning hurt feelings.

'Stop it, Elizabeth. I do love you. I have always loved you from the first day I saw you in your father's shop. I want to marry you. *Please,* Elizabeth. Will you consent to be my wife?'

'Oh yes Mathew, I sorry for teasing you. I have loved you for so long it hurts. Each time you came to the shop I made sure I was there to see you, hoping you would notice me and speak to me. Let us go and tell my parents; they will be so excited!'

Chapter Seven

On the same day that Mathew had returned to Hull, six riders entered the town through the Myton Gate. At first glance, they would have passed as merchants or gentlemen going about their business, with black riding cloaks and hoods covering their day clothes. But to anyone who took a closer look, indeed to any person who paid them just a little more attention, they would have noticed that three of them lacked the confidence of seasoned travellers and looked out of place on a horse, whereas the second three rode their powerful steeds with confidence and ease. Only the swords dipping below their cloaks gave a clue that these men were not gentlemen or merchants. The horses they rode bred for stamina and speed, in case of a fast getaway, and were not the steady beasts that most people would choose as a workhorse.

The riders entered the Hull in ones and twos, those riders bringing up the rear maintaining visual contact with their leader. The first three turned towards the White Meat Market and took lodgings at the Mermaid Inn. The second trio moved onto the quayside and took lodgings at an inn near the northern end of the quay, close to the town walls. The two groups of men didn't know of the other group's existence: it was pure coincidence that they had all arrived on the same day, but all six men were on similar missions.

The three who turned towards the quay took their horses to a stable close to Hull's North Gate and the River Hull, and after paying for a week's stabling and feed for the horses, entered The Deaf Cat Inn. The men surveyed the busy taproom, which was already filled with sailors and workers off the quay. Clouds of blue tobacco smoke hovered below the ceiling, mixing with the smell of stale ale, sweat and the damp dirty sawdust that covered the floor. The aroma of fish and whale oil was overwhelming, for this was an inn for fishermen and whalers: a place for hard men who lived hard lives.

A one-eyed fellow sat in the corner playing a thin wooden whistle, its shrill notes cutting through the noise of the drinkers who were relaxing after a day's work. The taproom was hot, and the three riders threw back the sides of their cloaks. The men were dressed in a similar fashion, with long riding boots, dark breeches and leather jerkins over plain linen shirts, and each of them also wore a battered broad-brimmed hat.

But the singular thing that marked these men out was the weapons that they carried. Each had hanging from his waist a 'mortuary' sword (a new cavalry issue weapon) and in his belt a large dagger and pistol. All of them were tall, lean and well-muscled with weathered faces covered in days of unshaven stubble and dirt from their travels.

Although they didn't fit in with the rest of the drinkers in the taproom, no one was going to question their reasons for being there, for it wasn't difficult to see that they were soldiers of fortune.   They had spent time in the Low Countries, helping the Dutch fight the Spanish invaders, who wanted to halt the spread of Protestantism throughout Europe, but principles were not their concern, they had fought for money.

It was only after three months of defending the Dutch town of Geertruidenberg from the Catholics and not being paid, that the English defenders turned on their allies and sold the town to the Spanish, returning home with purses full of gold, not caring what the Spaniards would do to the poor people of the town. Now their purses were nearly empty, and they were ready and willing to join any cause that paid the right fee.

After securing a room big enough for the three of them to share for the week, they went back down to the taproom. Of the three, John Franks was the leader. They had formed their bond in Holland fighting to stop the Spanish from crossing the only bridge over the River Donge into Geertruidenberg, saving each other's lives on more than one occasion. Franks carried a large burn scar covering most of the left side of his face, caused by an exploding keg of black powder. It gave his face a distorted look, since no hair grew through the scar tissue, while on the right side of his tanned face, was several days of unshaven stubble.

The mercenaries pushed their way through the throng of sailors to an alcove on the back wall of the taproom where four sailors sat drinking. John Franks didn't say a word: he just looked at the sailors meaningfully; it only took a few seconds before they got the message, stood up and left.

After they sat down Geoffrey Wilkes, the second member of the group, leaned across the table, and said, 'What are we doing here, Franks? Why are we in this godforsaken town on the arse end of nowhere? We're soldiers, not spies.'

'Money, Geoffrey, money,' John Franks replied. 'We're getting well paid for this job, and my old lieutenant wants it done, and that's good enough for me. We'll be safe in here—no one will come looking for us in this piss hole.'

Franks leaned into the corner of the alcove, his thoughts returned to Geertruidenberg, remembering how the Spanish soldiers took their revenge on the population for holding out against them. He wiped his hand down his face, trying to remove those terrible memories.

A serving girl with a smile on her face wandered over to the men, but before she could say a word Peter Martins, the last member of the three, had put his arm around her waist and dragged her across his lap. Holding her firmly with one arm, he gave her a long kiss on the mouth; with his free hand, he grasped the firm flesh of her ample bosom. When he released her, she jumped to her feet, slapped Martins hard across the face, that's going to cost you an extra two pennies on their bill for the liberties he had taken.

All three men laughed.

'Bring us three bottles of brandy-wine, some meat, cheese and bread, then piss off and don't come back,' Franks ordered.

The girl stood staring at them.

'NOW!' snapped Franks as he threw her a look that turned her cold inside.

She turned and ran from the table to the kitchen. The incident with the popular serving wench hadn't gone unnoticed and had drawn the attention of sailors close by, but they quickly went back to their own conversations after receiving a cold stare from Franks. The girl soon returned again with three bottles and horn cups, leaving them on the end of the table, keeping clear of Martins' reach.

Each of the men filled their cups with the stiff drink and swilled it down in one, clearing the dust of the road from their throats. The girl returned with the plates of food, a scowl still on her face. Martins dropped his purse on the table with a thud and removed two silver shillings, sliding them slowly to the end of the table where the girl waited. At the sight of his purse, her smile returned and, with a swish of her hips, she moved closer. Martins raised his face to hers.

'Come on then, give us a kiss!' He jangled the coins in his purse.

The girl bent lower, and Martins' right arm went around her neck, pulling her closer, while his left hand went up her skirt to caress her inner thigh. As his fingers went up inside her the muscles in her pelvis tightened, she twisted her hips from side to side, and he could feel her senses warming and arousing to his touch. It seemed that the girl had no shame, her only thought being the money in his purse on the table and how much she could coax from him. Martins could feel her wetness and warmth; she was arousing him quicker than he had expected and all he wanted to do next was to take her to the back of the inn for some sport.

'Put her down!' demanded Franks, sternly. Martins pushed her away reluctantly, saying, 'Later, my lovely, later.' He dropped sixpence on the floor to ease the expression of loss written across her face. She bent down to snatch up the coin; a sailor on an adjacent table caressed her raised backside. She screamed, jerking up quickly, then turned around and grabbed the sailor's tankard of beer and threw it over him.

'You only get what you pay for,' she yelled at him, her face red with anger. The customers round about who had seen what had happened roared with laughter, and the girl stormed off indignantly.

Wilkes stood up, saying, 'I'm going for a piss. Make sure there's some food left when I get back.' Outside, he stood at the quayside to relieve himself.

The River Hull was quiet, and Wilkes could see the town's eastern defensive wall across the other side with Hull Castle at its centre. The castle was little more than a circular tower within the wall, but it was sufficient to accommodate the soldiers who patrolled that side of the river. As he stood there finishing his piss, a group of sailors came towards the inn. Wilkes heard one of them ask in a loud voice what a soldier was doing hanging around a sailors' inn. Wilkes, re-buttoning his breeches turned to face the sailors.

'I'm improving the smell of the place,' he replied, his hand moving across his waist for his sword. The three men in front of him were only armed with daggers—they would be no match for an experienced soldier with a mortuary sword. The three sailors stepped back, and Wilkes started to relax. Then, out of the darkness stepped a giant of a man with a belaying pin in his hand. Before Wilkes had got his sword halfway out of its scabbard, the belaying pin hit his upper sword arm. The blow took him off balance, and a fist caught him under the chin. His head was swimming; he could feel himself falling—he hoped it wasn't into the river. Hands grabbed at him and dragged him along the quay to a dark corner away from the inn.

The last thing he knew was the pain in the side of his head as he was struck with something hard.

The four sailors entered the Deaf Cat Inn. Franks gave them a cursory look and returned to his food, still keeping an eye on who was entering and leaving the inn. It was a habit he had formed many years ago allowing him to watch for trouble coming his way. Wilkes had been gone a few minutes when Martins commented on the food that was still left waiting for him.

Franks gave Martins a look of concern. 'Something's wrong,' he stated unemotionally. Both men stood up together and push their way to the door. The large sailor in the group who'd just entered spotted them first as they were dressed in a similar fashion to the one they had left outside. He indicated their presence to the other sailors.

Once outside, Wilkes's two friends used the light from the windows of the inn to search along the edge of the quay, looking down into the mud of the River Hull. The door to the inn swung open again, adding an extra pool of light to the quayside. The four sailors who had attacked Wilkes stepped into the night.

'Are youse two looking for your pal?' one of them asked. Out of the shadows stepped a huge man with curly red air and a Scottish accent. 'He's over there bleeding if he's not dead already.'

The Scotsman's companions, who looked small and insignificant in comparison to the giant, stood a step back from him. The Scot stepped towards Franks, belaying pins in his massive fists. The first swing of the Scotsman's pin missed Franks' head by a whisker as he dodged the incoming blow. The distinctive ring of swords being drawn pierced the night as Franks swerved to miss a second blow from his colossal assailant.

Of course, the three sailors who confronted Martins reckoned they had the better of the split: three against one was far better odds than one against three. While two of them probed at Martins' sword with their long 'Bollock Daggers', the third slipped into the shadows to manoeuvre around and behind their quarry.

Franks swung his blade at the head of the Scot, but it was blocked by the hard wood of the belaying pin, splinters spinning through the darkness as the mortuary sword bit deep. The Scotsman was extremely fast for a man of his size, and his skill at wielding the belaying pins had come from years at sea, running coal carriers down the coast from Newcastle to Hull, Boston and London.

The Scotsman's second club caught Franks on the shoulder, sending a searing pain up his neck and down his left arm. He brought the sword down slicing at his enemy's left arm, but he had jumped back in anticipation of the move.

As the three sailors stalked Martins, he stepped back towards the quayside. A glint of light reflected off the blade belonging to the sailor who had tried to circle him. Martins' blade cut to his right and back again in a flashing sweep. From the darkness came a cry of pain and the noise of metal clattering to the stones. The sound of running feet disappeared into the night.

Martins took a small step forward, and the two sailors moved further apart.

Franks, meanwhile, who had underestimated the Scotsman for the last time, ignored the pain in his left arm as he withdrew his own dagger. He lunged at the Scotsman with his sword, knowing it would be knocked aside with the belaying pin, and deftly thrust his dagger towards his opponent's belly. Both attacks were blocked, but Franks brought his left foot forward and kicked the Scotsman between the legs. The Scotsman froze for a moment then moaned as the pain in his groin registered in his brain. Seizing the moment, Franks brought his dagger free and thrust it into the Scotsman's upper arm, and a belaying pin hit the cobbles of the quay. The Scotsman cursed loudly in a language Franks didn't understand, and both men separated.

Martins lunged at one of the sailors, who instinctively danced to the side and then back, drawing Martins in his direction. The second sailor moved in to attack in a coordinated manoeuvre they must have used before. But Martins had anticipated the move when the two sailors separated. He checked his advance on the first sailor, turned and swung his blade low, catching the advancing sailor across the thigh. As the man crumpled down to one knee, Martins used the pommel of his sword to hit him in the face. The sailor keeled over to one side and lay on the ground moaning, semi-conscious. In the short time, Martins took to turn back ready to fend off the attack from the last sailor the latter had disappeared into the night.

Franks stepped forwards; his sword held levelled at the Scotsman. He drew his sword upward signalling a blow to the Scotsman's head. The Scot raised his belaying pin to block the strike but it was a faint, Franks drove his dagger into the Scot's right shoulder. The wounded giant cursed again in his native tongue and fell back, dropping the second belaying pin. Realising that he was now on his own, he too turned and fled.

'Did you kill any of them?' asked Franks, as Martins joined him.

'No. I reckoned you wouldn't want me to, having just arrived in town.' Martins sheathed his sword.

'Good. Our paymaster wouldn't want the attention. Let's find Wilkes.' Franks put up his own sword and dagger. It didn't take long for the two men to find Wilkes slumped against a wall in the dark corner. His face was severely swollen; blood seeped from the corner of his mouth, and he had a cut across his cheek.

'I would have happier if you'd killed the bastards for me,' he mumbled through swollen lips.

'Come on, you've got good food going to waste inside,' said Martins.

Across town, the other trio of men had settled in at the Mermaid Inn. They were sitting eating a meal of meat-and-beer stew, bread and tankards of ale.

These characters were not soldiers. In fact between the three of them, they didn't look as if they had done a hard day's work in their lives. They were the kind of rogues whom you see and instinctively put your hand to your purse to check you still have it. Surprisingly, they were all educated men, but, for one reason or another, had decided that working for a living, in the conventional meaning of the word, was not for them.

This week, however, stealing money was not their game, and their talents as conmen and thieves were to be turned to different purposes, for now. Their job was to observe and report on the movements of the aldermen of Hull, including Sir John Hotham. Captain Legge wanted to know the business of all the key people in the town, and especially with whom their loyalties lay.

Each of these ne'er-do-wells had been assigned a mission. Henry Walker was to follow Sir John Hotham, Joseph Fox's mark was the ex-mayor Henry Barnard, and Thomas Potter was to report on the comings and goings from the Guildhall, the administrative centre for the town and port of Hull.

Henry Walker had decided that the drudgery of following Sir John Hotham was not for him. Walker's father had been a prosperous wool merchant in the north of Yorkshire but had died young of some disease he'd caught from the sheep's fleeces. Inheriting his father's business, Henry had soon gambled and squandered the money away. Now he used his tongue to ingratiate himself into the favour of unwitting people, before defrauding them of what money they had. Talking his way into employment among Sir John Hotham's clerical staff had not been difficult. His new job gave him access to the workings of the Guildhall, as well as most of the documents that passed between the clerks. As Potter had told him before, knowledge was the key to extorting money from the careless or greedy and that knowledge could be found in the Guildhall.

Thomas Potter had taken a ground floor room in the building opposite the Guildhall on the pretext of needing an office. From there he made notes of everyone entering and leaving the Guildhall. There was no way he could know their names, but with his keen eye, he picked out the key features of each person and listed them.

The aldermen and wealthy merchants were the easiest to identify, with their vibrant and colourful clothes; next came the clerks, always carrying piles of documents, their hands and cuffs stained with ink, then there were soldiers with coloured scarves, signifying that they were officers.

Identifying distinguishing features in people was easy for a 'Street Pirate'; however, the hard part was spotting the person who may look like an ordinary member of the public, but who acted out of character. Detecting such figures could be significant, and relieving them of their secrets could be more important still. With the aid of Henry Walker, Thomas would soon be familiar with their names and their business. He also provided a convenient drop-off point for any documents that Walker wanted to be copied, before passing them on to Captain Legge. All intelligence would then be passed on to Sir John Belasyse at Newburgh Priory, where it would be coded and sent to the Earl of Newcastle.

Joseph Fox's job was to exploit Henry Barnard, the disaffected ex-mayor of Hull. An accomplished conman, Fox, was to befriend the ex-mayor and learn the gossip of the Hull councillors. Joseph Fox was the third son of Francois Renard, a French Protestant, who had come to England soon after the old queen, had died, and changed his name to Francis Fox to enable his family to better fit in with English society. Joseph Fox had broken away from the family belief in Protestantism and converted to Catholicism when he came of age. For doing so, he had been ostracised by his family and had been forced to survive on his wits.

The newly converted Catholic had learned the social graces and had quickly taken advantage of anyone who believed his stories of business ventures he owned in England and France. But he had eventually been caught for this wrongdoing and sent for trial which, should he be found guilty, meant that he would hang.

Luckily for him, a benefactor had stepped in and paid a substantial fine to have him released and put in the care of the Earl of Newcastle's, for 'charitable reform'. With a small income from the earl's purse and protected from the law, such people soon decided that they were far better off working for the Earl than reverting to the uncertain prospects of their previous lives.

* * * * * *

John Franks' men were a different breed, with a different task; it was their job to check on the disposition of the military in Hull. They had each been given different objectives. Their first priority was to report on troop numbers and movements. Secondly, to identify any weaknesses in the town's defences and thirdly, to mix with the off-duty soldiers and learn anything of importance which would help the king when he came to take Hull. Like Henry Walker's group, they had been caught committing a serious crime—highway robbery—and their punishment should have been hanging, but Newcastle's agents had stepped in to save them from the noose.

They had been caught drunk in a tavern after a robbery on the road from York to Tadcaster. Had they not been drunk, they would have put up a better fight and either escaped or died fighting. At York Assizes they had been about to be sentenced when the trial was stopped. Officials had removed the prisoners and given them a stark choice: to work under the direct command of William Legge or be returned to the court and face their punishment.

They chose wisely.

Chapter Eight

Mathew approached Mr Moor with a little trepidation.

'Sir, may I speak with you privately?' Elizabeth was sent to the kitchen to help her mother while Mathew took her father aside. Mathew shuffled from one foot to the other, his hands wringing the brim of his hat nervously.

'Sir,' he repeated embarrassedly.

'Well?' retorted Mr Moor. 'I haven't got all day. A customer may come through that door at any moment, so you had better get to the point.'

Mathew stumbled and stuttered, eventually saying, 'Sir, I have asked Elizabeth to marry me, and she has accepted. May we have your blessing?'

At that moment Mrs Moor and Elizabeth came into the shop from the kitchen.

'Well, lad, you don't waste much time, do you? But like any father with a daughter, I have both wished for and dreaded the coming of this day.' Mr Moor looked at his daughter with pride and then turned back towards Mathew with a serious expression. 'I have no doubt that you'll be a good husband to my daughter, Mathew, and I will be proud to have you as a son. So, yes, you have my blessing.'

'Thank you, sir.' Mathew's face lit up with delight. 'If you are willing, sir, I would like you all to meet my family in Beverley this Sunday, if that would be agreeable to you of course? You would be able to set a date with my father for our betrothal.'

'Well, lad, you may have trouble getting your words out, but you plan ahead fast enough. We'll go to meet your family as you wish,' Mr Moor said agreeably, as he took his wife's hand and giving it a gentle squeeze.

Mathew beamed and put his arm around Elizabeth, while she nestled close to him, resting her head on his shoulder.

Mr Moor closed his shop early on Saturday afternoon and travelling in a hired wagon, the Moor family and Mathew set off for Beverley early on Sunday morning. Along the way, Mr Moor insisted that they stop off at the church in Woodmansey to give blessings to the Lord for the couple's forthcoming union.

The small church had an equally small congregation. The family filed into the church and with due deference to the regular gathering, sat at the back. Mr Moor took the seat nearest to the aisle, and Mathew sat next to Elizabeth. Though pleased to be there with Elizabeth, Mathew found the church claustrophobic; he had never given much thought to prayer and God since the death of his mother.

The vicar, a short, stout man, late in his years, addressed his flock in a slow monotone voice. His hands trembled as he turned the pages as he read from the Bible. Mathew couldn't wonder how long the service would last and how much of a delay it would add to their journey, but the Moor family were deep in prayer, while Mathew merely bowed his head in respect and wished he was somewhere else. The vicar was part-way through his sermon when he began to lose his way, forgetting the words, fumbling through the notes he had made, and dropping his papers to the floor. A woman of similar years to the vicar went to help him pick up the papers. She took him by the arm and led him to a chair against the wall, sitting him down. The small congregation stood up in silence and filed from the church, while a middle-aged woman joined the elderly couple to give what assistance she could.

While Mr Moor helped his wife up to the front seat of the wagon, Mathew assisted Elizabeth into the back. An hour or so later, they were in Beverley, with Mathew pointing out the Minster and the different streets of the town. He told her about the different gates on the roads into Beverley, but that unlike Hull it had no town wall or defences. Being a Sunday, the streets were clear of people and traders, so they soon arrived at Mathew's family home.

Mathew introduced Mr and Mrs Moor and Elizabeth to his family. Mary looked from Mathew to Elizabeth and forced a smile she hoped would seem sincere, and that no one would notice, hid her true feelings. She couldn't understand why she was jealous of Elizabeth, but she envied the girl.

'Come, ladies, let's leave the men to their talk,' Mary said to Elizabeth and Elizabeth's mother. 'We can sit over here and get to know each other and become good friends.' Mary led them across the kitchen to sit by the fire. The dog Bess came over to snuggle at Mary's feet.

'Oh, this is little Bess,' Mary explained. 'She keeps me company while the men are working.' Mary picked up the young Border Collie and sat her on her lap. The three women fussed over the black-and-white puppy as they talked about life in Hull, how they had met their husbands and their hopes for the future.

While Mathew chatted with his brothers, William Fletcher and Mr Moor sat at the big table' a large leather jug full of ale waiting for them. Mr Moor, grateful for the opportunity to relax with a man of his own age, talked freely with William Fletcher, glad to be away from the 'women's talk' of his wife and daughter, to which he had become accustomed at home.

Sunday afternoon was drawing on when Mr and Mrs Moor, Mathew and Elizabeth said their farewells to the Fletcher Family, climbed into their wagon and began their journey back to Hull.

A week later Mathew and Elizabeth walked along Denton Lane towards the gardens on Scale Lane discussing their forthcoming wedding. Mathew had rented some rooms and began his surgeon's practice. He told Elizabeth about how he was using his room at the Drunken Monk Inn as a temporary surgery until he found a shop that suited him and his purse. Elizabeth listened dutifully, happy enough to be walking arm in arm with Mathew on this bright sunny day.

As Mathew walked Elizabeth back to her father's apothecary shop, crowds of people were filling the streets. Considerable excitement was in the wind, and people were flocking towards the Guildhall. Swept up in the frenzy, the young couple followed the streams of people through the streets. Mathew asked a man what had happened, but all he could tell him was that someone significant had arrived in Hull. 'Someone told me it was the King himself,' he proffered. Others Mathew asked just said it was a great nobleman who was close to the king, who had tried to enter the town secretly but had been spotted and taken to the Guildhall.

'Come on, Mathew, we must see who is there, we *must!*' Elizabeth persuaded him, apparently having been caught up in the emotion of the moment.

'But what about your father?' protested Mathew.

'Don't worry about him,' Elizabeth insisted, frustrated at his reluctance to follow her. 'He will understand when we explain.'

Unable to leave her in the jostling crowd, he followed, catching up with her and insisting that she held his arm as the crowds grew larger as they reach the market area. People were pouring from the streets that led to the markets and on to the Guildhall. Mathew could see folk cheering at a man standing at the top of the Guildhall steps.

From across the market where Mathew and Elizabeth stood the man looked like any other merchant in riding clothes, and it wasn't until they drew closer that the quality of his clothing under his riding cloak became apparent and they could see he was no merchant. He wore a suit of sky-blue silk with gold trim, calfskin, thigh-length riding boots and he was carrying a basket-hilted backsword at his waist, the hilt of which encrusted with gold. A black beaver felt, broad-brimmed hat sat at an angle on his head, which sported a white ostrich feather attached to a gold coloured ribbon hatband.

Elizabeth and Mathew arrived at the Guildhall steps just in time to hear Sir John Hotham welcome the man to his town.

'It is a great and unexpected honour for our town to welcome his Royal Highness James, Duke of York, to our humble town,' Sir John gushed. His welcoming speech continued for a few minutes longer, the crowd dutifully cheering at the pauses before the duke was taken inside the Guildhall.

'Wasn't that exciting?' Elizabeth enthused, 'seeing a real duke!'

Mathew had never seen Elizabeth this excitable before. As they walked along the High Street, back towards Chapel

Lane and the apothecary shop, Elizabeth talked incessantly about the duke's beautiful clothes and how handsome he looked. Mathew was beginning to get frustrated at her non-stop babble, and he wondered if all young women were the same. Indeed, she was so taken up in her dreams of what it must be like to have riches and live in an elegant house, that had Mathew not been with her she would have walked into a pile of rotting offal, which had been thrown out into the gutter by a butcher. He dragged her aside just as a couple of dogs came to scavenge the putrid-smelling heap of animal guts.

Elizabeth's prattle paused for a moment; she had barely noticed the filth in her path. But as soon as they were able to walk on unhindered, her animated chatter started up once more.

The Duke of York, Prince Rupert of the Rhine, and the Lords Newport and Willoughby sat in Hotham's office inside the Guildhall. Hotham couldn't believe his luck at having the son of Charles, King of England in his office. Hotham took every opportunity to emphasise his loyalty to the King and to outline his plan to allow the King access to the town. He reassured the duke that with his son's help he would be ready for whenever the King arrived. Hotham suggested that the royal guests celebrate the duke's visit to Hull with a banquet to be held in his honour.

All the people of rank in the town received the urgent summons to attend the festivities to be held at the Guildhall that evening. Captain Overton decided to take Lieutenant Jack Maynard as his guest. Having a friend and colleague with him would be a distraction when everyone else in the room was clamouring to associate with the duke and to gain his ear.

As part of the evening's celebrations musicians played, and Andrew Marvell read some of his poems, after which the Duke of York thanked Marvell personally, the humble poet clearly embarrassed by the attention of the king's son. The dancing carried on late into the night, and by the time the evening's entertainment was over Sir John Hotham was congratulating himself on his newfound friendship with the Duke of York.

Chapter Nine

The following day, was the twenty-third of April, it dawned like any other for the people of Hull. But, Captain Overton was tired, having not slept at all that night as a result of his late-hours dining with Sir John Hotham, the Duke of York and the town's influential sons. He had preparations to make before the king's arrival. Sir John Hotham had provided the duke with accommodation in his own home after the banquet, but Captain Overton had too much work to do before he would see his bed. During the evening's celebrations at the Guildhall, the Duke of York had informed the gathering that his father, the King, had left York at the head of a great column of men and would be arriving at Hull the following day, and was expecting an enthusiastic welcome.

All the key men involved in the defence of Hull were present when the duke made his announcement, but Sir John Hotham wished that the young duke hadn't been so free with his words, knowing that not everyone present was a loyal follower of the king. A great cheer had echoed around the hall, only Captain Overton and one or two others didn't respond joyously to this outpouring of enthusiasm about the King's imminent arrival. Captain Overton had wanted to leave the gathering immediately but to do so would have given his hand away. He would bide his time before rousing the garrison and getting them to the walls of Hull before the King arrived. Once the dancing started

Captain Overton, and Lieutenant Maynard left the Guildhall to begin their preparation.

To Captain Overton, having to endure an evening watching Sir John Hotham and other members of the Hull Council wallowing in subservience to the duke, went against his fundamental beliefs, in that all men were equal. He believed that the country should be run by the people, for the benefit of the people and not just for a privileged few. God ruled men, and the only legitimate King, in his opinion, was King Jesus, not this monarch who raised taxes to fight wars in order to enforce his father's version of the Bible on peoples that didn't want it. The King was under the misconception that his sovereignty over England, Scotland and Ireland was ordained by God. This King of England was coming to Hull to lay claim to its arsenal and start another war, but this time upon his own people. Captain Overton, would do everything in his power to prevent it.

Captain Overton sent Lieutenant Maynard with a list of allied officers to find the sergeant of the guard. His orders, to find and raise as many of them as he could, even though many of them would have only just retired for the night after a long day, and have them come to Captain Overton. He had to act before the Hotham's, father and son, could prevent him from taking action. Now, after holding a brief meeting and showing his letter of authority from Parliament as evidence, Overton gave his orders. Officers from the Hull Trained Bands garrison brought the men under their command to readiness.

At eleven of the clock that morning, the king, his retinue and three hundred soldiers appeared at the Beverley Gate entrance to Hull. The soldiers on duty at the gate had been informed that on sighting the King they must close the gates and raise the drawbridge and that under pain of death, they were not to allow him passage into Hull. News of the King's arrival spread around the streets of Hull and crowds gathered in the streets close to the Beverley Gate.

Many of the ordinary people in Hull were loyal supporters of the monarch. So to reduce the possibility of unrest within the town, Lieutenant Maynard ordered his soldiers to clear the streets of people and to enforce a curfew while the King was outside the gates. Captains Overton and Meldrum took two companies of armed men onto the walls, posting a musketeer every few feet, ready to defend the town should the King decide to try and capture Hull by force. Under orders from Captain Overton, two sergeants and a junior officer were sent to find and escort Sir John Hotham from his office to the top of the wall above the Beverley Gate.

Sir John Hotham received the news of the King's arrival with delight, for it meant that everything he had been working towards over the past months was about to fall in his lap. He even allowed himself to dwell on the fantasies of what kind of rewards the King would bestow upon him.

As he gathered his cloak to go and greet the king, the officer and two sergeants burst into his room and informed him politely, but firmly that they had been ordered to escort him to the Beverley Gate. Somewhat perturbed at first by the abrupt entrance of the soldiers, Hotham dismissed their lack of respect towards him to nerves over the sudden arrival of the King. Sir John hurried through the streets in the direction of the Beverley Gate, paying little heed to the soldiers guarding and clearing streets. The officer and the two sergeants at Sir John's heels ensured that no one tried to stop or warn him of what was to come before he reached

Captain Overton. On arrival at the town walls, Sir John took the steps two at a time up the tower to the top of the wall. Waiting for him as he emerged on to the wall were Captain Robert Overton and Lieutenant Maynard. As Sir John appeared on the town walls, Captain Overton called him over.

'Sir John, we need to speak before you address the King.'

'You will have to wait, Captain,' Sir John snapped back at him. 'The King awaits and the gates are closed to him. I must offer our apologies at once.' Sir John's insistence on placating the King was the final piece of evidence that Robert Overton needed; It was clear that Sir John Hotham was ready and willing to allow the King access to the town of Hull—even to surrender it to him. Captain Overton stepped forward and took Sir John Hotham by the arm.

'I must insist that you listen to me, Sir John. Your loyalties to the King over Parliament have been known for some time. I have orders from Parliament to take command of Hull and prevent the King from entering the town. So this is what you are going to do if you want to live a moment longer.'

Captain Overton then briefly explained that Sir John's letters to the Earl of Newcastle had been intercepted and that he was going to be arrested and put on trial for treason against Parliament. His only chance to redeem himself was to stand atop the walls of Hull and inform the King that he and the three hundred horse that accompanied him, would not be allowed access to the town. That as a compromise, if the King and six of his officers would like to enter the town to dine with Sir Jon and Captain Overton, rest and refresh themselves after their journey, they would be welcome to do so.

Seeing that he had little choice, Sir John Hotham agreed to do as he was told. While Hotham tried to negotiate terms with the king, Henry Barnard—the ousted mayor of Hull—called out to the King and wept that he and the people of the town were faithful and loyal subjects to His Majesty and that the King should be allowed unconditional access to their town.

King Charles tried to negotiate with Hotham, but with Captain Overton holding a sword at Hotham's back, the King was unable to bribe or cajole his way into the town or change the conditions of his admittance. Finally, outraged at the refusal to allow him entry to Hull on his own terms, the King declared Sir John Hotham, a traitor, and that, '*He be thrown down from the town walls.*'

The King turned his horse away from the gates and took the road to Beverley. En route he ordered that most of his horse regiments and artillery stay at Anlaby to begin a blockade of the roads leading to and from Hull. The King needed to capture Hull to bring about a speedy end to parliament.

After arriving in Beverley, the King was invited by Lady Gee to stay in her house adjacent to Beverley Bar. Its walled garden would not only provide security and privacy, but its flowers were some of the best to be found in East Yorkshire.

Captain Overton ordered patrols to follow the King to ascertain what he planned to do next and where he was going. It wasn't long before they returned with news of a camp that was being established at Anlaby. Overton realised immediately that the King intended to lay siege to the town. With the Kings bigger and better guns, it would only be a matter of time before he breached Hull's defences and forcibly secured its arsenal. Captain Overton only had a day or two before the King would be ready to attack the town. In a desperate attempt to prevent the Kings artillery from coming within range of Hull's defensive wall. Captain Overton ordered the irrigation sluices in the banks of the River Hull, north of the town, to be raised, and the banks of the River Humber to the west to be cut through. The low-lying land outside the town would be flooded, preventing the King from deploying his siege guns. Captain Overton knew the submerged land would only be a temporary hindrance to the king, as summer drew closer there was the risk of the flooded areas drying out, allowing the King the freedom to bring his guns up close to the town walls and level them at his leisure.

Overton called an officers meeting at Hull Castle. With its isolation on the eastern side of the River Hull, it was an ideal location for him to plan Hull's strategy of defence.

Captain Meldrum put forward a plan for a direct attack on the Royalist position at Anlaby. The Hull garrison would approach by the royalist camp by raft across the flooded land. The King's men wouldn't expect an attack to come across the flooded land when they were still setting up their own defences. Overton pondered the plan: with the area around Hull flooded, the town was protected from the King, but the flood also imprisoned the town's occupants, severely limiting their movements. Overton desperately needed intelligence on what the King was planning and the strength of the force he had brought with him. He also needed to inhibit the King's ability to use his heavy artillery, before they could be used against the town.

After studying Meldrum's plan with his fellow officers, the commanding officer gave permission for a reconnaissance mission to go ahead. For three days the men of the East Yorkshire Trained Bands built their rafts, aided by boat builders from the town. When all was ready, dozens of small floating platforms had been made to take two companies of lightly armed men out of Hull towards Anlaby.

As the next evening's high tide began to flow up the River Humber, Captains Overton and Meldrum, along with Lieutenant Maynard, and two company's of musketeers set sail on the rafts. Keeping close to the shoreline, the rafts were easy to control in the shallow water at the edges of the River Humber. One or two rafts strayed and snagged on mudflats but were soon released by the rising tide. Moving inland through the breaches made in the banks of the River Humber and onto what had once been the dry land of Boothferry, the rafts sailed north. Each soldier used a pole to propel his craft through water which was little more than two feet deep. Their silence was total, their progress steady, and the moon was hidden behind a dense black cloud. They had less than a mile to travel before reaching the higher ground of Anlaby Common.

Lights up ahead showed the location of the King's army camped on the common. By the time Overton brought the flotilla to a halt a steady drizzle had set in. Everyone on the rafts was already soaked to the skin from water which had lapped over the simple rafts, so a smattering of rain was not going to stop them now. They were only around four hundred yards from the camp.

Overton split his command into three. Captain Meldrum's men were to spike and disable as many guns as his men could reach. Lieutenant Maynard was to take his men and enter the horse lines, sabotaging equipment and freeing the horses, allowing them to wander off. Captain Overton wanted to learn the layout of the camp. Everyone was given strict instructions, that under no circumstances was anyone to be killed unless in self-defence. After all, the King had not attacked Hull yet, and Overton was determined that it would not be Parliamentarian forces who were going to be the first to draw blood.

Captain Overton wanted to get inside the perimeter of the camp, even if it was just for a short amount of time. Taking his trusted sergeant with him, he decided to try and bluff his way into the camp, suspecting the guards would not be expecting an enemy officer to walk into camp, especially while it was raining. As Overton had expected, they were not challenged as they entered past the guard post. When a sentry came out of the guard tent to greet the officer and sergeant, Overton merely waved him away, the guard being grateful to return to his dry tent. The two men wandered around the camp, making mental notes on the location of the baggage train, the officers' camp and the ammunition stores. After about fifteen minutes the sergeant suggested that it might be a good idea to return to the rafts and not push their luck any further. His captain agreed: this first 'assault' on the Anlaby camp had proved to be a great success, and showed how ill-prepared the King's army was for starting a military campaign.

The pair made their way back to the rendezvous point from which they had started. Maynard and Meldrum were already there, frantic at the amount of time Overton had been missing. Completely satisfied at the night's reconnoitre, Overton ordered his men to return the way they had come. They shoved the small craft out into the darkness and rain using their poles to manoeuvre their rafts back to the break in the backs of the River Humber, only to find the tide still rising and too strong to fight against. Their commander, therefore, had no choice but to order his men to abandon the rafts and enter the water. At waist depth, none of his men was in danger of drowning, and by following hedgerows visible above the height of the water, they made their way back towards Hull. It was early morning by the time they reached the Hessle Gate and passed back into Hull.

The night's work had been a success, Captain Overton and his men were tired and wet, but none had been lost. The sodden wool of their breeches and leather boots left raw flesh on the inside of their legs, and many of the men trembled uncontrollably with the cold. Before Captain Overton returned to his quarters to write a report on the night's events for Parliament, he ensured his men were fed and given warm, dry clothing. It was almost midday before he was finally able to take to his own bed and get some sleep.

The captain slept for four hours before being woken up by hunger and to the noise of soldiers' boots on stone floors outside his room. He still had to write his report to Parliament, but right now he was hungry and thirsty, and his news would have to wait a little longer. Overton made his way to a tavern favoured by most of the garrison officers. On entering, he looked around for a table near the fire and found Lieutenant Maynard sitting alone.

'Good day to you, Lieutenant, may I join you?' he asked.

Jack Maynard waved his arm over an empty stool. 'Be my guest, Captain.'

Overton called over a serving girl and ordered a bottle of brandy, meat and bread. 'Will you eat with me, Jack?' Captain Overton could see the weariness in Jack's face fall away a little at his kind gesture. They shared a meal, enjoying the warmth by the fire, but Jack Maynard was not in a mood for conversation, he spoke out of politeness to his senior officer, rather than a desire to make conversation. Jack was feeling too ill to make small talk or deliberate on the success of the night before. After they had eaten, and feeling the effects of the brandy, Lieutenant Maynard decided he'd better return to his quarters.

'I will take my leave of you if I may, Captain—I don't feel well after our wet night. There is an apothecary close by; I intend to buy some warming cordials and take to my bed.' Maynard took two steps and staggered across the tavern before falling across an empty table. Overton ran to rescue his comrade, helping him to his feet.

'I will assist you to the apothecary, steady yourself on me.'

The two men rolled out of the tavern like two drunken sailors after their first night ashore, but Robert Overton suspected that Lieutenant Maynard was iller than he had been letting on. They reached the door of the apothecary and burst through. The apothecary, Mr Moor, was serving a customer and Elizabeth, who was sweeping the floor, jumped back in alarm as the two men fell through the door.

'A chair for my friend, if you please,' panted Overton, out of breath after helping his sick lieutenant along the streets. Elizabeth fetched a chair that her father saved for sick customers, and set it in the middle of the floor for Lieutenant Maynard to sit on.

'He has spent a night in the cold and damp and is developing a fever, I think,' Overton explained. 'He was on his way here to buy some warming *cordials* when he collapsed.'

The customer in the shop took a look at Maynard's sweating face and quickly left the premises.

'Where does he live?' asked Mr Moor.

'In one of the blockhouses with the other soldiers,' replied Overton.

'That's no good for him in this state,' answered Mr Moor indignantly. 'The damp air from the river will lie on his chest. Does he have money?'

'He can pay for the cordials if that's your concern.' Robert Overton was getting annoyed at the apothecary's brusque manner.

'No, no, that isn't what I mean,' said Mr Moor. 'This man is sick and will need care—I have a bed in a storage room where I can treat him if he has no proper home to go back to, but it will cost me money to administer to his needs.'

'Don't worry about the money; he can pay. I will leave you five shillings to start with. When he is well enough, he will be able to make good any monies outstanding.' Captain Overton placed the money on the counter. 'Please, will you make sure he is well cared for? He is not only one of my best officers, but he is also my friend—I will be back to look in on him later.' Overton left Maynard in the apothecary's care and returned to his office.

Elizabeth was sent to put a mattress and blankets in a back room for Jack while Mr Moor examined Jack. Elizabeth and her father helped the semi-conscious man to his bed, and while Elizabeth went to fetch a basin of water and a cloth to cool Jack's face and neck, Mr Moor stripped him of his clothes, leaving him in his shirt, doing his best to make him comfortable on the bed. As Mr Moor administered cooling cordials to his patient, Elizabeth washed jack's face with water to cool the fever.

For the rest of the day, the young officer tossed and turned as he fought the fever. Every hour Elizabeth returned to his side to feed him a few more drops of cordial and wipe the sweat from his face.

That night Elizabeth lay in her bed thinking of the sick man in the storage room. It wasn't often that her father took in a patient; he usually visited sick people in their homes in order to administer medicines. She lay in the darkness thinking about the handsome officer, lying helpless in the room below hers. She convinced herself that she needed to check up on him to ensure that his temperature was not rising to a dangerous level and to see if he needed a drink of water.

Creeping downstairs, she sneaked into Jack's room. As she put her head around the door, she could see that he was lying on his back and had kicked off his blankets. Closing the door behind her quietly, she moved across to the bed and knelt down beside it. She tenderly mopped his sweating brow with the damp cloth before drawing the blankets back over him as the night was turning cold. She stared down at the vulnerable man on the mattress.

She couldn't help but notice the shape of his body through his sweat-dampened shirt before she had covered him with the blankets. Her eyes lingered on his loins as she lifted the blankets off him again. Still kneeling by his bed, she brushed a lock of hair from his face and placed her left hand on his chest. She could feel his heart beating rapidly and could see the gentle rising and falling of his chest as he breathed. She noticed too how her own heart was beginning to race.

Apart from her father, this was the first man she had ever been alone with. She replaced the blanket over Maynard but couldn't tear herself away from his side. Her head was buzzing as she found her hand sliding beneath the blankets, slowly making its way down to his stomach. Her hand moved lower until she could feel his manliness. She let it linger there for no more than a few seconds before Jack moved slightly. She flinched, pulling her hand back quickly, shocked and ashamed at what she had just done.

After returning to her own bed, she lay there with her heart racing, thinking of how Jack had felt beneath her hand. She felt her nipples rise and a strange tension deep in her loins. Elizabeth ran her hands over her own body, its softness contrasting with the hard muscles of the officer in the room below. Her body stiffened as her hands brushed against her skin, the sensations in her loins became more intense, as her hands slid downwards between her legs. She began to caress herself—it felt so natural, so warm and pleasing. She couldn't stop, she didn't want to stop. After a few moments, her breathing changed to gasps as the tension in her loins intensified. Her body arched and finally jerked, as a feeling of contentment flooded through her and the tension was released. She had never done this to herself before, her feelings were confused over what had happened, but the tension was gone, replaced with relaxed contentment. Sleep soon followed, dreaming of the man downstairs.

The next day Elizabeth awoke early and dressed. Before starting a fire in the kitchen as she would typically do, her first thought was to check on Jack Maynard. Elizabeth paused at the door to Jack's room and blushed as she remembered the previous night's events. Opening the door to his room quietly, she peered in. Jack lay there, his body glistening with sweat after a restless night. He'd kicked off the blanket that had been covering him, and his shirt had ridden up, exposing his private parts. Elizabeth stood in the doorway, staring at him. She was about to enter the room when a noise from upstairs warned her that her father was out of bed. She shut the door and went through to the kitchen to lay the fire before lighting it.

Her father came in just as the fire was taking hold and Elizabeth was putting bread and cheese on the table. 'How's our guest?' he enquired.

Elizabeth flushed red. 'I don't know, Father,' she lied. 'I've not been in to check on him.'

Over the next couple of days, to her mother's annoyance, Elizabeth took every opportunity to spend time nursing Jack as he fought the fever that was burning inside him. It seemed to her mother that the only time Elizabeth could tear herself away from Lieutenant Maynard was when Mathew Fletcher called on her.

By the end of the week, Jack's fever had abated, and he had begun to recover. Elizabeth spent time sitting and talking with him as he told her about his own family and his duties as an officer. The day after Jack left the care of the Moor family, Elizabeth made an excuse to her father, saying that she was going to meet Mathew. They were going to view a shop he wished to buy. Before her father could object, she ran to the door and was gone. Mr Moor followed her, intending to call her back. But, he was too late to stop her, and the last he saw of that morning was seeing her walking arm in arm down Lowgate with Jack Maynard.

Late that afternoon, Mathew arrived at the apothecary shop to find Elizabeth in tears. Her parents had clearly been scolding her for something she had done wrong. Elizabeth flew across the shop to greet him as he stepped through the door, declaring her undying love for him.

118

Mathew stared at her parents, embarrassed at this overt sign of affection, while Mr and Mrs Moor smiled in return, but gave no details of why they had been admonishing their daughter.

The young couple left the shop intending to stroll in the old monastery garden, where Mathew had taken her on their first walk. At first, Elizabeth didn't want to talk about the argument she'd had with her parents. It wasn't until they reach the garden that Elizabeth finally turned to Mathew and, throwing herself into his arms, sobbed uncontrollably.

Mathew was totally confused. She would neither tell him what had happened nor stop crying. It was only when he insisted that he would return to the apothecary shop, and confront her parents as to why they had upset her so much, that she managed to bring her tears under control. She explained that she had been careless and clumsy in the shop, breaking a jar of very expensive spice from India. 'It only happened because I was daydreaming about you, instead of concentrating on my work.'

Her fiancé wrapped his arms around Elizabeth, telling her, 'I could never get that angry with you, even if the jar had been full of gold. I love you, Elizabeth; I love you more than life itself.' He tightened his arms around her as she laid her head against his chest, while one final tear escaped from the corner of her eye, rolled down her cheek and dropped to her feet, to be lost forever.

After Mathew had taken her back to the shop and returned to his lodgings, Mr Moor turned to Elizabeth with a severe expression on his face. 'Well; what are you going to do?' he asked her. 'You are going to have to make up your mind about which one of those young men you want. Or, I will make up your mind for you!' Mr Moor was angry. He had set his mind on his daughter marrying Mathew and here she was enthralled by a soldier.

Captain Overton, alerted by the sound of running feet down the corridor outside his room, looked up from his work. Sergeant Armstrong knocked on the door and stepped inside, breathing heavily.

'Sir,' Armstrong began, 'please, forgive the intrusion, but this is for you.' He handed his commanding officer a letter. 'Right now there are heralds at the gates proclaiming to every soldier that a full pardon will be given to all those who will lay down their arms and offer allegiance to their king.'

'Have all the sergeants tell them any man think of joining the king or speaking sedition or leaving his post without permission is to be arrested. I will send a reply back to the King.'

Shortly afterwards Overton approached the leader of the heralds and handed him his reply, adding, 'You can tell the King that the armaments within the town are safe and in good hands. Remind him that they are for fighting the enemies of England and until such time arrives will remain here until they are needed.'

Wilkes and Martins stood outside the blockhouses that housed the town's soldiers. They were telling tales of their campaigns in the Netherlands to any soldiers who would listen and in return were asking questions about the strength of the garrison in Hull. Whether they had been there too long or someone had become suspicious about them questioning the soldiers, they would never know. The first they were aware that they had raised the suspicions of the officers inside was when they were confronted by a sergeant and four of his men, carrying pole-arms.

'Easy, Sergeant,' Wilkes told them. 'We're just two old soldiers enjoying a drink and telling tales of our foreign service to your men.' Wilkes pulled a bottle of brandy from the bag which hung over his shoulder as though it was evidence of him telling the truth. Meanwhile, Martins had taken backwards away from the armed men, his hand instinctively drifting towards his sword. Unfortunately, his actions didn't go unnoticed by the soldiers, as two of them stepped around Wilkes to confront Martins.

'I think you two had better come with us and explain yourselves to the captain of the guard,' continued the sergeant. Martins panicked and drew his sword with one hand and a dagger from his belt with the other. He sidestepped the first soldier's pole-arm as he swung at Martins, and in one deft manoeuvre, the sword blade sliced through the neck of the first bill-man, severing his carotid artery. At the time he ran his dagger across the exposed left forearm of the second soldier, slashing through his brachial artery. The first soldier toppled forward, spraying blood in front of him, while the second dropped his pole-arm, clutching at his wound, trying to stem the blood pulsing from his injured limb.

In the two seconds that the sergeant and the remaining two soldiers took to respond, Wilkes had let his bag fall to the ground further distracting the soldiers and drawn his sword, bringing it up between the legs of the sergeant, severing his femoral artery. He was dead in less than two minutes, his life-blood pooling in the gutter of the High

Street. The remaining two soldiers stayed rooted to the spot, stunned, unable to comprehend what had just happened. Wilkes and Martins turned and fled down the High Street towards the White Meat Market, hoping to get lost in the crowds that filled the narrow streets.

One of the remaining soldiers leant against the wall and vomited, while the other staggered back inside the blockhouse to raise the alarm. A couple of minutes later, officers and soldiers poured from the blockhouse. Captain Overton sent his men out in groups of four in different directions to try and find the killers. Standing over his dead soldiers and gave a short prayer, and swore an oath to find those responsible.

More men came from within the blockhouse to carry their slain comrades inside, and out of sight of the gawping passers-by. Overton began to question the two surviving soldiers, wanting to fully understand how the attack had unfolded and get a better description of the two murderers. It soon became clear from what the evidence the two soldiers gave him that the killers were highly skilled in the arts of war, unlike his Trained Bands soldiers. They had done no more than drill and practise with their weapons in case the town or surrounding district came under attack.

Captain Overton along with his friend Thomas Fairfax had spent a few years fighting in the Dutch-Spanish war, and both were well versed in the ways of how professional soldiers fought. Kill your enemy as quickly as possible, go for his vulnerable spots, save your energy and move on to the next opponent or alternatively get away fast.

Martins and Wilkes ran down the street, keeping just ahead of the soldiers who were chasing them. They were getting tired and attracting attention from passers-by, they needed somewhere to catch their breath and think before making good their escape. They turned off the High Street and burst through the first shop door they came to and threw the door's bolt to lock it behind them.

Mr Moor stepped forward to protest at the men's actions, but without skipping a beat, Martins drew his sword and cut the apothecary down with a downward blow that sliced through the base of the apothecary's neck from the left side, severing the jugular vein right through to the carotid artery. Blood sprayed across the ceiling and walls as Mr Moor turned and collapsed to the floor like a discarded rag doll.

Elizabeth, who had been in the back of the shop, came through carrying a glass bottle that needed replacing on a shelf. She froze in her tracks as she first caught sight of the two men in the centre of the room, one of whom had his sword drawn. Then her eyes fell to the body of her father and the blood which ran across the floor from the wound in his neck. Before she could scream and without a word from Martins, he stepped over the body in front of him, thrusting his sword forward over the shop counter and into Elizabeth's side. The shock of the blow pushed her body backwards, thrusting her hands forward, releasing the bottle she'd been holding. The vessel crashed against the counter and hilt of the killer's sword, shattering and splashing *oil of vitriol* over Martins' hand. As the acid bit into his skin, he screamed in pain and jerked his arm back, dropping his sword on the counter. Elizabeth fell back against the door through which she had just come, unconscious before she slipped to the floor.

As the corrosive liquid burnt deeper into Martins' hand, he grabbed a cloth from the end of the counter and wrapped it around his injured limb, yelling at Wilkes, 'I'm hurt *bad*! I need help!'

'Well, you ain't gonna get it 'ere, are you?' Wilkes snapped. 'Are you ready to go?'

Wilkes showed little sympathy for his comrade's suffering; his only concern was to escape and not get trapped in the shop. He drew back the bolt on the door and looked outside. Seeing no soldiers in the street, Wilkes signalled for Martins to follow him. He did so, abandoning the sword he could no longer hold.

The two killers made their way out into Chapel Lane. Mrs Moor entered the shop from the kitchen, alerted by the disturbance. Finding Elizabeth first, as she lay slumped against the wall close to the door, then seeing her husband lying in a pool of blood in the middle of the shop, she gave out a heart-stopping scream.

The two men had bundled out of the door and down Chapel Lane towards Lowgate and on into Denton Lane. Passers-by cleared out of their way as the desperate killers barged their way through: the locals had become accustomed to rough men from trading vessels drunkenly running amok in the streets of Hull and knew better than to get in their way.

At the end of Denton Lane, well away from prying eyes, the pair banged on a dirty weather-worn door, as soon as they heard the bolt being drawn back, they pushed inside out of sight. Inside the shabby little room, John Franks had been sitting at a table compiling the information they had been gathering, waiting for their return.

Mathew came down the street to find a crowd of people outside the apothecary shop. Confused as to why the place was drawing so much attention, he stepped through the doorway to see a constable and three soldiers standing over the carnage in the middle of the room. One of the soldiers was explaining to the constable that they had been chasing two men who had killed two soldiers and seriously injured another outside the blockhouses and that the killers had been chased in this general direction. This informant said he had sent one of his fellow soldiers back to report the incident to his commander, Captain Overton.

Entering further into the shop Mathew couldn't believe what he was seeing and wondering what had happened. He saw two women kneeling on the floor behind the counter, one cradling Elizabeth while the other held a bloodstained cloth against her side. Mrs Moor sat in a chair close by, sobbing uncontrollably and calling out to God in her pain, asking Him why he had brought down death and devastation on her family.

Mathew found it hard to comprehend the scene that confronted him. Mr Moor was dead and beyond his help, but since there were two women attending to Elizabeth, he prayed she might still be alive. Kneeling next to her, he could see the blood draining from her wound. He instructed the women to help him take Elizabeth up to her bedchamber so that he could attend to her injuries. Collecting what he needed from the shop, he followed the two women up to a small room on the first floor. The two women looked at him suspiciously as he followed them into the bedchamber.

'I am a surgeon, and we are betrothed,' he told them bluntly. 'Quickly; remove her dress and let me try and stop the bleeding.'

One of the women produced a pair of scissors from a pocket in her dress and cut the cord that laced up the back of Elizabeth's dress. Unhooking the bottom of the bodice from the skirt she pulled the bodice forward, and Elizabeth's arms slipped out from the sleeves. Mathew ripped open her chemise to see where the blade had entered her body.

The two-inch wide wound was not long, but it was deep. Dark red blood began to run down Elizabeth's pale skin onto the bed, staining the sheet. Mathew had been taught never to perform surgery within the thorax. He had been told that it was impossible to repair any damage to the internal organs and opening up the thoracic cavity would only allow more bad humours to enter Elizabeth's body, making the injury worse. The best Mathew could do was to suture the wound closed in order to stop the bleeding and hope that he would have done enough to save her life.

Instructing the two women to stay with Elizabeth and telling them that he would be back shortly with more help, Mathew ran from the building. He needed a second opinion, and his first thought was to return to Surgeon Adams for help. Surgeon Adams's premises were not far from the apothecary shop, and it took Mathew only a couple of minutes before he burst through the door into the surgery. Surgeon Adams jumped to his feet, alarmed at the unexpected intrusion. It took a few seconds before he recognised the sweating man gasping for breath as Mathew.

'Elizabeth, she needs you, I need your help—*please* hurry!' he pleaded.

Surgeon Adams left the ledger in which he'd writing open on his table. Mathew was not the first person to have burst into his surgery this way over his years, but if Mathew needed his help, the situation must be desperate, as Mathew should have been able to cope with most medical problems on his own.

The older medical man's thoughts flashed through various scenarios of what may have happened to alarm Mathew in this way, which only added to his sense of urgency. As Mathew hurried his old master along the street back to the apothecary shop, he explained the scene and what he had done for Elizabeth so far. Surgeon Adams refused to comment until he had seen the girl for himself. Almost shoving the ageing surgeon through the shop and up to Elizabeth's room he waited for Surgeon Adams to examine the injured woman. After several minutes Adams stood up and turned to Mathew.

'You have done an excellent job of suturing the wound,' he told his old apprentice. 'Your hands are skilful, and you have a fine touch. But the wound is deep, and I believe her spleen has been ruptured. I'm sorry, Mathew, but you need to prepare yourself for the worst. There is nothing more that anyone can do for her—she is in God's hands now.'

Downstairs, the constable, out of his depth in dealing with such a savage attack, sent men out to look for the murders, declaring a 'Hue and cry.'

Captain Overton entered the apothecary shop accompanied by the soldier who had been sent to fetch him. Seeing Mr Moor dead on the floor and the mortuary sword still lying on the counter, he recognised this was the work of the men he was already looking for, and that they would stop at nothing to make good their getaway. With the sword left in the shop and a broken bottle of acid on the floor, he deduced that it was likely that one of the assailants might have acid burns to his hands.

Mathew came downstairs to the shop to attend to Mrs Moor and to learn more about what had happened. Finding the army officer with the constable, Mathew demanded to know what had happened.

'Captain, what has gone on here?'

'What is it to you?' Overton asked curtly.

'Elizabeth, the injured girl upstairs, is to be my wife— her father had given his consent but a few days ago. Who has done this to them, and why?'

'I'm sorry, Sir. Two of my men were killed by the men we believe did this. They had been chased in this direction, and I suspect they came in here to dodge their pursuers, and in their desire to leave no witnesses, did this. The men we are looking for were dressed like soldiers and were well armed. One of them seems to have been injured; he pointed to the broken glass and sword. As you can see, one of them left his sword behind, and there is acid splashed all around. He must have been badly burned and in a desperate hurry to get away to have left his weapon behind. My men are out there now, searching the streets, but I suspect they have a bolt-hole somewhere. I suspect they will try to leave town as soon as they can and probably before nightfall. I'm sure you know that the King was turned away from the town gates earlier today. It could be that these killers are his agents, since they were at the blockhouses, asking my men searching questions.'

'Thank you, captain. I must return to Elizabeth now.'

Captain Overton turned and left the shop followed by the four soldiers, leaving the constable to deal with the civilians massing outside on the street. Taking his men away some distance to speak to them freely. Captain Overton ordered his men to visit each of Hull's gates and warn the guards to be on the lookout for the assailants, with the additional information that one of them was probably severely burned on his hand or arm. Anyone fitting their descriptions was to be held, by force if necessary, until he could arrive and question them.

Later that night, Elizabeth lay in her bed, not moving. She had taken on a very grey sweaty pallor, and her breathing was slow and laboured. Mathew held her hand, and a tear ran from the corner of his bloodshot eye. He had tried every treatment he could think of, but he had been unable to stop the internal bleeding from her *spleen*. He knew that her time was close, and all he could do was to hold her hand and pray.

The memories of his mother's final hours ran over and over in his mind. He reflected that he had been just as helpless to do anything for his mother as he was Elizabeth, but all those years ago he had been too young and ignorant to know what to do. But now for goodness' sake, he was a surgeon: he could work miracles for people. Yet now, *even with all his skills* and *all his knowledge*, his efforts had proved useless.

There was a knock at the bedchamber door, and Mrs Harrington entered, carrying new candles, soup and bread for Mathew. 'I've brought some soup for Mrs Moor as well,' the considerate lady told him, 'just in case she'll try and eat something.'

Mathew thanked her for her kindness and set the soup down next to him. He placed the two extra candles on the table alongside the candlesticks. The candles in them were burning low giving off long tails of black smoke which spiralled up to the low ceiling. Mrs Harrington had come from the cordwainer shop next door and was the one holding the cloth to Elizabeth's side, trying to staunch the flow of blood. Mrs Harrington had known the Moor family for the ten years they had been neighbours and knew the Moor's well. She had volunteered to stay with Mrs Moor until Mrs Moor's sister in Pickering could come down and take care of her.

As Mathew watched Elizabeth lying on her bed, he tried to work out why he had been powerless to stop the bleeding. He knew where the spleen was and what its functions were, so why had it not been possible to operate to repair it?

Another question followed: if he could investigate and dissect her spleen, would it give him some vital clue that would enable him to save someone else's life? He shook the idea from his head and cursed himself for thinking of such things. Elizabeth was not a dog from the streets to practice on; she was the girl he had chosen to have become his wife. What kind of a man was he, he wondered? What kind of a person had these cold-hearted analytical thoughts about a loved one? Was he possessed? Had he really loved Elizabeth?

Seething with anger and confusion over his own thoughts, he focused his mind on the men who had done this to her, revenge. Yes, revenge on the person who had destroyed his life, and his one true love. For a moment doubt crept into his mind. Or, he wondered, was he more angered by his own thoughts, and his relentless search for knowledge about the workings of the human body? No, it wasn't that; his life and the woman he loved were being torn away from him. Without Elizabeth, he could not foresee any vestige of optimism for his further happiness.

Elizabeth gave a slight moan. Her body arched slightly and then lay still. Mathew held her hand more firmly as her breathing faltered and finally stopped. He desperately felt for the pulse in her neck, he called her name, but she did not respond. He knelt on the floor beside her bed, once more feeling like the helpless child he had been all those many years ago.

Mrs Moor sat on the opposite side of the bed mumbling, for it appeared that the terrible trauma of losing her only daughter and husband, had caused her to lose her wits. She did not even respond to the loss of her only child, for she was as much a victim of the attack as her husband and daughter had been. The lives of her husband and daughter had been ripped away, along with her sanity.

It was left to Mathew to sort out the funeral arrangements. Money had been found in a strongbox in the room behind the shop. There was enough to pay for a humble service for Elizabeth and her father, leaving a few pounds spare for Mrs Moor future. It was decided that she would go to Pickering with her sister after the funeral, and once the sale of the shop and its contents had been organised. At least the proceeds of the sale would ensure that poor Mrs Moor would have enough to live on for the foreseeable future.

Captain Overton called on Mathew at the Drunken Monk Inn. He knocked on the door of his room but received no response. The captain knew Mathew was there, the landlady had told him. So he entered the room anyway to find him lying in his bed at mid-morning.

'Excuse me asking, Mr Fletcher, but I would like to attend the funeral if I may?'

Mathew looked up at the officer. 'Why?'

'Because I feel partly responsible for what happened to those people,' said the captain. 'Had my men put up a better fight, or had they chased after then sooner, we may have caught the murderers while they were still at the blockhouse instead of letting them escape to kill again.'

Mathew continued to stare at the ceiling.

'Pull yourself together, man!' the military man said firmly. 'The funeral is later today. If you loved Elizabeth as much as you profess to, get your arse out of that bed and prove it!' Overton snatched the jug of water from the small table and threw it over Mathew's face.

A few hours later, the two men stood together in the churchyard as the preacher read a prayer over the coffins as they were lowered one by one into the ground.

The Moor family did not have many friends, so there were few mourners at the graveside, and for a man who had helped so many people in the town, it made the proceedings even more sombre. Mathew wept inconsolably and unashamedly as the service ran its course. The church bell rang six times and then another three times and paused, marking the deaths of father and daughter. It then tolled again: one ring for each year of the lives lived by the two victims who were now being given back to the earth and their souls to God.

And so the mellow toll of the death knell rang out across the town, its hollow sound reminding all that listened to it that, one day, the bell would toll for them. Mathew had insisted that he would be the one who would cover the coffins once they had been laid in the graves. He wanted time alone to say his farewell to Elizabeth. In some way, he felt that it was his means of coming to terms with, and accepting that, Elizabeth would no longer be in the apothecary shop waiting for him with her warm, shy smile and her furtive glances when he stepped through the door.

Later, Captain Overton took Mathew back to his own rooms and suggested that he may like to spend the evening there rather than being alone. Mathew accepted the kind offer, but there was little conversation between the two men. The younger man stared into the flames of the fire and thought of what could have been, his soul burning with anger, demanding revenge.

Captain Overton sat with his new friend, refreshing his cup of wine as required. He completed some reports that needed to be sent to Parliament as well as some written orders for tomorrow's garrison duties. He had prepared a palliasse and blankets for Mathew, and in due course, he took himself to the bed in the corner, leaving Mathew transfixed on the fire in the hearth.

'I'm going to find them and kill them.' Mathew spoke the words to the flames, as though he was making a vow to some unseen deity. 'Tomorrow, I start my search to find them, and no matter where they go, no matter where they hide, I will find them.'

From his bed, Overton issued a warning: 'Be careful what you wish for, Mathew. These men are trained to kill, and you are not. They don't have a conscience like you do—they have killed too many people for that.' Robert Overton knew all too well that Mathew stood little chance of finding the killers, but Mathew's promise sounded too sincere to ignore.

'I need to know what they look like. I want to know where to find the murderers. Will you help me, Robert?'

Mathew's voice was steady and resolute. His face set firm as he looked across at the other man.

'I can give you a brief description of the men. They were tall and lean and dressed as soldiers, but do not belong to any of the Trained Bands Companies of East Yorkshire. I think they served the King and were sent here to spy on my men and town defences.'

'What the hell happened to you two?' Franks shouted.

'What indeed?' repeated Wilkes, nodding his head in the direction of Martins. 'This brainless bastard decided it would be a good idea to fight our way out of a situation that I was happily dealing with, by talking to some soldiers outside the blockhouses. I had just about talked them round when one of the soldiers saw Martins put his hand on the hilt of his sword. Next thing I know, all hell breaks loose! After killing two of the soldiers, we ran for it. Then we stopped to hide in a shop on the corner of Chapel Lane and the High Street, and then he killed the owner and some girl who came from a back room. Now we've got half the town and the garrison on our backs.'

'You pig's bastard of a fool, Martins!' snarled Franks. 'It's always you who gets us into these scrapes. We'll have to leave town now, and you can be sure that I will tell Captain Legge of the fool's cock-up you've made of everything.' Franks returned to the small table and stool he had been sitting at moments before and kicked them into the corner of the room with frustration.

Martins said nothing and looked at the ground. He knew that Franks could kill him without a moment's hesitation when he was in a mood like this.

'Stay here and don't make a sound,' Franks told them. 'Don't open the door unless it's me wanting to come in. I'm going to get us out of here, and you fools damned well better just sit on your arses and stay out of trouble.' So saying, he threw a cloak over his shoulders and slipped out into the lane.

He headed across town to the Guildhall to find Sir John Hotham. The journey took him twice as long as it should have done because he had to check that each lane and street was clear of soldiers before continuing the next step of his journey. He walked straight into Sir John's office and apprised him of the situation. Sir John Hotham was not a man who was going to stand up to the likes of Franks.

'I want a letter of authority to travel for me, Wilkes and Martins, and I want it now!' Franks demanded. 'I ain't got time to waste. We are going to join up with the King's soldiers near Beverley. Don't put a destination in the letter. We will make our way via an indirect route. Just say we are traders leaving town after selling our goods.'

Hotham willingly wrote the letter and was glad to see the back of Franks as the man hurried from the office. If anyone questioned him about Franks, he would pass him off as an urgent messenger carrying letters to Parliament in London.

Franks made his way to the stables near the Deaf Cat Inn where they all had lodgings, to retrieve their horses. Disguising the horses as pack animals, he led them from the stables and back towards Denton Lane. Keeping his hat pulled down low over the scarred side of his face he attracted little attention as he made his unhurried way across town.

After collecting Martins and Wilkes, they each took a horse and led them towards the Low Gate exit from the town. The soldier on duty halted the three men wanting to know why they were leaving town when it was under siege. Franks pulled the letter from inside his jerkin and thrust it at the guard.

'Wait here,' said the guard. Because he was unable to read, he took the letter to his sergeant. When the soldier returned he asked Franks, 'So where are you going?'

'Bridlington,' lied Franks. 'We're going to meet a ship with goods from Holland. I can bring you back some Jenever if you like. How about it?'

The guard smiled, returned the letter of travel signed and sealed by the Mayor and let them pass.

The following morning, Mathew thanked Robert Overton for his consideration and kindness and returned to his lodgings at the Drunken Monk Inn. He sat for a while in the taproom, nursing a drink that he didn't really want. The serving girl had kept badgering him until, in the end, he'd bought a tankard of ale just so she would leave him to his thoughts.

After an hour or so of soul searching he left the untouched ale on the table and then left the inn to make his way back to the apothecary shop. It was all locked up, but he didn't need to go inside. He stood in the doorway; stopping people as they passed by, asking if they had seen anything of what had happened in the shop.

Most people had no idea what he was talking about, while some sympathised with him over his loss. The rest wouldn't even stop to talk to him. He stayed there all morning, asking questions and getting no useful information in return. Next, he decided to try the town gates. He passed from one to the other begging anyone who would listen for information. Most of the guards wouldn't even talk to him, and indeed, none were prepared to own up to seeing three desperate killers pass through their gate. He was at a loss as to what to do next. The frustration of his failure hung like a millstone around his neck.

He returned to the Drunken Monk to drown his sorrows.

Chapter Ten

Before first light, Captain Overton stood in front of his men with Lieutenant Maynard by his side. 'Time to start, Lieutenant,' he said. 'Are your men ready?'

'All present and correct, sir,' came the snap response.

The column of soldiers shouldered their weapons and the entire body of men, three officers, four sergeants, thirty-six bill-men and thirty-six musketeers, armed with matchlock muskets, stepped off in unison. Captain Overton took the head of the company, followed by the ensign carrying the company colour, the flag of the East Yorkshire Trained Bands.

The company had four miles to march to reach the royalist fort at Hessle. The fort had been built to prevent ships landing goods at the river port of Hessle and sending them to resupply Hull.

The few townspeople who were on the streets at that time in the morning stopped to watch Captain Overton's men march by, before carrying on with their daily lives; the sight of soldiers on the streets of Hull was becoming commonplace. Captain Overton needed his men to be in place by daybreak. He hoped that he would catch the small royalist fort unprepared for an attack.

The sun had not shown itself above the horizon when they arrived on the outskirts of Hessle. The company had made good time along the well-used road, with only a few cattle and sheep to note their passing. Outside the village,

Overton split his command into two units—musketeers and bill-men. Lieutenant Maynard took charge of the musket division and with the aid of the ensign, led them off to the right: they would approach the fort from the north, leaving Captain Overton to attack the main gate of the fort with his bill-men. The plan was to capture the fort and destroy it if possible but failing that, to let them know that the occupants of the place would not be allowed to stay there in peace.

As planned, Lieutenant Maynard led his musketeers towards the northern side of Hessle, to a copse of trees, from which he would launch his attack on the wooden fort. While they waited out of sight, the sergeants gave the order to load muskets. All thirty-six musketeers loaded with gunpowder and ball, lit the match they held in their left hand, and then returned their muskets to the 'shoulder position' to show that they were loaded, and were ready to move off.

Lieutenant Maynard viewed the fort from the cover of the trees. There seemed little activity from within. He led his soldiers out of the woodland about one-hundred-and-fifty yards from the fort, with Maynard in the lead, the Ensign at his side and his musketeers reforming their division as soon as they were on the open ground, the sergeants hurrying them into position. They were there to be seen and draw the attention of the fort's occupants.

The musket division was spotted immediately by sentries on the fort's walls. Maynard could hear the shouts of alarm and the beat of a drum calling the fort's defenders to arms. At this distance he was in no danger from musket fire from the fort, they were out of range.

The small wooden fort on the edge of the village had been hastily constructed. Its twelve-foot high walls made from felled trees, which had been sunk into a trench, surrounding a camp of tents. Twenty musketeers, officers and four gun crews, were stationed there to operate and defend the four artillery pieces that were aimed at the quayside of Hessle.

Maynard's Musket Division stood its ground waiting for orders, the weeks of training now paying off, as the men stood patiently in the crisp morning air. Addressing the musketeers and his two sergeants, Maynard ordered firing by what was termed 'forlorn files', a recognised military manoeuvre for musketeers. The two external files of men lowered their muskets to the 'give rest' position and marched forwards twenty yards, the sergeants leading the way. At the correct distance, the sergeants ordered the files to 'form line and make ready to fire'. And so a thin line of grey-coated musketeers faced the fort, one hundred and thirty yards from the fort's walls. The senior sergeant, taking charge of the firing line called out the orders.

'Present—giiiiive—fire.'

Bringing the muskets to the firing position, the musketeers squeezed the triggers on their long matchlock muskets (these had a burning 'match' with a trigger-activated mechanism designed to apply the match to the powder at the time of firing). The line of musketeers fired as one, and twelve musket balls flew across the open ground to strike the wall of the fort. A cloud of white-grey smoke billowed away from the Musketeers, the noise from their muskets causing birds from nearby trees to rise screeching into the air. No one in the fort was injured, but it kept the defender's attention focused in the direction of the Musketeers. As the Musketeers on the firing line filed back past the sergeant to return to the rest of the division, the second two files moved forwards to pass them, heading for the sergeants on the firing line, and take their turn at firing on the fort. This 'forlorn files' bombardment continued by rotation until all the Musketeers in the division had been up to the firing line and loosed two balls of lead at the fort.

Maynard was playing for time. After his musket division had reformed and reloaded, he ordered the musket division to double its front. The musket division did as ordered and reformed its order. It was now three men deep and twelve men abreast. Maynard led his men forward, and at about one hundred yards from the fort, he stopped the musketeers and ordered the musket sergeants to fire on the fort by ranks, maintaining their ground.

The sergeants acknowledged the order and gave the musket division the command to make ready, firing by ranks, without advancing any closer to the fort. The front rank brought their weapons to bear and fired then, turning to their right, filed away to the back of the division to reload, while the next rank stepped forward into position, ready to fire on the fort.

By now the musket balls were striking the fort with more accuracy, the fort's defenders, flinching away from splinters of wood and the lead balls that were narrowly missing the men on the walls. Maynard needed to be closer, another fifty yards, and his musketeers would then be in the killing zone. Maynard, standing to the right-hand side of the Musketeers, ordered: 'Firing by ranks, gaining ground.' The sergeants barked the orders and this time after each rank of musketeers had fired their muskets and retired to the back, the division took five paces forward. The tension in the ranks began to rise as the men drew closer to the fort and the enemy musketeers. Even in the cool morning air, the men were beginning to sweat, the smoke from their muskets drying their throats when they breathed in the sulphurous gases. The heat that was now building up in the musket barrels was making them too hot to handle, and the fort's defenders were now returning musket fire.

By the time Maynard's musketeers had reached seventy-five yards distance from the fort, the gunfire from the fort was becoming accurate: men from the attacking force began to fall each time the royalist fired. Maynard's sergeants ordered the gaps to be closed up and for the injured to be left where they fell: there was no time to stop for friends or to take pity on those crying for help. Maynard knew he could not capture the fort this way, but he was there to do a job, and his lost men would be replaced. He split his musket division into two and ordered his senior sergeant to take command of half the remaining musketeers. They were to lead off with orders to fire on the West Wall of the fort.

At the sound of the musket fire, Captain Overton took his men forward. They had to keep their approach to the fort unnoticed for as long as possible for his plan to work. Staying off the road, his men used all the cover they could find to get closer to the fort. He needed to get as close as possible before launching his attack. He split his bill-men into two divisions: the larger group were to assault the fort directly. The smaller group ordered to deliver the *coup de grâce*.

Overton watched Lieutenant Maynard's men firing on the fort. Captain Overton offered up a prayer as the Musketeers drew closer to their target. It was time for his own men to play their part in the assault. He ordered the larger group forward, but they were not to draw attention to themselves by shouting. After Maynard's musketeers fired their next shot, the bill-men were to run as fast as possible up to the walls of the fort. If they got caught on open ground, Captain Overton warned them; they ran the risk of being cut to pieces by grapeshot from the fort's artillery.

The bill-men made a headlong assault on the walls of the small wooden fort. Their minds focused on the long-range weapons that could be used against them. What they were not aware of was that the fort's artillery pieces, mounted on raised platforms, were useless against the Parliamentarian forces now attacking the main entrance and walls. The primary purpose of these guns was to deter ships from docking at the small quay of Hessle. The guns had been secured in their positions and were pointing in the wrong direction.

With the onslaught of lead coming from Maynard's musketeers, the small number of men inside the fort found it too difficult to return sufficient fire on the two divisions parliamentarians musketeers attacking both walls. As a result, Overton's bill-men made it to the walls of the fort unnoticed. Lieutenant Maynard ordered his musketeers to cease fire. The fort defenders quickly appeared atop the walls, resting their muskets on the wooden wall, ready to fire on Lieutenant Maynard's men.

As the barrels of the muskets appeared over the side of the wall of the fort, from below Overton's unseen bill-men hooked their branch-lopping bills over the musket barrels, dragging them downwards and out of the hands of their owners. Those that managed to hang on to their muskets withdrew them quickly, surprised at the close-quarter attack. While some of the occupants of the fort used pistols against Overton's bill-men, others realised their desperate plight and reengaged Maynard's musketeers.

Captain Overton led his reserved force forwards, their sole objective to place a petard (a box filled with explosive powder) on the main gate of the fort, and detonate it.

So while the main force of bill-men and musketeers kept the King's men inside the fort busy, two of Overton's unarmed soldiers hammered large spikes into the centre of the fort's gate. Before they were finished, Captain Overton signalled for the remaining two more men to move in with their weapon. These two soldiers carried a petard (a keg of gunpowder that was bound with ropes). The pair ran forward towards the gate, carrying the petard by its ropes. Their job was to hang the petard by its rope supports over the spikes hammered into the gate. A fuse hung down from one end of the petard, waiting to be lit. On seeing the two bomb-carrying soldiers break cover, Lieutenant Maynard's musketeers delivered a hail of lead towards the fort as a distraction, to keep the heads of the Royalist musketeers directed away from the bomb.

With little regard to the safety of Overton's bill-men, the Parliamentarian musketeers kept firing. Some aimed high, not wanting to hit their comrades, while others did as they were ordered and watched bill-men fall to the ground injured or dead. By the time the bill-men had realised it was their own Musketeers who were firing on them, the shooting had stopped. The petard had been secured, and the fuse had been lit. Captain Overton and his bill-men ran for their lives to escape from the imminent blast.

As the petard hangers and bill-men ran for cover; from over the walls either side of the gate, royalist musketeers fired on them, unaware of the danger attached to the gate. They managed to let loose a single volley before the petard exploded, destroying the gate and killing the musketeers closest to it.

Captain Overton fell to the ground along with his billmen. Just before the petard exploded, some of the fort's musketeers who had fired that last volley had hit their targets. Captain Overton had been hit, the bullet ripping through his jacket and taking a thick line of flesh from the top of his right shoulder, the force of the one-ounce bullet pushing him off balance, and rolling him in the dirt. Stunned and with an intense burning feeling in his shoulder and neck, Captain Overton tried to stand, but the searing pain made his head spin, and his knees buckle; he fell unconscious to the ground. Next to him, a soldier had been hit in the back of the head. The bullet had shattered his skull, tearing apart his face as it made its exit, carrying with it a mass of torn flesh, brain and blood, his body tumbling to the ground like a rag doll.

Stunned by the exploding gate and the realisation that the fort was indefensible, the Royalist soldiers in the fort soon indicated their surrender with a white flag. Overton's men stopped running and turned back to take stock of the damage they had done to the fort. The gates had gone, blown from their hinges. The petard had been more substantial than it had needed to be. Those Royalists within the fort had lost the will to fight.

As soon as Lieutenant Maynard had seen the surrender of the fort he had rushed his men forwards to capture it, unaware Overton was nowhere to be seen. Inside he found the Royalists in total disarray and unable to fight on, their commanding officer, Captain Herbert Maydew, severely wounded and dying. Captain Maydew had been mortally wounded trying to turn and fire one of the four artillery pieces. The canon had exploded, the breech shattering into thousands of fragments of hot metal, shredding its gun crew and the brave captain. He lived only moments after Lieutenant Maynard had found him, his wounds so numerous and severe that blood surrounded him in a large pool, his clothes tattered and torn.

With the fort secured, Lieutenant Maynard looked to the needs of his own men next, sending six men out to collect the wounded. He had not expected his commanding officer and friend to be one of them.

Captain Overton was still breathing, but unconscious. Maynard removed Overton's silk scarf and folded it to make a pad and slipped it inside Overton's jacket to cover the wound.

While the dead from both Royalist and Parliamentarian armies were buried in a local churchyard, wagons had been procured locally to transport the Parliamentarian wounded back to Hull.

A sergeant banged on Mathew's door calling his name and demanding that he report to the officers' quarters in Hull Castle to attend to the wounded.

'Why me?' yelled Mathew.

''Cause I was told to get *you*,' replied the sergeant. 'Now, are you coming, or do I have to come in and drag you there?'

Mathew put on his jacket and ran his hands through his unkempt hair. He didn't want to go; he just wanted to stay in his bed and drink until the pain of losing Elizabeth could be washed from his mind. Befuddled with drink, it was fortunate that he remembered to pick up his surgeon's kit of instruments from the small table before he left his room to follow the sergeant.

They crossed the bridge over the River Hull and followed the base of the town's defensive wall to the castle. Mathew stopped for a moment while to vomit up the beer he'd been drinking.

'Never seen a sober surgeon yet,' muttered the sergeant just loud enough for Mathew to hear.

Relieved of the burden of drink and but with his head still thumping, Mathew continued to follow the sergeant until they reached the gates of the castle. The guards on the gate stood aside as the sergeant rushed Mathew through.

'Up here!' The sergeant indicated stairs to an upper floor. Mathew took them slowly—his feet still felt like lead, and his head was starting to swim again. He was led to a sparsely furnished room, with a table in its centre, upon which a man was lying on his back. As he drew closer, he could see that it was Captain Overton, his jacket torn and covered with blood that needed his attention. Lieutenant Maynard stood by the table, concern showing on his face, which turned to shock when he saw the dishevelled state of the surgeon.

'Are you fit enough to tend to the sick?' Maynard's question was harsh and demanding. Mathew wiped the sweat from his forehead onto his jacket sleeve. The sight of the injured officer helped him focus his mind.

'Yes, I'm fit,' Mathew snapped back. 'Send someone to fetch hot water and towels.' He pushed passed the lieutenant to get to his patient and began to cut away Overton's jacket and shirt. Maynard sent the sergeant for the necessary items.

'What caused the wound?'

'A musket ball, I believe,' was the reply.

'He's a lucky man, your captain. If the bullet had caught him in the neck he would have died before you could get him off the field; had it struck lower down, it would have gone through his lung, and he would have died slowly and painfully, and there'd be nothing I could to help him.'

Mathew turned to look at the sergeant. 'I'm going to wash the wound with vinegar, and then cauterise it. I need you to fetch a couple more men to hold the captain down while I work on him.'

The sergeant went pale at the thought of a red-hot iron being applied to human flesh. He left the room to do as he had been told, while Mathew prepared the captain for his operation. When the sergeant returned, he brought two of the tallest and most formidable-looking men Mathew had ever seen.

'Pikemen,' explained the sergeant without being asked.

There was a small fire burning in the fireplace, into which Mathew placed a cauterising iron. He gave his instructions to the men who were now to be his assistants.

'Now, Sergeant, I want you to hold his legs down. You two men take an arm each and hold the captain still. When I start to clean the wound, he'll wake up and try to get off the table. It is important that he moves as little as possible. Lieutenant if you would be kind enough to hold the captains head still I'll get started?'

With tweezers, Mathew carefully searched the wound for torn shreds of clothing as he could, painstakingly cleaning the wound. Satisfied he'd removed all the debris, he poured a generous amount of wine vinegar into the channel the bullet had made as it had passed through the top of the captain's right shoulder. Captain Overton screamed and tried to rise from the table, but the pikemen held him down.

'Captain, I'm sorry,' Mathew apologised. 'I must do this, or gangrene will set in.' He gave Robert Overton a few sips of wine laced with laudanum, and then inserted a piece of wood, wrapped in linen, between his teeth. Taking the red-hot cauterising iron from the fire, he slowly ran it across the open wound.

Robert Overton jerked violently, giving a gargled scream and then fell still on the table. The two pikemen had turned their heads away at last minute, not wanting to see the flesh shrink away from the hot iron. But, they could smell the sickly-sweet aroma of burning, tortured, flesh and blood as the smoke drifted past their faces. Instructing the two pikemen to sit the unconscious captain on the edge of the table while he dressed the wound, Mathew quickly finished his work.

'Put him to bed,' he told the lieutenant. 'I'll go check on the rest of the injured men you brought back. I can help the company surgeon; he'll probably be glad of the assistance. I'll come back later, to check on the captain.'

Mathew spent the rest of the day helping the company surgeon, pleased to have the distraction, to stop him from sitting alone, thinking of Elizabeth.

By the time the young surgeon returned to see Captain Overton later in the early evening, his head had cleared, and he'd eaten his first solid food since the funeral. He found the captain sleeping with the sergeant sat by the side of the bed. The sergeant stood up as Mathew entered.

'Would you like me to wake him, Sir?'

'No, let him sleep, Sergeant, and when he does wake up, give him three drops of this *laudanum* in a cup of wine—it will help with the pain and send him to sleep again. Don't let him try and move around too much or he'll open that wound. I will call in the morning to renew the dressing.' Mathew left, satisfied with the work he had done that day.

Mathew returned at eight of the clock the following morning to find Robert Overton sitting on the edge of his bed.

'Captain! Really, you must rest and give yourself time to heal,' surprised to see that the injured man was already awake.

Robert Overton slowly turned his head to look towards Mathew, the smallest movement sending ripples of stabbing pain through his shoulder and up the side of his neck. Although Robert's face was pale and drawn, he managed to give a little smile. 'Forgive me if I don't stand up,' he said with a trace of humour.

'I've brought you some more *laudanum,* and I need to change your dressings.' Mathew sat on the chair next to the captain.

'Help me up; I want to sit at the table.' Robert Overton placed his left hand on Mathew's shoulder and forced himself to his feet.

'You will be better off in bed; you need to rest.'
The captain ignored him and shuffled slowly to the table.

Why me? Why did you send for me?' Mathew asked. 'You have surgeons in the army who could have treated your shoulder.'

'You're the only surgeon I know who's not one of the army-trained medical men. I've seen them work; they're more like butchers than healers. I wouldn't let my horse be treated by one of them.' He looked into Mathew's face and smiled. 'Besides, I checked up on you with Surgeon Adams after I met you in the apothecary shop. He thinks very highly of you.' Overton sat on a stool, resting his left arm on the table while Mathew re-dressed his right shoulder.

'You will not be unable to use your right arm for some time, but as soon as you are able to move it without too much pain you will have to start exercising it, or it will stiffen up. But take it gently, a little movement at a time. I will check on you every day until the scar is granulated.'

While they sat and talked, Overton's servant entered, carrying a new shirt and jacket for his master. After helping the captain dress, he left, to return with cups of wine and a bacon tart for the captain and Mathew.

Chapter Eleven

At dinner, with Lady Gee, the anger returned to the king's face, 'how could they turn against us? Hotham assured us the town was loyal to their king. It was supposed to be a dignified entrance to the town, but he turned against us! He defied his king. I gave him every opportunity to surrender the town peacefully, and what did he do? He made me look the fool. Well, Sir John Hotham, we are the King of England, appointed by God to rule this land and I will have you pay for this day's humiliation!'

Lady Gee picked at her food while the King vented his frustration. She had not wanted the King in her house but had felt it her duty to offer up her home for his use when he arrived in Beverley. Her former husband, now long dead, had always spoken highly of the monarch, his eloquence and his intelligence. She was discovering that he was decidedly petulant and behaved like a spoilt child.

Captain Overton, recovering well from his wounds, sat talking to Mathew Fletcher while the young surgeon changed his dressing.

'The swelling is reducing, and there is no sign of infection, you have been very lucky,' Mathew informed his patient, feeling proud of his handiwork. 'You know, you do not need me to dress this for you anymore. You could get one of the army surgeons to take care of you now,' Mathew told the man who'd become his friend.

'I still need help with many day to day things while my arm is weak, but Mortimer here looks after me very well.' Captain Overton indicated to his servant, who was entering the room with a bottle of wine and two glasses. 'I have added to his duties of late. He also doubles as my secretary, which I trust he will continue to do until I can write legibly again with my injured arm.'

Mortimer gave a respectful smile to Mathew as he placed the opened bottle of wine and glasses on a small table between the two men. 'He has also turned out to be very useful at keeping an eye on what's happening in the Guildhall,' Overton continued, 'when he goes to collect letters and news from London and Parliament.'

After a pause in the conversation, the captain confessed, 'the thing is, I trust you, Mathew. You have not seen the poor standard of work our army surgeons do. We do not always get the best men available, you see, Parliament has taken the best medical men and given them to the navy.' Overton smiled, embarrassed by what he had just confessed. 'I will have to be careful what I say around you, or I will be giving away all our military secrets.' It was as he said the words, he realised that Mathew's quiet manner and personal involvement in his patient's recovery had loosened his own tongue. He was allowing himself to confide in his surgeon, sharing more information than he ought to. At that moment the spark of an idea occurred to him.

'Mathew, I have something I would like you to consider. I have not thought through all the details yet, but I would like to ask if you would consider working for me, for

Parliament—gathering information that may be of use to our cause.' Overton knew he needed more time to think the plan through thoroughly, but he needed to test the water first, to find out how Mathew Fletcher would react to the suggestion.

'Me? Spy for you and Parliament!' Mathew replied, aghast. 'I'm no spy, Captain. I don't know anything about spying, and they would kill me if I were caught. I'm a surgeon; I help people. I don't sneak about in the dead of night. No. No. I cannot think that far ahead. I need time to grieve for the loss of my Elizabeth.'

William Fletcher screamed in pain and fell to the ground, clutching his lower abdomen.

Charles and Henry left the wheel they had been working on and dashed across the yard to their prostrate father. Between clenched teeth, William confessed that he may have a 'stone', as he had not been able to piss properly for several days. As they looked at their father lying curled in pain on the ground, the brothers watched a wet stain appearing in their father's breeches and spreading outwards.

Embarrassment spread across William's face. 'I've pissed myself like a babe,' he confessed, 'but the pain has eased. I think I need Mathew's help. I can't stand the pain anymore, and I can't lie down each time I need to take a piss.'

The pressure, having been released from his bladder, William Fletcher got to his feet, removed his breeches and washed them in the horse trough. Leaving them to dry hanging from a peg in the workshop, and returned to the house to get a dry pair. Mary stared at her father-in-law as he passed through the kitchen heading for the stairs. With his shirt almost down to his hairy knees and his socks held up with a cord just below its hem, he looked like he had just got out of bed. Mary turned away, not daring to ask what had happened to his breeches—she would get Charles to explain later.

That evening, Henry took it upon himself to be the one who would go to Hull, and inform Mathew that his father needed him. 'I have given the matter a great deal of thought,' he told the family 'I will go by boat, travelling down the River Hull. By staying off the roads, I will avoid the soldier's patrols.

Later that night, Henry slipped a small boat he had borrowed into the water. There was near blackness on the water under the shadows from the bank. A faint moonlight rippled over the water as it flowed swiftly towards its freedom at the mouth of the River Hull. With the tide in his favour, it would only take a couple of hours for Henry to row the boat to Hull. As he made his way down river, he found that it was only two barge-widths wide at the start and with its high riverbanks to prevent flooding onto the fields either side, it made the waterway feel dangerous and claustrophobic.

Occasionally, trees leaned their branches across the river, casting eerie shapes and shadows against the dim sky which was only marginally brighter than the darkness in which Henry found himself. Startled waterfowl disturbed by the small boat passing close by flapped and crashed through the reeds to escape the strange unseen craft, as it steered an unsteady course through the East Yorkshire countryside.

As Henry approached the outskirts of Hull, he passed the breaches which had been cut in the eastern riverbank to allow water to flood the fields around Hull when the tide was full. He didn't understand the reason for these openings in the riverbank. To him, they were just curiosities on his journey to a reunion with his brother and to get the help that his father so desperately needed.

It had been a few days since Elizabeth's death, and Mathew had done nothing about setting up his own business. He had done very little at all except to sit in his room and dwell on what might have been had they married. His visits to Captain Overton had helped fill his days, but later, when he returned to his room at the Drunken Monk, he fell once again into despair. His room stank of his unwashed body, soiled clothes and the un-emptied night bucket. He barely ate but drunk a lot.

Mathew lay in a stupor on his bed, an empty jug of beer and cup on their side upon the table. When Henry arrived at his brother's lodgings he was unaware of Elizabeth's death, Mathew had been so wrapped up in misery he couldn't face putting pen to paper to notify his family. So when Henry hadn't received an answer to his knock on Mathew's door, he had forced his way in. At first, he was angry with Mathew for being in such a filthy state, but as he listened to his brother and tried to console him as best, he could. He understood his brother's deep sorrow and loss.

'Mathew, you have to throw yourself into your work,' Henry told him. 'You have to give yourself something to focus on other than Elizabeth's death. You are too young to give up on your future happiness; people need you.'

Mathew turned towards his brother, ready to strike him for questioning his grieving. With tears running down his face and his heart broken, Mathew snapped at his brother. 'What do you know about love, Henry? My heart is in pieces! She died in my arms, and I couldn't save her! Like our mother, I was helpless to do anything to save her. I have sworn an oath to help and heal people, but now, all I want is revenge on those men. It fills me up; I know it's wrong, but it's tearing me apart because I'm powerless to do anything to relieve it. Am I evil; is it normal to feel like this after the loss of a loved one?' At first sitting, then falling sideways onto his bed, his face covered by his hands, Mathew wept openly. Henry would have done anything to help his brother but didn't have the time to indulge him. He still hadn't broken the news of their father's ailment and needing Mathew's help. But, he had waited long enough, and even though he knew the news would cause his brother more distress, Henry had no choice but to inform his brother of the real reason for his sudden arrival.

'I'm sorry, Mathew, I'm really sorry, but I have to tell you. Father is ill with the 'stone', and he needs your help. Father is asking for you. We need you to come home.'

Mathew sat up on his bed and stared at his brother in disbelief. 'What? I need time to think. Father has a stone? But how? Why? His questions were rhetorical, as he struggled to digest the news. 'How much more bad news do I have to take?'

The young surgeon felt as if the world he knew was being turned upside down. Mathew put his feet to the floor and his head in his hands.

'I will come with you; there is nothing left for me here. Everything reminds me of Elizabeth.'

Henry explained the difficulty he'd had in getting to Hull, and that he was unsure if they would be able to return by the same way.

'I know someone who may be able to help us.'

Mathew washed his face before the two brothers made their way to the military quarters of Captain Robert Overton.

Mathew was determined not to let his father down: he was not going to lose another person that he loved. Finding Captain Overton preparing himself to leave on military business, he begged his new friend for just a few moments of his time. Henry explained to the captain how he had left Beverley by rowing boat, travelling down the River Hull at night, and that he had been lucky that there had been little moonlight to give away his silent passage down the river to Hull. With the siege around Hull growing tighter each day, the return passage via the same route would be almost impossible.

'I'll see what I can do, Mathew, but I can't make any promises,' Overton explained to the brothers. But an idea from earlier had never left the captain and was now growing; he needed to give it a little more time to flourish. Mathew wanted to protest at Overton's apparent lack of commitment, but the captain held up his hand to Mathew to silence him.

'Sorry, Mathew, but I need to work this out. If I am going to get you back to your father safely, I will need the help of some fellow officers.'

Overton had decided to take advantage of his new friend, but he would need the help of Sir John Meldrum.

Captain Overton made his way to Sir John Meldrum's quarters. Knocking on the door, he entered before being asked. Meldrum was taken aback by the sudden intrusion and was about to complain, but Overton butted in first.

'Sorry, Meldrum,' he began, 'but this is urgent, I need your help.' He took a seat next to his friend and explained about getting Mathew and his brother back to Beverley in return for getting Mathew's help with intelligence on the king's forces stationed there.

'The problem is,' he continued, 'we have to keep the Hotham's in the dark as to what we are up to. If word got out that we had dropped one of our agents in their midst, he wouldn't last very long. I suggest we take them with us when we leave on the raid tomorrow. That will get them most of the way to Beverley, after that, they will have to make their own way, and take their chances.'

'With Mathew do as you ask him, Overton?'

'Yes, I believe his to be a man of his word. I will also give him an incentive to do as I ask.'

After Overton had spoken to some of his fellow officers, the plan was agreed. Mathew and Henry Fletcher would leave Hull with Captain Meldrum's horse company the next day, and when Meldrum made his attack on the king's forces at Beverley, Mathew and Henry would be allowed to break away from the company.

That evening Mathew Fletcher sat at a table with his brother Henry, as they ate their meal of pork stew with apple and small suet dumplings. The brothers were making plans for their return to Beverley unaware of what Captain Overton had arranged for them. They decided that, if Captain Overton would not help them, they would devise their own route back to their hometown. The brothers were planning to take a small boat from the quay in Hull and to travel down the River Humber the short distance to the village of Paull, from where they would travel overland to

Beverley. While they sat discussing these things, Captain Overton entered the Drunken Monk Inn, finding the brothers in the corner of the taproom; he removed his large black felt hat and crossed to where the brothers were sitting.

'I'm sorry for delaying your return to Beverley,' Overton told them, 'but to get you back as quickly as possible I needed to be sure I could get the help of some loyal fellow officers. I am pleased to tell you that they have agreed to help you, but there are conditions.'

Mathew had expected to have to repay the favour he had asked of the captain, but from the serious expression on Captain Overton's face, it looked as if the price was going to be high.

'I want you to reconsider my request to gather information on the King's forces in and around Beverley.' Captain Overton stared at the brothers, his face devoid of expression waiting for their response, he wanted them to understand they had no choice but to accept his terms.

'Before you give me your answer, there are a few things you need to consider. I believe the men who killed Elizabeth and her father are in Beverley on the King's business. But, by volunteering to join and spy on our king, you will increase your chance of finding the men you are looking for. Two soldiers were killed in Hull on that same day, by two men who had been stopped for questioning. They made their escape down the High Street and Chapel Lane, where the apothecary shop is located, then on towards Lowgate. They have not been found in Hull, and one of them, as you know, is thought to be injured. I do not know how they have managed to get out of Hull, but they may have masqueraded as merchants, and slipped out that way.'

Mathew pushed his meal away from him and sat back, studying Captain Overton and considering what he had just said. He was incensed at being manipulated in this way, but the news concerning Elizabeth's killers changed things. He had never known he could harbour such feelings of hatred for another person as he did for the men who had killed Elizabeth and the opportunity to find them, persuasive. Overton's conditions were harsh: help him or be unable to leave Hull and save his father. The captain had offered him a way to find Elizabeth's killers, and for that he was grateful. What harm could it do if he collected information about the King's army at the same time as he was searching for the murderer's, he would still get his revenge on the killer?

'How soon can we be on our way, Captain?'

Overton gave a small sigh of relief at Mathew's response, but he noted the formality in the way he had been addressed and was saddened by it. He liked this young man who had treated his wound so diligently. He was a man of peace whose nature had been altered by the cruel hand of fate. Although Mathew wasn't much younger than he was, the latter having seen war in the Low Countries. Mathew's vocation was that of being a surgeon. The two men had evolved very different roles in life, but both were intelligent and determined.

Robert Overton was the eldest son of a modest landowner in Easington, East Yorkshire, and had joined the army after gaining a degree at Oxford University. He had chosen a military life for a career and had learnt his trade fighting the Spanish alongside Thomas Fairfax, a family friend.

The captain informed Mathew and Henry of the plans that had been made for them. 'Tomorrow morning, a company of horse will escort you to Beverley,' he explained. 'I will have two horses ready for you outside the Inn at six of the clock, tomorrow. Before I leave, I need to give you details of how to pass your messages to me. I will send you a courier; you will give him any news you discover of the King's plans—we'll want any information, no matter how insignificant it may seem. With the information you provide, added to intelligence we have gathered from other sources, it may be you who provides the vital piece of knowledge that tips things in our favour, or saves many lives. The courier will identify himself by informing you that: *'He comes from our friend in Hull.'*

Overton stood up and replaced his hat. 'I will leave you to your meal. Thank you, Mathew. I am aware that I have tested our new friendship, but I am an officer who has been forced to take sides against my King for the sake of a country I love and a people that deserve better than to be ruled by a corrupt tyrant.' He gave a slight bow. 'So, gentlemen, I wish you Godspeed tomorrow, and hope that your father makes a fast recovery.'

Chapter Twelve

Mathew and Henry slept little that night. The anticipation of the following morning's ride with a company of mounted soldiers was not something they did every day. They awoke early and ate a small breakfast: nerves getting the better of their appetites before their horses arrived. By six of the clock, two sturdy mounts from Captain Meldrum's Company of Horse were waiting for them as promised. Outside the inn, in the growing light of morning, they mounted their horses, apprehension of what was about to come making their hands shake.

From the shadow cast by the overhanging first floor of a shop front, Thomas Potter, on the instructions of his confederate, Henry Walker, watched as the two brothers prepared to leave with the half-dozen heavily armed troopers. Unable to move from the shadows for fear of discovery, he was unable to get a good view of the brothers' faces or hear the words that passed between them. His heart was thumping as he watched the troopers and the two civilians mount their horses. He followed them as they walked up the street to join more troopers, all of them heading in one direction; to form up on the road outside the town walls. Potter turned back up the street.

163

This was news that Captain Legge had to hear.

Mathew turned in the saddle to face his brother, saying, 'Whatever happens, Henry, we stick together. We'll break away from this lot as soon as we get the chance and head for home.'

Henry nodded back his assent.

They had not expected to join such a large force of Parliamentary horse and asked the soldiers around them about why they were all assembled. They soon learned that they were about to attack the king's forces in Beverley. This was something Mathew and Henry had not bargained for.

When they found Captain Overton, he explained that as they knew the King was using Beverley as his headquarters for maintaining the siege on Hull, it was a legitimate target for attack. As soon as the Parliamentarians were in Beverley, Overton assured Mathew and Henry that they would be free to break away and get home as best they could.

With the sounding of trumpets, the soldiers brought their mounts to order and prepared to set forth. The horses sensed the tension of their riders, shifting from hoof to hoof, jostling their fellow creatures nearby. Tack and swords jangled and added to the sounds of horses snorting and whinnying.

The squadron of cavalry had formed up into three smaller squadrons of two troops each, on the open ground to the north of Hull. The order sounded to move off, and the column fell into order to make their way up the Beverley

Road. Mathew's mouth soon became dry from the dust thrown up by the horses.

'Henry,' Mathew called across to his brother. 'I hadn't expected us to get involved with an attack on Beverley. I'm afraid of what will happen.'

'Me too,' replied Henry. 'We'll just have to hope we can escape in all the confusion.'

The brothers rode on in silence, wondering what they had let themselves in for and if they had made the right decision to return to Beverley in this way.

Henry, after speaking to a junior officer, had learned that the plan was for the attack on Beverly to come from two different directions at the same time. One from the north of Beverley Bar, along the Driffield road into the Saturday Market, the second attack being launched along the road from Hull leading past the Beverley Minster into Wednesday Market. Mathew and Henry were to follow the troops entering the town from the north of Beverly Bar on the Driffield road. The two assaults on the town were to be fast, the idea being to assess the strength of the forces in the town, to cause confusion amongst the king's soldiers, and then leave as quickly as they had entered, leaving Mathew and Henry behind.

Outside the hamlet of Woodmansey, Meldrum and Goodricke's cavalry column split into two. Captain Meldrum led his men towards the village of Weel, where they crossed the ford on the River Hull, skirting the eastern edge of Beverley to come into the town from the north.

Captain Goodricke was to hold his position for one hour before he led his two troops of horse forward into Beverley from the Hull Road. Mathew and Henry were ordered to follow Meldrum, but now that the pace had increased they soon found that they began to lag behind the more experienced riders as they galloped towards Weel.

Captain Meldrum's troopers refused to slow down for the two stragglers at the back. However, Mathew and Henry managed to catch up to the troop as they slowed to cross the ford but soon found themselves dropping behind again when the more experienced troopers increased the pace once they had passed through Weel. The brothers managed to keep the others in sight until they finally caught up with them once again when they gave their horses a breather before entering Beverley. A sergeant rode to the rear of the column to find Mathew and Henry.

'A message from Captain Meldrum, sir,' he told the non-military pair. 'Once the attack starts, you are on your own. The captain regrets he will not be able to offer you any further aid once we start our attack. He wishes you both Godspeed and safe deliverance to your family.'

Mathew and Henry watched the sergeant return to Captain Meldrum. Mathew's throat was dry once again, and he wished he'd thought to bring a drink with him. He could feel his body trembling with fear as he looked across to his brother for reassurance.

'We'll be fine,' his elder brother reassured him. 'They're the ones doing the fighting—we've just got to keep our heads down.'

From up ahead, the brothers heard the order to 'trot on'. The troop reformed into an orderly column as it advanced towards the Beverley Bar. The pace quickened to a canter, and then to a charge as they passed through the arched gate into Beverly Bar Within. The cavalry thundered through the narrow street scattering the citizens of Beverley as they headed for the Saturday Market and the heart of the town.

Meldrum's troop had met little resistance at Beverley Bar and quickly dispatched the few sentries on duty there. His confidence grew as his troop advanced on the market without a shot being fired at them.

Mathew and Henry did their best to keep up but perpetually lagged behind the troopers. As the gap between the brothers and the other riders opened up, they found their entrance to Beverley unopposed, the troopers having cleared the street as they rushed forwards. They eased their mounts to an easy trot before entering Cuckstool Pit Lane and then into their father's wheelwrights' yard.

By the time Meldrum's force entered the Saturday Market, the royalists had been alerted and were preparing to defend against the income attack. Once the first shots had been fired at the guards on the Beverley Bar, pikemen had assembled at the entrance to the market to allow the royalist musketeers to be ready themselves.

Meldrum's troopers were surprised to find the pikemen waiting for them and were forced to split up. In the mayhem that ensued, they were channelled down the narrow streets either side of the rectangular marketplace. The captain's inexperience with mounted troops had lost him half his command, and he was now at risk of being trapped in the narrow streets around the market. Musketeers started to come forward to protect pikemen, firing at close range as the troopers rode past looking for their lost commander. Men and horses fell wounded and dying on the cobbled streets. Here and there, dismounted Parliamentary troopers fought hand to hand in small clumps with the king's men. The attack that was meant to have been a quick 'in and out' of Beverley, to give the King a bloody nose, was quickly falling apart.

At the end of Silverlesse Lane, Meldrum regrouped what was left of his troop and turned north towards St Mary's Church looking for a means of escape and leaving the fallen behind. In the narrow streets and lanes around the market, the few unseated soldiers who had been left behind were soon overwhelmed and died in a hail of musket fire, or else were cut down by pikemen.

By thirty minutes past seven of the clock, Potter was banging on the back door of the Barnard house. It was the cook that answered the impatient clamour at her home. Clearly unhappy, the heavy-set woman glared into his face.

'What do you want, making all that noise, this time of the morning?' she demanded.

'I need to see the captain,' Potter told her. 'It's urgent.'

'It'll have to wait 'till he's had his breakfast. Come back later.' She made to shut the door, but Potter pushed past and stood in the large kitchen that took up the greater portion of the back of the house. The room's warmth was inviting after standing in the chill of the night watching the two men at the inn.

'I want to see Captain Legge, and I want to see him now, woman! Tell him Thomas Potter needs to see him urgently!' Potter held his ground, glaring back at the cook, who stood facing him, her complexion going from pink to bright red.

'Tillie, Tillie, go get the master,' the woman ordered one of her helpers. The cook didn't take her eyes off Potter. Tillie the kitchen skivvy; a young lass in her early teens, ran to the door, glad to get away from the cook's rising temper.

'Don't you move,' ordered the formidable woman, 'I'll bash you if you pull any tricks with me.' Folding her thick arms under her ample bosom, she made herself look like an immovable obstacle: she was determined to stand her ground against all comers, no matter how important they thought they were.

It wasn't long before Barnard, and Captain Legge appeared in the doorway. Legge recognised Potter instantly.

'With your pardon, sir, I need to interview this man immediately,' Legge asked the cook's master, 'may I take him to the library?'

Barnard nodded his consent. 'It's all right, Ruth, he'll be leaving shortly,' he tried to reassure his servant. 'Please have our breakfasts made ready. We will eat as soon as this man leaves.'

While Captain Legge sat at the desk in the library taking notes, Potter told how he had been keeping an eye on Robert Overton. The spy informed the captain that one of the men, who had been collected from the Drunken Monk Inn this morning, had been seen more and more frequently in Overton's company. He didn't know for sure where they had all gone, but he could guess.

'I want you to go back to the inn and find out who they are,' Legge instructed. 'Then watch the inn to see what they do when they get back.' Captain Legge sat back in the brown leather chair, wondering who the two men could be. He had thought that he and Newcastle knew all the key players in the struggle to restore Hull to the Crown. So who were the two new men working for Overton?

Potter bowed to the captain and left the library, leaving the house the way he had entered, without a second look at the cook.

Barnard and Legge sat down to breakfast.

'Is everything all right, William?' Henry Barnard asked as he looked at his friend, who was deep in thought.

'Yes, yes, everything in fine. It's just that something unexpected has cropped up, but the matter is in hand.'

Thomas Potter asked at the Drunken Monk Inn about the two men who had been staying there. The only information he was able to get from the innkeeper was that they were brothers, and the younger one had lost someone close to him. She had overheard them talking about getting back to Beverley because their father was ill and they had told her that they wouldn't be returning anytime soon. The physical description he got was vague: the brothers were both tall, young, and had brown hair. It was not much to go on.

After entering the wheelwright's yard, Mathew and Henry closed the gates and rushed into the house. Henry stood by the front door, holding a large hammer, ready to attack anyone who tried to break in off the lane. Mary sat at the back of the kitchen, hiding under the stairs with Bess on her lap.

They had heard the shooting at the Beverley Bar and seen the troop of horse flash by the end of the lane. They waited for what they thought was going to be a ransacking of the town by the Parliamentarian army. Upstairs, William Fletcher called for news from his sickbed. He had heard the sound of the yard gates being closed and the house door bursting open. Mary had screamed, and Bess had started barking when she heard the kitchen door burst open. Charles turned to face the attack a knife in his hand, only to be confronted by his two exhausted brothers. Relief spread across the brother's faces as the family was once again safely reunited.

Leaving Henry with Charles and Mary, Mathew hurried up to the bedchamber to see his father. Entering without knocking, he covered the distance from the door to the bed in two large strides.

'Father, what ails you—what can I do to help?' Mathew's voice betraying his anxiety. He now regretted all the time that he had spent away from his family. He feared losing the father who had sacrificed so much for him while he was growing up in Hull learning to be a surgeon, and making plans for his own future, made him feel guilty.

William Fletcher lay helpless in his bed, ashen-faced and sweating. He looked nervous at the sounds of pistol shots, shouts and horses' hooves clattering over the cobbled streets outside.

'What's happening, Mathew?'

'Calm yourself, Father, it will be over soon.'

'I am in great pain, Mathew. Greater pain than I have ever known. I believe I have a stone. I haven't been able to piss properly for many days. The pain has been growing for weeks, but I daren't tell anyone, or seek help, until now. Will I die the same way your mother did?'

The suffering man grasped the sides of the bed as another spasm of pain ran through his body. He stretched out, his body rigid, as though the unnatural position would help relieve some of the pain. As the spasm passed, Mathew was able to examine his father and ask about his symptoms.

'The stone is in your bladder not in your kidney, so there hope. I will do what I can, Father, and God willing you will make a good recovery.'

Mathew did his best to reassure his father, knowing that what was to follow was something he would not wish on any man and that his father's recovery would be more in God's hands than his own.

The first part of the treatment would be easy: the relieving of the pressure in his father's bladder due to the build-up of urine. He went outside to collect some instruments from his surgeon's kit and, calling on his two brothers to help him, returned to begin his father's treatment.

The chaotic sounds from outside dropped away, to be replaced by the noise of townsfolk coming onto the street to see what had happened after the troopers had left the town. It was time for Mathew to see to his father's needs.

Mathew asked his brothers to hold their father in a standing position, supporting him, with one of his arms around each of their necks. Unable to stand on his own William Fletcher hung from the arms of his sons, his knees slightly bent. Mathew set the night bucket between himself and his father.

'Father, there will be some pain to start with,' Mathew explained, 'but it will soon be over, and then you will feel relief as the piss comes away.'

Mathew knelt on the floor in front of his father and unfastened the sick man's breeches, letting them drop to the floor. Taking up the bottom of his father's shirt and giving it to his brothers to hold out of the way, Mathew picked up a long, thin, brass catheter which had a slight bend to one end. He covered this instrument in fine lard, then gently, he inserted the curved end up into the opening at the end of his father's penis. The patient began to groan, his body stiffening with the pain. Slowly, Mathew pushed the catheter deeper, until it was well inside his father's body, and then, after he had given it a little twist, urine began to flow through the tube into the bucket.

William Fletcher relaxed as the pain from his over-enlarged bladder started to ease. It seemed to last a long time, but eventually, the flow of urine stopped, and Mathew was able to remove the catheter. William recovered almost instantaneously, his normal colour returning to his face. Charles and Henry congratulated Mathew, both relieved to see their father on his feet again and recovering. Pulling up his breeches, William thanked his son.

'Come, we all need a drink after that,' said their father.

They returned to the kitchen where Mary had been waiting anxiously.

'We need to talk, Father,' Mathew said sympathetically, 'about what must come next. You do realise that the terrible pain caused by trapped water will happen again, and soon?' Mathew looked at his father seriously, knowing that there was no point in trying to pretend that all would be well from now on. His father had to understand that he couldn't avoid what was to come next; the alternative was to suffer a long and painful death.

'You are going to need an operation to remove the stone, or it will continue to grow, and you will die.' Mathew looked into his father's face and saw the fear, the first time he had ever seen fear in this bear of a man, who had always stood tall and proud. 'You know it must be done, and you know I will do everything in my power to bring you through it safely.'

Mathew's father nodded, putting down his horn cup of beer.

'Just for now, my son, please let me rest and enjoy the company of my family,' William answered. 'We can talk it over tomorrow—after we have all recovered from today's little drama.'

Mathew didn't sleep well that night; he knew what he must do. He had seen it done many times and had assisted Surgeon Adams on several occasions. He had even performed the surgery himself under Surgeon Adams's supervision and received praise for his skill, but this was different, he would be doing it for the first time on his own, and operating on his own father. Again and again, he ran through the procedure mentally, picturing in his mind each step he must take, muttering over and over again, as he talked his way through the operation until he finally fell asleep from exhaustion.

The next morning Mathew informed his father that there would be no work for him today, as the sooner the operation was performed, the easier it would be. Mathew led his father back to his bedchamber.

William dutifully drank the foul-tasting preparation that Mathew gave him. Within a minute he felt his stomach begin to churn, and, lurching across the room, he only just made it to a bucket by the door, to vomit up the remains of the food he had eaten the night before. He heaved so much that the pain brought tears to his eyes; so intense was the urge to vomit, he thought his stomach would rupture as it emptied its final contents of solids. The only substance coming up now was the yellow bile of his digestive juices, which burnt his throat as he spat it into the bucket.

He rolled onto his back wondering what was to follow. Feeling weak after the ordeal, he went to his bed and slept for a while. When he opened his eyes, he found that he was alone. He got up slowly, making his way to the door. For the sake of his own self-esteem, he was going to make it to the latrine out in the yard. Mathew followed his father back into the house after he had finished voiding his bowels in the latrine.

'Rest now, Father,' Mathew said. 'I am going to prepare for the operation.' He asked Mary, who had just returned from the market, to scrub down the kitchen table. When she had finished, he washed his instruments and dried them on a clean cloth, then laid them out on the table, in the order, he would need to use them. The young surgeon then asked Mary to fetch Charles and Henry from the yard; he was going to need their help. He gave his father a small cup of *laudanum* to drink and asked him to undress. Mary returned with her husband and his brother. Charles was carrying two lengths of rope.

'You had better leave, Mary,' Mathew told her. 'This is not going to be a pleasant sight for a woman to watch.'

'No, I want to help. I've helped with the birthing of my sister's babies, it can't be any worse than that, and I know what a naked man looks like.' She smiled. 'Don't worry; I will make myself useful.'

Mathew returned her smile. 'Good, I shall be glad of your help.'

They sat the naked patient on the end of the big table, with his heels on its edge and his knees tucked up against his chest.

'Right, Henry. You tie the rope around his ankle as I told you,' ordered Mathew. Mary, help Charles hold onto father to stop him falling off the table, now the *laudanum* is taking effect. While Henry tied the longer of the two ropes to his father's right ankle, Mathew wound the rest of the rope around his father's calf, then up to his knee. From there it went over his right shoulder to his left shoulder, then after winding the rope down his leg from the left knee to the left ankle, he tied the rope tight.

The second, shorter rope, Mathew looped around the first rope where it came above the knees and drew it under his father's armpits and behind his back, pulling it tight so that William's legs were pulled apart and could not move forward or close together again.

Inserting a piece of wood wrapped in linen between his father's teeth for him to bite down on, Mathew was ready to start.

'Mary,' he commanded, 'I will want you to pass me the instruments as I ask for them, and have a cloth ready to wipe away the blood.' Mathew didn't wait for a reply. 'Lean father back a little,' he instructed his brothers ' and hold onto him tightly.'

With his left hand, Mathew inserted two fingers deep into his father's anus, feeling around for the bladder stone. On finding it, with his free hand, using his scalpel he made an incision through the skin that was situated between the scrotum and the anus, directly above the location of the stone. Removing his fingers from his father's rectum, he wiped off the remnants of any faeces and then opened up the incision he had made into the skin. Separating the sphincter muscles, he found the peritoneum and cut through it, asking Mary to hold each incision open with a retractor (a device used to hold open a wound). He found the bladder and made a small cut into it, feeling around inside with his fingers for the stone. It was there, and it was a large one. With a pair of his surgical scissors, he snipped a larger opening in the bladder and inserted his duckbill forceps to extract the stone.

Mathew was working as fast as he could. The *laudanum* he'd given his father only eased the pain of the operation, but did not protect him from all of it. William fought against the bonds that held him screaming out in pain.

Charles and Henry did what they could to hold their father as still as possible.

Mary was the only one in the room who seemed to stay calm, patiently doing whatever she was asked. With the stone removed, Mathew set a silver clamp on the open bladder in order to close the wound. Because of the clamp, he was unable to close the operation site. If he sutured the bladder closed, the internal stitches would eventually rot, causing a lethal blood poisoning infection. All Mathew could do was to keep his father heavily sedated with *laudanum* and wait a few days for the edges of the bladder to start to knit together, while they were held closed with the silver clamp. He would have to close the peritoneum in the same way, and finally, days later, suture the skin between his father's legs.

If his father could endure the pain, combat the infections that would bring on fevers, and if Mathew had sealed the bladder correctly, there was a chance that his father might survive.

But if Mathew had damaged the sphincter muscles, his father would be left incontinent, and that was something that William Fletcher would never forgive him for.

The days passed slowly for William Fletcher while he was kept sedated with large doses of *laudanum*. Between them the family took it in turns to watch over the suffering man, cleaning the large wound between his legs, and checking for signs that the bladder had healed and stopped leaking.

After three days Mathew was eventually able to remove the silver clamp from his father's bladder and use it to close the peritoneum, and three days later he closed the wound between his father's legs, washing the operation site with wine or sometimes with vinegar, to keep away any infection.

It would be many weeks before his father was on his feet again, eating and drinking normally, but as each day passed Mathew knew his father's chances of recovery improved. Charles and Henry had returned to their work, so it was left to Mathew and Mary to nurse William back to health.

After a week, Mathew reduced the amount of laudanum he was giving his father. William needed to eat and drink more than the few spoonfuls of broth they had given him to drink if he was to build up his strength. However, caution was needed; too much fluid would put a strain on his recovering bladder. After ten days William was out of danger and eating and drinking small amounts, though he was still in lots of pain. Mathew assured his father that he was safely through the trauma of the operation. As the sick man recovered, Mathew remembered the deal he had made with Captain Overton. He would soon have to inform the family of his changed plans for the future.

On the morning his father was out of bed for the first time, Mathew made his announcement.

'I am going to volunteer to join the King's army, and work as a surgeon,' he explained to everyone as they ate breakfast. 'It's the quickest way for me to earn the money I need to set up my own surgery practice. I won't be too far away from home; I'm only going to Anlaby Common so I will be able to get back to see you all from time to time.'

Of course, he had lied. He had not told them his main motive for joining the King's army was so that he could track down Elizabeth's killers. If he had explained this, they would have tried to stop him. Mathew was bombarded with protests from his family, most of all from his father, but Mathew had given his word to Captain Overton, and now his father was recovering it was time to fulfil his promise. Mathew waited a couple more days relaxing with his family, but the time came when he couldn't delay his departure any longer.

Chapter Thirteen

Taking a horse and a mule from his father's stable, Mathew put his portable surgeon's roll in one of the saddlebags along with his clothes, he loaded his large surgeon's chest containing salves, essential medicines and the bulk of his surgical instruments onto the back of the mule. He said his farewells to the family, and with a last promise to keep himself safe, he waved goodbye.

He turned south through Beverley and passed the Minster out onto the road to Anlaby. He bypassed the villages of Cottingham, and Skidby, when he reached the hilltop outside the village of Willerby, he could see Anlaby mile or two away, where a detachment of the King's Army had set up their military headquarters. Driven by thoughts of revenge on Elizabeth's murders, he had decided on a means to disguise the real motives for joining the army. He would become the best bloody surgeon the King's army had ever seen. He would save their lives, he would patch them up, he would learn all the secrets they would tell him in their pain and delirium, and then sell them down the river to the Parliamentary forces and Captain Robert Overton. Anyone, even remotely associated with the death of Elizabeth was now his enemy.

Mathew arrived at Anlaby shortly after noon. 'Hello the camp!' he called as he caught sight of two sentries at the entrance to the settlement. They had a large tent with a brazier burning outside.

'HALT!' shouted one of the guards. 'What do you want?'

'I've come from Beverley to join the king's men,' Mathew replied as enthusiastically as he could.

'Why? Apart from riding into battle on that old nag, what can a farm boy offer us?' Both guards laughed.

'I'm a surgeon,' Mathew replied indignantly, trying to sound more superior than he looked.

'Step down then, *Surgeon*,' the taller guard said. 'I'll take you to the sergeant of the guard.' Mathew tied his horse and mule to one of the guy-ropes of the guard tent and followed the soldier inside. Bits of armour lay on the ground close to the canvas walls, polearms stood in racks ready for use, and the ground was freshly covered with straw to reduce the amount of mud.

Mathew saw a man sitting at a trestle table scratching away with a quill on a tatty piece of paper. 'This is the guard rota for that day,' the scribe said, thrusting the document at the soldier standing next to him.

'What do you want?' the man at the table said, glancing up at Mathew as the guard brought him forward.

'Sergeant, he says he's a surgeon and wants to join the army,' the guard said crisply.

The sergeant gave Mathew a searching look. 'And why would a lad like you want to join the army?' He asked suspicious of anyone volunteering for the army of their own free will.

'I have just qualified as a surgeon,' Mathew explained, 'and I need money to set up my own practice. I can gain experience and get paid at the same time working for the army.'

'Uuum.' The sergeant took a drink from a bottle on the table and stood up. 'I'll take you to the captain—he can decide what to do with you.'

Mathew followed the sergeant to another tent close by. Standing outside, the sergeant cleared his throat before calling out, 'Excuse me, sir, may I see you?' His voice was strident yet deferential.

'Come in, Sergeant,' said a voice.

Once inside the tent, Mathew saw a young officer sitting at a table eating a meal of venison and carrots. His clothes were of fine quality: made from dark-blue wool, with yellow trim and silver buttons.

'Begging your pardon, Captain Hewitt,' the obsequious sergeant began. 'This man claims to be a surgeon and wants to join the army. I thought I'd better check with you.'

'Thank you, Sergeant. You may go.' Captain Hewitt dismissed Sergeant Pickles with a flick of his hand. 'What's your name, boy?' Captain Hewitt asked, continuing to eat his meal.

'Fletcher—Mathew Fletcher, sir.' Mathew stood with his hat in his hand, not sure how he should be addressing a gentleman and soldier.

'Sit there.' Captain Hewitt pointed with his eating knife to a stool close to the wall of his tent. Mathew sat and waited in silence for the captain to finish eating. Captain Hewitt didn't rush his meal. He mopped up the gravy from the venison with a slice of bread and finished his goblet of wine. He wiped his hands and mouth on the white linen napkin he'd had over his shoulder and finally, adjusting his seat, he turned to face Mathew.

'Let me see your papers.'

Mathew stood up and handed him the signed contract from Surgeon Adams, releasing him from his apprenticeship and the seal of membership from the Barber-Surgeons Guild of Kingston upon Hull.

The captain studied them for a moment. 'You have only recently qualified. You don't have much experience, do you?' Captain Hewitt shot a questioning look at Mathew.

'I have more knowledge than you think,' Mathew snapped back, his emotions getting the better of him. 'What's more, I learn quickly, and I need the money and experience to set up my own practice.'

Captain Hewitt rounded on Mathew, glaring at him. 'Be careful, Fletcher, for I am an officer in the King's army and I can have you flogged for insolence.' He paused before continuing so Mathew would have time to digest the danger of crossing the forbidden line.   'If you want to join us, you will need to understand a few things. You join as a civilian worker, not a soldier of the army. Though you will still be senior to all non-commissioned ranks; but, you *will* show due deference to officers. You will get paid two pennies per month from every man in my company, as and when we get paid, you get paid. You will treat the men, no matter what malady they are suffering from, and officers are to be given preference.' Captain Hewitt silently accessed the man in front of him for a moment.

'You have turned up at the right time. I need a surgeon. The army is losing more men to the pox than to military action.'

'Thank you, sir. I will serve the men well, I promise, I won't let them down.'

'You had better not do, Fletcher, you are under military law now.'

      Captain Hewitt poured himself another drink. 'I'll write you a pass, enabling you to come and go as needed, including permission to collect supplies from the baggage train. Get some men to help you set up a surgeon's station. You can see Sergeant Pickles if you need help and before you receive your note of authority and pass.'

Mathew had achieved his first objective.

The sergeant was waiting outside the tent as Mathew stepped through the tent flap.

'Come with me, lad,' Sergeant Pickles told him. 'Jenks! Todd!' he yelled across at two soldiers, who were standing talking. 'Get your sorry arses over here!'

Sergeant Pickles led the three of them through the camp to where the baggage train was encamped. It was set apart from the rest of the camp and had its own set of guards to prevent pilfering.

After being introduced to the quartermaster sergeant, Mathew requested two tents: one as a treatment tent and the other for use as a store and for his own personal use. The Quartermaster found the tents, tables, benches, pots and pans that Mathew needed and he Jenks and Todd ferried the kit to the area that Sergeant Pickles had found for him. Mathew noted it was close to the cook's tent. When all the kit had been collected together, Sergeant Pickles ordered Todd and Jenks to help Mathew set it all up. Jenks brought over Mathew's surgical pack, and chest from his horse and mule then took the animals away to a field to join the other horses of the company.

By evening the tents were erected, the tables, benches and the other equipment were all laid out to Mathew's satisfaction. Finding that he had been set up close to the cook's tent—a definite advantage—with bowl and spoon in hand, Mathew made his way over to the sutler to enquire if he could get anything to eat. A large round man with a red, sweaty face and dirty apron turned away from the tub in which he was washing some fine plates and glassware as Mathew approached.

Before Mathew could say a word, the fat cook introduced himself: 'I'm Ethan Goodman,' he said. 'You're a lucky bastard like me. We have what they all want, don't we? I feed them—you mend them. We'll look after each other, eh?' Ethan Goodman smiled, dried his hands and took Mathew to a table standing close by. He placed a thick slice of lean beef and some buttered bread in Mathew's bowl. 'The officers won't miss that bit; I've got some good strong ale to wash that down with too, so just sit here.'

Mathew was bemused and surprised at the cook's apparent generosity and openness.

'See here, this is how it works,' Ethan told him. 'We look after each other. We *work* for the army, but, we're not *in* the army. I look on it as a bit of give and take because we can go weeks without getting paid, so I reckon that gives us the right to take what we need to get by. What's your name?'

Mathew finally got to introduce himself.

'When you've finished that my friend, I've got some nice bag pudding with a drop of cream put by for you? As their surgeon, the men know they've got to keep you sweet in case they need you. They keep me sweet so that they don't get a plate of gristle! Give n take, that's how it works around here.'

Mathew thanked Ethan for the food and the information. The thought of the bag pudding made him think of Mrs Adams and the way she used to feed him when he was still an apprentice. She had taken a shine to him right from his first day, and whenever she was making bag pudding, the smell of the cinnamon, cloves, ginger and mixed dried fruits, coming from the cauldron as it boiled over the fire, never failed to make his mouth water.

Returning to his tent, his belly full and feeling bloated, he set out his blankets and pillow on his rope bed ready for sleep. He lay listening to the men talking, singing and laughing around their campfires in the distance. Happily, he was far enough away from the main soldiers' camp to avoid the worst of the noise the soldiers were making.

Tomorrow he would have to familiarise himself with the layout of the camp, but for now, he was both emotionally and physically drained. He was in the camp of his enemy. What would he do *if* he did find the men he was looking for, he wondered? After all, they were trained killers, while all he had ever done was his best to save lives. Those were problems for the following day. The large meal and the long day took its toll on Mathew, and before he'd realised it, waves of tiredness overtook him, and he was asleep.

After an unsettled night, of strange dreams, Mathew awoke tired, to the sound of the military camp coming to life. The noises from soldiers coughing, sniffing, spitting and talking together woke Mathew out of a dream. He sat on the edge of his bed and ran his hands through his hair, stretched, stood up, and wandered over to a small table on which a bowl and jug of water were waiting for him. After washing his face and dressing, Mathew stepped out of his tent to see the camp preparing for the day.

Ethan Goodman was busy cooking bacon at his campfire. 'Captain Hewitt likes bacon in a morning— would you like some?' Ethan prepared all the food for the officers.

'Eh? Oh, sorry, good morning,' Mathew replied; still only half awake. 'I had a bit of a rough night. Do you have anything to drink?' He stretched again and walked over to the cook.

'And bacon? Yes please, I'd love some.' Mathew tried to gather his thoughts in the unfamiliar surroundings.

Ethan put a large jug of ale on the table. 'Help yourself. There are some wooden cups over there.'

'Do you cook breakfast for everyone?' enquired Mathew.

'God no, just for the officers,' Ethan told him. 'The men have to fend for themselves. They get their daily food ration.' He looked across at the surgeon. 'Tell me, what brings you here?'

Mathew paused before replying. He couldn't tell him the truth, but he had to give a plausible answer. 'I finished my apprenticeship a couple of months ago. I need the practice and the money before I can set up my own surgeon's shop.'

'There's plenty of money to be made on the back of the army all right, but you'll earn every groat. It must be a sorry business being a sawbones; I haven't the stomach for it. What made you choose such a profession?' Ethan's question seemed quite personal, but Mathew found himself warming to cook's friendly open manner.

'My mother died when I was young, and no one could help her. So I vowed I wouldn't watch another person die while I stood by helplessly in the same way I did that day.' Mathew's thoughts returned to the day he watched Elizabeth die at his side and remembered his feelings of frustration and helplessness.

Ethan looked embarrassed by Mathew's disarming confession. 'I'm sorry for asking. Please forgive me for being nosy. I can't help it, you see? I just like to talk.'

Mathew finished his fried bacon, bread and ale, thanked Ethan and returned to his tent. He wasn't sure what the day would bring but guessed that he would soon be busy or the captain wouldn't have been so keen to hire him.

It wasn't long before his first patient turned up. The musketeer walked slowly towards his tent. Mathew saw him coming closer while he was laying out his surgical instruments on the table. The musketeer kept stopping. He'd walk to and fro, kick at the ground with his boot, and then take a few steps closer. Mathew watched him getting nearer, fascinated by the soldier, who was obviously struggling with the notion that he needed the surgeon's help, but was either too frightened to see him, or was wondering whether his condition would get better on its own. Eventually, the soldier arrived at the open entrance to the surgeon's tent.

The musketeer looked at Mathew. 'Are you the new surgeon?' he mumbled.

Looking at the man's face, Mathew had a good idea what his problem was.

'Aye, that's right. What can I do for you?' Mathew moved away from the table and brought a stool over for the soldier to sit down on.

'I've got a bad tooth,' the musketeer mumbled, the slurred words coming from a badly swollen mouth.

'Then you'd better let me have a look,' Mathew said as sympathetically as possible.

The musketeer opened his mouth, revealing a pit of rotten teeth. Mathew stepped back from the foul smell that was so strong it could have turned cream sour. Holding his breath, the surgeon moved closer to look around the inside of the soldier's mouth. There wasn't a sound tooth to be seen. However, a noticeably rotten tooth in the middle of a red and swollen gum made it clear which particular tooth was causing today's problem.

'I'm afraid it's got to come out,' Mathew said, confirming the soldier's worst fears.

'Can't you just give me summat fo' tha pain?' the musketeer pleaded.

'You'll feel better with it out, and I will give you something for the pain, don't worry,' Mathew reassured him.

Mathew poured brandy into a small earthenware cup and added three drops of concentrated *laudanum*. 'I'll be back in a minute.' Mathew rested his hand on the musketeer's shoulder for a second, before leaving the tent and heading off in the direction of the sutler's tent. Shortly afterwards he returned to the musketeer, followed by Ethan Goodman. Before the man with a toothache could protest, Ethan had his arms pinned behind his back preventing the soldier from getting off the stool.

The unfortunate patient opened his mouth to protest, and as he did so, Mathew inserted a jaw clamp. As the surgeon turned the screw at the bottom of the device, the two metal plates of the clamp separated, forcing the man's jaws apart. Satisfied that the clamp was tight and the musketeer couldn't close his mouth, Mathew took a pair of pliers from the table. Gripping the tooth between its jaws, he pushed down hard. The musketeer gave a gurgled scream. Mathew then rocked the tooth from side to side, and with a slight twist of his wrist, the tooth came free. The soldier gave another gurgling scream. Quickly releasing the clamp, Mathew gave Ethan the nod to let the soldier go. While the soldier leapt to his feet and spat blood and pus on the ground and held his face in his hands, Mathew filled a small cup with brandy.

'Here, rinse your mouth with this,' Mathew told him, giving him the cup. 'Don't drink it, rinse it around your mouth and spit it out.' More blood and pus came away as the musketeer spat on the ground. 'Sit down,' said Mathew, 'and open your mouth. I need to see the hole where the tooth was.'

The soldier looked at Ethan and decided he'd better comply with the order. Looking in the soldier's mouth, Mathew could see that the hole left by the missing tooth was oozing pus. Inserting a pack of lint, he dabbed at the open gap in the jaw and mopped up the pus, applying slight pressure to force the remaining putrid liquid to the surface. The soldier flinched back as Mathew applied more pressure, but stayed in his seat. Satisfied with his work Mathew stood back. The *laudanum* and brandy were taking effect on the soldier. Standing up, he staggered slightly to one side, his arms flaying for something solid to grasp and to steady him against.

'Thank you, Surgeon,' the suffering man muttered. 'That weren't 'arf as bad as I expected.' He bent down and picked up his hat which had fallen to the ground when Ethan Goodman had grabbed him.

Leaving the tent, he staggered away. Mathew and Ethan looked at each other and smiled. 'Your first satisfied customer,' Ethan said as he chuckled. 'You know you're gonna have to get someone to assist you when the real work starts.'

Mathew nodded. 'Thank you very much, Ethan. You're right. I'll see the captain about getting some help.'

Chapter Fourteen

Charles Mortimer walked into the surgeon's tent, saying urgently, 'Surgeon Fletcher, can you help me, please? I think my arm may be broken.'

Mathew turned to see the newcomer cradling his left arm. 'Take a seat over there,' he told him. 'I will have a look at it for you.'

As Mathew started to examine the man's arm, the stranger whispered to Mathew: *'I've come from our friend in Hull.'*

'What?' exclaimed Mathew, far louder than he intended. Looking intently at the man sitting in front of him, Mathew had been caught unprepared.

'Shhhh!' said Charles Mortimer. 'Don't you remember me? I work for Captain Overton.'

Recognition softened the shocked expression on Mathew's face. Examining Mortimer's arm for a break, Mathew slowly manipulated the limb.

'I don't think your arm is broken,' Mathew blurted out, a little too loudly. He was still a little nervous, but bringing his voice under control, he went on to say, 'I think you must have a bad muscle strain. Tell me, how did this happen?'

Mortimer smiled and explained. 'I told one of the soldiers that I made and supplied small lead ingots for the army. Short lengths of lead that can be given to the Musketeers, so they can melt them down to make their own lead bullets, it saves the army the trouble of making, supplying, and transporting bullets to its musketeers. I simply asked the soldier to take me to you. Captain Overton needs to know what you have found out so far about the army's intentions on blockading Hull. Are there signs of a long siege being set up, or are they going to move on?'

Mathew's head was still reeling from the sudden meeting with Mortimer, and now his insistence for news so soon after arriving made him realise the enormity of what he had let himself be talked into.

'I've got nothing yet,' Mathew whispered back hoarsely. 'I've not been here long enough yet.'

'Well, I'm going to stay close by. I'm going to make up some bullets from my lead ingots and sell them ready made. So you can find me somewhere in the baggage train when you need me.'

'I wasn't expecting *you* to act as the courier,' Mathew informed Mortimer.

'The captain has been a good master. When I learnt about what you were going to be doing, I volunteered to help.' The smile on Mortimer's face seemed reassuring.

'I still need to earn the trust of the men here and anyway; there has been so little action against Hull since the sluices were opened on the River Hull most of the soldiers have nothing to do. So much of the land surrounding the town of Hull is flooded so that the artillery cannot get close enough to have an effect on the town defences. The army is blockading the roads, but supplies still reach Hull by boat along the River Humber. Until there is some action, I have very few patients.'

'Well something will happen soon, or the King may as well pack up and go home,' replied Mortimer.

After Mortimer had left, Mathew went to explore the camp. Most of the men sat around their fires talking, playing dice or cards, repairing their kit or cutting wood for fires. Some of the sergeants had taken groups of men aside for musket or pike drill, but there was an air of listlessness about the camp as they all waited for the action to start. What secrets or news he was going to find was a total mystery to him at that moment.

Mathew noticed the lack of officers around the camp and wondered if they must be keeping to their tents or away finding distractions in Beverley. That deduction in itself, he realised, was worthy of note: if an attack were made on the Anlaby camp while the King's Army was so unprepared it would put them in total disarray and must prove successful.

Deciding to walk along the eastern perimeter of the camp, Mathew made a mental note of how the camp was spread out on both sides of the road leading into Hull, but the baggage train had been placed on the western side of the camp, on the Beverley side. The settlement looked as if it had once had some formality to it, but the men were beginning to spread out, and some of the walkways through the once orderly encampment had become blocked with refuse or piles of firewood. The main thoroughfares through the camp remained clear of obstacles but were heavily used by both men and horses.

Mathew noted the baggage-train was guarded by men with the new 'Doglock muskets.' He had learnt that only the best musketeers where given these new weapons, with its flint sticker instead of the piece of burning match cord to fire the gun. With a Doglock a musketeer could fire and reload much more quickly than a man with a matchlock musket.

Returning to his tent, Mathew made a careful notation of all that he had seen and added a suggestion that an early morning attack on the camp would catch the Royalist Army totally unprepared. After he'd finished writing down the details of what he had discovered, he hid the note in a large jar of dried lavender flowers. Feeling satisfied he had something useful for the captain, he decided to go in search of Ethan Goodman for some food. It was gone the dinner hour, and Mathew had lost track of time, he'd been so engrossed in his wander around the camp and his note-taking.

'Master Ethan, how goes your day?' Mathew smiled as he approached the cook.

'Bloody officers,' Ethan replied as he turned to look at who was speaking to him. 'I spend the morning preparing food for them, and then most of them go off somewhere without a word, this lot is all going to waste. Can I tempt *you* with a few morsels of chicken pie and honeyed parsnips, Mathew?'

'You've read my mind, Ethan.' Mathew laughed and sat on a stool close to where Ethan had set some covered pots.

'What would you have done if I'd been an officer when you made that remark?' asked Mathew. He found it easy to talk to Ethan Goodman. He was a typical Yorkshireman, you could take him at face value, and you knew where you stood. Ethan cut Mathew a big wedge of pie and poured him a tankard of wine, taking the same for himself and putting it on a wooden plate. The two men sat and ate in silence for a few minutes.

'I say sod 'em. Officers don't come looking for me, they send someone else,' said Ethan through a mouthful of pie.

Mathew looked at him and smiled. 'Well, you make a bloody good pie.'

Both men laughed, spitting pie crumbs in the air as they did so, which made them laugh all the more.

Mathew took a deep drink from his tankard and immediately felt the effects of the strong wine.

'I'm not pissing about this afternoon, cooking a meal for tonight,' the cook moaned. 'They can have what's left from dinner. Anyway, they might not come back at all tonight if they've gone into Beverley.'

Ethan topped up Mathew's tankard. 'I'm having a slow day as well. You know, if we both sit here, anyone who needs us will be able to find us.' Mathew took another pull on the tankard, his words beginning to slur.

'How come you joined the army?' Mathew asked.

'Oh, I was cooking meals in the Riverside Tavern near York Castle. Lots of the officers would call in for a drink and something to eat. Colonel Duncombe was one of them. It was him that talked me into joining the army to cook for the officers. Said he needed a cook of my calibre to cook for his officers when the army moved on. Well, it was fine at first, I had lots to do, everyone enjoyed the meals I prepared, but now most of them prefer to stay in Beverley, close to the colonel. They only come back here when they need something, or they have been assigned some duty or other.'

The young surgeon took another swig from his tankard. 'A right pair of silly bastards we are. You got talked into joining the army, and I bloody volunteered.' Mathew started laughing. Anything and everything became funny to him as the effects of the strong drink took effect. He laughed so hard it hurt, and Ethan joined in. Ethan wasn't as drunk as Mathew, but Mathew's laugh was infectious. Both men laughed together. Mathew took another drink from his tankard, and the world around him swam out of control. Before he was aware of it, he had fallen off the back of his stool and was asleep on the grass.

Looking down at Mathew, Ethan stopped laughing. 'You silly bugger,' he said to the unconscious form on the ground. Leaving Mathew where he lay, Ethan set about clearing away the leftovers from dinner.

It was three or four hours later when Mathew awoke. The evening was drawing in, and the air had cooled. His head was banging, and his body was stiff from lying on the hard ground.

A booming voice from above said, 'Here drink this!'

Mathew forced his eyes open a little and squinted at Ethan, who was holding a tankard.

'I couldn't drink any more wine; I'll throw up.'

'It's not wine, you fool; it's small beer; it'll help clear your head.'

The drunken man took the tankard and drank the beer down in one. The wine had left his mouth dry, and he found himself very thirsty.

'Good stuff, that officers' wine,' Ethan said, smiling at Mathew's suffering.

'I normally stick to beer. God, my head hurts.' Mathew sat on the stool he had vacated earlier in the day.

'I'll do you some bacon and bread—it'll help make you feel better. You know, you're the one with the medical training; you should be looking after yourself.'

'I couldn't eat anything right now, I feel like shit.'

'Trust me; I've put more people back on their feet this way than any of your fancy medicines.'

Mathew ate the thick slices of bacon with the fresh bread and butter, followed by another tankard of small beer to wash it all down. Standing up, he looked at Ethan.

'Thank you,'; he said, 'I needed that. I needed that more than you'll ever know,' feeling some of the worst effects of the wine beginning to dissipate.

The younger man felt like something had changed in him, it wasn't the hangover, his head was still pounding with pain; it was the tension he had felt since he'd arrived in camp, it had gone. The stress he had been under caused by Elizabeth's death had gone. He still loved her, he still missed her, and he was still determined to find her killer, but he felt like a weight had been lifted from his shoulders.

That night Mathew slept without the usual nightmares about Elizabeth's death and awoke refreshed the next day. After breakfast with Ethan, he spent the morning checking his medical supplies and looking for anything that he might be short of. He had decided that he would use Mortimer to collect any medicinal supplies he wanted. Mortimer would then have an excuse for leaving the camp at regular intervals. If asked why Mortimer was fetching and carrying for him, he could say that Mortimer had volunteered to help him. By dinner time he had a short list ready, along with the note he had made on the weaknesses in the camp's defences, he was ready to send Mortimer off on his first mission.

Thomas Potter brought his horse to a stop at the water trough in the Saturday Market of Beverley. No one took any notice of him. The soldiers were too busy with their own duties to take any interest in a small merchant who was riding a tired old horse.

As he surveyed the scene around him, the enormity of his task sank in. How was he going to find two men in a sea of men? He had guessed that the brothers he was looking for must be locals when he heard about the concerns they had over their father. He would start by frequenting the taverns, asking questions and listening to gossip. When someone is ill enough to bring two men home from another town, in a time of conflict, there is likely to be talk about it around the town. His friends and family will be talking about their father's recovery or about his funeral. It was the only thing Potter had to work on in his search to find the friends of Captain Overton.

Chapter Fifteen

Late in the afternoon, Mathew sat outside his tent. None of
the soldiers had been to see him, Ethan and Mortimer were
busy doing other things, and so he was left to his own
devices and with his own thoughts. He had been hoping
someone with at least a minor ailment would need his
services. So all afternoon he had enjoyed the warm summer
day in his own company. He would talk to Mortimer later
about taking his message to Captain Overton.

He'd checked his surgical tools, sharpened his scalpel
and large curved flesh knife, and he'd checked his supply of
roller bandages. There were one or two tinctures, salves and
tonics he could do with replenishing from Mary's stocks,
but they could wait. He returned to his medical book,
finding that his stomach felt bloated after the dinner that
Ethan had given him: slices of tender beef with onion
pickle, crusty bread with fresh salty butter and, as always,
plenty of ale.

Mathew looked up from his book, hearing the sound of
an explosion. The sounds of distant cannon fire were
common enough, but this sounded closer—much closer. He
stood up to look around the camp, curious about where the
sound of the explosion had come from. Over on the far side
of the encampment, he could see a large column of smoke
billowing into the air. *They must be practising with some of
the larger guns*, he thought, so he returned to his book. A
few minutes later, two men carried a stretcher into the

surgeon's tent, Mathew followed them in. The two soldiers placed the stretcher gently on the table ready for Mathew's attention.

'Who is this?' asked Mathew as he started to examine the badly injured man in front of him.

'He's Gunner Atkinson, Surgeon,' one of the stretcher bearers explained. 'The gun he was in command of exploded prematurely while it was being loaded. He was in a new team that hadn't worked together before. The rest of the gun crew are all dead. It was only because Gunner Atkinson was bending down to get some more slow match out of his tool chest when the gun exploded, that saved him from being killed instantly.'

The pieces of the fragmented gun barrel had sliced through Atkinson's flesh. He had a gash from his left buttock along his thigh, where the fragment of metal exited close to his knee. The back of his jacket and breeches were shredded and burnt black from the burning gunpowder. The back of his legs, his buttocks and his back looked like he'd received a multitude of lashes in some horrible kind of corporal punishment.

Getting the two stretcher bearers to help him, Mathew stripped Atkinson of his clothing, to better access the damage to his body. He'd been lucky: most of the wounds to his legs, buttocks and back were superficial, and though some would leave scars, he would recover from them.

However, the long, deep laceration to his left thigh was a different matter. His fleshy thigh hung open as though a butcher was preparing a joint for deboning. It appeared that no major arteries had been severed, but several veins were oozing blood as their ragged ends tried to shrink and stem the flow of escaping life fluid. Mathew tied a temporary bandage around the torn thigh to close the wound, while he prepared his surgical tools.

When he was ready, he removed the temporary bandage, allowing the wound to fall open again. The two stretcher bearers held Atkinson over on his right side so that Mathew could work. He first cleaned the wound with *rosewater,* washing out the threads of cloth and dirt from Atkinson's shirt and breeches. Removing a red-hot cauterising iron with a crescent-shaped head, like that of a curved axe, from a small brazier, he ran the hot iron along the length of the wound. The flesh sizzled and recoiled at the touch of the red-hot metal. The smell of burning flesh filled the tent as wisps of smoke and steam rose up from the gunner's leg. The rich, sweet smell of cooking meat filled their nostrils, as one of the helpers lurched for the door of the tent to empty his stomach, just out of sight of Mathew.

'Don't you faint on me,' Mathew spoke calmly to the one soldier who was left holding onto Atkinson, as he staggered sideways.

'No, sir, I won't,' came the reply, in a weak voice.

'There'll be a large cup of brandy for you when we're finished, that'll steady you up.' Mathew smiled reassuringly at his unhappy helper.

After stopping the bleeding with the cauterising iron, Mathew double-threaded his large suturing needle, the one he used for closing amputation wounds, and started to draw the two sides of the wound together. He used large stitches to join the edges of flesh: two sutures, two fingers' distance apart along the length of the wound, leaving a wider gap in the middle. The gaps were there to leave places for the pus to escape, and, should Mathew need to reopen the wound to clean it, there would be fewer stitches to remove.

Gun Captain Atkinson had not recovered consciousness during the whole of the surgery, for which Mathew was grateful. It had taken time to close the leg and wash and treat all the minor wounds. Atkinson was going to be in enough pain when he came round, never mind having to suffer being awake while Mathew worked on him. When he was finished, and the gunner had been placed in a cot, Mathew took the time to enjoy a brandy with Jefferson and Daniels, the two stretcher bearers. They weren't in a talkative mood: both looked pale and shaky as they sipped at their cups of brandy. Mathew thought back to the early days of his apprenticeship with Surgeon Adams. He had fainted at the sight of his first operation, and Mrs Adams had taken him aside to wipe his forehead with a cool damp cloth and then given him sips of brandy.

While the three men sat with their drinks, a stirring came from the cot behind them. Gunner Atkinson was beginning to regain consciousness. Forgetting his two aides, Mathew jumped to his feet and went to see his patient. Kneeling by the cot on which Atkinson lay, Mathew held a small cup of *laudanum* to the gunner's lips.

'Take a few sips of this. It will ease the pain and help you sleep,' he told him. Atkinson did not open his eyes; he just sipped at the strong liquid until it ran down the sides of his cheeks and then he was asleep again.

The following day Mathew was awakened by Atkinson calling out in pain. Mathew had prepared more *laudanum* ready for when he awoke, for he knew there were going to be many more days like this until the wounds and burns healed. Over the following days, as the large doses of *laudanum* took effect, Atkinson began to want more and more of the drug. Most of the time he was asleep, but occasionally he called out to unseen people who were around him as if he was involved in some kind of vivid dream.

'You wait till the Cornish engineer gets here,' Atkinson rambled on. 'He'll break the walls of Hull. He'll teach you how to use an artillery piece.'

Mathew listened to the drug-induced ravings of his patient recalling memories from his recent past. At last Mathew had some real news to pass on to Captain Overton. Gunner Atkinson continued to talk freely, but incoherently in his delirium.

Who was this Cornish engineer that was going to break the walls of Hull? Mathew tried to question his patient, but couldn't get an answer he could understand. After a couple of days, a pattern emerged. It seemed that Atkinson was at his most vocal a few minutes after he received a fresh dose of *laudanum*. Mathew decided to let his patient wake from his drug-induced sleep. After checking on the leg wound and cleaning away the pus, he gave the Atkinson some soup and bread, and then checked his pulse and temperature. His pulse had stabilised, but he was a little weak. His temperature felt higher than it should, but at least he wasn't burning up.

'You've been talking in your sleep,' Mathew told him. 'About some Cornish engineer who's coming to knock down the walls of Hull.'

'He's good, this Cornish man, good with guns,' Atkinson answered.

Mathew eased Atkinson into a sitting position to continue the conversation to confirm the information he was getting. 'When's this Cornish man arriving?' Mathew prepared a few more drops of *laudanum* in some brandy and offered the laced drink to his patient. The gunner drank it greedily, looking into the empty cup as though there might be more hiding in the bottom, before handing it back to Mathew.

'I've been told he's arriving by ship and that he's bringing a lot more guns with him, from Holland, of all places.' Atkinson was beginning to slur his words as the *laudanum* made him feel more and more drowsy.

'So what's his name, this Cornish man? What's his name? When will he arrive? Atkinson? Stay awake!' Mathew sat Atkinson upright and gently slapped the sides of his face to bring him back to his senses.

'Stop it! Let me sleep, damn you!' Atkinson protested.

'When will the Cornish man arrive?' Mathew shook his patient a little, which aggravated the wound in his thigh, making Atkinson cry out as the pain overrode the effects of the drug.

'Aaaah! You bastard that hurts!' Atkinson's eyes flared opened wide for a moment before the drug began to get a grip on his senses again. In less than a minute, his head began to fall back as the arms of Morpheus beckoned him away.

Mathew had got all the information he was going to get out of Gunner Atkinson for the moment, so he let him sleep. He had given him more *laudanum* than he should have done: indeed, if he had given him much more, he might have fallen asleep and never woken up.

There was nothing left to do, for now, Mathew let him sleep. Leaving his tent, he wandered over to the sutler's tent to find Ethan Goodman. With Ethan, Mathew didn't need to bother with making the effort of conversation, because Ethan always took the lead, and Mathew was happy to listen to his tales while eating the officers' food that Ethan called 'a perk of the job'. Mathew had no sooner caught sight of Ethan than the jolly fat cook was calling him over.

'How's your patient?' he asked as he placed a wooden plate of cold duck and boiled eggs with mustard into his hands.

'The wounds are deep and will take a long time to heal. If Atkinson survives the infections, he'll be fine, though he'll probably walk with a bad limp for the rest of his life. I've done all I can. He's in God's hands now,' Mathew replied, though his thoughts were more on how he was going to get the rest of the information about the Cornish man.

Eight hours later the gun captain began to stir, as the medication which Mathew had given him began to wear off. Atkinson had started to sweat, and fidget about in delirium as the pain from his wounds began to ravage his body. Mathew checked the gunner's thigh and found it red and swollen: the amount of pus coming from the wound had increased. He would have to remove some stitches and find the seat of the infection.

Mathew prepared more *laudanum* for Atkinson. While the gunner lay in his bed, Mathew cut through the stitches over the worst part of the infected thigh. The wound burst open as soon as a couple of stitches were removed and thick grey-black pus poured down the gunner's thigh. Mathew washed the site with vinegar and then prepared a small amount of weak *oil of vitriol* to take away any decaying flesh and clean the infected area. He closed the wound again and re-bandaged the leg. When Atkinson awoke later in the morning, the first thing he wanted was his drink of brandy and *laudanum*.

'You've been talking about the Cornish engineer again; he must be an important person.' Mathew passed the comment as though it was everyday conversation.

'John Lanayan,' Atkinson muttered. 'What the sodding 'ell do you want to know about 'im for? Give me the brandy!'

Atkinson's eyes focused on Mathew's hand which was holding the cup of brandy and *laudanum*. Snatching the cup from Mathew's hand, he gulped down the drink, then ran his finger around the inside of the vessel and sucked his finger for the last remaining essence of the drink that he was now completely addicted to. Satisfied for the moment, he sank back on his bed and closed his eyes.

'When's he arriving, this John Lanayan?' Mathew pestered.

'When he arrives,' Atkinson replied without opening his eyes.

'I have some more medicine for you.'

Atkinson's eyes opened as Mathew held the cup of medicine just out of his reach. The wounded man stared, his full attention focused on the cup in Mathew's hand. Atkinson licked his lips as Mathew went to sit on a chair next to the table, leaving the cup in full view of his patient, but just out of his reach.

The surgeon asked the question again. 'When is Lanayan arriving?'

Atkinson continued to lick his lips and a thin film of sweat formed on his brow as he stared at the cup that was sitting on the table. 'Soon, all I know is he is going to arrive as soon as possible.'

'How?' asked Mathew.

'By ship. He's coming by ship into York from Holland, disguised as a merchant.' Atkinson answered without hesitation.

The questioner placed the cup in the gun captain's hands and watched him drinking it, his patient savouring every drop, before laying back on his cot and falling asleep.

With the information gathered on the weaknesses of the camp layout, and the news about the Cornish man, John Lanayan, Mathew felt that he finally had enough good intelligence to send back to Captain Overton.

He went off to find Charles Mortimer's wagon amongst the baggage train while Atkinson slept. He found Mortimer beside his wagon, sitting at a fire over which hung a small cauldron containing molten lead. On his left was an open bullet mould next to a bucket full of water and musket balls waiting to cool before their gate-plugs and blushings could be trimmed off, after being released from the bullet mould. On his right was another bucket containing freshly dressed bullets, ready for use.

Mathew sat down on a log next to Mortimer. 'I have a message I would like you to take to Captain Overton,' he said in a low voice. 'When will you be able to take it?'

'I'll leave a word with one of the sergeants this afternoon,' his contact replied. 'I'll tell him that I need to arrange for more lead to be delivered. I'll leave first thing in the morning.'

'Well, I'll tell him you're collecting medical supplies for me as well,' the surgeon continued. 'It may help you get permission to leave camp. How are you going to get the information back to Captain Overton?'

'I'll go to Howden, and get a boat travelling from York to Hull. The traders are always happy to pick up passengers for a few shillings. There are a lot of folk travelling via the boats that way, now that the roads into Hull are blockaded.'

'You'll need to be ready to leave when I give you the word,' Mathew explained.

'As you wish,' Mortimer replied. 'Just tell me when.'

Chapter Sixteen

Colonel Duncombe issued a decree that soldiers stationed in Beverley were to be billeted in houses around the town, and since the Fletchers had plenty of space in their house and in the stable within the wheelwright yard, they had been forced to take the unwanted lodgers. But, one by one, all the soldiers who had been billeted with the Fletchers had fallen ill with fever. They were not alone. Soldiers were falling ill, not just in the Fletcher household, but across the town.

Mary was rushed off her feet trying to see to the needs of the sick in the Fletcher home. The house had begun to stink from the sweat and dirty clothes of the military men. Adding to the families woes, when the fever was at its highest, the men would vomit where they lay, and often be too ill to ask for a piss pot, and so they'd wet their breeches as they lay on their mattresses.

Charles had given-up helping his father and brother repairing and making wheels in the yard in order to help Mary look after the soldiers. Everyone in the household was becoming bad-tempered and tired looking after the unwanted boarders who had been forced upon them. Those that had not fallen ill would come and go as they pleased at any time of day or night. Household items were getting broken or going missing, and all the time the men wanted feeding.

The family feared that they too would succumb to the sickness and while incapacitated, the soldiers would ransack the house and they would be unable to stop them.

Mary did her best with her limited medical experience to help the soldiers but was struggling to cope. Her mother had taught her how to treat a fever, but this was a different kind of illness. It was more than just a summer fever; the men were covered in a pink rash, the flu-like symptoms and lethargy, later turning to delirium. There had also been reports of soldiers dying. It seemed as if all the soldiers in the town were coming down with it. Mary wished that Mathew was there to help.

Sergeant Pickles woke Mathew early. 'Begging your pardon, Surgeon,' he said urgently. 'I have orders for you.'

Mathew opened the note the sergeant had handed him. He had been ordered by Colonel Duncombe to return to Beverley, where he was to help deal with the outbreak of fever that was spreading through the town.

'What's wrong with them?' Mathew asked.

'I don't know, do I? You're the quack, that's for you to find out. Come on, be quick, it's the Colonel himself that has sent for you.'

The chance to live with his family again was going to be a welcome relief from living on a campsite. Mathew had found that the ground of the campsite turned to a deep foul-smelling mud every time it rained because of all the horse shit and the daily refuse of a thousand soldiers. A lot of the time, he had little to do, but then there would come moments of frenzied activity when injured men would be brought to him. It was difficult to get into a routine when most of your patients' injuries came from random accidents.

Mathew roused himself, and, after a quick breakfast with Ethan. He showed the colonel's letter to Charles Mortimer and asked him not to leave camp until he got back. Mathew set off for Beverley wondering what he would find when he got there.

The first thing he noticed when he arrived in the town was fewer people were out and about on the streets and in the lanes than usual. Reporting to Lieutenant Colonel Duncombe's command post in the Push Inn on the corner of Lady Gate, Mathew found he was rushed in to see the colonel quicker than he had expected. Without waiting for the formalities of introduction, Colonel Duncombe explained that he was calling into Beverley everyone he could find with medical experience, to help deal with the fever that now had the town and his soldiers in its grip.

'In your opinion, what kind of plague are my men suffering from?' asked the colonel, putting Mathew on the spot. Mathew hesitated, if he gave the wrong answer, he would lose the colonel's respect and trust.

'Colonel, I have come here straight from the camp at Anlaby,' he explained. 'I need a little time to examine the sick. I am a surgeon, not a physician, but if you allow me the rest of the day to visit the sick, I will report back to you this evening with my opinion on the disease.' Mathew hoped he had bought himself enough time to figure out what was blighting the town.

'Very well, Surgeon Fletcher, I will expect you here at six of the 'clock.' With that, the colonel returned to his business with the two officers at his side.

The orders given to Mathew were simple: stop the fever in any way possible.

Leaving the colonel after promising to do whatever he could, Mathew made his way home past the soldiers' camp which had been set up on the site of the Saturday Market near to the Push Inn. Mathew could see the camp was in disarray with sick men milling about aimlessly.

As he arrived home, two soldiers were leaving the yard at the side of the house. He was surprised at first to see them, his mind being distracted by what the colonel had told him. Mathew then realised that his home too was being used to billet soldiers. It annoyed him to think his home had been invaded by strangers but realised dozens of other households were in the same predicament. As he walked his horse into the yard, both the stalls that the horses should have been kept in were occupied by soldiers. He tied his horse to the post between the two stalls, glanced down at the obviously sick soldiers, then turned and went inside the house.

Mary was at the fireplace, removing boiled lined shirts from a steaming cauldron. Mary looked up as the door opened, and Mathew caught sight of the sweaty and strained expression on her face. Henry came down the stairs to see who had entered the house.

She was the first to speak as Mathew crossed the room to greet them both: 'Thank God, you're here, Mathew! There's disease in the town, all the soldiers are going down with fever, and it's spreading to the townsfolk. There's a proclamation up in the market that everyone in the town has to open their homes to sick soldiers, or the army will move us out of our houses and move the soldiers in.' Mary dropped the wet linen back into the cauldron, and gave Mathew a hug, tears of joy and relief coursing down her cheeks.

212

'Good to see you, brother,' said Henry. 'We need all the help we can get. All the physicians that were in town seem to have left. I guess they're more interested in saving themselves and their families than helping the sick and risk catching the disease themselves. All we have left in Beverley is a couple of surgeons, and a couple of barber-surgeons to deal with all these men. There are so many people getting ill that it's hard to cope.'

'Where are Father and Charles?' asked Mathew.

'Charles is upstairs removing soiled clothing from soldiers who are too sick leave their beds. Father is out trying to buy food for everyone,' said Henry.

Mathew soon noticed how the house stank of unwashed bodies, dirty, sweaty clothes and vomit. He knew the bad air in the house would only make the disease worse, but said nothing, not wanting to add to the family's worries. He guessed that the fever had probably come from the stink of the overflowing cesspits in the town, now that the town's population had doubled in size due to the influx of soldiers. With so little medical help in the town, Mathew knew he was going to have his hands full. He had been summoned to deal with the medical emergency, but it was only now that he began to realise the size of the problem he faced.

First of all, he examined the soldiers in the Fletcher household. They all had the same high temperature and a red rash, but none had died so far. Mary had been in charge of the soldiers' welfare, and Mathew needed to know how she had been treating them. Mary explained that once they had fallen ill, she had got Henry to strip and wash them, while she washed their clothes. They were put to bed and fed on a light diet of broth and kept cool; it was all she knew about treating fever. Cleaning the soldier's clothes had been her first priority since so many of the soldiers were fouling their clothes and bedding. Henry also made new paillasses for them whenever they had become too badly soiled and needed replacing. Mathew praised Mary for doing such hard unsavoury work.

Mathew reported back to Colonel Duncombe at six of the clock.

'At the moment, sir, all I can suggest is that due to the overcrowding in the town, the filthy condition of the soldiers and the overflowing cesspits giving off foul odours, it must be the air that is causing and spreading the disease. Thirty years ago the town suffered badly with the plague and lost a quarter of its population to the disease. Also, Beverley no longer has its most profitable business of tailoring, and the town has been in decline ever since. Beverley has been neglected for years and is run down; it cannot cope with demands your army is putting on it. I haven't discovered what the disease is yet. Once I do I will work out a solution on how to deal with it. If you will allow me a little more time to complete my investigations I will report back to you as soon as I discover anything.'

Mathew left the Push Inn wondering what he had let himself in for with this unknown plague and the run-down state of the town. As he crossed the market, he thought about the problem. *The patients at his family home would make a good starting point. He would experiment on them first, and with the help of his medical books, he may be able to find a cure.*

Mathew entered his house and looked about him, a soldier lying on a blanket in the corner of the kitchen was as good a place to start as any. He began his examination by taking his pulse and feeling how 'hot' he was. The soldier was indeed hot and sweaty with a racing pulse. When he opened the patient's eyelids, his eyes rolled back in his head. The man was delirious and deep in the grip of the fever. Opening the man's shirt, Mathew saw that his chest was covered in pink blotches.

Was it measles, he wondered? No, measles wouldn't infect this many adults at the same time, most people caught measles while they were children.

Fever. Why was everyone coming down with fever? Had they not prayed every Sunday? Was this God's punishment for man's wrongdoings, he mused? Mathew remembered his Sunday school days and how the preacher had said 'God had put diseases on the earth to punish men for their sins'.

Mathew had seen many fevers during his apprenticeship in Hull with Surgeon Adams. Sailors would often come back from long sea voyages from faraway lands, suffering from strange diseases. Somewhere in the back of his mind, a memory stirred, of something he had been told.

A Hollander had visited Hull and told stories of his time fighting the Spanish in the Low Countries. He had been held prisoner on an old hulk in one of the ports, where men were dying of fever. There had been a riot, and a number of prisoners had escaped. This Hollander had jumped overboard and swum across the river to escape, getting swept up by the outflowing tide. The only thing that stopped him from drowning was a tree branch that floated within reach which he grabbed. As the river widened, the water had slowed to a point where he felt confident enough to strike out for the muddy shore. The story concluded with the revelation that he, along with the other prisoners on the hulk, had started to acquire red blotches on his skin, but after his time in the salty water, no more had appeared and he subsequently only suffered a mild bout of fever, and then recovered.

There were similarities: Beverley was full of men living close together in dirty conditions, and the men who had arrived in the Fletcher house first, were the ones showing the best signs of recovery. Because Mary couldn't stand the stink of them, she had insisted on washing their clothes, and this could be the key to it all.

Could this be 'Camp Fever', also known as 'Gaol Fever', he wondered? It had to be. It was the most likely explanation that Mathew could come up with. The bad smells from the dirty clothes and the stink of the overflowing cesspits around the town were what was obviously causing this terrible illness to spread through the population, but washing the men and their clothes could be the cure.

Mathew started his treatment by purging his patients (giving them medicines to evacuate their bowels), followed by bleeding them, working on the principle that removing the bad humours from their body was the best way to aid recovery. The body, with its humours back in balance, would then help to heal itself. He remembered the old saying by Francis Bacon: *'Cleanness of body was ever deemed to proceed from a due reverence to God.'*

With God's help and some help from Mary, Mathew was sure that he would be able to beat the fever attacking the people of Beverley and the soldiers of the army. He would report his findings to the colonel the following evening.

He decided to call on the two surgeons who had stayed behind in Beverley when all the others had evacuated. He wanted them to accompany him when he went to see Colonel Duncombe that evening. Having his fellow medicos with him would give him some much needed moral support, even if they contributed little to the conversation. These men had been courageous enough to stay to fight the disease, and Mathew would need and value their support to fight it. The two barber-surgeons were not as well trained as the surgeons were, but they could act as assistants to the two surgeons.

Mathew spoke to his two medical colleagues, Bartram and Jenkins, and explained that he needed their support when he went to meet Colonel Duncombe at the Push Inn. They were not keen at first but agreed to go when Mathew told them that he would be mentioning their names anyway, during his report to the colonel, so implicating them in his work regardless of whether they wanted to help him or not.

So Mathew, with Bartram and Jenkins accompanying him, made their way to the Push Inn. Mathew explained to the guards at the door who they were, and that they were to report to Colonel Duncombe. One guard told them to wait until called for, while the other disappeared inside. Unlike on his previous visits, this time they were kept waiting, but eventually, they were summoned inside. All the tables and chairs that once filled the main room of the inn had all been moved out, apart from three tables placed end to end along the right-hand wall of the room. Sitting behind the centre table was Colonel Duncombe, with an imposing gentleman sat to his right and junior officers and aids sat either side of them.

Mathew felt as if he was on trial. He stood in the centre of the room, with Bartram and Jenkins just behind him, aware that all eyes were upon him. Fearful of what was going to happen he decided the only thing he could do was tell the truth as he understood it. After all, people were dying, action needed to be taken, and they had asked for

Mathew's help. They were the ones in the real problems, and they needed him. But at that moment he still wished it was someone else standing there instead of him.

Lieutenant Colonel Duncombe was the first to speak, saying, 'Surgeon Fletcher, this is My Lord the Earl of Newcastle, advisor and officer to The King of England, Charles Stuart. You will give your report about the disease that is spreading through the town and amongst our soldiers, to him.'

Bartram and Jenkins both took a step backwards and stared at the floor. Mathew knew he was on his own. He cleared his throat, and in a voice that was not as confident as he would have liked, he started to speak: 'My Lord, Colonel Duncombe, I believe that all the sick are suffering from Camp Fever, also known as Gaol Fever.'

A murmur went through the officers who were seated at the tables in front of him. Mathew waited to be asked another question, not daring to volunteer more information than he'd been asked for.

'Well, what are you going to do about it?' an officer on the far right asked.

This was the question that Mathew had feared most: they were going to put the responsibility for curing the disease on his shoulders, and if he failed his career as a surgeon was effectively over. With a boldness that comes from desperation, Mathew stood up straight and looked Lord Newcastle directly in the eye.

'My Lord,' he began, 'the first thing that must be done is for all the soldiers who are still fit and well to be moved from Beverley and onto the Westwood Common, or they will catch the disease. All the remaining sick soldiers are to have their clothes and bodies washed. Bartram and Jenkins will help me tend to the sick and dying who are left in the town.'

Once again there were mutterings amongst the officers sitting at the tables in front of him, though Lord Newcastle sat silently weighing up the man who stood in the centre of the room.

'How long will it take to cure my men?' Colonel Duncombe was blunt and to the point.

'I'm not sure. Three weeks, a month maybe, it depends on how bad the fever gets. What I can say for certain is that the longer your men are in Beverley, the more of them will die. We need to act as soon as possible.'

Mathew was getting the feeling that the officers could not afford to lose men unnecessarily and that they were becoming desperate to find a cure for this mystery disease. It was the only reason he could think of as to why they hadn't chastised him for being so forward in speaking to his betters.

'What will you do to restore the health of the men?' This time his questioner was an officer from the opposite end of the table.

The young surgeon decided to push his luck a bit. 'We will cure your soldiers. But what we will need from you is a team of men to help empty the cesspits, plus another team to remove the dead and bury them. Until this disease is stopped, no more soldiers than absolutely necessary are to enter the town. With the clearing of the cesspits and dead, we can remove the bad ague from the town.

Not accustomed to being told what to do by a subordinate, and not foreseeing these obvious first steps himself, Colonel Duncombe shuffled forward in his seat with a thunderous scowl, his face, at being embarrassed in front of the earl. Before he could say anything Lord

Newcastle put a hand on his arm to stall his response. Colonel Duncombe looked at the earl and settled back in his seat.

The Earl of Newcastle spoke for the first time in Mathew's presence. 'Wait outside while we discuss the matter,' was all he said.

Mathew bowed to the earl and the officers and turned to leave, just in time to see the backs of Bartram and Jenkins, who were exiting through the door as quickly as they could. Outside in the street, they looked at each other. Bartram and Jenkins were clearly rattled by the experience of being in the same room with an Earl and men of power, but Mathew had got the impression that had he not been honest with them, they would have seen him as weak and not up to the task in hand.

'What the fuck have you got us into?' Bartram yelled at Mathew. 'I shouldn't have let you talk me into this!'

Jenkins paced back and forth, muttering that he wished he'd left Beverley when he had the chance.

After what was an agonisingly long wait, Mathew alone was summoned back inside.

'We will comply with your request,' said Colonel Duncombe. 'We will give you a dozen men for one week, to use as you will. Surgeon Fletcher, you will cure these men, do you understand?' The colonel was leaning forwards with both hands on the table, looking directly into Mathew's eyes. This was not a request or an order; it was a threat. And if Mathew failed, it would be he alone who bore the responsibility.

The homes and shops surrounding the Saturday Market were turned into makeshift hospitals for the sick soldiers. As many infected men as possible were brought in from homes around the town to these temporary 'hospitals.' Mary's job was to go from house to house telling the tale of the Hollander who had been cured of the fever by washing in salt seawater and advising the womenfolk to wash the soldiers' clothes. While she was at home, Mathew got her to brew up large batches of cooling 'decoctions', (preparations used to reduce a person's temperature). He would take these decoctions on his rounds to administer to the sick. He advised the army quartermaster that he would be buying more medicines from Mary, for she made the decoctions he needed and according to his recipes, the quartermaster agreed without question.

Mary also made a soothing cream to go on the red blotches, concocted from *pork dripping, Lavender, Chamomile, and Dock Leaves,* ground into a paste. The cooling decoctions she made from *lettuce, water-lilies, Great Houseleek, and Garden Night-Shade,* boiled down into a concentrate.

Mathew and his team of medicos worked hard and slept little, but after the first week there were no more new cases of the disease, and after the second week there were no more deaths. Under Mathew's direction and with the aid of Mary's medicines they had stopped the spread of the disease, and sick soldiers were returning to their regiments, now encamped on the Westwood Common.

By the time the month was up, and all but a few of the soldiers who had been taken ill were back with their regiments. Mathew was lying in his own bed, staring at the roof beams supporting the thatch that covered the house. For the first time in four weeks, he didn't need to rush around Beverley tending to sick soldiers. He had made sure that his home had been cleared of soldiers as soon as possible, for what sleep he had managed to grab over the past weeks, he had wanted to take in his own bed. As he lay there, he heard a little scratch at the door as it gently swung half open, then came the tap of feet on the wooden boards, and Bess, the family dog, laid her head on his arm. She had become used to him rising early each morning and had come to remind him it was time to get up.

'No rest for the wicked, eh, Bess?' he said with a smile, as he reached across and gave her a quick scratch behind the ear. Mathew could hear movement downstairs—no doubt Mary was up and had sent Bess to wake him, and before long the whole family were up and eating breakfast.

For the most part, all that was left for Mathew to do was check on his last few patients and then his job would be done. Breakfast was only just over when there was a banging on the door. Mary opened it to find a sergeant standing there with a letter for Mathew. He handed it to Mary, touched the rim of his helmet with his finger and left. Mathew broke the seal and read the contents: he was to meet Colonel Duncombe at the Push Inn at noon that day.

'I am extremely happy with your achievements, Surgeon Fletcher,' the colonel informed him when they met at the inn. 'You may be aware that I had my doubts, and that I didn't think you would be able to stop the spread of disease. But it seems that due to all your hard work, you have been proved correct, and for that, your efforts have been reported to the King by Lord Newcastle. You have probably saved the King's Army in Yorkshire, and as a reward, His Majesty has sent you twenty golden angels.' The Colonel dropped a purse containing the coins on the table.

'I also have a request of you,' the colonel went on. 'You weren't afraid to take charge of things at the height of the epidemic. You were willing to take responsibility when others stood back, but, most of all, you did what you said you would do and saved my men, and for that, I am very grateful. If you are willing, I would like you to be my personal surgeon. You would still have to work with the men, but you would attend on me when needed. For this, you will receive an allowance from me as well as the pay you get from the regiment. You think it over, and let me know.'

The colonel shook Mathew's hand, then turned and left the room, leaving Mathew wondering what he would do, not only with the money but as regards his new benefactor.

But for now his work in Beverley was over, and he knew that he must return to Anlaby.

Outside, in the Saturday Market, Mathew was about to return home when he heard a voice addressing him, saying, 'Ah, Surgeon, a moment of your time if you please?'

Mathew turned to see a short man in well-worn woollen jacket and breeches, his hat held in his hand, showing Mathew deference as if he was a man of status. 'I understand you have done an excellent job in saving the town and His Majesty's army from this terrible plague,' the man continued. 'Congratulations, sir, you must be very talented indeed.'

The hairs on Mathew's neck stood on end. He instantly took a dislike to this obsequious stranger who was clumsily leading up to some kind of proposal or question.

'Thank you, er, Mr—'

'—Potter, sir, my name is Thomas Potter. I was just wondering. As a man who must know so many people in Beverley, would you be able to help me find someone? You see, I am a lawyer's clerk, and I have been tasked with finding two men who left Hull last month before I could make their acquaintance and make them aware of a relative's last will and testament. All I know is that they returned to Beverley because their father was ill. Have two brothers approached you seeking medical help for their father?'

Mathew stood in silence for longer than he had meant to. Altering his shocked expression to one of pensiveness, he knew that he needed to give a convincing answer. 'No, no I haven't. Do you know the illness their father was suffering from?'

'No, just that they left Hull in a hurry for Beverley.'

'I'm sorry,' Mathew lied. 'Maybe one of the other surgeons can help you. I'm sorry I must leave you, duties call.'

He left Potter standing outside the Push Inn. Without looking back, Mathew made his way home, wondering who the strange little man was and why he was on the trail of him and his brother. Potter watched the surgeon leave; he didn't know why, it was just a feeling, it was a feeling that told him that the surgeon had not told him all he knew. Potter made a mental note to learn more about Surgeon Fletcher.

At home, Mathew warned his family about the strange man asking questions and told them to say nothing about their father's illness. The following day, taking his horse from the yard and after saying his farewells to his family, he trotted back to the Royalist camp at Anlaby.

At the home of Lady Gee, Lord Newcastle requested an audience with the King. The news he had to impart was not good. Parliament had clearly been informed of the King's intention to capture Hull, and Hotham's refusal to allow the King admission to the town indicated that he was probably the informer and had changed sides.

To help soften the blow of the bad news, Newcastle informed His Majesty that money was being raised by royalist supporters in the northern counties. Gold and silver plate was being collected, melted down and turned into coin. The donated money was being used to raise more soldiers and equip them with the arms. Lord Newcastle advised His Majesty to return to York where he would be more comfortable and able to oversee the administration of his growing support. The King, comfortable in the home of Lady Gee, decided he would stay for the time being.

Chapter Seventeen

Back in Anlaby after four weeks in Beverley, Mathew went to see Ethan, to catch up on the latest camp gossip and partake of one of his of excellent meals. Ethan was, as usual, preparing dinner for the officers of the camp but he was pleased to see the surgeon return.

'Welcome back, my friend, it's good to see you,' Ethan welcomed him cheerfully. 'Since you've been in Beverley performing miracles I've had more bloody officers pestering me for a cooked meal than you can shake a stick at. There're never bloody satisfied, with their constant, 'I don't like this', or 'I don't like that'. With a bit of luck, they'll go back to Beverley now and leave me in peace. Here, sit down and tell me about how you saved Beverley and the whole of Yorkshire and maybe England from the plague.'

Mathew laughed. 'You're exaggerating again. It wasn't the plague, it was Camp Fever, and it was mostly the soldiers that caught it, not the whole of Beverley. Still, I think I did a good job, even if I do say so myself.' He accepted the tankard of ale offered by Ethan, and after taking a long pull on the drink, he wiped his mouth on his sleeve and sighed with satisfaction.

The two friends sat and exchanged stories for a while until Mathew decided it was time to find Charles Mortimer. He needed to tell him what he had been doing.

He found Mortimer sitting by his wagon with another bucket of half prepared musket balls at his side.

'This is a boring job,' Mortimer complained as Mathew walked over to him.

'Welcome home to you too,' Mathew said sarcastically.

'I'm sorry, but it is. I am pleased you're back safe. There's been lots of talk around here about you 'saving Beverley'. *The brave young surgeon, defeating the deadly disease.*' Mortimer smiled at Mathew's embarrassment.

'Yes, yes, I know. I just heard it all from Ethan. Now that I'm back, I need to send a message to Captain Overton,' Mathew said in a low voice. 'But, I want to have a look around the camp first, find out if there have been any changes.'

'There's no need; I've been keeping an eye on things here. Nothing much has changed, apart from the arrival of all the officers and men that fled Beverley. A lot of them came here, rather than staying too close to the town. I'll take the news you have about the disease to Captain Overton. I'll leave in the morning if that's agreeable to you.'

Mortimer was keen to return to Hull and getting away from the boring life at camp.

Mary busied herself by mixing the ingredients for the medicines she was making, all the time thinking about Mathew and the ability he had to cure people. She was happily married to Charles Fletcher, but she wished that she too, could have something to focus her mind on, other than taking care of three men and cleaning house. If only she could help people in medical need, as Mathew did, she

227

thought about how wonderful it must be. She knew how to make lots of medicines: her mother had taught her the skills, just as her mother's mother had taught her. In the same way that she had been taught, it was probable that she also would one day teach her daughter, if she had one. So evidently, she reasoned, she ought to be able to use the knowledge she had to help people. With no sign of a baby on the way and a life spent more as a servant than as a wife and mother, there was little for her to look forward to.

It wasn't long before an opportunity to use her medical knowledge presented itself. A couple of days later she learned that Margaret, a pregnant friend she met regularly in the market, had gone into labour earlier than had been expected. The two of them didn't have much in common, except they bumped into each other regularly and had started to chat.

Charles had suggested that she visit her friend in her confinement, to see if she could offer any help to the family, and so Mary had decided to take some of her soothing herbs, and a recipe for a salve to her friend. The salve was to be rubbed on her friend's skin, to reduce the swelling of her abdomen after the baby had been born. The visit would also give her the chance to offer some medical opinions of her own, on what might help this friend who was in premature labour.

On arriving at Margaret's home, she found her in bed, and in a great deal of discomfort. The house was little more than one large room downstairs and two small rooms upstairs. The small windows allowed in little daylight, and damp ran down the walls in long green-and-black patches. The floors were dirty with filth trodden in from the street, and the fire in the hearth was small and smoky, giving off little warmth.

Margaret and her mother were very poor. The young mother-to-be had taken what work she could find but had never stayed in a job for very long. The two women were squatters in this house, and the only reason they hadn't been thrown out was that it was in such a sorry state that no one else wanted it. What little rent they paid, when they could, kept the landlord away. Margaret couldn't afford to pay for the help of a midwife and knew that if the baby was born now, the chances were that it would be dead or die soon after the birth.

Daisy, Margaret's mother, was the only other person in attendance as Margaret fretted over the early onset of labour. Daisy reassured Mary that she'd had plenty of practice delivering babies and that even though this one was a few weeks early, there was no significant concern. She was in fact lying; she cared little for her daughter apart from when she earned enough money to keep them both drunk.

It seemed that Mary was the only person who had Margaret's welfare in mind. Unhappy with Margaret going into labour so early and getting urges to push, Mary wondered if she could somehow stop the labour pains with one of her home remedies.

'Margaret, do not push,' Mary told her. 'I'm going home to get some more things that I need. It's too early for you to have this baby. I want to try and slow its coming, until the right time.'

Mary had helped with delivering her sisters' babies, and her mother had given her many recipes for medicines that could help with labour problems.

'What will be, will be, it's God's will,' declared Daisy as she blew her nose on the hem of her dirty apron, while she sat on the stool next to Margaret's bed. Daisy was enjoying sucking on an empty chipped clay pipe that hung from the corner of her mouth. The pipe was there out of habit, and the continual abrasive movement of successive clay pipes against her rotten teeth had worn a gap in them. Taking one last look around the simple room, Mary left.

When mother and daughter were alone, Daisy turned on her daughter: 'I told you that lad was no good. He's had his fun with you, and now he's buggered off. You silly cow, you'll never learn.' Daisy wiped the spittle from her mouth onto the sleeve of her dress and sat with her back leaning against the damp wall. The pipe twitched in her mouth as she ran her tongue around its stem, playing with the tip of the clay tube.

'Ma, it hurts, I'm frightened,' moaned poor Margaret.

'Not as much as it's gonna, young 'un, you ain't had no pain, not yet.'

Daisy had no sympathy in her voice for her daughter. Fate was a terrible master. Daisy's remembered back to the handsome young man who, eighteen years ago, had left her to face the birth of Margaret on her own. Since that day she had scavenged, worked, stolen, begged and sold her body, to keep them both alive. She sometimes asked herself, 'What was it for? Was it really worth the effort?' They were two—soon to be three—lives lost in a world of poverty and squalor.

Back at the Fletcher home, Mary prepared a tonic to keep Margaret's strength up and medicine to try to stop the premature labour pains. Some good food for Margaret would also encourage the baby to stay where it was, and not seek sustenance from outside the womb. Mary had noticed that there was very little in Margaret and Daisy's house that would aid in the birthing of a child, or give it a healthy future. She wondered if the best thing for Margaret would be if the child were not born alive. Mary dismissed the notion and looked through her mother's old medicine recipe book for something that would delay the oncoming of a child. Finding the correct recipe, she prepared the ingredients. The *Spodium, eggs and white wine* were all to hand, but the *twelve leaves of gold* were beyond the means of the family so Margaret would have to make do without them. She took a large pot and filled it with the leftovers from last night's meal of mutton and barley. A jug of strong ale, bread and cheese also went into her large basket. The warming cordial was on the shelf already made, along with the tonic that would help to give Margaret strength.

Returning to her friend later that day, she gave her the tonic and food, leaving the medicine with Daisy, with instructions when to administer it. Margaret and Daisy shared the mutton and barley stew. The bread and cheese they kept for later, but Daisy drank most of the strong ale.

'Keep in with her, lass, we can milk her for a while, a bit of easy living, eh?' Daisy whispered to Margaret when Mary's back was turned.

Two days later Mary received the news that Margaret's labour pains had ceased soon after her visit and that she was resting comfortably. Mary felt very pleased with herself, and she couldn't wait to tell Charles and the family about her success with Margaret, but most of all, she wanted to tell Mathew the news of her medical success. She had seen how proud his father and brothers were of him and listened to their hopes for his future. She sighed and thought: *if only I could be like him.*

Sir John Hotham had had plenty of time to think about the ramifications of refusing the King admittance to Hull over the past weeks and how he would redeem himself. First of all, he decided that he must re-establish contact with Lord Newcastle and explain what had happened on the town walls, and reaffirm to him that he was still loyal to the King. Sir John was desperate to convince the King that with his help, Hull would soon be in royal hands. A knock at the door disturbed his train of thought, annoying him.

'Yes!' Hotham roared.

The door opened and his servant Bottomley stood there looking sheepish. He was all too familiar with Hotham's outbursts, and violent tirades against those who could not fight back.

'I have Charles Mortimer waiting to see you, sir.'

'Send him in,' Hotham snapped.

Charles Mortimer shuffled into the room. He had once worked for Sir John Hotham at his family home at Scorborough. Mortimer's sister, brother and mother still worked at the Hotham home. His father had been a cordwainer, and Charles and his brother were going to his apprentices, but their father had died while they were still young. The only way they could earn any money was to go into service, and it was their bad luck that they ended up working for Sir John Hotham.

Mortimer had run away from home at fourteen and taken any job he could find in Hull. After a number of temporary appointments, it had been his good fortune to meet a young Lieutenant Overton who was in need of a servant, which is what brought him into service for the now up-and-coming Captain Robert Overton. Overton had arranged for him to learn to read and write, offered him steady employment and was a good master.

Robert Overton was not only a religious man with a high intellect, but he was also one of a rare breed that had the idea that all men, regardless of rank, should be treated equally.

It was while he was carrying out his duties for Captain Overton one day that Mortimer met Sir John Hotham again. As Overton gained rank within the East Yorkshire Trained Bands, and Hotham embarked on his bid to become Mayor of Hull, the latter had used a number of threats against Mortimer's family to intimidate him into double-crossing Overton.

He had called Charles Mortimer to his office and made it clear that his family were at risk of losing their jobs and had hinted at more darkly veiled threats if Charles did not keep him abreast of Overton's activities.

In short, Mortimer had had no choice in the matter, and he hated himself for what he was doing.

'Do you have news for me, Mortimer?' Hotham snapped, looking up impatiently from the letter he was struggling to write.

'Yes, sir. I know the name of the Parliamentary spy in the King's camp at Anlaby. He is Mathew Fletcher, a surgeon, and he is working for Captain Overton.'

After betraying his friend, Mortimer hung his head in shame, but his own family must come before any other loyalties.

Hotham put down his quill, a smile lighting up his face. It was the cruel smile of a man who had found the chink in his opponent's armour, one that would give him that vital advantage. He listened intently to what Mortimer had to report.

'Good,' Sir John answered. 'Very good. I need time to think about how best to use this information. You go and tell Overton your message while I make up my mind about what to do next.'

After leaving Hotham's office, Mortimer went to find Captain Overton.

Reading the letter from Mathew, Captain Overton slammed the flat of his hand down hard on his desk.

'Great news! Well done, Mathew!' Overton exclaimed aloud, looking up from the letter to Mortimer. 'We can attack the Anlaby camp where and when it will hurt them most. I will set up a plan with the other officers, and we will strike as soon as possible. You have done a good job in bringing this news to me, Charles.'

Charles Mortimer's face flushed crimson as much from the compliment, as from the guilt of knowing that he had let down the one man who had helped him more than any other, apart from his own father.

'Do you have a message for me to take back, sir? Surgeon Fletcher has also asked that I return with some supplies he is running short of. I will need time to get them for him before I return.'

'No, no message yet. But don't return to Anlaby. I need time to work out a plan of attack on Anlaby, and you will need to warn Mathew about it. I wouldn't want him to get hurt when it happens. Go and do your errands and then report back to me tomorrow.'

Mortimer left Overton in a state of excitement and optimism. He felt worse than ever, and before going to get the supplies he'd been sent for, he headed for the nearest tavern.

Captain Overton gathered his officers together in his office to plan the attack on the King's Army at Anlaby.

The next morning Charles Mortimer arose early to buy supplies for Surgeon Fletcher. Having filled his saddlebags and also carrying a large sack of supplies, he returned to Captain Overton around mid-morning.

'How long will it take you to get back to Anlaby?' Overton asked Mortimer.

'I can be there late tonight. A boat leaves with the high tide at two of the clock this afternoon. But, I cannot arrive too early—I have to make it look like I have been to York for the supplies. It's a long way to travel via Howden, but it's the closest place that boats from both York and Hull stop. I also had to leave my horse at the Ferry Inn at Howden, so I need to return the same way I came here.'

'You must make haste. We will strike at dawn the day after tomorrow. I cannot prepare for an attack and delay its implementation in case news of it leaks out. Godspeed you on your journey.'

Mortimer returned to the Guildhall to report to Sir John Hotham on Overton's intentions to attack the camp at Anlaby. Hotham received the news with interest and wondered how successful it might be.

Knowing that Mathew Fletcher had found a weakness in the camp's defences at Anlaby gave Hotham an opportunity to take advantage of the situation and try to rescue his reputation. Informing Colonel Duncombe of the attack that would come shortly by the East Yorkshire Trained Bands

Companies would save many lives, but Colonel Duncombe would get all the credit.

Hotham had to make it clear that he could still be useful to Lord Newcastle and the King. The best way of doing that he decided, was by letting the attack on the Anlaby camp go ahead. Trusting it to be successful, it would embolden Captain Overton and his men, especially after their success in destroying the fort at Hessle and their first raid on Beverley. The captain's victories could make him overconfident, and therefore easier to draw into a trap. With Overton out of the way, he could retake control of the council and the garrison at Hull, enabling him to give the town up to the King.

Allowing another defeat of the King's arm at the hands of Captain Overton to go ahead, would trick Lord Newcastle and the King into being more willing to listen to him, especially if he could deliver the spy working in the midst of the Royalist camp. He could then complete his accomplishments by giving the King Hull as a prize. He would explain to the King that he had been held at sword point, and had been in fear of his life, the day the His Majesty had tried to enter Hull and that it had not been his fault that he'd been forced to turn the King away. It had all been the fault of that son of a jumped-up farmer, Robert Overton.

Mortimer stood impatiently as Sir John thought through his plan. Hotham stood, walked from his desk to the window of his office and looked down upon the street traders, beggars and townspeople milling in the street. He ran his forefinger around the inside of one of the diamond-shaped pieces of glass, held together with strips of lead which made up the window. Looking at his fingertip, now smeared with dirt, he wiped it on a handkerchief. He exhaled through his nose and adjusted his doublet, lifted his hair, which had become trapped behind the stiff collar of his doublet, and let it drop onto his shoulders.

Turning to look directly at Mortimer, he said, 'I want you to return to Anlaby. Do nothing. Say nothing about this planned attack. The very next time you come to me I want to know more about this Surgeon Fletcher, where he is from, who his family are, everything. Now go.'

Mortimer bowed low, glad to be able to get out of the office and away from this man. Bottomley looked up from his desk as Mortimer came through the door. He smiled, his thin lips turning it into a sneer.

Charles Mortimer left the Guildhall to make his way to the boat waiting at the quay, feeling more wretched than ever. His only solace was that he was doing what he had to for his family's sake. As he arrived at the boat, it was still being loaded with goods for York. He climbed aboard and paid his fare to the skipper. Looking for a place to sleep off what was left of his hangover; he moved to the front of the boat and settled on some coils of rope covered in canvas.

He was soon asleep and slept through the boat's departure from Hull. He only awoke as he felt the boat juddering, and heard shouts and curses from the crew. The afternoon was passing to dusk, the sun low on the horizon. It soon became apparent that the boat had run onto a mud-bank, one of many that plagued the Humber and shifted and changed with each tide.

Leaving his nest amongst the ropes and canvas, he found the skipper to ask about the delay. He was informed that the wind and tide had changed, and unless they could get the boat free from the mud-bank in the next hour, they would be stuck there until the next high tide.

237

Chapter Eighteen

The day dawned with a blood red sun making its appearance over the horizon, through the clouds. There was very little wind, the air was cool, and above the sound of the horses and mumble of men's voices, the dawn chorus was the loudest sound that could be heard. A heavy dew lay on the grass and on the leaves of the trees. The horses skittered nervously, feeling the tension in their riders.

Everyone could smell and see the Royalist camp spread out on the common ahead of them at Anlaby. They had ridden through the darkness of night to be in this position before the light of day. Captain Overton had brought three squadrons of horse from Hull. Taking them north, then west before reaching Cottingham, they then turned south through Kirk Ella to come upon the Royalist camp from the west. The encampment was silhouetted against the sunrise, while Overton's cavalry was still hidden against the darker sky.

Captain Overton rode out the front of his men, conversing with the officers and quietly reassuring the troopers. They had formed a line the full width of the Anlaby camp. Surprise was to be their greatest asset. They knew where the strongest and weakest points of the camp were located all they had to do was ride fast and hard, and of course, kill or maim as many royalists as possible.

For most of Overton's men, this was to be their first action, but their bravado of the previous day was now completely gone. Their mouths were dry, their hands shook, and many felt sick at the prospect of what was to come. As he passed along the line, Captain Overton assured his men that God was with them. 'Pray to the Lord, and he will protect you,' he said reassuringly. His religious belief was unshakeable, and he carried it like a protective shield. It gave him a confidence and integrity that most men could only dream of, and that confidence, he instilled in those around him.

In the camp the sentries struggled to keep their eyes open, while men slept around the remnants of last night's campfires, pulling their blankets close around them, cursing the sound of the birdsong and the chill damp air of morning. They knew they would have to be up soon, but every moment they could maintain that last bit of comfort before rising and starting their daily duties was a bonus.

At first, the sound that came to their ears was like a distant roll of thunder, getting louder as it travelled across the common towards them. Reluctant to move at the prospect of a rainy day, they huddled further into their blankets. The thunder like noise grew louder and with it came a new sound, that of hundreds of swords rattling in their scabbards, horse tack straining and pulling as the horses raced on. The sound changed to that of horses' hooves, hammering across the ground, accompanied by the shouts of men, venting their fear in a roar that released the tension which had been building within them, in anticipation of the morning attack.

They came through the camp like a tidal wave. Pistol shots rang out as the riders discharged their weapons at the first men they came across. The sound of pistol shots was followed by the scraping sound of swords leaving scabbards. The confusion in the camp was total. One moment they were sleeping, now the men were wide awake running and falling over each other in disarray as they scrambled about looking for a weapon, any weapon. Muskets took too long to load—their only use was as a club. As the Royalist soldiers looked to where the attack was coming from, the lead riders of the attacking force were passing them by.

The defenders were faced with a wall of horseflesh and steel that came at them out of the darkness. The royalist officers were falling out of their tents, tripping over guy-ropes, unable to issue coherent orders as men of all ranks ran around looking for a place to hide or a weapon to fight with. The wave of horses, riders, steel and death passed through the camp in just over a minute and was gone. Sergeant Pickles ran to what was left of the campfire around which his division of musketeers had been sleeping.

'On your feet, you lazy bastards, and fall in on me!' Pickles yelled at them. 'They'll be back in a minute. Get your muskets and load them. Shoulder your muskets when ready!'

Captain Overton reined in his squadron a quarter mile from the Royalist camp. The other officers came to join him.

'All right, gentlemen, reform your squadrons and we will go in for another attack before they can organise themselves,' Overton ordered. 'Meldrum, I want you to find their baggage train and burn as much of it as you can. Lieutenant Maynard, I want you to follow me through the camp. If we can destroy their powder store, we will have done a good morning's work. It's time for your men to light their torches. Once the powder store is found, the guards are to be killed first, then send in the men with torches. The guards will have loaded Doglocks—they can load and fire much quicker than the other musketeers, so it's important that they are taken care of first. Once the powder store is torched, get your men out and home as quickly as possible. If we don't meet you on the way back to Hull, we will all assemble in my office at noon. Right, now back to your men. We all charge together at the signal of my cornet, good luck, and God be with you!'

Sergeant Pickles had managed to gather a division of twenty-four musketeers under arms, with their guns loaded. Formed up in two ranks of twelve he stood behind them, not from fear, but so he could give his orders from a place they could all hear him, and he could stay out of the way as they fired and reloaded *if* they got the chance to reload. In the distance, the sound of a cornet cut the air. For a moment the camp fell into total silence, then came the sound of orders being shouted from all directions as officers and sergeants brought the remnants of their commands together. Scattered groups of pikemen and musketeers formed defensive positions where they could, but there was no time to set up a coordinated defence of the camp, all they could do was to wait for hell to fall upon them.

The first of the attacking horse soldiers came crashing into the camp moments later. Sergeant Pickles' men were ready. The front rank was primed to fire as the first of the Parliamentarian cavalry came into sight, perfect targets now with the light of the new day silhouetting them against the skyline. Pickles gave one order: 'Fire!' and the front rank of his small division fired as one. As soon as their muskets had been discharged, they filed away and reformed behind their sergeant to reload.

Then the second rank raised their muskets to the present. The Musketeers were ready to fire as more horsemen came into sight: Sergeant Pickles gave the order to fire once again. Smoke from the discharged muskets obscured their view as the front rank reloaded. The second rank lowered their weapons and began to retire behind the first rank, reloading as they went.

Sergeant Pickles now stood in front of his men, yelling: '*Salvee* lads, we only have time for one more shot, so we'll give 'em all we've got.' Standing to the side, Sergeant Pickles gave the front rank the order to kneel. They all went down on one knee. The rear rank stepped up close behind them. All the muskets were ready for firing. The sight of another troop of horse came into view, charging towards them, the riders with their swords drawn, and their horses at full gallop. 'Wait for my order!' Sergeant Pickles called.

The troop of Parliamentary horse was rushing down on them. One of the musketeers fired before the order was given, and the sound of a horse whinnying in pain carried to their ears just before they heard Sergeant Pickles give the order to fire. Twenty-three muskets fired in one thunderous volley. The black smoke of the burnt powder hung in the air, blocking their view of the scene ahead of them. Pickles lowered his halberd into the defensive position, just in time for three riders to break through the musket smoke and into the two ranks of musketeers. The horses bowled the musketeers aside like skittles.

The riders swept their swords down across the waiting musketeers, slicing through their unprotected heads and shoulders. Blood spurted into the air, covering attacker and defender alike. Men screamed in pain. Sergeant Pickles turned his halberd on the closest rider, sticking its long sharp point into his side. The rider arched backwards as he felt the point enter his left side and travel up into his lungs and towards his heart. The force of the action and the forward momentum of the horse tore the halberd from the sergeant's hands, spinning him around just as another rider came by. Seeing the sergeant's unprotected back, the rider thrust his sword between the shoulder blades of the sergeant who had rallied his men so bravely.

On the other side of the camp came a series of explosions and the sounds of screams from men dying. Fewer riders were passing through the camp now. All they were interested in was getting away; all their fight had gone. Men, horses, tents and debris lay all around. The sun had risen above the horizon, with very little cloud; it was going to be a perfect summer's day, except there was no birdsong to welcome the new morning. It had been replaced with the groans of mutilated men, and the screams of injured and frightened horses. The attack had been an almost total success.

The camp was in tatters; its defenders were taken by total surprise.

Mathew and Ethan came out from their hiding place under the wagons. The baggage-train had remained unmolested, and Mathew's surgeon's tent was intact. When the attack started both Mathew and Ethan were suddenly woken by the noise and went to cover between the wheels of their wagons. The two friends stood surveying the devastation in silence, stunned at the damage and loss of life in such a short period of time. Shouts for help from wounded soldiers quickly brought Mathew to his senses. The two men went in search of anyone they could assist.

An officer was ordering a corporal to get a party of men together, to collect the dead and to place them behind the wagons, out of sight of the main camp. Ethan and Mathew brought back one wounded man with a severe sword wound across his face and left arm. By the time Mathew had removed what was left of his left eye and stitched his wounds, more wounded men had been placed on the ground outside his medical tent. Ethan Goodman knelt amongst the wounded, wiping their faces, giving them sips of water and binding the worst wounds with whatever material he could find.

Mathew had seen wounded men before; he had helped Surgeon Adams deal with some horrific injuries, but not so many at one time. There must have been thirty to forty men lying on the ground waiting for attention. Moving from man to man, looking at their injuries, he was beginning to panic, thinking *which one do I deal with first?*

Ethan came over and tapped him on the shoulder, asking in a quiet voice, 'What do you want me to do?' his face was drawn and pale.

Mathew looked at him blankly for a moment—it was the distraction he had needed to clear his thoughts.

'I need the most badly injured to be brought into the tent first, while I get the table ready for more surgery. As soon as that is done, I'll need lots of hot water. But first, can you find a couple of men to help build a makeshift hospital to protect the injured in case it rains. Get Sergeant Pickles to organise things; he's a good man.'

'He's back there with the others. He was one of the few that put up a fight,' said a wounded musketeer with a cut on his face, pointing to where the dead were being piled up.

Ethan dropped his chin to his chest and shook his head slowly. 'Poor, brave bastard,' he muttered to himself, then went and put a cauldron of water over the fire. Mathew worked on the wounded all the rest of the afternoon and through the night. Most of the men were suffering from sword cuts. The deep wounds he cauterised with a hot iron, the smaller wounds, he stitched with black silk thread.

Those suffering from gunshot wounds were the least in number. Firing a pistol accurately from horseback was hard enough, but in the dim light of dawn and at full gallop, most bullets had missed their targets. Those that had been hit had died quickly or had minor injuries. None of those who had been shot needed bullets removed, however, the wounds still needed cleaning. The smaller wounds were cauterised, the more serious treated with a mixture of *nut oil and egg yolk* combined into a paste and applied on an emplaster.

There was only one amputation required. The bullet had smashed the Humerus of a man as it passed through his upper arm. The bone was too badly damaged to be splinted, so the damaged part of the arm had to be removed below the break.

Mathew saw the devastating effects of battle at first hand, and the waste sickened him.

The primary concern of the officers of the camp was to hide the evidence of battle as quickly as possible: the dead had to be buried, and the wounded moved out of sight before replacements were brought in. Only Mathew and the other surgeons saw the true cost of battle in lives lost and destroyed.

Robert Overton met with his officers at noon on the same day. They were going to discuss the morning's attack over a meal before retiring to sleep. Earlier in the day, each officer had ensured that the wounded in his squadron had been taken to the infirmary in Trinity House, and the remainder had received a hearty breakfast. Overton's injured shoulder pained him as he massaged it with his left hand. Visually the wound had healed, but the muscles were taking far longer to recover.

'Now, gentlemen, your reports if you please,' Overton asked, feeling worn out with tiredness. The officers had not changed their clothes from the morning's foray. None were wounded, but they were covered in mud and splashes of blood. The raid had been a total success: nineteen troopers lost, fifty-six injured. From the reports of those junior officers who hung back to survey the Royalist camp, the raid had destroyed most of the camp's powder store, and they had released or stolen many of the Royalist horses, and countless men had been killed or injured. The only part of the attack that didn't succeed had been that on the baggage train, due to a heroic stand by a group of musketeers and their sergeant.

Chapter Nineteen

John Franks led the way as Geoffrey Wilkes helped his friend Peter Martins up the street in Beverley. Matins' hand and arm had become severely infected, and fever raked his body, making him shiver and weak. Every joint in his body flared with fiery pain; each muscle felt like it was tearing itself apart. He was soaked with sweat, and the pain in his head made his vision blur and his stomach retch.

Franks spotted the sign of the surgeon above a door as they passed the top of Cuckstool Pit Lane, and he beckoned Wilkes to bring Martins over. Without knocking, Franks opened the door and stepped inside, closely followed by Wilkes, half dragging, half carrying Martins.

'He needs the surgeon,' Franks exclaimed as he moved towards a chair at the table.

Mary had turned towards the door when she heard it open, expecting to see her husband enter. Startled by the intrusion of the three rough-looking men, Mary had frozen to the spot, but at Franks' request for help and seeing him sit down at the table, followed by the sight of the other two men, one of whom was apparently in distress, Mary regained her wits. She wiped her hands on her apron and stepped towards Wilkes and Martins.

'The surgeon's away with the King's Army in Anlaby for now, but I help him when I'm needed,' she lied.

This was her chance to practise some more medicine, and this man's need was urgent. Though Mathew was not at home, the man, who was clearly in distress and pain, needed help urgently, and she was determined that she would be the one to give it.

'Put him on the bed by the wall,' Mary told the two men. 'What has happened to him?'

Wilkes explained that Martins had burnt his hand in a fire and it had now become infected. Mary looked at the raw flesh: there was no skin covering a large part of his right hand, and the fingers and wrist were covered in patches of the same flesh-eaten wounds. As Wilkes went to join Franks at the table, Mary took hot water from a pot on the fire. From the shelf where Mathew kept his medicines, she took a clean cloth, a bottle of *laudanum* and a jar of *willow bark*.

First of all, she made Martins drink half a cup of *laudanum*, then filled the cup with broken *willow bark* and topped it up with some of the hot water and put it aside for later. The *laudanum* soon started to take effect, and Martins began to relax on the bed. Mary took his hand and washed carefully around the wounds.

Wilkes and Franks spoke secretively together so that Mary could not hear what they were saying, but it was clear from their mutterings that they were in disagreement about something. Mary continued to clean Matins' hand of dirt and pus. She coated the burns with O*ils of* B*en and Hypericon, egg yolks and Turpentine*, then covered the arm with a clean piece of linen and bandaged it. Lifting the injured man's head, she made him drink the now cooling tea of *willow bark*. Its bitter flavour made him gag, but he was too weak to resist and had to swallow it.

'He will have to stay a few days so I can help him fight the fever and redress his wound,' Mary informed Franks and Wilkes, feeling confident that she had done a good job.

The two men stood up; Wilkes dropped some coins on the table.

'He's coming with us,' said Franks as he walked to the door.

Wilkes picked up Martins from the bed, and half carried, half dragged him out through the door. Three strangers made Mary's flesh crawl, and she was pleased to see the back of them, even though she would have liked more time to treat the injured one.

She went out into the yard where Henry and Charles were working. They had been unaware of the three strangers in the house and looked up at Mary as she stood in the doorway.

'Is everything all right, Mary?' ask her husband, Charles.

She wanted to tell them about what had just happened—about how she had treated a sick man on her own, and how proud she felt about herself. Then she thought better of it. After all, Charles would not have been happy with her, letting three strangers into the house without at least one of them being there with her. At the back of her mind something told her that those men were dangerous, and telling Charles and Henry about their presence would not be the wisest thing to do.

'I just wondered if you fancied a mug of ale.' Mary smiled at the brothers. 'You have been working so hard.' She decided there and then to say nothing of what had just happened.

The following day Wilkes returned, this time knocking at the door. Mary opened it, looking up at the stranger she recognised from yesterday.

'He's burning up with fever,' Wilkes said in a matter-of-fact voice, with no feeling of humanity. He made no attempt to enter the house, and from his statement, Mary was unsure if he had come for medicines or wanted her to follow him.

'I could go with you and check on him,' she offered. 'Or I could give you some cooling cordials.' Mary felt wary of him as he stood there impassively. Wilkes shrugged his shoulders.

'I'd better see him,' she said, grabbing a few things she would need from the shelf, and wrapping them in a cloth, before following Wilkes.

As they walked through the streets, Mary asked herself what the hell she was doing, going to see a sick man, accompanied by a total stranger whom she feared? It wasn't as if he had forced her to go. But maybe, she reasoned, that was the very reason she had offered to go with him. Perhaps she had misjudged him. Would Mathew have refused to help a stranger just because he didn't like his looks, she wondered?

They stopped at a small run-down cottage on the edge of Beverley Westwood. The single-storey building had a thatched roof, mud walls painted white, and a small window made up of triangles of glass held together with ribbons of lead. The door at which they stood was rotted at the bottom, leaving a gap through which rats would be able to pass with ease. Mary wondered why they had chosen to stay in such a place. Wilkes knocked on the door; there came a scraping sound as something was dragged away from its other side. As it opened, the smell of damp and mould was overwhelming. Mary took a deep breath and followed Wilkes inside. She saw Martins sitting on the earth floor, leaning against a wall at the back of the cottage.

The walls were damp and covered with mould, patches of plaster were missing revealing the mud-brick construction of the building. There was a stone hearth in the middle of the single-roomed cottage containing a trivet and a small fire. The only table was made from an old door placed across two upturned barrels, with smaller barrels for seating. Franks looked at her for a second, then at the things she was carrying, and stepped aside to allow her to pass by and cross to the sick man. He was sitting on a couple of blankets shivering and sweating, his face pale and clammy. Mary turned to look at Franks and Wilkes, saying, 'He's going to die unless you keep him warm and get him off this damp floor.'

'E's nowt but trouble anyway,' said Wilkes dismissively.

'If we had money to spare, we wouldn't be living here,' said Franks.

'If I bring you some things to make him more comfortable, will you help him?' Mary asked with a tone of anger, surprised at her forwardness with men such as these.

'If you like,' said Franks.

'Make him a tea from this bark I'm leaving you, and make him drink it every few hours. It will break his fever. Build that fire up, keep him warm. I will come back and bring you all some food and something better for him to sleep on.'

Franks and Wilkes looked at each other and smiled.

'Yes, *my lady!*' Franks threw back at her sarcastically.

Mary left the cottage and made her way back home, feeling that her fears about the strangers had been unfounded. They were just soldiers with no jobs and desperate for somewhere to live. She felt sure she could help the sick one, maybe even save his life. This was the start she needed—she was going to learn to become a healer, just like Mathew.

Arriving home late in the afternoon, she didn't have time to go back to the cottage; she had supper to finish preparing. She would make some extra food, save it for tomorrow, and then take it back to the soldiers in the cottage. That night, she lay in her bed thinking about the next day. She was feeling discontented with her life at home. She was beginning to believe that she could do more with her life, more than cooking and cleaning and fetching for three men. What she was doing in the run-down cottage was making a difference to a sick man's illness. She was needed because of her skill at healing, not just for doing humdrum chores around a house.

Charles cuddled up close to her; she could feel his arousal pressing against her thigh.

'Mary,' he said, brushing the hair away from her face.

'I'm tired, Charles, let me sleep, please?' She turned over, too distracted by the events of the day and by what was to come tomorrow, to be pleasing her husband tonight. Charles turned away from her, muttering something to himself under his breath, making a great effort to make himself comfortable as a means of expressing his displeasure at being rejected.

The next morning Mary was up quickly, getting breakfast ready for when her husband Charles, Henry and William before they came downstairs. Feeling guilty about refusing Charles's bed-time advances, she fussed around him, giving him a hug and a kiss when he stood up from the table.

'I love you; you know that, don't you?' she said to Charles.

Charles smiled and hugged and kissed her back.

'Now, now, you two, you'll make me jealous,' bellowed Charles's father, Henry laughed at his brother's blushes.

The three men left by the back door, entering the yard to start work on a seemingly endless supply of broken wagon wheels.

Mary rushed through her morning chores. She brought down the palliasse from Henry's room, removing most of the straw to enable her to fold it up and carry it. In a pot, she put the remains of last night's stew, and placed this, together with a loaf of bread and a bellarmine of small beer into a basket. Donning a cloak and with the palliasse and blanket under one arm and the basket in the other hand, she left by the front door.

While she was out, Charles came back into the kitchen to ask Mary to bring out some beers, as they were all getting thirsty. Not finding his wife where he expected, he helped himself to a leather jug and filled it from the beer barrel, returning to the yard with three cups.

By lunchtime, Mary was back home, acting as if all was normal. She didn't mention that she'd been out, and since there were fresh bread and cheese on the table, Charles assumed she'd been to the market.

The next morning Mary followed the same routine as the day before and had breakfast ready as soon as the family came downstairs. Putting the remnants of last night's supper and this morning's bread and cheese in her basket, she put on her cloak and left the house.

As she passed the yard entrance, the gate happened to be open, and Charles caught sight of her passing by. He noticed she was heading in the wrong direction for the market and that her basket was full and not empty. Curious as to where his wife was going, he followed her at a discreet distance.

Just before leaving Beverley she stopped at the little cottage near the Westwood, and with barely a pause, entered the property. Charles returned home to await Mary's return; curious as to whom she was visiting.

Inside the men's cottage, Matins' fever had broken during the night. With the food and medicines which Mary had brought, and the palliasse that the men were filling with dry grass to keep him off the earth floor, his strength would soon return.

'I will only need to make one or two more visits,' she said to Franks. 'Your friend is recovering well. I've treated his arm and changed the bandages each day, but his wound will take a long time to heal. He should see a surgeon, who can treat the wound better than I can.'

'When he's on his feet he can deal with that for himself,' Wilkes chipped in.

'I will call again tomorrow, but I hope it will be for the last time. I have done all I can do for you.' Mary left the cottage and made her way back home.

When Charles, his brother and father stopped work for dinner, Mary was in the kitchen waiting for them. While Henry and his father helped themselves to fresh bread, butter and beer, Mary carved smoked ham from a joint. Charles looked at Mary, wondering how to bring up the subject of her visit to the cottage.

'Been to the market again today, have you, Mary?' Charles asked as lightly as possible, trying to make it sound as though he was just making conversation.

'Yes—feeding you three is an uphill struggle,' Mary lied, her cheeks flushing slightly.

'Did you see anyone we know?' Charles asked, a bit more directly than he'd intended.

Mary threw him a guilty look as if she'd been caught red-handed stealing sugar from a jar.

'No,' she muttered, 'I just got some bread and cheese to feed you gannets—you get through so much.' She tried to make her voice sound as normal as possible, but she could read Charles's face, and she guessed he suspected her of lying.

After breakfast the following morning Mary set out to make her final visit to the men in the cottage. As she passed by the entrance to the yard, Charles glanced up and watched her go up the lane and turned left. She was heading towards Beverley Bar, away from the market, as he had seen her do the day before when she had said she was going to the market.

Making an excuse to his father and Henry, he left the yard and followed Mary out of town towards the Westwood. He hung back: she wasn't hard to follow. She turned left on the road leading out of town and to the Westwood Common. Charles stayed close to the wall which ran along the side of Lady Gee's house, then went on to the trees and bushes that lined the road as the buildings quickly became fewer in number and the spaces between the cottages grew larger. At the last cottage, before she reached the open common, Mary stopped, knocked on the door and entered without waiting.

Charles found a place to hide and observe the cottage from a small stand of trees almost opposite, and where he would be unseen from the cottage windows. Mary did not stay more than a few minutes, and as she left, Charles saw the man standing in the doorway give something to her. He couldn't see what it was. He only saw Mary take the gift and the tender way she placed a hand on the man's arm in thanks.

During the time Mary was inside the cottage, Franks and Wilkes gathered their few possessions together, while Martins sat at the makeshift table, cradling his bandaged arm. The three men had greeted Mary warmly when she arrived, as they had grown to trust this woman who had shown them kindness and asked for nothing in return.

'I cannot stay long,' she told them. 'There's bread and cheese in the basket. I'm going to re-dress your arm, and then I must get back. I think my husband suspects me of something; I'm spending too much time away from the house.'

Mary finished as quickly as possible, picked up her basket and walked to the door. Turning to take a final look at the men she wished them well, then, she opened the door to leave for the last time. Franks followed her, saying, 'Wait; I have something for you.'

While they stood in the open doorway, Wilkes took a silver sixpence from his purse and handed it to Mary. 'It's my touch piece; it's all I have to give you for your kindness. It will keep you safe.'

Mary smiled and thanked him.

As she walked back towards town, she passed the place where Charles was hiding. He jumped out from behind a tree. 'Who is the man in the house you are seeing behind my back?' His face crimson, as he bared his teeth and snarled at her in anger. Without warning he raised his hand and slapped her hard across the face, knocking her to the ground. Mary had never known him to act this way before. She tasted salt with her tongue as blood ran from her split lip. She placed a hand on the side of her face where she had been struck, feeling the heat in her cheek and the wet stickiness of blood.

Leaving Mary on the ground, Charles turned and strode off in the direction of the cottage. He banged on the cottage door, and as it opened, he was confronted by Wilkes. Charles demanded to know why his wife had been sneaking away to this hovel of a house and wanted to speak to the man he'd seen standing at the door with her. He tried to push past Wilkes in the doorway when it suddenly opened wide, and he stared into John Franks' scarred face.

The outraged husband didn't see it coming. He knew nothing at all about what was going on until the burning pain that surged through his chest, registered in his brain. His body felt one more shove of the blade, as the steel penetrated his heart, but he never felt the twist of the blade, because his heart had stopped beating and he was dead.

The light had faded from his eyes, and the pain stopped as he slipped to the ground, the front of his clothes soaked in his own warm, sticky, red blood. Franks and Wilkes took a swift look around from the doorway and decided nobody had seen what had happened and that it was safe to venture out. They dragged Charles's body round to the back of the cottage, to the woodpile. Laying Charles's body next to it, they piled cut logs on top of him until he was completely covered and out of sight.

Mary tried to stand but, with her senses spinning and her legs tangled in her skirts, she failed to get to her feet before Charles reached the cottage. She saw the murder happen, and was helpless to intervene. She didn't make a sound as she watched the events unfold. She just stayed on the ground out of sight, close to the bush where Charles had been hiding. She saw the body of her husband dragged outside and round to the back of the cottage.

She shivered as the realisation of what had happened struck her. It hadn't been Franks who had killed her husband; it had been *her*. If it hadn't been for her vanity, if she had simply turned the men away saying that the surgeon was away from home, she would never have got involved with those men, and her husband would still be alive. There was nothing she could do now, except report what she had seen to the constable.

Once Franks and Wilkes had back inside the cottage, she got to her feet and walked back into town. Taking the silver touch piece from her purse, she threw it into the road— there had been no luck in that coin, more likely it had been cursed.

Her thoughts raced. How was she going to explain what had happened to her father-in-law, and Henry and Mathew? Through her pride and deceit, she had got her husband killed. She couldn't go home. She didn't want to go home, for it would no longer be her home, not without Charles. Slowly, she walked back through the Bar. Her only hope to preserve her family life would be to continue the lie.

She would return to the family and explain that she had met Charles and they had taken a walk on the Westwood Common, where they had been attacked. Charles had stood up to the attacker after he had struck her, allowing her to make her escape and come for help. It was the best story she could think of, that avoided her having to explain why she had been seeing the three men without informing Charles beforehand.

Mary was pretty sure that the men were leaving the cottage, so when Charles did not come home, and a search was made for him, the empty cottage would be a logical place to look. The cottage would show signs that it had recently been lived in and deserted. The constable would guess this was the place the robber had hidden.

Her thoughts jumped back to Charles. *He shouldn't have hit me*, she thought, as she wiped the tears and blood from her face. The justification she concocted, granted her little solace. *If he hadn't struck me, I would have been able to stop him from going to the cottage, and I could have explained to him what I had been doing there. But no, he had attacked me without warning. I've been lucky after all;* her thoughts tumbled to make sense of events? *Would he have hit me at some other time in the future if she had displeased him? Maybe I have escaped a life of beatings from Charles. Yes,* she decided. She would tell everyone they had been attacked on the common. *Charles was a wife beater and deserved what happened to him she convinced herself.*

Chapter Twenty

Franks, Martins and Wilkes packed up what few belongings they had; it was time to leave. It wouldn't be long before there was a search for the missing man hidden in the woodpile.

'We're going to join the military camp at Anlaby,' Franks told the others. 'We can merge with the other soldiers, then, leave when they do.'

Mounting their horses, they headed down the York Road, away from Beverley. Heading towards Walkington, then Little Weighton, Willerby and on to Anlaby, they would arrive after dark and be able to slip into the camp unseen, three soldiers amongst many.

Mary returned to the wheelwrights' shop and staggered into the yard, tears running from her eyes leaving dirty streaks on her cheeks. The blood from her lip was smeared across her chin creating a crimson crescent on her skin.

'Help! Charles needs help!' Mary cried out desperately.

William and Henry dropped the wheel they had been assembling and ran across to her.

'What's happened?' demanded William, helping Mary to sit on a box against the wall of the yard. 'Where's Charles?'

'We were walking on the common, when we were attacked by a robber,' Mary choked out through her tears.

'He held a knife on Charles and knocked me to the ground. As the robber struck me, Charles attacked him and shouted for me to get away, so I ran home. Please; go and save Charles!'

Henry jumped on a carthorse without even saddling it and cantered through the streets towards the common. It took him little more than a few minutes, but there was no sign of Charles amongst the cattle and sheep feeding on the grass. He rode across the common towards the holding pens, the stockmen; the only people he could see who were out on that part of the common. No one had seen the attack on his brother and sister-in-law.

Heading further south, he went to the soldiers' camp. Even though this was not a direction that a walking couple would have naturally taken, he was desperate for a sighting of his missing brother. The guards had seen nothing. He turned the carthorse around and cantered across the common, scattering sheep and cattle as he went, but however hard he looked, there was still no sign of his brother. With no sign of Charles or a robber, there was little more he could do for now but return home.

William Fletcher had taken Mary into the house, and sat her at the table, awaiting the return of Henry and Charles. She sipped at a cup of brandy, while her father-in-law sat close by. Mary repeated her story of the attack, only this time she described the attacker. She described him as Wilkes had appeared: tall, lean, about thirty years old, and looking like a desperate soldier of fortune.

Henry burst through the door, sweat dripping from his chin, his damp hair sticking to the sides of his head. He dropped onto a stool in angry frustration. 'Nothing!' he announced to them. 'I found *nothing*, and the only people I saw were across the Westwood, too far away to have

261

noticed anything. I can't understand why I couldn't find Charles. If he had been injured, I would have found him. The only thing I can think of is that he's giving chase to the attacker.'

'Stay with Mary,' William told his son. 'I'm going to find a constable and raise a hue and cry to find Charles and the attacker.' He crossed the room, heading for the door. The concern on his face for his missing son showed clearly in worry lines that creased his forehead.

Mary sat shivering from shock at what had happened. Her head felt like it would burst under the tumult of thoughts that raced through her brain. She knew she had to keep up the pretence of the lie. If Charles's family found out that she was the real reason that Charles was missing and dead, she would lose everything. Keeping up the lie was her only hope, and she would deal with her conscience later.

Furthermore, had she not already reasoned that his death was not her fault? After all, he had knocked her to the ground, a vicious side to his nature she had never seen before. *So I couldn't possibly have prevented Charles's death,* she muttered under her breath.

Franks had killed Charles. The story I've told them is the real truth of what happened, for all I know those men probably were robbers and thieves. The new facts in Mary's mind made her feel more at ease.

William Fletcher found a constable on the edge of the Saturday Market. The man was nearly as tall and broad as William, he would have been a formidable man to challenge, but William was not to be put off. He dragged the bewildered man back to his house to hear the story from Mary.

'Tell him, Mary,' he encouraged her. 'Tell him what has happened!'

So Mary retold her story between sobs and tears.

'Now,' demanded William, 'let's get some men together and search the Westwood for my son.'

Starting at the edge of town the line of men walked up the road and out onto the Westwood. Using long hazel sticks, they prodded and probed amongst the bushes either side of the road, searching for a man lying injured and unseen. It didn't take them long to make their way to the old decayed cottage that Franks, Wilkes and Matins had been using as a hideout. The signs that the building had recently been occupied made them give it a thorough search.

Blood on the grass around the door and leading around the side of the house led to a search of the woodpile, where they found Charles.

William picked up his son in his arms and carried him back to the house. Passers-by cleared his way, then stood and stared as he trudged passed. Tears ran down his cheeks and, though the weight of carrying Charles was more than he could comfortably manage, he would not be helped. The description of Wilkes was posted around Beverley, with a reward of ten pounds for information as to his whereabouts.

Mathew returned from Anlaby, Henry having been sent to fetch him. The family buried Charles Fletcher in the graveyard of St Mary's Church in Beverley. Mathew had gained permission from the army to stay with his family for a few days, to grieve and to come to terms with his loss.

William and his two sons never once questioned Mary's version of the attack. They had no reason to; they were too stricken with grief to examine the chain of events that Mary had told them.

Chapter Twenty-one

Mathew was getting a reputation in the Anlaby camp for being an excellent surgeon, and though it was still early in the day, a few men were queuing outside his tent with the usual soldier's aches, pains and social itches needing his attention. None looked as though they were about to die so he decided that they could wait until he had eaten one of Ethan's excellent breakfasts.

He had returned to Anlaby as soon as his brother's funeral was over all the more determined to find the men he was looking for. The work he enjoyed so much, kept him busy and helped distract him from his brother's loss. Mathew greeted Ethan, and the two sat down to eat before starting work. He'd soon acquired a taste for Ethan's thick slices of fried bacon; bread dipped in bacon fat, all washed down with a mug of ale.

Refreshed after his breakfast, he called the first man into his tent. All he needed was some ointment to rub into his shoulder. He was in pain after helping to manoeuvre a particularly large artillery piece out of a ditch.

Later, as Mathew was in the process of administering mercury to a very embarrassed soldier, who had a large scab on his male member, a messenger arrived. The messenger smirked as he watched Mathew inserting the mercury syringe into the end of the soldier's penis. Mathew looked up at the messenger, then returning his attention to his patient, he sarcastically said to the newcomer, 'I bet I'll be doing this for you one day.'

The smirk quickly vanished from the messenger's face.

'I have a letter for you from Colonel Duncombe in Beverley,' the new arrival said curtly. 'Do you want me to wait for a reply?'

'No, I'm busy. I'll read the letter later, and send a reply if I need to then.'

If the letter had been urgent, Mathew reasoned that the colonel would have instructed the messenger to get a reply, so the letter could wait until he had finished his morning's work. The unfortunate soldier he was treating leaned back against the table grimacing as the brass tube of the syringe entered his body. The man was plainly in a lot of discomfort as the greased probe of the syringe slid up inside his penis and entered his bladder. Mathew's thumb applied pressure to the plunger, and the quicksilver flowed into the man's body. He withdrew the syringe and placed it on the table.

'You can get dressed now,' the surgeon told him. 'The mercury will feel heavy inside you, and you will continually feel like you want to piss. Eventually, you will piss the mercury out, but let's hope it does its job first. You are going to feel sick and weak for a long time. You will lose your appetite, vomit often, probably lose some or all of your teeth, and your hair will fall out. But, with God's grace and a lot of luck, you will recover. So next time, if you can't afford a clean girl, use your hand.'

The soldier walked slowly and carefully out of the tent. After the morning's roster of patients had been dealt with, Mathew went to sit with his friend Ethan, who was putting the finishing touches to a plate of fried trout with capers, almonds and butter.

'I'm ready for a mug of ale and a sit-down,' Mathew declared, sitting by the fire and staring into the flames. Removing the letter from inside his waistcoat, he broke the seal and started to read. Ethan went out to the officers' tent and then returned and picked up a frying pan.

'I've saved us a couple of trout for dinner,' Ethan announced cheerfully. 'I've made a mushroom, almond and lemon stuffing for them. They just need cooking, and while we wait we can share some ale, and you can tell me what your letter is all about.' Ethan sat his fat backside down next to Mathew and placed the frying pan on the trivet at the edge of the fire, where hot embers glowed as a gentle breeze blew across the fire pit.

'The letter is just a summons from Lieutenant Colonel Duncombe in Beverley, asking me to attend on him at my earliest convenience,' he told Ethan, he screwed up the letter and threw it in the fire. 'I'd better go and see what he wants, but it can wait until we've eaten.'

The aroma of the frying pan was making Mathew's mouth water. But he didn't relish going back to Beverley just to see what Colonel Duncombe wanted; not so soon after his brother's funeral, he would be pleased to call in and see his family again. It had only been a few days since the death of his brother Charles, and he still grieved for his loss. He wanted to see his family again, even though he knew it would bring back painful memories.

Once back in Beverley, he turned his horse into Cuckstool Pit Lane. He would leave his horse here, at the wheelwrights' yard, while he went to see the colonel, and then spend time with the family after his meeting. As he entered the yard, his father and brother Henry greeted him warmly, pleased to see him again. They all went into the house, where Mary was busy cleaning. Bess was curled up close to the hearth; she raised her head sleepily and gave a wag of her tail in greeting as the men came through the door, before stretching out lazily and going back to sleep. The family sat and talked, catching up on missed news. Only Mary seemed a little distant, but they put her quietness down to the death of her husband. But Mary found it hard to look at Mathew. The sense of guilt she felt in not trying harder to prevent Charles's death, and now having to keep the facts surrounding his murder a secret, was proving too much for her conscience to handle. But, as Mary welcomed Mathew, her feelings about him confused her. Mathew was here, and that pleased her, but she refused to talk or look at him so returned to her cleaning. Mathew only stayed for half an hour or so, before leaving to call on the colonel, as requested.

Colonel Duncombe instructed Mathew to sit and accepted the glass of wine he was offered by the colonel's servant. He waited patiently as the military commander finished the note he'd been writing.

'Surgeon Fletcher,' the older man began, 'I need to take you into my confidence. You managed the outbreak of sickness in Beverley well, and you spoke your mind when others dithered. The question is: can I trust you with another task?' The Colonel shifted in his chair, making himself more comfortable and fixing Mathew with his piercing stare. 'You know that I have sent troops from here at Beverley to Anlaby, to replace those killed in the attack by the forces from Hull. My senior camp surgeon was also killed in that raid, so I want to make you my new senior surgeon and for you to take on the responsibilities that go with the job. However, in order for me to do that, I must know that I can trust you with military secrets. Do you want the job? And are you capable of keeping the secrets to yourself?'

Mathew's first instinct was to say no. It would make it harder for him to fulfil his mission to find Elizabeth's killer or killers, but on the other hand, it would give him more freedom to search for them without being questioned. And the secrets he learnt would be useful to Captain Overton.

'What would be my duties, Colonel?' Mathew asked respectfully.

'You would supervise the other surgeons in the regiment and arrange medical supplies, as well as being my own personal surgeon. It would also mean I would have to trust you with the knowledge of future army movements so you can prepare for our future needs.'

Mathew studied the colonel for a few moments while he thought through the offer. 'Thank you, Colonel. It will be an honour to be of service to you and the regiment.'

The colonel smiled and nodded his head. 'Good, Mathew. Have another glass of wine.'

Mathew helped himself from the bottle left by the colonel's servant.

'The siege of Hull has proved to be a failure and will be lifted soon,' admitted the colonel. 'The King has decided to move his army and that we will find a stronghold in the Midlands. What I want you to do; is ensure we are prepared for the march and that we have plenty of medical supplies when we set up our next camp. Anything we are short of, I want you to arrange for it to be supplied.'

Before Mathew could ask when, and to where, the army would be moving, the colonel's servant arrived with a note.

'That's all for now. I will get word to you later with further details. I have an urgent matter I must deal with.' With that said; the colonel stood up and left the room, hurriedly followed by his servant.

Left alone to finish his wine, Mathew thought over what had just transpired. It was obvious that Captain Overton would be pleased with the news of his promotion, and being taken into the colonel's confidence. From a personal point of view, it would give him greater freedom to come and go as he pleased to search for the men he was looking for. It was a pity he had sent Mortimer to Hull already: this additional news would have saved a journey for his courier.

Mathew returned home keen to share his good fortune with his family. They would be pleased he was doing well.

However, he wasn't sure that he had done the right thing in accepting his new responsibilities. True, it would give him greater freedom to move about and ask questions and gain intelligence to pass back to Captain Overton, but with hindsight, he would lose his invisibility as one amongst many soldiers. As he walked away from the Push Inn through the Saturday Market towards Cuckstool Pit Lane, he felt the pride of his promotion pushing doubt to the back of his mind.

He had started out with just the intention of finding Elizabeth's killer. He had then taken on the role of a spy and joined the army. This had led to him being instrumental in saving Beverley and with it, the King's Army from a terrible disease. Because Mathew had achieved so much in such a short time, it had brought him to the attention of men of power, raising his status within the army, and giving him the potential to earn the money he would need to set up his own practice. He had achieved so much in such a short time. He looked at the people he passed, none of them knew what he had done, what his plans were or even who he was. But the people who loved him would know, and the thought of that filled him with pride.

The streets of Beverley were full of litter, soldiers, horses; people going about their business, noise and stink; he noticed the similarity to the army camp at Anlaby. What had once been open fresh pasture at Anlaby, was now a muddy, filthy 'tent town'. In reality, the only difference between the two places was that Beverley was built from brick and wood, while the Anlaby camp was built of canvas.

But the sky was still blue, with light white clouds drifting westwards. Then a thought occurred to Mathew, he lived less than twenty miles from the coast, and he had never seen the sea. He'd seen the River Humber, the mile-wide scar that separated East Yorkshire from Lincolnshire, but that was usually brown with silt or on a dark day filled with rain, a foreboding slate grey.

Was the sea really blue like they said it was, he wondered? One day, yes, he promised himself, one day he would find out. Lost in his daydream of sea and sky, he was surprised to find himself walking into his father's yard at the side of the house. He had been so lost in thought he couldn't recall his walk across the Saturday Market and up Beverley Bar Within. He laughed, thinking, *what if I'd been attacked by a cutpurse or trampled by a horse?* Putting his thoughts aside, he entered the house, where Mary greeted him more warmly than previously.

'Where are Father and Henry?' he asked, almost adding 'Charles name' before he stopped himself just in time.

'Oh, they've gone to collect some more timber to make wheels with. They'll be back after a while.' Mary smiled at Mathew. 'Would you like some beer? There's a jug and tankards on the table.'

Mathew sat down and poured two tankards of beer.

'Come, sit and talk to me, Mary,' he asked her. 'You work so hard, yet, since Charles died, you have said very little. Remember, I know what it is to grieve for someone you love. I still Miss Elizabeth terribly, and we didn't even get the chance to marry.'

Mary left the broom she had been sweeping with against the wall and sat opposite Mathew. She looked into her beer. Two large teardrops ran to the end of her nose and dropped into her drink. Mathew put his hand on hers, and she looked up, her eyes full of feeling.

'I don't know what to do,' she admitted, the tears flowing down her cheeks. 'Without Charles, I feel I have no right to be here. I'm frightened that your father will ask me to leave. Yet, every day I stay here reminds me of Charles. We had no children to tie me to your family. And if I left, I would have nowhere to go.' She spoke the words rapidly as though they had been bursting to come forth. She put the tankard down and grasped Mathew's hand in hers. 'What should I do?' she pleaded.

'Father would never ask you to leave. Mary, you are one of the family now, don't you know that? You mean so much to us all. Father always wanted a daughter, and that's how he sees you.' Mathew did his best to reassure her, but she went on.

'I feel like a lodger that's paying no rent. I don't contribute to the business, so I can't pay my way.' Mary was getting more and more distraught.

'Of course, you pay your way! For goodness' sake, you cook and clean and look after Father and Henry.' Mathew squeezed her hand reassuringly.

'So that's it then, is it? I'm to be the unpaid skivvy and run around looking after a house full of men and be grateful for a roof over my head, am I?' She let go of Mathew's hand, shouting the words at him.

'No, no, Mary, that's not what I meant. I'm just trying to say we all need you and love you. We're all upset at Charles's death. You'll see things differently in time.' Mathew did his best to make her see reason.

Mary went back to her birch-wood broom, taking her frustration out on the floor as she vigorously swished it back and forth.

'Mary, please, sit down and listen to me,' Mathew called to her. 'Look. I need you, and I can pay you for work. Please, just listen to what I have to say.' Mathew was standing, holding out his arms in a beseeching gesture.

Mary thrust the broom against the wall, wiped the tearstains from her eyes and sat back in her place opposite Mathew.

'Well?' she said petulantly.

'As you know, I've just been to see Colonel Duncombe. He was so pleased with the way you and I cured the sick soldiers, he's made me his personal surgeon and promoted me over all the other surgeons working in his regiment. He wants me to ensure that it is provisioned with all the medical supplies it will need, and I'm asking you if you will make the balms and tinctures and cordials I'll need.' Mathew had lied about the colonel including Mary in his praise for the curing of the soldiers, but she seemed to believe him.

'Really?' Mary asked in surprise. 'He mentioned me? He must think we are a team or something.' Mary's mood had changed in an instant and Mathew was beginning to wonder if he had said the right thing.

'Thank you, Mathew, thank you so much,' she told him. 'That's just what I needed, something to make me feel like I belong. And if I work for you, then I'm still part of the family, aren't I?' Her hands shot across the table and grasped his. 'Thank you, Mathew, that's wonderful news! I suppose that makes me your apothecary.'

Mathew smiled reassuringly, but inwardly he questioned the wisdom of what he had said to Mary.

While Mathew was in Beverley, Mortimer returned to Anlaby from Hull. The journey had taken longer than it should, his boat back to Howden getting stuck on a mud-bank delaying him by another twelve hours until the next high tide.

Chapter Twenty-Two

It was time for Mathew to see how many soldiers would be waiting outside his medical tent. He wondered what it was that made people go to bed the night before feeling well, to awaken the next morning feeling ill. Was it that while the body was lying prone and defenceless in the darkness of night, the devil took advantage of man, inflicting him with evil humours and diseases? He wasn't sure; there were so many things he wasn't sure of. Reluctant to stir from his bed, he marvelled at the progress that surgery had made over the years, and wondered when physicians would find a way to stop men dying from infections caused by bad humours entering wounds. Would he ever understand how to stop the bad humours entering a wound and destroying the skilled work of a surgeon? Would cleverer men than him work it out, or was it God's punishment for man's past sins that man would suffer forever? And if it was God's punishment, was he a sinner for trying to alleviate his fellow man's suffering? The thoughts ran around in his head until he became thoroughly confused.

'Bugger it,' he said aloud. 'It can't be right to let people suffer.'

Mathew looked outside his tent as he threw the door flap back on itself.

Not many patients this morning, he thought, as he looked at the scruffy gaggle of men stood talking to each other.

275

As the morning progressed, there were the usual amount of infected wounds that needed cleaning, skin rashes and aching joints. But Mathew's last patient had a more serious problem: the back of his right hand and forearm were badly infected. Some attempts had been made to treat the wound, but it was now dirty, and the bandage that covered it was inadequate, with just a basic salve as a treatment. Surely the surgeon who had treated this wound should have done better work than this, he thought? He concluded that it was probably some quack that had treated after a drunken night in Beverley.

'How did this happen?' Mathew asked as he removed the filthy dressing.

'Oh—err—it was while I was putting a rabbit over the fire,' his patient lied. 'The fire flared up and caught my arm.'

Mathew looked him in the face for the first time and knew this wasn't true. This was no fire burn caused by a cooking accident; the skin had been eaten away. In order to cause this much damage the man would have needed to hold his arm over the flames for a long period, and the burn would have been on the inside of the forearm too. Judging by the way the damage was spread across the top of his arm, it looked more as if a corrosive liquid had been poured or splashed onto the skin.

While he was thinking these things, the man simply looked back at him. Then, without warning, his patient interrupted his thoughts:

'Well get on with it then! It fucking hurts, so *do something!*' The injured man's face hardened. His curled-back lips made him look like a snarling dog, and the display of dirty brown teeth and the foul stench of his breath made Mathew want to pull away.

The surgeon was taken aback by the aggression in the man's voice and facial expression; this wasn't how his patients usually addressed him. The realisation that this man, all these men, in fact, could be dangerous had not, in reality, occurred to him before now. The realisation that he could be in danger from the men he was helping came as a shock. He had become used to people being grateful for his help, but this man was not like the other soldiers. This character had an air of sinister darkness about him as if he knew and revelled in the thrill of danger.

Mathew's mind began to race, was this one of the man who had set him on his path of revenge, all he could do was stare at him and wonder if it was. Mathew couldn't think what to do next. How was he to treat the wound?

Clean it, clean it first, come on, Mathew, get your thoughts under control! He was panicking inside, suddenly realising that he was frightened of this man. For the first time, he was actually afraid of a patient; this was something he had never expected would happen.

Taking a sponge and *rosewater* from the table, Mathew cleaned around the wound. Pus had formed on the unhealed areas, so he washed it away. The damage was deep and would take a long time to heal, that was always supposing he didn't die first from blood poisoning. The man didn't flinch as Mathew removed remnants of dead skin and old bandage from the infected areas.

'I need to put medicines on the wound, and it's going to hurt,' Mathew explained to his unpleasant patient. 'I want you to drink this, it's called *dwale*, and it will make you sleep until I finish treating you,' Mathew spoke as confidently as he could but didn't dare tell his patient about the risks of taking the sleeping draft. The drug *dwale* was similar in make-up to *laudanum* but much stronger; it would render the patient unconscious.

Moving the man to a rope bed in the corner of his tent, Mathew watched him drink the *dwale* in two large gulps, the bitter taste of the drug making him retched and coughed.

'What the fuck was that, poison, you bastard? I came here to be cured, not for you to fucking try and kill me!' He stood up and then staggered to one side, the *dwale* quickly taking effect.

'You had better lie down before you fall down.' Mathew took his arm and guided him back to the bed. The patient lay back with a groan and closed his eyes.

While his patient slept, Mathew anointed the injury with a mixture of *Mel Cum, Succo Cepar, and a Pulv and Iridis* mixture, he then washed the area around the wound with a *decoction of Hyoscyam, Malvar, Solan, Violar, Sem, Cydon, Psyllii and a third part of Lac Ebuty-Ratumand*, embrocating the rest of the arm and hand with *unguent of Stramon*. The only thing left to do for now was to cover the arm with a tent dressing to protect the flesh without touching it.

Mathew sat staring at the man as he slept. Something stirred in the back of his mind, but he couldn't think what it was. He puzzled over the elusive thought that wouldn't come to mind and then gave up. In need of better company, he went to find Ethan.

Ethan was one of those people who no matter how busy he seemed to be, he always found time to sit and chat, and invariably he had a nice titbit hidden away for such an occasion. Mathew found his friend skinning a rabbit for the captain's dinner. Mathew watched as Ethan dressed the rabbit. He had just finished removing its feet and was slicing through the skin on its back legs so he could draw the loose skin towards the head, which would allow him to remove the stripped pelt and head together.

'Good day to you, Mathew, are you well?' Ethan asked, wiping his bloodied hands on his apron, and then rubbing his nose on his sleeve as he gave a sniff. 'Always the same when I have my hands covered in blood and guts, I get a runny nose. Does happens to you?'

Mathew sat down in his usual place next to the fire; he looked up at his friend and just nodded, his thoughts still troubled by his sleeping patient.

'Ahh, what's up then?' Ethan picked up a jug of beer and two mugs and left the rabbit on the table while he joined Mathew by the fire. 'You had a bad one to deal with this morning, is that it?' he enquired sympathetically.

'Sorry, Ethan, it's just that I've got this soldier in my tent, and he's a real rough sort. I've treated a lot of skin damage to his arm. He lied to me about how it happened, he said it was from a fire, but the way the burn is spread over the back of his arm and hand doesn't fit with his account of how it happened. In fact, I've watched you working around the fire. It's the inside of your arms that are at most risk from the flames, not the back parts. It looks more like burning oil had been poured onto his arm to me, or maybe scalding water, but not fire damage. He looks a real mean bastard as well, so I didn't want to push my luck by questioning him too hard. It just, I don't know, something about the injury reminds me of something else, but I can't think of what it is.'

'Then forget it,' the chubby cook advised, as always offering his support. 'It's not your problem if he lies to you. Plenty of people lie about how they get injured. They just don't want to tell you the truth in case it makes them look foolish. Let it drop. If it's important, you'll remember what's nagging at you later. Here, have a drink and stop worrying. Once he's fixed up, he'll be gone, and you'll never see him again.'

'You're right. I'm just here to fix them up and get them back to work, but I simply can't help being curious about how and why things happen—the mysteries of medicine I suppose you could say. For instance, I know that if his arm is kept clean, it will eventually re-grow the skin that's been burnt off. But—how? And, when the skin does grow back, why will it grow back with a scar, and not as it once was? Surely if we are born with perfect skin, why can't the body remake skin in the same perfect way? It's all a puzzle, and I don't have the answers. There must be reasons why. Is it all part of God's mystery? It seems that the more I learn, the more I don't understand. Then I meet an oaf like that, and it makes me question why I bother at all.'

'It's because you care, and because you have too much time on your hands. All we do is sit here in this camp and look after the undeserving bastards around us. The army is supposed to have Hull cut off, but the King can't get close enough to the town to attack it. The men in Hull don't need to come and fight us; they get everything they need by ship. So we sit here with nothing to do most of the time. The whole affair is a waste of time.'

Mathew wanted to tell Ethan about his talk with the colonel and his planned move, but he thought better of it, especially as he didn't know where they would be moving to or when.

But then he changed his mind, not wanting to keep a secret from the warm-hearted cook who had been so kind to him.

'I saw Colonel Duncombe in Beverley yesterday,' Mathew said at last. 'He very pleased with the way I dealt with the outbreak of fever in the town and has asked me to be the regiment's senior surgeon.'

'That's good. That'll give you more to do. You know what you need, Mathew, is a girl to take your mind off things.' Ethan laughed aloud at his cheeky suggestion.

Mathew nearly fell off his seat. The look of shock on his face was one of horror. Slowly standing, he started to tremble. That was it, the thing that had been troubling him ever since he'd seen the boorish soldier's injury! He remembered the day when he walked into the apothecary shop. The way Elizabeth had died, and how there had been nothing he could do to prevent her death. The words of Captain Overton ran through his mind.

'One of them seems to have been injured. He has left his sword behind, and there's acid splashed all around. He must have been badly burned.'

Could the man sleeping in the tent be one of the men he was looking for? The injuries fitted the type of wound that acid would leave. The man had received only rudimentary medical treatment for the injury. And his description fitted that given by Captain Overton.

Ethan stood up and took hold of Mathew by the arms, yelling, 'What's the matter, Mathew? Are you having a seizure? Shall I get help? What on earth's wrong?'

Mathew looked into Ethan's face as the initial shock began to wear off. He could feel his heart thudding in his chest as though it was trying to break through his ribs. His face had gone cold, and his head was swimming. He had been holding his breath for what seemed an age, his knees were feeling weak, and his ears were ringing. He allowed himself to be lowered back down to his seat by Ethan.

Once seated, Ethan held a mug to Mathew's mouth. 'Here take a drink, my friend,' he said. 'Steady now, that's the way.'

As Mathew opened his mouth, he released the air trapped in his lungs; his breath came in great gulps. Holding onto the mug of beer with both hands he took a couple of small sips. Slowly, the realisation of the situation came to Mathew: he had found one of the people who had killed Elizabeth and her father.

Of course, he had to be sure—he couldn't just come straight out and accuse the man. What would he do if he were wrong? Should he try holding on to him? No, he couldn't, because Captain Overton couldn't come and identify him.

As his mind raced, he became aware of Ethan's voice, as his friend stared at him.

'Mathew, what's wrong? Mathew? Mathew?'

Ethan's concerned features came into focus at last.

'I'm sorry, Ethan, I don't know what happened,' he lied. 'I must have had a bad turn. I'm all right now. Thank you, Ethan, thank you so much for your concern. I'll just sit a moment.'

Mathew took a few sips from the mug of beer. He needed time to think about what to do next. The soldier in his tent would be asleep for hours yet, so there was no need to rush into a decision.

Ethan offered Mathew something to eat. Mathew took the food and began to nibble at it while he thought over the problem.

The act of eating and drinking was the distraction that helped to bring Mathew's thoughts back to what was going on around him. Finishing his meal, he took his leave of his friend, explaining that he would talk to him later.

Back inside his surgery tent Mathew stared down at the man asleep on the bed. It would be remarkably easy to kill him, here and now.

No one was looking, no one would know. But what if someone came looking for him? One of the other killers perhaps? Yes, he thought, *the others.* Captain Overton had said that there was more than one killer. Mathew realised that he needed to get them all, and besides, could he really kill this man while he slept? What if he wasn't the person he was after?

Doubts and arguments battled back and forth through his mind. *Find the other men first*, he finally concluded, *and then make a decision on what to do*. He decided he had to get a message to the captain—he would be able to advise him.

The sick man slept through the night and was awake by the time Mathew entered the tent the next morning with his breakfast.

'Thank you, surgeon,' the patient told him. 'That was the first full night's sleep I've had since this happened.'

'What's your name?' Mathew asked as he passed him the food.

'Martins, Peter Martins.' Taking the buttered bread in his good hand, he tore a mouthful off with his teeth.

'You're going to have to stay here for a while, as I haven't finished treating you. I need to remove the bad blood from your infected arm in order to give the new blood your body will make a chance to heal the wound. You don't look like you've been eating very well, so I'll need to feed you up. You need to rebuild your strength for the wound to heal quickly.'

Mathew couldn't believe what he was saying. He was telling this man that he was going to help him to recover. The contradiction with the way he felt about him seemed so absurd that it made him smile.

Martins lay back down. This was better treatment than he had expected. Far better than that small damp ramshackle hut that he had been forced to sleep in on the edge of Beverley Westwood, or else to sleep in the open with the other soldiers. The pleasant lascivious thought of the young woman who had helped him while he was in the hut crossed his mind. *Oh well*, he thought to himself, *you can't have everything.*

'You may develop a fever if I can't stop the infection from getting worse,' Mathew told him. 'Once I'm sure you're out of danger, you can leave, but you'll need to come back each day to have your arm re-dressed.'

Martins nodded his acceptance.

Mathew looked down at the killer laying on the bed, taking in his features, his weather-beaten face, with its wrinkles of age beginning to show on his forehead and around the eyes. He had a fine scar, running from the front of the right side of his brow to his ear. He was a slender, muscular man in dirty well-worn clothes. But, his most striking features were his eyes, which were deep-set, dark and menacing.

They weren't the eyes of an intelligent man: there was no light or inquisitiveness behind them. This man was not a leader of others; he followed orders, took his pleasures where he found them and moved on, be that from place to place or from person to person. With no thought of the future or the past, he probably lived for the moment and took what he wanted without conscience or remorse, living more by animal instincts than human feelings.

284

Mathew left him to finish his food and shuddered. He couldn't begin to imagine what life must be like for this man—his existence was so far removed from his own understanding of what 'being human' was.

About an hour later, after a walk around the camp, Mathew returned to administer a clyster to empty the man's bowel and give him a *pear julep and barley ptisan*. By the time Mathew had finished giving him a '*cupping*' to the shoulder in order to draw away the bad humours from his arm—Martins had had enough of the discomfort and pain from the treatments and was getting uncooperative, so Mathew left him to rest.

While Mathew and Ethan sat eating their evening meal, Ethan leaned closer to Mathew. 'Have you heard the news?' he whispered.

'What might that be?' Mathew stopped eating to give Ethan his full attention, wondering what gem of gossip the cook had picked up.

'We're moving off soon—to Doncaster.' So saying, Ethan looked around, checking that there were no eavesdroppers.

When they met in Beverley, Colonel Duncombe had already told Mathew that there would be a move, but only to the Midlands.

'Where did you get that from?' asked Mathew, eager for news.

'I overheard the officers talking before I took their dinner into them. They stopped chatting while I was there, but some of them think the walls of these tents are enough to keep private everything they say.'

'If that's true, it'll be strange moving away from Beverley and Hull, there the only places I have known.' *Will I get to see my family again?* He had become accustomed to being able to drop in on them during his visits to Beverley.

Mathew wasn't looking forward to giving them the unwelcome news, but for now, he had the dilemma of what to do about Martins. Killing him while he slept would be the simplest way of dealing with him, but Mathew didn't feel that he could do it. And, besides, if someone was to miss him, they might ask some difficult questions.

He'd already been told there was someone else involved in Elizabeth's murder; Martins hadn't been working alone. The man's injuries would mean that he would have to keep returning to have his wound dressed. *Once Martins is back on his feet, I could follow him back to his friends.*

A couple of days later Martins was over his fever and able to return to his comrades. Instructing him to return every day to have his dressing changed, Mathew prepared to learn more about this man and his friends before taking any action.

The Royalist camp on Anlaby Common was spread out over the entire common. Mathew planned to follow Martins back to his friends. He had decided to do it a bit at a time so as not to arouse Martins' suspicions. He would make it look like he was tending to men in the camp, but at the same time, keep an eye on where Martins went. Once he had established the direction Martins would always take, he would find a reason to search that area of the camp and wait for Martins to pass-by again. Each day he would move ahead of Martins projected path and wait for him until he discovered Martins with his accomplices.

Mathew followed Martins the very next day. He carried his portable surgeon's kit in a large bag. The ruse was to give the impression that he was checking on the health of the men, looking for signs of camp fever or plague.

Martins slowly walked away from the surgeon's tent nursing his arm which hung in a sling, picking his way between the small groups of men who sat around communal campfires.

The camp had organised itself so that each discipline of soldier was grouped together. The cavalry was the furthest from Anlaby village, on the outermost part of the camp: they needed the space to corral, feed and exercise their horses. The pikemen and musketeers also kept themselves apart. The pikemen looked upon themselves as the 'gentlemen of the pike.' The pike is a noble weapon, once used by the Greeks and Romans was looked upon as senior to the musket. It took a man of stature and skill to wield the sixteen-foot ash pike and stand against a formation of charging horses.

The Musketeers were deemed to be the 'lower status' section of the army: it didn't take long to teach a man of limited ability to load and fire a musket, and working with gunpowder was dirty and dangerous. In fact, a musketeer could be in as much danger from his own gun, or from that of the man standing next to him, as from the enemy facing him. A poorly-made musket could explode when fired, or a 'hang-fire' might later go off unexpectedly, while the musketeer was trying to clear the miss-fired musket. His bandolier, holding twelve wooden bottles of gunpowder, could go off like a set of Roman candles if one of these had a badly fitting lid and a spark were to ignite its contents. Added to this, the Musketeers also needed to be close to the gunpowder store, to draw more gunpowder when it was needed. The musketeers were also responsible for protecting it from sabotage and from anyone careless enough to get too close to it with a naked flame. Finally, the officers had their tents closest to the village of Anlaby, not only to separate them from the men but because it was less distance for them to walk into the village alehouses. The baggage-train sprawled through the camp and was closest to the road. The camp, needing constant resupply, wagons would be coming and leaving every day.

Martins set off in the same direction each day after his arm had been re-dressed. Once Mathew was sure of the general direction that Martins headed, he decided that he would explore a little further, in order to find the area of the camp where Martins and his comrades lived.

The soldiers recognised Mathew as he passed amongst them and called him over to look at the minor ailments they suffered from, such as sore feet, splinters, small scalds from cooking spills, while many asked for 'medicinal' brandy to ease an aching joint or muscle. He enjoyed the encounters with the mainly good-natured men, but all the while he kept a lookout for Martins.

Eventually, he found him sitting on an upturned barrel, staring into a small cooking pot that was standing in the embers of a fire. As casually as he could, Mathew made his way closer to his quarry. Two men lay on the ground near him, and both were dressed in a similar fashion to that of Martins. Their clothes may have been just as dirty as everyone else's, but they actually seemed to fit their wearer, unlike the jackets that the rest of the soldiers had been issued with, which had been made as quickly as possible to a standard pattern.

Martins and his comrades weren't mixing socially with the other soldiers either: the three of them seemed to stay apart, whereas the other soldiers had set their camps up in groups of six or eight, depending on the size of the file of men in their division.

Mathew noticed that one man from this trio carried a large burn scar on the left side of his face; while stubble grew on the right side, the left cheek was clear of any hair growth.

The surgeon realised that these must be the men he was looking for, the men who were responsible for the death of his beloved Elizabeth and her father. Anger built up inside him, and a bead of sweat broke out on his brow, but he could do nothing, not now, not while he was alone. He wanted to yell 'Murderer!' but everyone would think him mad if he did. The frustration at not being able to act was getting too much for him.

He walked back into the surgeon's tent and dropped his kitbag on the table. 'Bastards!' he shouted, as he gave vent to his frustration at being powerless to do anything about Martins and his band. Seconds later, Ethan Goodman put his head through the door of the tent.

'You'll be needing a drink then and a tasty morsel, maybe?' Ethan Goodman disappeared as quickly as he had shown up.

Mathew sat on a stool to think. He couldn't match Martins in a fight, even if Martins only had one useful arm, for Elizabeth's killer was clearly far more skilled in weapon-craft than he was. Mathew cursed his lack of manly skills with weapons. He thought about poisoning or drugging Martins, then killing him while he slept, but Mathew was no cold-blooded murderer, no matter how much he would like to be as far as Martins was concerned.

He couldn't turn Martins and his confederates into Captain Hewitt for arrest, without having to explain why he knew who they were and why he was here. No, he would have to wait. With Mortimer's next trip to Hull, he would report finding them to Captain Overton; he would know what to do. For now, the best action he could take was to keep an eye on Martins and his pals. Mathew went to see Ethan. If his good friend Ethan Goodman couldn't cheer him up, no one could.

Chapter Twenty-Three

Mathew didn't delay in sending Mortimer to Hull to inform Captain Overton that Martins, Franks and Wilkes had been found. On his arrival, Mortimer made his way to Sir John Hotham in the Guildhall. Hotham read Mathew's latest intelligence report with interest.

'So,' Sir John mused, 'the King is thinking of moving to Doncaster, and Fletcher is on the trail of the Royalist spies that escaped from Hull.' That bit of information worried Hotham: If in spying on the king, Fletcher discovered that Hotham was still plotting against Parliament and the Hull Council, Captain Overton would turn on him instantly.

'This letter to Captain Overton, also tells of the success of the attack on the Anlaby camp, and suggests that a second attack would probably leave the camp undefendable,' Mortimer replied to his employer.

'Hmm. You will need to go to Beverley and inform the commander about the second attack as soon as you get back, but I want you to keep quiet about the surgeon. As long as you bring me his messages before they go to Overton, I can use them to my advantage,' said Sir John. 'I want you to go now. But, before you return to Anlaby, report back to me with Overton's reply to Surgeon Fletcher.'

'Yes, sir,' Mortimer acquiesced.

'See my clerk outside; he will give you money to get a return boat and repay your expenses. See to it that this

Surgeon Fletcher gets all he needs. I want him to feel secure while I make use of the information you bring me. I don't want anything to go wrong. I want to know everything this Surgeon Fletcher gets up to. What news do you have of Fletcher's family?'

'There is no news yet, sir. I will have to engage him in conversation and somehow win his trust. He has been very busy of late, but as soon as I am able, I will talk to him about his family and his plans for the future.'

'Make it quick, Mortimer, there may not be much time left. Now go.' Hotham shooed Mortimer away, still troubled at the possibility that there may be spies in Hull he was not aware of.

As Mortimer opened the door, Hotham shouted through to Bottomley to give his man enough money to see him back to Anlaby and to buy the supplies he needed. Bottomley gave Mortimer two 'half angel' gold coins to pay for his swift travel, plus five shillings in groats for food and lodging. Mortimer accepted the purse and hung it from his belt.

'Mind you don't waste that money,' Bottomley sneered. 'It all has to be accounted for.'

Mortimer sneered at Bottomley with an expression of such hatred that the clerk took a step backwards, turned and said no more, just giving Mortimer a sideways glance as he left the room.

Walking away from the Guildhall, Charles Mortimer headed for Captain Overton's office in the blockhouses on High Street. It tortured him to think he was betraying the master who had treated him fairly at all times. He stopped at a tavern before carrying on: he needed a drink to settle the nerves in his stomach.

While he was in the tavern, he had time to contemplate his disloyalty to Overton. He bought another drink. No matter how much he hated what he was doing, he had to protect his family, and do as Hotham ordered. Mortimer bought one more tankard of ale before setting off to find Robert Overton, and give him the letter from Mathew Fletcher. The surgeon was yet another person he had now betrayed. Captain Overton could wait a little longer. He finished his ale, then, ordered rum: he was going to need a lot of courage for what he was going to do.

After Mortimer had had a few more drinks and before he got too drunk to visit Robert Overton, he finally left the tavern and decided to visit the market to start buying the supplies he needed to take back for the surgeon. That way he could walk off the worst effects of the ale and rum before heading to his meeting.

A pie would help, he thought, as he spotted a pieman at the edge of the market. The delicious mutton pie, heavy with meat and thick gravy was flavoured with herbs and tasted good. Mortimer finished the pie quickly; he had been hungrier than he realised. He shoved the last remnants of pastry into his mouth and licked the gravy from his fingers, and let out a loud belch. Eating the pie had helped to clear his head. Now, with a full stomach and the courage of the drink inside him, he felt up to the task of facing his master.

The guard at the blockhouse entrance waved him through with a nod of recognition, which he returned. He made his way to Overton's quarters and, finding the office empty, decided he would wait, and took a seat by the door. Leaning against the wall, it wasn't long before the effects of the alcohol and the pie started to make him drowsy, and before long he was asleep. He had no idea how long he'd been dozing on the stool, but the next thing he knew, he was on the floor, having been tipped off the stool. Captain Overton was sitting at his desk, and the sergeant of the guard was looking down at him.

'You drunken bastard, how dare you fall asleep outside the Captain's office?' the sergeant snarled, the sergeant grabbed him roughly by the shoulder and hauled him to his feet.

'I'm sorry, Captain, it's been a long day, and I was tired. I promise I won't let it happen again.' Mortimer fumbled for his words of apology as he tidied himself.

'Thank you, Sergeant, that will be all,' Captain Overton dismissed the man, and then looked Mortimer up and down. 'This had better not happen again. You are on an important mission, and I need you sober.' The disappointment was evident in Overton's face and voice.

'What news have you, from Surgeon Fletcher?'

Mortimer passed over the letter. The captain read the report without speaking. Putting the paper down, he looked hard at the dishevelled courier.

'It seems that our raid on Anlaby was very successful. With the outbreak of disease in Beverley, their men will be weak and their numbers depleted.' Overton reclined in his chair, thinking. 'We need to take advantage of the situation while they are vulnerable. I will arrange for another attack on the camp as soon as possible. If we are as successful as we were last time, we may be able to defeat the King before he leaves for Doncaster. You must warn Mathew; tell him to find somewhere safe to hide or, better still, he must find an excuse to get out of the camp for a few days until the attack is over.' Overton was getting excited by the idea of another successful attack on the Anlaby camp. 'I want you to go now and get back to Anlaby as fast as possible to warn him.'

Charles Mortimer returned to the Guildhall to repeat to Sir John Hotham the message he was taking back to Surgeon Fletcher. He left the bulky items he had bought in the hall and carried the expensive smaller things in saddlebags, which were now hanging over his shoulder. He entered Bottomley's office without knocking, placing his saddlebags on Bottomley's desk, shoving aside papers to do so, and putting them right in front of the little man, who was scratching at a document with a quill pen. He looked the clerk straight in the eye as he said,

'I spent your money on expensive medical supplies. Most of them are poisonous if you don't know how to handle them correctly, so do please examine the contents. Please make sure that I spent your money wisely.'

Bottomley shuffled out from behind his desk, muttering under his breath, giving Mortimer the evil eye.

'I hope you're wasting Sir's time, he's a vengeful man,' Bottomley sneered. 'I'd look forward to a trip to Scorborough, to throw your family out on the street or have them all locked up for stealing.' Bottomley sniggered cruelly, then had to duck quickly out of the way, as Mortimer's fist flashed past his ear.

Bottomley reached the door to Sir John's office, knocked quickly and entered before waiting for a reply, in case Mortimer was following up his first attack with another one.

'Charles Mortimer to see you, sir,' Bottomley puffed out.

Mortimer brushed roughly past the man, stepping on his toes as he entered Hotham's office. Bottomley squirmed in pain and left the room.

'Well?' said Hotham.

'Captain Overton is planning another attack on the Anlaby camp. He believes that another successful attack will break the king's resolve on blockading Hull and could lead to the King's defeat.

'Good, good. When Colonel Duncombe finds out about the next attack, he can prepare an adequate defence. That will be the end for Overton, as for his surgeon friend I may be able to turn him to work for me, but regardless, I will have proved my loyalty to the King.' Hotham rubbed his hands together in anticipation of the revenge he was about to take on Captain Robert Overton.

Hotham wrote quickly, sanded the ink when he had finished and carefully folded the letter, top and bottom to the middle and then folded the sides in to make a neat square. He melted a large amount of sealing wax over the folded ends of the paper and thrust his seal into the centre of it.

'I now want you to go to Beverley first,' Sir John ordered. 'This letter goes into the hands of the Earl of Newcastle and no one else. Do you understand? No one else!'

Mortimer took the letter and turned to leave.

'Don't let me down, Mortimer,' Sir John called out a warning as he walked away. 'Remember, your family need you.'

As Mortimer left Hotham's office, Bottomley was waiting for him.

'I do enjoy the little trips into the countryside, especially to Scorborough,' Bottomley muttered, just loud enough for

Mortimer to hear. Mortimer didn't react. He took hold of his saddlebags and dragged them across Bottomley's desk, knocking the inkwell and papers off the desk and onto the floor.

'Oops, sorry!' Mortimer called out. 'I do hope those papers weren't anything important.' He gave a brief nod to Bottomley in a mock sign of respect and strode confidently out to the hallway, while Bottomley scrabbled on the floor to retrieve his ink sodden papers.

At Hull quay, Mortimer found a boat taking goods to York that would drop him at Howden, where he'd left his horse. The tide was coming in, and the ship set sail soon after he was aboard. With the wind in its sails and the advantage of the incoming tide, the vessel made good headway up the Humber and, within a few hours it was turning into the River Ouse, with the ferry crossing at Howden soon coming into sight.

By nightfall, Mortimer would be in Beverley.

Chapter Twenty-Four

Lieutenant Colonel Duncombe arrived from Beverley to supervise the defence of the Anlaby camp himself. 'Captain Hewitt, how are the new men I sent you settling in?' were his first words to his company commander.

'Very well, sir,' Hewitt replied. 'I've set them to work already. I will show you the preparations we are making. I can only hope they will be ready before the attack comes.'

'My guess,' Colonel Duncombe informed Captain Hewitt, 'is that Overton will make another assault in the manner of the first one. I want you to send riders out into the countryside to watch for his forces leaving Hull; I want to be sure from which direction they will come. These observers must be your smallest, lightest, best riders on the fastest mounts you have. They are to be given no weapons and must carry as little weight as possible. They will need to be able to ride like the wind to bring back news of Overton's departure and direction of attack.'

'Yes, sir, I will see to it immediately,' replied Hewitt. Turning to a lieutenant, he dispatched him to arrange everything the colonel had requested.

'Now, Hewitt,' continued Colonel Duncombe, 'show me these defences you are preparing.'

Captain Hewitt led the colonel on a walk around the perimeter of the camp. On the northern and southern sides of the encampment was something that resembled a giant hedgehog: twelve-foot long posts that were being driven into the ground at an angle of forty-five degrees, pointing outwards from the camp. Once secured, their tops were being sharpened into vicious points.

'As you can see colonel, the defensive spikes are to deter cavalry from entering the camp and thereby channel the attack to come along the road which runs through the camp from east to west. This was the direction that Overton used on the last attack. The baggage train has been brought inside the cordon of spikes but is still dangerously close to the exposed ends of the lines of defence, but we have nowhere else to put it, and not enough time to extend the spikes around it. Overton's attack, Colonel, will meet our prepared musketeers and pikemen. The woods to the north and south of the common, along with the cordon of spikes we are setting up, will funnel his attack into one of two prepared directions. This will be like the French attack on the English at Agincourt, only Overton's cavalry will meet our musketeers.'

'You have done well, Captain,' Colonel Duncombe congratulated him. 'Let us retire, for I am hungry and thirsty. Keep the men working—let them know that their lives depend on these defences working. After we have eaten, I will see your men at drill. I want to be sure they are well disciplined in their arms.'

'It will be my pleasure, Colonel. I have asked our sutler to produce a special dinner in your honour. All the camp officers will be there so you will be able to question them about their progress in preparing for the attack.'

The two officers walked back through the camp to the officers' pavilion, where Ethan Goodman had prepared a splendid repast for the assembled officers. In the centre of the pavilion stood a large table covered with a rich Persian carpet, on top of which was a fine linen tablecloth. Places had been set for all the officers.

Pewter plates were at each place with fine glassware and white linen napkins. Next to each place setting lay the eating implements of the officers who were to dine. It was a chance for the officers to show off their finest cutlery.

The officers, recognising their own place settings, stood behind their chairs as Colonel Duncombe and Captain Hewitt entered the pavilion. The colonel was shown to his place at the centre of the table, while the other officers stood to wait for their commanding officer to be seated first before they could sit. As they all took their seats, the stewards, who had been standing quietly to one side, stepped forward with silver jugs, and as the officers held their glasses aloft, filled them with expensive wine.

Outside the pavilion, watching for a signal from one of the stewards, Ethan Goodman waited to bring in the dishes he had been preparing all morning. With his limited equipment at the sutler's tent and the complications of cooking outdoors, he hoped that the assembled officers would be grateful for what they were about to receive. There were Spinach Tansies, Tench with currents, cinnamon, rosemary and breadcrumbs, butter beans, parsnips with black pepper and vinegar, to be followed by apple fritters with sherry syllabub. One by one the stewards came to collect the dishes he had prepared and then disappeared back into the pavilion with the trays of rich food. Ethan had done his best with what he had, and what he had been able to obtain and it was too late now for him to worry about it. He would hear from Captain Hewitt later if they had been disappointed.

Colonel Duncombe had ordered that Bartram and Jenkins, the two Beverley surgeons, to join Mathew in Anlaby, and to give assistance dealing with the wounded after the night's attack. Mathew set Bartram and Jenkins's to work preparing his surgeon's tent and medical equipment, get everything ready for the casualties to come. They worked hard all day, preparing *splints, splenia, bandages, medicated plegits, and emplasters.* The sky was dull and overcast as Mathew commandeered two soldiers to cut wood and store it under wagons to keep it dry. If it was going to rain he would need plenty of wood to keep the fire going to heat water. By around six on the clock, they were ready, and Mathew took Bartram and Jenkins over to Ethan Goodman for their evening meal. There was plenty of beer, but only bread, cheese and some leftover gammon from dinner time to be had.

'Orders from the colonel,' Ethan told them. 'Everything is to be stored away, except the essentials. He's keeping the men working until it's too dark to continue, and then he'll give them a rest before the attack he's expecting tonight. But, he's gonna look pretty stupid if it don't come.' Ethan was not happy about having to store all his sutler's equipment for just one night, knowing he would have to unpack it all again in the morning.

Mathew sat and listened to Ethan telling Bartram and Jenkins all about his time in York cooking great meals for his wealthy clients. But the senior surgeon was preoccupied, wondering what had happened to Mortimer. He hadn't returned from his visit to Hull, after delivering Mathew's information regarding a second attack on the Anlaby camp.

Had Mortimer been captured? How had the colonel known to prepare for another attack so soon after the first one? If it was not Mortimer, who had given away the intelligence, he had sent to Hull? It was big a coincidence that Colonel Duncombe was here, planning for the coming attack, that he had suggested should take place as soon as possible, and for Mortimer to be missing at the same time. Had Mortimer been found out, captured and tortured to get the information? If that had been the case, why hadn't he been arrested? If Mortimer had betrayed him, surely he would have been by now. It didn't add up. Where was Mortimer?

Mathew sipped at his beer, while Ethan bored his captive audience with his tales from York. His nerves were taut, he was more scared than he had ever been in his life, but he couldn't escape. He wondered if Bartram and Jenkins had been brought in to replace him, once he had been arrested. Maybe they were waiting until after the attack to detain him because they knew they were going to need his help with the wounded? He was trapped with no one to advise him, no one to share his anxiety with.

In the meantime they enjoyed Ethan's jolly distractions, the three men and their genial host stayed together at the fireside as the night drew on, Ethan keeping them supplied with small beer and tasty morsels.

Mathew didn't want to be alone until he had discovered what had happened to Mortimer, and more specifically if he'd been exposed as a spy. As the darkness fell, so did the rain, just the odd spot at first which they could feel on bare skin, then steadily increasing, making it uncomfortable to sit in the open next to the fire. They took shelter under the awning of the surgeon's tent. The cooler air brought by the rain sent a shiver down Mathew's spine as he looked out across the camp, where darkness had set in completely. The preparations for the defence of the camp having ceased, men now went in search of food and rest.

Just before midnight, Captain Overton led his officers out through the Myton Gate to the waiting troopers, who were formed up into their squadrons ready for another attack on the Anlaby Camp. A light drizzle had set in, which was common in the counties close to the North Sea.

There was no wind, and the fine rain fell straight downwards from the low clouds. Overton looked up at the clouds, 'this type of drizzle is likely to last all night,' he thought. It was a deceptive rain: it penetrated clothing by steady accumulation. It added weight to the riders as their clothing became saturated, and little by little, it would add to the weight the horses had to carry. It was a depressing rain that didn't vary in its direction or intensity. While it would muffle the sound of their approaching attack, it would make for a miserable ride for both man and horse.

However, the confidence of the men was high, and a cheer rose as Captain Overton rode passed the assembled riders. The troopers slapped their swords held in their scabbards, by way of a salute to their leader. Overton blushed at his unexpected greeting, thankful that the darkness hid his embarrassment. Nevertheless, the cheer from the troopers appealed to his vanity, and he straightened his back and held his head erect as he rode slowly to the head of the column, water dripping from his broad-brimmed hat. Overton's plan was going to be similar to the one he had used on the first attack. He didn't expect it to be as successful as the first—the Royalist camp would have learnt from that mistake—but he did anticipate a successful raid, breaking the spirit of the officers and men who were continuing their blockade of Hull. As he moved along the road, the formed-up squadrons of horse fell in behind him.

The column set off in the direction of Cottingham, first, then on to Kirk Ella, finally coming to the same spot where they had waited prior to their first attack. As before, Captain Overton formed the cavalry into a line, two riders deep, so that they could sweep through the Royalist camp. As he rode across the front of the line of waiting troopers, he wished them luck and told them to pray for God's blessing. Cantering back to join his fellow officers ahead of the centre of the line, he took one final long look over his shoulder at the troopers standing ready in the rain, steam rising from the flanks of the horses, every man's attention focused on him, waiting for the signal to attack. He gave his final orders to the officers. Each captain was to lead their squadron, and Captain Jackson was to have the honour of the centre. Overton would take the right side of the camp and Maynard the left. When the attack was finished, each officer would assemble his men on the road to Hull, after which they would return home together.

The surgeon stood under the awning, listening to the raindrops playing their melancholy tune on the canvas over his head. It was getting late, and they were tired, but they couldn't retire, for the darkness and the chill rain seemed to be like a portent of the oncoming danger. There were no boisterous noises coming from the men in the camp as would have been normal on any other night, just a low constant murmur as men huddled under cloaks, cassocks and blankets trying to keep dry and to stay warm, unable to sleep. The Musketeers stayed close to the tents where their muskets, powder and match were being stored to keep them dry. The pikemen had left their pikes close to the positions where they would need to put up the main defence of the camp. All the officers, now in the colonel's pavilion, seemed oblivious to the night's forthcoming peril as they drank wine and shared jolly conversation.

Late in the night, as though the hounds of hell were chasing him, a rider came bursting into the camp. He didn't stop at the camp entrance; he simply rode his horse hard up to the colonel's pavilion before reining it in, its hooves slipping in the mud, as the rider jumped from the saddle, and almost tumbling into the tent. His arrival didn't go unnoticed by the rest of the camp. By the time the officers emerged from the colonel's pavilion, the rank and file were already starting to rouse themselves, getting ready for their expected orders.

The Drum Major on duty outside the officers' pavilion beat the call, the rest of the regimental drummers joining him, the drum beats sounding flat and dead in the damp air. Men all around the camp threw off their protection from the rain. The pikemen ran down to their defensive positions at the western end of the camp, while the musketeers gathered their guns, bandoliers and match. The rain continued to fall relentlessly, and the musketeers wondered how they would be able to keep their match lit and their powder dry.

The musketeers formed up in divisions of twenty-four men, each under the command of a sergeant or senior corporal. Some were marched down to where the pikemen were already in their defensive positions and placed into one long line in front of the pikemen; the musketeers were given the order to make ready and kneel when loaded. With muskets loaded and their match lit at both ends, in the hope of keeping it alight in the rain, the musketeers waited down on one knee, water soaking into their breeches and dripping from their broad-brimmed hats. The pikemen lowered their pikes into the defensive position over the heads of the kneeling musketeers, ready for an attack by horse. They waited for the onslaught that was about to come out of the darkness and the rain. Along the line, the occasional man retched with fear, but all else was silent apart from the sound of the rain.

Captain Overton gave the order for the attack. The glow from the distant campfires could be seen through the haze of the rain, which gave the scene an unreal, dreamlike appearance. The horses started forward, steady at first, but gathering pace, men and horses tense, wanting the night to be over with so they could return to their warm beds and stables. The gentle downward slope of the terrain helped to keep the momentum going as some horses began to slip.

Faster and faster, they raced towards the camp, as the riders remembered their success in the previous attack. The speed of the horses caused the rain to beat hard against the faces of their riders, almost blinding both horse and rider. As they drew closer to the camp, they found themselves bunching together. Unbeknown to the attackers they were being funnelled closer together, into one point on the camp perimeter, by the obstacles that had been set up earlier in the day. Consequently, the line of attack that should have been two horses deep was thickening as the riders on the outside were forced inwards. Captain Overton realised what was happening and reined in his horse, calling to those closest to him to do the same, but the noise from the horses' hooves and the sound-deadening effect of the rain meant that only those closest to him heard his order.

The rest had given their horses their heads and charged relentlessly towards the camp.

The sound of rattling horse tack and sword scabbards came first, then the mud-deadened sound of the horses' hooves. Sergeants shouted the order to 'Present' as out of the darkness and rain the attackers came into view. Musketeers brought their muskets to their shoulders ready to fire.

The order came: 'Fire!'

A ragged volley of flame shot out from the muskets sheltering under the defensive pikes. Horses and men could be heard screaming. Some fell, but the Parliamentarian horse kept coming. Some had seen the pikemen waiting for them and tried to rein in their horses, but the muddy ground and the downward slope gave the horses' hooves no purchase to manoeuvre. The riders pulled hard on the horses' reins, forcing the animals to sit back on their haunches, their forelegs stretched out straight before them, but they couldn't slow down or stop. Men and horse impaled themselves on the sixteen-foot ash pikes with their razor-sharp steel points. The pikes snapped as more and more horses were forced forwards.

The Musketeers at the front of the line and below the defensive pikes were crushed under dead and dying horses. The bodies and necks of the horses were ripped open, entrails steaming on the ground. The carefully planned defensive line broke; Parliamentary horses and riders

307

entered the camp in scattered groups. But most of the attacking force had come to a halt at the barrier of death that lay before them at the camp entrance. Those that could turned and fled back into the night.

A dozen Parliamentarian troopers made their way into the centre of the camp and found themselves confronted by a small division of musketeers, who fired into their midst. Six of the riders were dislodged from their mounts, while the remainder brought their horses under control and, before the Musketeers could reload, changed direction and headed for the nearest camp perimeter, away from the trap they had found themselves in. The large fires outside the surgeon's and sutler's tent showed that going in that direction was probably the quickest way out, being close up to the camp's perimeter. Working their way through the defensive spikes on the outside of the camp would now be easier on the way out since their points were facing away from the riders.

There were sounds of battle coming from the western side of the camp, and growing louder. Mathew watched as the Parliamentarian troopers were attacked in the middle of the camp, and how the remainder were heading in his direction. As the riders approached, Mathew, Bartram and Jenkins hid beneath the closest wagon.

The six riders came storming from the centre of the camp, wildly discharging their pistols into the surrounding tents, hoping for a chance kill. They drew their swords ready to kill anyone who tried to prevent their escape. The riders, spinning their mounts around looked for a way past the wagons when they were suddenly stopped by a volley of shots which rang out from the far side of the sutler's cooking fire. The musketeers assigned to protecting the baggage-train had spotted the Parliamentarian troopers breaking through the camp's defences and anticipated their line of progress through the tent line. They had been formed up ready to fire as soon as the troopers presented themselves as an easy target.

All the riders were dismounted. Two horses lay mortally wounded, screaming and thrashing their legs around in shock and pain. The Royalist musketeers reloaded their guns and left to find other mounted Parliamentarians that might have broken through the camp's defences, leaving the fallen troopers where they lay.

While the riders were down, Ethan chose that very moment to step into the light thrown out by the campfire. But three of the dismounted troopers, only stunned by their fall from their horses, got to their feet. Gathering up their swords, all three focused on Ethan Goodman, the bloodlust of battle was upon them, and they needed an enemy on which to vent it.

From his hiding place below the wagon, Mathew was hidden by the shadows created by the wagon above him; he watched the three troopers approach Ethan. He wanted to help his friend, but he had no weapon and fear held him rigid. He felt his heart pounding in his chest, as the enemy riders closed on Ethan, he could hear his blood pulsing in his ears. He could feel himself becoming hot and sweaty and start to tremble, then his vision narrowed to slim tunnels of intense light before his vision disappeared altogether.

When his vision returned he was standing by the campfire, a sword in his hand and three dead Parliamentarian troopers lay close by. He dropped to his knees, letting the bloodied sword fall away. Ethan Goodman was the first to reach him, followed by Bartram and Jenkins. Mathew stayed on his knees trembling, while Ethan, Bartram and Jenkins looked at him in amazement. Ethan and Bartram bent down and, taking an arm each, lifted Mathew to his feet, 'You need a stiff drink, lad,' Ethan said as he led Mathew to the surgeon's tent.

'Brandy, get him some brandy,' Ethan Goodman ordered. Jenkins fumbled amongst the pots, jars and jugs on a table, finding a bellarmine containing brandy. He filled a horn cup and placed it in Mathew's trembling hands.

'What happened?' Mathew asked. His voice sounded hoarse and dry, his vocal chords strained.

'You don't know? Can't you remember?' Jenkins said in a disbelieving voice.

Mathew sipped the brandy. 'The last thing I remember I was under the wagon. I was shit scared. I saw riders shot from their horses, then as Ethan stepped into the light of the fire some of the riders got to their feet. I thought Ethan was going to die. Finally, everything went black.'

'Well, fuck me rigid!' Ethan exclaimed. 'I've never 'eard nowt like that afore. You really don't know what you did, do you? You bloody killed 'em, that's what you did! You came out from under that wagon. I thought, *you silly bastard, they'll kill us both now.* You picked up a sword from one of the dead 'uns and sliced it across the nearest trooper to you. As he went down the other two turned and went for you. The big 'un swung his sword at your head, I thought you were going to lose it, but quicker than anything I've ever seen, you blocked his blade with your sword and, with a short back slice, you took 'im in the throat. Blood sprayed everywhere. The last one came at you at a run. His sword was held over his head, ready to split you in two.

Cool as anything, you stepped to the side, shoving your sword into 'is heart and it was over. You stood there for a second or two, then dropped to your knees and let the sword fall away. It was all over in a flash. I'd be dead, but for you.'

Bartram and Jenkins nodded in agreement. 'That's how it happened,' Bartram added. 'As God is my witness, I've never seen anything like it.'

The four men didn't have long to dwell on the events that had just unfolded, as the first of the casualties were brought to the surgeon's tent.

At the start of the attack, Captain Overton sat astride his horse full of hope and with undoubted success in mind. With him, three hundred men had set forth to strike the Anlaby camp. But now, only ten minutes later he was ordering his Cornet to play 'He gave the order to the young officer with a heavy heart, knowing he had lost many good men. The young officer stood up in his stirrups and blew the 'recall' to bring back the troopers to their officers. The lad, not much past his eighteenth birthday, sounded the recall again and again. The poignant notes betraying the emotion of what the young soldier had just seen; there was a tremble in the notes as they carried shrill and mournful through the night and rain.

Overton looked down on the camp to see riders already returning, others hearing the cornet's recall, glad to be pulled away from the carnage at the edge of the camp. Captain Overton wondered where God had been that night. Men had prayed to Him to keep them safe. Had *God* been busy elsewhere or turned His back on them all, he wondered bitterly.

It was obvious that the camp had been ready for them. Not just better fortified than usual, they actually *knew* that an attack was coming.

So who had betrayed them?

Was Mathew Fletcher dead or alive?

More men arrived from out of the darkness. Lieutenant Maynard appeared by Overton's side. The look on his face telling of the death he had seen that night.

'We'll go home to lick our wounds, gentlemen, let us leave this place.' Overton turned his horse towards Hull. 'If the others are coming they will find us on the road.'

It rained all the way back to Hull, with Captain Overton leading a disordered column back through the bar into the town. The day would dawn to the wailing of many a widow and orphan that morning.

He felt ashamed: he had let his men down and lost so many lives for nothing.

Chapter Twenty-Five

Mathew, Bartram, Jenkins and Ethan worked all through the night. One after another the wounded were brought to Mathew's table, many with broken limbs, some of which were damaged beyond repair, requiring amputation.

The cauterising iron hissed continually as it was applied to wounds they would normally have stitched, but they didn't have the time to do so because of the number of injured. Mathew would never have managed to deal with the number of wounded without Bartram and Jenkins's help, and he still could have done with more assistance.

They were running out of medicines and bandages. Ethan Goodman worked tirelessly, keeping them supplied with hot water, and, when needed, he would hold a man down while his arm or leg was removed. Colonel Duncombe appeared once at the entrance to the tent, looked in, and left without interrupting.

Outside in the rain, men lay on the wet, cold earth waiting to been seen, many of them dying before they could be helped. These unfortunates could feel their blood leaking into the grass, before drifting into unconsciousness, then dying silently, alone, in the chill of the coming dim morning light. And still, it rained.

The rain finally stopped around mid-morning, the clouds slowly breaking up, allowing through a weak, hazy sunlight. A steady breeze came in from the south-west, bringing with it slightly warmer air.

By early afternoon the last of the wounded had been seen. All four men were exhausted. The attack that had lasted minutes had left many men maimed for life; many would need weeks to recover from their wounds, some might need months. The long process of recovery would now start. However, the work of the surgeons was not over, for the wounded would still need constant care and would be looked on as a burden to the army. Mathew, summoning up the last of his ebbing strength, made his way through the camp in search of Captain Hewitt, finding him directing a group of soldiers digging a mass grave.

'Good day to you, Captain, may I speak with you a moment?' Mathew asked.

'Ah, good day to you also, Master Surgeon, a sorry night's work, I guess,' came his response as he turned to give Mathew his full attention.

Mathew noted his muddy and bloodstained clothes and a shallow cut to the side of his face that had stopped bleeding but needed to be cleaned and stitched.

'We have dealt with the wounded as best as may be expected,' Mathew explained, 'but we are very low on medicines and other essentials. The wounded will need more than I can supply. I have need to go to Beverley to obtain more. I would also like to ask if I can return with four women nurses and my sister-in-law, as she is a fine apothecary and nurse. With your permission, I would like her to assist me in my work. Having the nurses to help us will free Bartram, Jenkins and me more time to healing the men, rather than us having to do the unskilled but vital jobs, such as fetching them piss pots and feeding them.'

Mathew had an ulterior motive for speaking to the officer, didn't need to ask permission to go to Beverley: as senior surgeon, he had every right to go and replenish his stores and hire help as he saw fit, but he needed to know if the officers had discovered that he was the spy in the camp. Captain Hewitt's friendliness and attitude of respect towards him, reassured him that the officers weren't aware of his clandestine activities. It was a few seconds before the thought occurred to him, but he suddenly realised that he had never been addressed as Master Surgeon before. He liked the feeling. Captain Hewitt agreed to his request.

'May I also suggest that the more seriously wounded be billeted in the cottages close by the southern edge of the common? The locals could provide them with shelter and food while they recover.' Mathew knew that if the more seriously wounded men did not get shelter from the weather, they would be dead in days.

'All good suggestions,' Hewitt replied. 'I will arrange it with the colonel. I will send men to you later, to transport the wounded you have selected. Is there anything else you need?' The captain became concerned, losing interest in Mathew as he noticed that the men digging the giant grave were beginning to ease up on their work, while he had been distracted.

'No, thank you, Captain, that's all I need for now.' It seemed clear that no order had been made to arrest Mathew, but he wondered how they had known to strengthen the defences of the camp on that particular night.

Turning back towards his tent, he had no time for sleep: wounded men lay everywhere, some asleep, some unconscious, many demanding water or crying out in pain. He looked at the wrecked bodies he and the other surgeons had repaired. Mathew, Bartram and Jenkins carried on working tirelessly seeing to their patients' needs, while Ethan made broth to feed them.

Overton, Maynard, Meldrum, Hotham and Pelham met in Overton's rooms.

'How many did we lose last night?' asked Overton.

'Twelve from my squadron,' Maynard volunteered.

'I lost sixteen, and Captain Jackson lost twenty-seven men,' Meldrum added. 'He lost his own life trying to protect his men.'

Overton hung his head in shame. 'How did they know we were coming?'

'Why was I not informed of the attack last night?' Captain Hotham asked tersely.

'Because we couldn't all go. We could not leave the town undefended.' Speaking in a tone that established his seniority, Overton spoke the truth, but he didn't make common the knowledge that he knew Captain Hotham and his father to be untrustworthy. Overton couldn't be sure if either one of the Hotham's had got wind of last night's attack and somehow informed the king's men of Overton's intent.

Overton's orders from Parliament had been clear: leave Sir John Hotham to govern the population of Hull. He was to take command of the garrison and keep the town secure for Parliament. Nonetheless, he wished he could arrest Sir John Hotham and his son, and remove what he suspected was their intervention in undermining the town's security.

'I should have been better prepared,' Captain Overton confessed. 'I should have had more intelligence on the camp's defences before we attacked. The failure is my fault, gentlemen. I let you down. I beg your forgiveness.'

Secretly, Overton wondered if Mathew Fletcher had deliberately misled him.

Colonel Duncombe gathered his officers in his pavilion. 'Well, gentlemen, we survived the night—just,' he announced to them. 'It was costly, but we repelled the attack. A lesson learnt, I think. We will maintain a vigilant watch for further intrusions. You all put up a valiant defence. I don't think the East Yorkshire men will be back in a hurry; you are to be congratulated.'

The assembled officers in the colonel's pavilion raised their glasses and gave a loud, 'Huzzar.'

Mathew told Bartram and Jenkins he was going to Beverley to get the supplies they were running short on. Bartram was the first to voice his disapproval, saying, 'When are we going to get the chance to visit our families? You come and go as you please. But we're stuck here, not knowing what's happening to our kith and kin, just because you got Colonel Duncombe to conscript us in to help!' Bartram's words of complaint were bitter and angry.

Mathew could see his point, but he wasn't going to give in. He told them about the extra help he was bringing back from Beverley so they would all be able to enjoy more free time. Mathew needed to get away from the camp to think. The stress of his active part in the skirmish and the worry of not knowing how the attack on Anlaby had been discovered was constantly on his mind. He had to get away from the camp; his colleagues would just have to put up with it, for now.

'I'll speak to the colonel about releasing you both when I return,' Mathew told the griping surgeon. 'I should be able to manage with just the nurses in a day or two. Just keep an eye on these men for now, and I promise to do what I can for you both when I return. You've both done a great job, and I couldn't have managed without you. Thank you, gentlemen, I will be back as soon as I can.'

Hoping he'd said enough to appease them both, he set off.

Arriving at his family home, Mathew rode into the yard and found his father and Henry shaping the spokes of yet another wagon wheel. The two men welcomed the excuse to down tools and greet Mathew. While Henry stabled Mathew's horse, his father took him in to see Mary.

'Look, Mary, Mathew is safe,' William Fletcher announced. 'We heard about the attack on Anlaby the other night, and we prayed for your safety. All we heard was that the camp had been attacked and many men on both sides had been lost. Rumours are flying around Beverley of a battle that lasted most of the night, with a great loss of life. Come, Mathew, sit and tell us what happened. Mary, bring us some beer, would you please?'

Mathew sat at the table opposite his father, just as Henry came in from the yard. Mary placed a jug of beer in the centre of the table with four tankards and sat down next to Mathew. William and Henry were eager for first-hand news of the battle.

'There is nothing much to tell,' the returning brother told them. 'It was over so quickly. It was dark and raining, and I didn't see much at all. The events of the night must have been greatly exaggerated, but there were many killed and wounded.' Mathew went quiet for a moment as he remembered what he had been told of his exploits during the battle, and of the many wounded men, he'd had to deal with during the remainder of that night and the following day.

His silence was broken by his father, 'you look tired, son, was it that bad?' His father noticed the strained look on his son's face as the memories of that night reappeared as flashing images before his eyes.

'I didn't see much of the fighting, it was dark, and I was safe with the baggage-train. It was later, when the wounded started coming for treatment, that I—we—couldn't save them all, there were just too many.' Mathew's voice faltered as he remembered the men lying on the ground around his surgeon's tent. Left where they had been placed by soldiers who were glad it was not they who were injured. The wounded, no longer the responsibility of their officers, had then become the responsibility of the surgeon.

Changing the subject, 'I've come to town for more medical supplies and some nurses,' Mathew went on. 'I need to arrange a constant supply of bandages, ointments, unguents, balms and salves—the men get through so much I can't make them quick enough. I've come to ask Mary to help me if she is willing.'

Mathew turned to look at her. 'Mary, you are skilled at making many of the medicines I need, and I will be able to pay you well for your help. If Father and Henry can spare you, you could bring the medicines to me at Anlaby. It will not be for long; I don't think the camp could hold out against another attack. But you must not say a word to anyone about what you see there. If the colonel got to hear any loose talk, it could be dangerous for you all.'

319

Mary looked at the faces around the table, all waiting to hear what she would say.

'It's up to you, lass,' the older man volunteered to break the silence. 'Henry can accompany you on the journey when you make deliveries to Mathew. You keep the house nice and clean, but I see the sadness in your face every day since we lost Charles. Helping Mathew may help lift your melancholy.'

This was what Mary had secretly desired all along: to work with Mathew, to heal people as he did, to feel important. She no longer felt the guilt of how this situation had come about, and the terrible circumstances of Charles's death. She knew what she wanted.

'If it's what *you* want, then I cannot refuse.' Her eyes darted from father to son. At that moment both men believed she was following their bidding.

At dinner that evening in the officers' pavilion, Colonel Duncombe addressed the officers.

'It has been decided to abandon the Anlaby camp. It is too close to Hull for it to remain a defendable position. I am bringing all the men back to the main camp on the Beverley Westwood. Until I receive further orders from the king, we will send out patrols from there. It is time to start breaking camp.'

On Mathew's return to Anlaby, he arranged with the company sergeant for a wagon and driver to be made available for the wounded. His plan was to move the more seriously injured men into the village homes around Anlaby

Common. Mathew had agreed with each household that they were to keep an account of the expenses incurred in caring and nursing for the maimed soldiers in their care. The costs were to be later recovered from the Mayor of Beverley, once the injured soldiers had recuperated.

It was common for the costs of caring for the wounded to be exaggerated, resulting in the homeowners making a profit from the care they offered. However, the men who were left in the care of the villagers of Anlaby were those who were least likely to survive their injuries, and if the soldier died, the care-giving householder would not get paid. Unfortunately for many soldiers, care on these terms amounted to a death sentence at the hands of those entrusted with their welfare: for there was no incentive to feed a man who may die anyway.

The nurses Mathew needed to hire were to be four destitute widows; this would be an opportunity for them to earn fourpence a day, for washing, feeding and tending to the needs of the less seriously injured men, the ones that could possibly return to service once they had recovered from their injuries.

Mortimer wandered the streets of Beverley, pondering on his dilemma of what he should do next. It was common knowledge that the attack on Anlaby had been repelled, but at a high cost to both sides. He had informed Colonel Duncombe of the attack as Sir John Hotham had instructed, and now the feelings of guilt from which he was suffering were almost too much for him to bear. He had no way of knowing if his master, Robert Overton had been killed or injured in the attack. He was too frightened to re-join

Mathew at Anlaby and face the man who had entrusted him with the message to arrange the attack. And he could not go back to Hull in case he was seen by Captain Overton, who, if he were still alive, would be looking for the one who had informed the enemy about his plans to attack Anlaby that night.

For now, all he had in his possession was the money in his purse and the letter that Sir John Hotham had given him, instructing him to travel to York, and deliver it to the Earl of Newcastle. Unable to decide what he should do next, he found the nearest tavern and went inside.

Captain Hewitt entered the surgeon's tent to find Mathew changing the dressings on a soldier who had received a sword cut across his back.

'Surgeon Fletcher, a moment of your time if you please,' his tone was respectful since he could see Mathew was doing important work.

'Just one moment, if you please, Captain,' Mathew apologised. 'I am nearly finished with this man; he will benefit greatly from the egg white I am putting on his wound being allowed to dry before I re-dress it.' He spread the last of the egg white over the length of the sword laceration on the soldier's back and dried his hands.

'Now, Captain, how can I help you?' asked Mathew still wondering when he would be arrested, but as the captain had come alone, it seemed that this was not to be the time.

'We are moving the camp to Beverley, to join the main force camped on Beverley Westwood Common. I need you to prepare these men for transportation as soon as possible. Now that the worst cases have been moved into the village, these men can finish their healing in Beverley. Good day to you, surgeon,' Captain Hewitt gave a quick nod of the head to his surgeon, turned and left.

Mathew broke the news to Bartram and Jenkins.

'That's ridiculous!' exclaimed Jenkins. 'We've only just started to get their wounds to close up and stopped the bleeding. The journey will open everything up again. Mathew, you must see the colonel—explain what even this short journey is likely to do to these men.'

'I know, I know, of course, I will do what I can, but we can hardly stay here without the army to protect us, can we? I will ask for wagons to help move those that cannot walk. When we get there, I will find billets for the men in Beverley; they will fare better in the town rather than camping out in the open.'

'It will be hard on the men,' said Bartram, 'but I agree with Mathew, they will recover faster if they are indoors out of the weather.'

'I will go speak to the colonel and ask for his help and if he will tell me when we will be leaving here,' Mathew told them.

Mathew removed his bloodstained and dirty apron, straightened his dark blue woollen jerkin and rolled down his shirtsleeves. He picked up his hat as he left the surgeon's tent, and set off in the direction of the colonel's pavilion. As he walked through the camp, he noticed preparations were already being made for the change of location. At the colonel's pavilion, two sentries with halberds stood guard at the entrance, and voices could be heard from inside.

The surgeon approached one of the guards, asking, 'I would like to see the colonel—I am the sergeant surgeon,

Master Mathew Fletcher. I need to speak to the colonel about his plans for moving the wounded.'

The guard disappeared inside, returning moments later, holding open the pavilion entrance for Mathew to enter. He found the colonel sitting at a desk that was set to one side of the long tent. Captain Hewitt and a couple of other officers were also there. As Mathew entered, he removed his hat and bowed to the colonel.

'Forgive me for disturbing you, Colonel, but I am here on behalf of the wounded men in my care.'

'Yes, Mathew,' Duncombe answered agreeably. 'And how are the men faring? Are they recovering well?'

'Yes, Colonel, they are making good progress, thank you. I understand from Captain Hewitt that the camp is to move to the Beverley Westwood. I need to inform you that the wounded men are just starting to heal and will suffer greatly with the upheaval of moving. I was wondering if you would give me some idea as to when you plan on moving the camp, and if I may have some wagons to help move the wounded?'

'Straight to the point as always, Master Surgeon,' the colonel said bluntly. 'I would have discussed the matter with Captain Hewitt in due course and as senior surgeon in the camp, with you, but as you are here I'll tell you now— we move in two days. Speak to Captain Hewitt he will give you any wagons he can spare when the time comes.'

All officers the smiled as Mathew received the mild rebuke from the colonel for circumventing military procedure. The fact that Mathew was the senior army surgeon in camp didn't put him on the same level as the officers, and he had been well and truly 'put in his place'.

'Thank you, Colonel.' Mathew gave a short bow, replaced his hat and left the tent. He glanced at the two guards, who sniggered at him as they had heard what had been said inside. He was angry with himself for assuming that he could go straight to the colonel to get what he wanted, and for assuming that he would be treated differently now he was now the colonel's personal surgeon. It also rankled that he had been humiliated in front of the other officers of the camp.

Returning to the surgeon's tent, he felt utterly frustrated. All he had wanted was to do his best for the men in his care, and he was being treated like a schoolboy. He went to find Ethan: somehow Ethan always had an answer for everything and had the knack of making him feel better. He sat down on a log next to the cook's fire; it wasn't long before his friend found him.

'What's up with you then?' the cheery cook enquired. 'You look like someone's slapped your face.' Ethan placed a tankard of beer in Mathew's hand before he could answer.

'I've just made a fool of myself in front of the colonel and Captain Hewitt,' Mathew explained. 'I know I should have gone to Captain Hewitt first rather than go straight to the colonel, but after he told me about the change of camp, he just left abruptly, without even giving me the chance to ask any questions.'

'Trouble is though, Mathew, the army has its own ways of doing things, and, rightly or wrongly, they won't let you do things as you think fit. You're not a *gentleman*.'

'You're right of course, but I still find it hard to take, when I just have the best interests of the men at heart, and they put their own bloody protocol and social order over the men's welfare.'

The two men talked and ate for a time. 'Thank you for listening, Ethan—it helps to get it off my chest.'

The following morning Mathew humbled himself before Captain Hewitt when he requested wagons for moving the wounded. The latter had left Mathew standing outside his tent for an hour before admitting him and after that had merely said that he would see what he could do. However, when the wagons did finally arrive, it was not until late the following day.

After Mathew had loaded his surgeon's tent and equipment, into the wagon, and there was only enough space left for the most seriously wounded. Mathew, Bartram, Jenkins and the four women nurses walked with the wounded that weren't lucky enough to get a ride in the wagons, the six miles to Beverley Westwood.

It was dark when they arrived, the unloading of equipment would have to wait until the following day. They left the wounded in the wagons, everyone else spent an uncomfortable night on the ground, each covered only in a blanket, but at least they had arrived without further injury.

Once dawn broke Mathew set the women to work feeding the men bread, cheese and small beer, while the three surgeons set up the medical tent and equipment and checked their patient's wounds. Later that day, Mathew planned to visit Mary and pick up the medical supplies she hopefully would have ready for him.

Mathew walked the half mile from the Beverley Westwood camp into town. His patients were settled and had come through the journey well. The nurses complained about being taken away from Anlaby, but as they were being well paid for their caring work and they were getting fed better meals with Mathew than if they had stayed behind, Mathew paid them little heed.

Bartram and Jenkins started talking about going home again, for their work, as far as they were concerned, was done. Mathew could manage alone, with the nurses helping to change the dressings as and when needed. However, before they could leave the army, Bartram and Jenkins, would need the colonel's permission. He would probably let them go, but Mathew was in no rush to aid them in their quest to leave.

Mathew entered his family home via the front door, the familiar sights and smells suddenly making him feel very tired after the tensions of the previous week. He was back where he could be himself, and where he was welcome. Mary was busy decanting a liquid from a cauldron into two large brown earthenware Bellarmines. She looked up at the sound of the door opening and gave Mathew a big smile.

'I've been busy ever since you left,' she told him. Eager to show what she had been doing, Mary pointed to the corner of the room, where Mathew spotted lots of jars and pots of various shapes and sizes. She wiped sweat from her brow on the hem of her apron and tidied her hair, pushing a few loose strands back inside her coif. He noticed she was wearing the same blue dress she had worn on the first day he had met her. It was of a colour that suited her well.

'Thank you, Mary. The men are in great need of fresh medicines. I will tell them about you as I use them, it will help to take their minds off the discomfort they suffer.' Mary blushed at the compliment.

Henry came in from the yard, 'Hello, Brother! Father's out, he's arranging to buy some oak and elm to make more wheels, but he'll be back soon.'

'I can't stay long, as I must return with these medicines, but I will wait for Father and share a meal with you.'

The thought of returning to the camp didn't enthral Mathew. The humiliation in the colonel's pavilion still rankled. Mathew had many questions bothering him, not knowing what had happened to Mortimer, how the attack on the Anlaby camp had been discovered, whether or not the colonel was aware that he was spying for Captain Overton, not to mention caring for a large number of sick soldiers, all these matters were now putting him under a great strain. The simplicity of being home with his family, even for just a few hours, was a very welcome respite.

He watched Mary working, and suspected she was only a couple of years older than Elizabeth. The swish of her dress when she flicked her hips as she turned, as well as the loose strand of hair that continually dropped from below her coif, reminded him of her. He turned away feeling guilty, as his thoughts turned to Elizabeth, but she was dead, along with his brother Charles. They had died at the hands of soldiers brought to Hull and Beverley by the King, the very people he was now helping. It was just another complication in his life. Mathew looked for a distraction and called Bess over, to give the dog some attention and fuss.

With a heavy heart, Mathew decided he needed advice and that he needed to talk to his father about what he planned to do. He needed someone to confide in, someone he could trust. His father may be angry with him, but he needed to talk to someone.

It wasn't long before William Fletcher returned bursting into the room like a giant bear, with his thick bushy hair and beard, shouting about his return with his booming voice. His brown woollen jacket was speckled with sawdust, his latchet shoes scuffed and muddy. He welcomed his youngest son with a spine-crushing hug.

'I'm hot and thirsty and in need of news,' William said. 'I hear the camp at Anlaby has been abandoned, and it has moved to the Westwood.'

'Yes, Father, I will be much closer to home now, and it is good to see you well. No more trouble with the stone, I hope?' Mathew didn't really need to ask; he could see that his father had recovered well from the bladder-stone removal surgery.

Mary had prepared a midday meal, and it was lucky it was pea and ham soup, for it was easy to make the thick soup stretch for one more person. After washing down the soup and fresh bread with more beer, Mathew was feeling a bit bloated, but satisfied. It was time he to return to his patients.

'Father, will you walk with me? I could do with some help to carry these supplies back to camp, and it would give us time to talk. There are matters I need to discuss with you.'

William Fletcher's face lost its smile as he noticed his son's serious expression. 'Surely, Mathew, you know that I always have time for my sons.' His voice had taken on a reassuring tone.

The two of them walked back towards the Westwood, each with a sack over their shoulder. They walked in silence at first, but once through the Beverley Bar, Mathew began to confide with his father.

'Father, please don't be angry with me, I have something to confess. I have been gathering intelligence about the king's camp at Anlaby and passing it on to those in Hull, who support Parliament.'

His father stopped walking for a moment and looked at his son. 'Go on.'

They walked a little further until William Fletcher stopped once again.

'Well? Are you going to tell me all of it, or are you going to leave me hanging?' They continued to walk as Mathew went on to explain why he'd decided to help Overton.

'He can help me search for Elizabeth's killers; he also believes that they may be the same people involved with the death of Charles, from Mary's description of one of them. It has made me all the more determined to find Elizabeth's and Charles's killers.' It was when he explained about Mortimer's part in the plan, and that he had disappeared and not returned, that William Fletcher stopped again, staring at his son in outrage.

'You fool!' William barked. 'You bloody fool! What are you going to do now?'

Mathew shrugged his shoulders. 'I'm sorry, Father, but so much has happened. I just don't know what to do next.'

They walked on in silence a short distance.

Stopping again, William turned to his son and said, 'Tomorrow I want you to find a way to come home again. We will talk this through.'

Father and son walked the remainder of the journey in silence. Mathew sensed the anger in his father, who had marched on ahead, eager to deliver the medicines and return home. Mathew wondered if he had done the right thing in telling his father about what he had been doing, but it was too late now. He was glad the cat was out of the bag.

Come what may, his father was the one person he knew he could trust with his burden, but he wasn't looking forward to their next meeting

Back in the camp, the three surgeons did their evening check on their patients, cleaning wounds and changing dressings. The four pitiful old nurses fussed around, dispensing food and seeing to the men's other needs.

Although Mathew had not resolved anything by talking with his father about his activities, when he sat down to his evening meal with Ethan and the others, he felt more relaxed than he had done for some weeks. Mathew stared into the flames of the campfire, thinking about tomorrow, his father wanted him to leave the army since finding the killers of Elizabeth and Charles was a pointless cause, as even if he found them, there was little he could do about it.

But he began to enjoy his work, and he felt an affinity with the soldiers and the camp lifestyle, he knew he was doing valued work. After all, most of these men were decent ordinary soldiers, who would have nothing to do with the murder of innocent people. Mathew's patients needed him, and they had genuine needs, he wasn't doing unnecessary, cosmetic medical work, such as removing the wart from the daughter of the dreadful Mrs Milburn's.

He would return home tomorrow to hear what his father had to say, but he was resolved to stay in the army and carry on with his work.

'I've told them everything,' his father said as Mathew sat at the table in the kitchen. 'They have a right to know what you are doing.'

Mathew looked into the faces of his family, each one set with a concerned expression.

'We have decided that the best thing for you to do is to leave the army,' William went on. 'I—that is *we*—understand your feelings over the death of Elizabeth and Charles. But if you get yourself killed chasing the killers and working for this Captain Overton, then I will end up losing two sons for no good reason.'

Mary gave William a quick sideways look, her face reddened, and then she looked away.

'You mean, *you* have decided I should leave,' Mathew replied. 'Well, I can't. You haven't thought it through. If I leave and they have any suspicion I was involved in betraying them, it will point the finger of guilt at me for sure. There are three things working in my favour: firstly if I stay and don't run, it will show them I've nothing to hide. Secondly, I was in the camp when the attack took place, and third, Mortimer is the one who is missing. What's more, I killed three of the Parliamentary soldiers that—'

'WHAT!' Mathew's father roared. 'Why is this the first we have heard of it?'

Mathew sat back on his chair and took a deep breath. He hadn't meant to mention his part in the Anlaby battle, but his blood was up, and he had confessed more than he had intended. 'I didn't mean to get involved, Father, it just happened. One minute I was hiding, watching as my friend was about to be slaughtered by the troopers. The next, I'd killed three soldiers. I don't want to talk about what I did, it just happened.'

There was a long pause as they took in the news that their surgeon son had also been a killer.

'I can't leave Beverley or the army until I find out what's happened to Mortimer, and I am determined to find those bastards that killed Elizabeth and Charles. I can't stop now until I have peace of mind. What would you have done if someone had killed Mother? You've just left the death of Charles in the hands of the constables, and you know they won't do or find anything now and so you have just given up. Someone has to put things to rights.' Mathew was raging, his words pouring out in a torrent of stress and anger.

William Fletcher stood up and slapped Mathew hard across the face, knocking him from his chair and sending him sprawling across the floor.

'You spoilt little shit!' William roared. 'Who in God's name do you think you are? Don't you think I want revenge on the ones that killed Charles? I wish I could tear them limb from limb with my own hands, but I have the rest of the family to think of, Henry, you and Mary, not to mention the family business that pays to feed us and houses us. You have nothing but your own selfish pride to worry about. One day, maybe one day, when you grow up and have a family of your own, you might just see that.'

Henry sat his father down, while Mary went to Mathew's side. Mathew picked himself up, nursing the sizeable red handprint on the side of his face and stormed out of the house.

Mortimer sat with his hands around a tankard of ale. He'd lost count of how many he'd had, the events of the past few days playing on his conscience, the drink fuddling his mind. What had started as simply passing on small amounts of information to Sir John Hotham had now trapped him in a more complicated dilemma. If he'd gone straight back into camp he might have been able to fool people into thinking that the preparations for the attack were a coincidence with the message he had carried to Hull, but he'd stayed away too long now, and that would have made Mathew suspicious. Mathew would contact Captain Overton, and ask questions about why he was missing. If he went back to Hull, Sir John Hotham would find out he hadn't taken the letter to York, thus putting his family at risk. As he sat in his drunken state, he didn't notice Mathew Fletcher entering the inn.

Finding a private corner in which to sit and hide the red mark on his face, Mathew called to a girl, to fetch him a tankard of ale. He'd chosen The White Horse because of its many small rooms on the ground floor, ideal places to sit and talk in private or to skulk away and nurse one's pride.

The inn was dimly lit, the rushes on the floor had been changed from the night before, but the table felt sticky from spilt ale and food. He knew he would have to go back and apologise to his father, but decided that it could wait for an hour or two. He needed to calm down, put his thoughts in order first, the doubt about what he was doing in the army, tearing at his nerves. He drank his ale, emptying the tankard in one throw. Chucking his pennies on the table, he ordered another along with some bread and cold mutton.

Tasting the fresh bread and chewing on the mutton helped to ease his tension. Sitting back, he washed down a mouthful of food with the ale, his thoughts dwelling on his father's words. As he sat quietly a noise broke out from another of the little rooms in the inn. *A fight*, Mathew thought to himself, thinking: *I'm not getting involved—I'm not here to put drunkards back together again.* He could hear the raised voice of one of the serving girls shouting at a customer.

'Bill, Bill, come 'ere!' the girl shouted. 'This pig's thrown up all over the table, and 'e's pissed 'imself as well. Get 'im out. I can't lift 'im!'

Mathew watched as a man, the size of his father, made his way slowly past the tables. He was bald-headed with stubbly whiskers on his face, and stank of sweat and stale beer. His woollen breeches had smooth, shiny fronts to them, doubtless as a result of rubbing against beer barrels. His shirt, once white, was now grey and covered with sweat and beer stains. His stout arms and legs gave testament to the man's strength; there was no way anyone was going to argue with this giant.

Next, came the sound of table legs scuffing on floorboards and then the dragging noise of something being dragged across the floor. As Mathew looked from his corner, he saw Charles Mortimer being pulled by one arm along the floor towards the door and the yard at the back of the inn. Mortimer was dropped unceremoniously outside in the sewage gutter which ran through the centre of the yard.

The giant cellar man, Bill, was coming in from the yard as Mathew reached the back door. The man filled the doorframe, the room dimming as he blotted out the outside light which his massive body. Bill hadn't said a word: he didn't look the type to say much at all.

He passed Mathew without a glance. Mathew stepped outside into the yard, recoiling at the smell of human and animal waste which was so strong he could taste it in the air. The area had evidently not been cleaned for days. He had to fight back the urge to vomit, but he had to talk to the drunken Mortimer and get to the bottom of why he hadn't returned to camp.

Finding a bucket by a horse trough, he filled it with water and sluiced down the prostrate Mortimer. It took three buckets of water before the unconscious man began to stir. Mathew dragged the half comatose body to a wall, propped him up against it and left him in a sitting position, his chin resting on his chest. If Mathew could get him home, he calculated, and then he could sober him up and get to the bottom of where Mortimer had been and what he had been doing.

Stepping back inside the White Horse, Mathew found the serving girl who'd had Mortimer thrown out and paid her half a groat to leave Mortimer where he sat until he could return with a cart to retrieve him.

Chapter Twenty-Six

Racing home, Mathew's firstly apologised to his father. He found him in the yard with Henry. The pair had returned to working on a wagon wheel they'd started that morning, glueing and tapping home the spokes into the hub before attaching the second section of felloes. They both looked up as Mathew entered the yard. He stood at the entrance and looked at his father, 'Sir, I'm sorry,' he said quietly. 'I was wrong to talk to you that way; it was childish of me. I beg your forgiveness.'

'In some ways, you spoke the truth,' William replied. 'Had I been younger, I would have dashed after the killer without thinking; at least you have a plan,' replied his father, pleased for the chance to mend the rift with his son. 'How's your face? It still looks a bit red.'

'Nothing more than I deserved, Father. But enough of that, something has happened, and I need your help.' Mathew explained about finding Mortimer at The White Horse and wanting to bring him home to question him. His father agreed immediately, wanting to prove all was forgiven.

It didn't take long for the three of them to retrieve Charles Mortimer from the yard at the inn and bring him home on one of the repaired carts that were waiting to go back to its owner. Mary took one look at Mortimer and refused to have him in the house until he'd been washed and his stinking clothes removed and burned. Bess, the dog, standing next to Mary with hackles raised, sniffing and growling at the unconscious man in the yard, she didn't want the foul-smelling stranger in the house either.

Once he was stripped, scrubbed and wrapped in a blanket, Mortimer was carried to the truckle bed in the corner of the kitchen. The man was alive, and breathing, which was the best that Mathew could say about him for the moment. All the family could do now, was wait until Mortimer woke from his drunken stupor. Time was pressing; Mathew had to leave Mortimer in the care of Mary since he needed to return to the Westwood camp with the medicines that she had made for him.

Bartram and Jenkins were waiting for him when he arrived.

'Have a jolly time with the family?' Jenkins remarked sarcastically.

Ignoring him, Mathew put the refreshed medicine containers on the table in the surgeon's tent. All he wanted to do was to go home and wait for Mortimer to wake up, but there was work that had to be done here first, but listening to Bartram and Jenkins's complaints was getting too much to bear.

'If you please, gentlemen, we shall check on our patients,' Mathew announced. 'Anyone we find that can be returned to duty, we will release. If we can reduce the numbers enough so that I can manage them on my own, I will speak to the colonel in the morning and ask him to release you from service. Would that be agreeable to you both?'

'Let's get on with it then,' Bartram replied grudgingly, clearly jealous of the freedom Mathew had, to come and go as he pleased. 'It's been near on a week since I was last home, and I will want paying for my services before I leave.'

With the severely wounded having been left in the care of the Anlaby villagers, the surgeons were left with those who were suffering from the lesser wounds. Most of the lacerated wounds were knitting together well: another week and they should all be able to have their stitches removed. Those with broken limbs, however, would be unable to fend for themselves for some weeks yet, but it would be the nurses who dealt with their needs: fetching and carrying, feeding and washing. All the men who had developed fevers after their injuries were either recovering or dead. As Mathew took stock of the numbers, he made a decision. All the men with broken arms could go back to their companies and be put on light duties or given leave. Those that had lacerations that had stopped suppurating would be able to return to light duties in a few days, as their wounds only needed to be kept clean. So long as those patients were fed well, and given healing cordials to encourage agglutination of the skin, they would be fine.

'Very well, gentlemen, our patients are healing nicely,' Mathew told his reluctant colleagues. 'There is no need to keep you here. I will recommend to Colonel Duncombe that you be released from your service to the Crown. I cannot though, insist that you be paid before your return to your families—that is a decision that only the colonel can make.'

Mathew knew that he would be kept busy for a while when Bartram and Jenkins left him, but at least he wouldn't have to listen to their constant complaints. Later that day he spoke to Captain Hewitt about discharging Bartram and Jenkins, and the captain promised to take it up with the colonel. Mathew recognised the smug expression on his face, that all-knowing smirk that told him Mathew had learnt to follow the army's chain of command, rather than going straight to the colonel himself, as he had done before. Mathew hated him for it.

As they sat and ate their evening meal around Ethan Goodman's campfire, Jenkins informed Mathew that the colonel had agreed that he would release them at the end of the week. 'Good. I know you want to be away from here, but those extra few day's help will make a lot of difference to me. Mathew was keen to return home himself, to see if Mortimer was still there. He would have liked to have returned today, but if he was to ensure he would have any free time at all, he needed to make certain that his remaining patients were in the best possible condition before he left them in the hands of the nurses for any length of time.

Back at home at the end of the week, he was surprised to see Charles Mortimer waiting for him.

Mathew looked at Henry enquiringly. 'He's been no trouble,' Henry told him, smiling. 'He only woke up the day after you left. He was unconscious for the best part of two days.'

'I'm sorry Mathew. What do you intend to do with me?' Mortimer mumbled.

'That depends on what you have to say for yourself.'

'I suspect you warned the colonel of the attack on the Anlaby camp and you were too scared to return in case you got hurt. Is that what happened?' Mathew looked accusingly at Mortimer but kept his voice calm. Getting aggressive with him wasn't the way to get results.

'I'll tell you everything; I have no choice now. Whether I live or die for my actions, I can't carry on living a lie.' Mortimer hung his head in misery. 'I am ashamed of what I have done, but I had my reasons. With the losses you have suffered, Mathew, you are probably the only person who will understand my plight.'

'Go on, tell all,' Mathew said unsympathetically.

Mortimer explained how he and his family had been employed by Sir John Hotham and were still working for him. 'Sir John Hotham is holding my family, blackmailing me into working for him as a spy on Captain Overton.' Mortimer went on to explain 'Sir John reads all the messages between you and Captain Overton and uses the information to further his own career, hoping to regain favour with the king.

'That explains this letter we found on you which is addressed to the Earl of Newcastle.' William Fletcher interrupted.

'Yes. I decided to warn the colonel of the attack, but I didn't mention your name, and I didn't want to deliver the letter to the earl in Beverley and betray Captain Overton any more than I have done already. When Hotham finds out I haven't delivered the letter, he will know I have failed him, and he'll take revenge on my family. Captain Overton, who has been very good to me, will also find out that I have betrayed him. My family will lose their jobs on the Hotham estate at Scorborough when Sir John gets to know what I have told you. I have made a mess of it all. I have lost everything. I'm lost. I don't know what to do anymore.'

The Fletcher family and Mortimer sat in silence for a moment before Mary offered a solution.

'Take the earl's letter to Captain Overton,' Mary advised him. 'Throw yourself on his mercy.'

'We couldn't trust him to go to Overton,' said Mathew's father.

'You could if I took him,' interjected Henry. Everyone's eyes turned towards him, then back to his brother, in anticipation of an answer.

'Well?' said Mathew to Mortimer.

Mortimer knew he was out of options, and that this was his only chance he had to redeem himself, but the cost, at the very least, would be his job with Captain Overton. He didn't even want to contemplate what might happen if Captain Overton arrested him.

Later that day, while he was outside with Henry, in the lane preparing to return to Hull, Mortimer had a moment when he asked himself if he was making the right decision in returning to face Captain Overton. He felt like Judas. No matter what he did next, someone he cared for would probably suffer for his failings.

But there could only be one decision, so the two men set off towards Howden and a boat on to Hull.

Late that same day, the pair arrived in Hull, the boat tying-up close by the King's Stairs on the River Hull. They walked along the High Street, and on past the markets, turning left towards the blockhouses and the main entrance to the soldiers' quarters.

Mortimer approached the guard and asked, 'Is Captain Overton in his rooms?'

The guard recognised him, replying, 'Aye, he's in.' He pointed the way with his thumb. Mortimer's fears intensified as he walked through the familiar building. If Captain Overton wouldn't listen to his explanation, he was lost. He would be arrested and no doubt hanged.

He found Captain Overton in his rooms, sitting with a cup of brandy while waiting for his evening meal to be brought to him. Mortimer tapped on the open door and entered, with Henry close behind him. Overton put down his drink and looked over his shoulder to see who had entered the room. He was surprised to see the two men standing before him, and it took a moment before he recognised Henry as Mathew's brother.

'Good evening to you both,' Overton welcomed them. 'I didn't expect to see you, Henry. Is everything well with Mathew?'

Henry explained that he had escorted Mortimer to Hull and that his companion had a confession to make.

At first, Mortimer just stood there in silence, looking at his feet.

'Come on, man!' Captain Overton asked him urgently. 'Tell me what news you have. What is wrong with you?' Overton's voice was filled with concern as he waited for his servant to open his mouth.

'I'm sorry, sir,' Mortimer muttered miserably, unable to look his master in the eye. 'I do have news from Mathew Fletcher, but first I have a confession to make.'

Overton rose from his desk and stood stony-faced, wondering what had happened or gone wrong. His mind racing, trying to imagine various scenarios, such as that the surgeon had been discovered spying, or dead. What else could it be, he wondered?

'Well, man? For goodness' sake, spit it out!' Overton demanded.

'I've been under the control of Sir John Hotham. I have been passing him copies of your meetings and any intelligence I could uncover. But please, sir, let me explain the hold he has over me.' Overton glanced across at Henry for support.

'Sir, please give him a chance to explain,' Henry pleaded.

Overton, without a word, sat down to listen to Mortimer's explanation.

'Most of the information that I gave away was of no great importance, but Hotham now knows of Mathew and his intelligence gathering for Parliament for you. Sir John also gave me this letter to take to the Earl of Newcastle. I should have delivered it days ago, but I couldn't bring myself to do it.'

Taking the letter, Overton broke the seal and read its contents. It explained that Sir John Hotham was still loyal to the King and that it was Overton, holding a sword to his back, who had forced him to refuse to open the gates of Hull for the monarch. It went on to explain that Hotham would work to bring about a change of order in Hull, allowing him to surrender the town to the King at a later date.

Looking up at Mortimer, Overton thought for a minute before speaking. 'Well, Gentlemen. This letter is of such great importance that it has condemned Sir John Hotham as a traitor to Parliament and has also saved your life. You will return to Surgeon Fletcher, if he is prepared to trust you again, you will continue to report to Sir John Hotham, any news that Surgeon Fletcher gives you. Only there will be two messages: the one that you give Sir John will continue to be of little importance. What you bring to me will be encoded, so that you can't understand it and betray me again.'

Mortimer took a step back and then fell to his knees, clasping his hands together, as though to pray.

'Sir,' he begged, 'I will do anything you say to redeem myself. You have been more than fair to me in the time I have been in your service. You are a just and godly man. It is for my family that I fear, not for myself. Do with me as you wish, but please, help my family escape from Sir John's control.'

Captain Overton called in a guard. 'I want you to watch this man and ensure he does not move from the spot. If he does, you are to kill him instantly, do you understand? I will be back shortly. Henry, please, take a seat, as I say, I will be back very soon.'

Overton left the room with the guard standing over Mortimer, who was still on his knees.

'Yes, sir.' The guard lowered his halberd with its fifteen-inch steel spike atop a sharpened axe blade and pointed it directly at Mortimer's chest.

Overton went to the room next door and sat at the table to write in private. He wrote the code for his cypher which Mathew was to use from now on. He also enclosed instructions about opening the letter, if he found that the message had been tampered with prior to him receiving it, he was to disregard the contents and return to Hull immediately by any means possible because it meant that Mortimer had betrayed him again. The code was a conversion system, letters for numbers, some letters with duplicated numbers, some numbers used as spaces; know as a Caesar shift code.

Folding the letter carefully, Overton returned to his own room and gave it to Henry. 'If you fail me again,' he told the kneeling man, 'I will see you hang, and your family will be left to the mercy of the Hotham's. I will decide on your punishment later.' Overton dismissed the guard.

'Captain, with your permission, sir, I need to take back some medical supplies for Surgeon Fletcher and more lead to make bullets,' the kneeling man said quietly. 'I still have money given to me by Sir John for my journey to Beverley. I can use that to buy the medical supplies and lead from the merchants. Those were the reasons I gave for leaving the camp at Anlaby. I will have to take back evidence of my errand in case the guards question me.'

'Fine, do what you must, but remember, Mortimer, your life and the lives of your family depend on Surgeon Fletcher receiving that letter unopened. Henry will deliver the letter to Mathew and escort you back to Beverley. I will keep this letter for the Earl of Newcastle.' Overton placed the earl's letter in the drawer of his desk and locked it.

Henry and Mortimer left Overton's office. Standing in the street outside, Mortimer took a deep breath and turned to Henry. 'I've been a fool, but, now that I have confessed to Captain Overton, and I have corrected one of my errors, I feel much better for it.'

'You ain't out the woods yet,' Henry said in a cold, matter-of-fact voice.

'No matter. If I can put things right again, even if I'm no longer trusted as I once was, I will be able to live with my conscience,' sighed Mortimer.

Meanwhile, Overton sat back in his chair and once again read the letter from Sir John to the Earl of Newcastle. He could arrest Hotham here and now, for what was written in this letter, but he had to be sure he was doing what Parliament would want him to.

Deciding that he needed to share this information with those senior to him, he wrote a letter explaining everything to Lord Fairfax, dispatching a messenger to leave by boat for York, and then on to Denton Hall. Overton gave him explicit instructions that the letter should be destroyed rather than allowed to fall into the hands of those loyal to the King. All Captain Overton could do now was wait.

Five days later, Overton got the reply he had been waiting for. He was told to arrest Hotham and his son and to deliver them to the Tower of London until they could be questioned by Parliament.

Sir John Hotham sat at the desk in his office, putting some amendments to a contract for transporting whale oil to York. The increased trade in fishing and whaling was turning Hull into a prosperous town. The royalist siege of Hull had had little impact on the comings and goings of merchant ships from the port with the navy remaining loyal to parliament. The King had raised forts at Paull and Hessle to try and prevent vessels reaching Hull. But Captain Overton and Lieutenant Maynard had destroyed the fort at Hessle, and a ship of the Royal Navy had destroyed the fort at Paull.

As Hotham went through his contracts, Bottomley scribed the figures into a ledger. Bottomley's ink-stained fingers held the quill-like an artist, as he neatly wrote the characters into his book. His head, slightly cocked to one side and close to the work as his failing eyesight caused him to stoop closer to the page.

Captain Overton, accompanied by an armed guard of eight men carrying halberds and wearing swords, entered the Guildhall that afternoon. Before Hotham's two red-coated bodyguards stationed at his office could react, Captain Overton ordered four of his men to subdue them before entering Sir John's office. Leaving the guards in the

347

secretary's office, Overton marched up to Hotham's desk, ignoring Bottomley, and declared that Sir John Hotham was under arrest.

'This is absurd!' shouted Hotham in protest. 'Have you gone mad, Captain? I am the Military Governor and Mayor of Hull! You have no authority to arrest me.'

Sir John sat back in his chair, his hands gripping the armrests, the whitening of his knuckles the only sign that he was showing any stress at the unexpected intrusion. Bottomley closed the ledger and laid down his quill. His jaw had fallen open as his gaze switched from Overton to Hotham, wondering what was going to happen next.

'You have betrayed the trust that Parliament has put in you,' Overton declared. 'You have been in secret negotiations with the Earl of Newcastle and the King to surrender this town to them.'

Overton remained relaxed, his voice even and calm. He stood in front of Hotham's desk; his eyes fixed on those of the other man. He noticed the bead of sweat that appeared on Hotham's forehead and ran down the bridge of his nose into the corner of his eye, causing the accused man to blink away the salty perspiration.

'Have you gone insane?' Hotham protested. 'I am loyal to Parliament! It was Parliament that gave me this appointment. Pym himself signed the warrant of authority. I make the law in Hull and, Captain Overton; I am going to make you wish that you had never stepped into this office.'

Bottomley pushed his stool away from Hotham's desk and stood up, putting the ledger under his arm. He hadn't moved more than a step or two before Overton ordered him to leave the ledger on the desk.

'Sit back down, you!' he ordered. 'I will want to question you as well.'

Overton maintained eye contact with Hotham while Bottomley slipped back onto his seat, still clutching the ledger to his chest. Overton's right hand lifted the flap on the satchel he was carrying and produced the letter that Hotham had written to the Earl of Newcastle.

Sir John went pale. He opened his mouth as though he was going to say something, but no sound came out.

'Sergeant!' It was the first time that Overton had raised his voice above a normal conversational level. The soldier ducked his head as he came through the door, the morion helmet he was wearing making him seem even taller than he was. His soldiers tuck hung in its baldric over his grey jacket, his halberd in his right hand.

'Take Sir John to the castle, along with this one,' Overton told the sergeant. 'Let them speak to no one, and place a guard on these rooms. No one is to enter these rooms until I have had time to search them.'

The sergeant beckoned two more soldiers into the room. They took up their positions either side of Hotham.

'You can't do this.' Hotham's voice was almost a squeal. Bottomley, still holding the ledger close to his chest as though it would give him some kind of protection, was visibly shaking, his face a deathly white.

'By the by, I almost forgot,' Overton added. 'Your son has been arrested as well. He will be waiting for you in your cell. Take them away, Sergeant.'

Captain Overton had waited weeks for this day to come; Hull was now under his control.

Mathew, his father and Mary returned to the kitchen table. 'I hope Henry will be safe with Mortimer,' said Mary.

'Don't worry, lass, Mortimer knows this is the only way he'll be able to salvage any of this mess he's got himself into.' William Fletcher gave his daughter-in-law a reassuring smile. 'What do you intend to do now?' he asked his son.

'I will return to the camp; there are still wounded men that need my help. Now that Bartram and Jenkins are leaving, I'm not going to have any free time.' He gave a sigh.

'Could I not help in some small way?' asked Mary, flashing Mathew a hopeful smile.

'It's a camp full of men. I don't think it's the right place for a woman,' Mathew responded instantly.

'You've got four women nurses there helping you. Why is it different for them?' Mary replied indignantly.

'Er, they are older, destitute, they—er—they have to do things that a good respectable woman and wife shouldn't have to do.' Mathew's face flushed.

'I am not unaware of what men's bodies look like,' she replied firmly. 'After all, I was married to your brother for over a year.' She stood away from the table; tears filled her eyes leaving glistening trails down her reddening cheeks as they fell. She pulled a handkerchief from her pocket, blew her nose and wiped away the tears. Mathew looked at his father, a plea for help written across his face.

'Don't look at me, son, I'm not getting involved with this. You must decide between you.'

Mary replaced the handkerchief in her pocket, giving Mathew a determined look, before saying 'Listen, Mathew, I can help you-you know I can. I would be someone you could trust, and I wouldn't complain like those other women probably do. I could even help you keep them in order. If needs be, I could come home each night so you would know that I was safe.'

'Well, – you are right, I could do with the help. But Father and Henry need you here. 'If Henry were here, he would agree with me.'

'How about a compromise?' Mathew's father interceded. 'Supposing Mary spends every alternate day with you. After all, she may find the work not suited to her after she has tried it.'

Mary gave him a big smile and looked at Mathew expectantly. Her hands clenched in front of her.

'As you wish,' Mathew conceded. 'But, it's just to see if it works out. Things change rapidly in a military camp, and if there is any sign of danger, you will have to leave.'

Mary gave a squeal of delight. 'I promise I will do exactly as you say,' she said excitedly.

'Thank goodness that's settled, because I'm hungry. Can we eat now?' William asked.

At least I won't have her to put up with for long, Mathew thought. *If the King is moving into the Midlands, he will have to take his army with him, and Mary will have to stay behind with the family.*

Chapter Twenty-Seven

Mary was determined to make a good impression on her first day with Mathew in the military camp. She started by washing all the surgical instruments in Mathew's surgeon's chest, using warm water infused with lemon juice to remove any grease and dirt. She dried them carefully on a clean piece of linen and replaced them neatly back in the tray that fit into the top of the very large box. She checked the contents of all the medicine bottles and jars, making a note of which would soon need topping up.

Mathew watched as she worked, still unsure that agreeing to let her come was the right thing to have done. Ethan Goodman, come across.

'Good day, Ethan. You know I won't be able to find anything by the time she's finished,' Mathew said quietly indicating in Mary's direction.

Ethan gave a little laugh. 'Come and have a drink, Mathew. Leave her to get on with what makes her happy.' With a look over his shoulder, he agreed and went with Ethan to sit by the campfire. Mathew always felt at ease sitting by the fire staring into the flames and sharing a drink with his friend for company.

'She's certainly a willing helper,' said Ethan. 'She'll be much more useful to you than those moaning, half-hearted surgeons you had helping you.'

Mathew nodded and sat down in his usual place on the tree log. 'I know, but, ...'

'Here, try some of these,' Ethan suggested, putting a plate of spinach tansies into Mathew's hand. 'I'm going to make a batch for the officers tonight. Eat them while they're hot, they go a bit chewy when they're cold.'

'Um, not bad!' Mathew said appreciatively. 'What are they made of?'

'Eggs, cream, spinach, breadcrumbs and nutmeg, then you fry them on a griddle, fold them back on themselves to keep them warm and eat them while they're hot. I'm going to serve them to the officers with some summer greens and pigeon pie.'

'Maybe you could give the recipe to Mary? Father and Henry would really enjoy these.' Mathew picked up another folded Tansy from his plate. It was gone in two bites. He licked the grease from his fingers, took a swallow of beer and belched loudly. 'Just what I needed,' he sighed.

'Glad you enjoyed them.' Ethan smiled. 'You'd better let Mary have something to eat she's been working hard, while you've been sitting here.'

The four elderly nurses watched from a distance. They had been left to cook for themselves and the injured men, eating only regular camp rations of potage, dried fish, bread and cheese. They came together to grumble about not getting any tansies.

Mathew and Mary returned home just as daylight was starting to fade. The air had chilled, and after their meal with Ethan, the walk home was a pleasant end to a summer's day.

'Thank you, Mary. You worked hard today. I wonder how Father managed at home left all on his own.'

Mary gave him a sideways look. She couldn't decide if he was just making conversation or dropping hints that her proper place was back at home. They walked on side by side, Mathew still making small talk, and Mary giving answers where needed. As well as admiring Mathew's skill as a surgeon, she toyed with the thought that maybe, just maybe, she could get Mathew to look on her as something other than a sister-in-law.

Henry and Mortimer had arrived back in Beverley late that afternoon. Mathew greeted his brother, but ignored Mortimer, just giving him a quick glance as if to say: 'What are you doing here?'

Mary cleared scraps of bread and cheese from the table and took them over to Bess, who was curled up on her bed of rags near the chimney. Bess raised her head and flicked the end of her tail to and fro in welcome. She could smell the titbits from the table in Mary's hand.

'What happened in Hull?' Mathew asked his brother quietly before he went to sit at the table with Mortimer. 'And what's he doing here? I thought Captain Overton would have had him arrested.'

'It seems Captain Overton has other ideas,' Henry informed his brother. 'He gave me this letter for you. He wrote a note on the outside, saying that you had to check it hadn't been tampered with before you read it. But it's fine, I haven't let it out of my sight and Mortimer hasn't even tried to get close to it.' Henry took the letter from inside his jacket. Mathew looked at the seal for a moment and then broke open the letter.

Written in Captain Overton's neat hand, he read.

Mathew

I have decided not to arrest Mortimer at the moment; he has explained how he became entrapped and blackmailed into working for Sir John Hotham. I am seeking advice from others on what to do about Sir John and his son and will tell you more about those developments at a later date. I'm still not sure if Mortimer can be trusted, so I have enclosed a cypher that you are to use in all future correspondence. Keep it safe, NO ONE must see it. It is for you and me to use only. I want you to continue to use Mortimer as your messenger; it is too late to try and recruit someone else and at least we both now know about Mortimer's past. He assures me that no one other than Hotham knows you are working for me, as he wants to use the intelligence you provided to develop his own plans and schemes. I don't think Mortimer will double-cross us again now that his treachery is in the open, though I will still have to find a suitable punishment for him later.

God be with you and keep you safe.
Your friend
Robert Overton

Mathew refolded the letter carefully and placed it inside his jacket. He looked at Mortimer. 'It seems as though I have to keep you on. I don't like it, but the captain must know what he's doing.'

The room fell silent, with everyone wondering what to say next. After a few moments, Mathew stood up, 'Well I can't stay here, I need to get back. The camp guards don't like it when anyone returns after dark. You had better come with me—I'll tell anyone who asks about your absence, that you had been taken ill and stayed in Beverley for a few days.'

As Mathew and Mortimer walked up North Bar Within, the only illumination in the street was from the lights shining through the windows of the taverns; all the other buildings had their shutters firmly closed against the night. They passed under Beverley Bar. High above their heads, candlelight escaped into the dimming sky through the small twin leaded-light windows, and the faint sound of a minstrel playing his lute drifted down to them. Mathew looked up above the gateway to the windows.

'The King is still in residence with Lady Gee,' Mathew said to his companion, without even looking at him. 'He must be reluctant to leave Beverley just yet.'

While he was unhappy about working with the treacherous Mortimer, he knew he still had to work and talk to him, but it wasn't going to be easy to be civil to him.

They turned left after passing under the bar, and soon came within sight of the Westwood Common. The growing darkness of the oncoming night masked the untidy scene which was evident during the daytime. In the distance now, they could see small campfires, spread out across the common as they lit up the gentle slopes of the undulating ground of the Yorkshire Wolds. It was as though the stars in the heavens were reflected over the earth: small flickering lights as far as the eye could see, each fire illuminating a tiny patch of the common. It would only be when they drew closer that they would hear the noise of the camp as it settled for the night and the illusion was spoiled by soldiers playing dice or cards, singing and drinking themselves to sleep.

There had been no more attacks from Hull on the king's forces after that rainy night at Anlaby. Mathew thought about the numbers of Parliamentarians that had died or been injured that night, and he wondered how many had made it back to Hull alive, and how many had died of their wounds on the way home.

The attack had been his fault, his and Mortimer's. It was *his* message that had encouraged the attack at Anlaby. The thought of all that death and pain he had caused grieved him. Mortimer's betrayal of that information that had allowed the camp to put up a strong defence, and it was the rain which had made the ground slippery and prevented the charging horses from stopping as they raced down that deceptively long gentle slope which had brought them crashing into the camp's defenders.

His mind filled with the horrors of that night and the thought of what he had done to the three troopers, even though he had no recollection of killing those men. Why couldn't he remember killing them? He could recollect seeing the sword in his hand at the end of the carnage, and Ethan had given him a blow-by-blow account of what had happened, but all Mathew could remember was seeing the soldiers about to attack Ethan, then blackness, until he was looking at their bloodied corpses lying on the ground around him.

They arrived at the entrance to the camp; the guard waved them through, recognising Mathew from his frequent comings and goings.

'We'll go and join Ethan,' Mathew told Mortimer. 'Your wagon and stores have been brought from Anlaby along with ours, you can check it in the morning.'

Mortimer nodded his agreement. When they arrived at the campfire, rather than stay with Mathew and Ethan,

Mortimer went over to his wagon and extracted a waxed groundsheet. 'I'll turn in if you don't mind,' he told the two men. 'It's been a long day.' He wrapped the sheet around himself and lay down beneath his wagon.

'Where's he been?' Ethan asked in a hushed voice.

'I found him in Beverley, said he'd had a fever over the past week and had taken to bed in one of the town's inns,' lied Mathew.

'And you believed him?' Ethan asked incredulously.

Mathew just gave Ethan a blank look and shrugged his shoulders.

Changing the subject, Ethan asked, 'Tell me more about Mary. She's a fine looking lass, is she going to come again?'

Mathew smiled. 'That's my sister you're talking about.' He spoke with mock indignity.

'No, my friend, she's your *sister-in-law*.'

Mathew looked at Ethan's smiling face. He didn't know if he should be offended at Ethan's remark. It was an innocent correction, but somehow he took offence as if it had been a jibe. Mathew explained about his brother and how Mary had volunteered to help him with the wounded and keep him supplied with medicines.

Next morning Mathew was awaked by the usual sounds of the camp. The 'camp-cough' seemed louder this morning, as soldiers cleared their throats and spat the mucus onto the ground. The smell of tobacco drifted through the air as hundreds of clay pipes were lit for the first smoke of the day. The delightful odour of fried bacon wafted across from Ethan's campfire. The officers had got used to their bacon and bread in the morning, washed down with a tankard of small beer, and so had Mathew.

He stretched his arms wide and arched his back—sleeping in a tent, even though he'd been lying on a bed, made his muscles ache in the morning. How he longed to be in a proper bed, inside a house again, and out of the cold morning damp. The soldiers all around him slept out in the open, under hedges, rolled up in waterproof sheets as Mortimer had, or with just their woollen jackets pulled tightly about them. Some slept with a blanket, as close as they dare to the campfire, none seemed to mind too much.

It was still summer, and the day had dawned early and bright. Mathew decided that he would eat first, and then take Mortimer to see Captain Hewitt and provide the man who'd been missing from camp for so long with a fabricated reason for his absence.

The elderly women nurses were up and about their business: one was preparing a cauldron for boiling bandages, while the other three had prepared a meal of bread and cheese left over from the night before, to give to their recovering patients. Mathew watched them work. With each passing day, there was less and less work for them to do as men recovered and returned to their regiments. But, there was still enough work for them to do, for now.

His thoughts in the main, however, were occupied with the killer Martins and the untrustworthy Mortimer. With Mortimer to keep an eye on, how was he to deal with Martins and the others? The only way was to send Mortimer back to Hull so that Captain Overton could deal with him. Mathew no longer felt comfortable having Mortimer around. He would have to find some news to send Mortimer back with.

'Good day to you, Ethan, you are about your business early, as usual, this fine morning,' said Mathew greeting him warmly.

'Bloody good-for-nothing officers,' Ethan huffed angrily, just loud enough for Mathew to hear. 'Most of them spent last night dining in Beverley at the house of Lady Gee with the King and Lord Newcastle, and now they don't fancy eating breakfast. They'll eat later when they rise. If it weren't for the sergeants and corporals, this army might as well pack up and go home. I'll be glad when we move on.'

Having vented his frustration about the officer classes, Ethan greeted Mathew: 'Sit yourself down, there's bread, fresh butter, bacon, a bit of cheese, some boiled eggs and plenty of beer—help yourself.'

Mortimer joined Mathew at the table, plate in hand. 'Good day,' Mortimer said tentatively.

'And to you,' Mathew returned coldly.

Mathew had no sooner finished eating than a young lad in the livery of the King came running up to the three of them.

'Begging your pardons, sirs, I'm looking for Sergeant Surgeon Mathew Fletcher,' the boy panted.

'That'll be me,' Mathew volunteered.

The boy thrust a message into his hand. 'I've been told to tell you, sir, that you are to make all haste to Beverley Bar and the house of Lady Gee. You are to follow me back.' Mathew read the note, which was written on fine paper, folded, but not sealed.

It read:

Surgeon Fletcher

Lady Gee has been taken ill, and at the recommendation of Lt Col Duncombe, the King requires you to attend on her urgently.

Lord Newcastle

Mathew and the boy arrived at the walled garden gate of Lady Gee's house. The lad hammered on the thick oak door and waited for it to open. Once inside, the guards recognised the boy and stood aside, allowing them to pass. They followed the gravel path between formally landscaped gardens, laid out in geometric designs. The box-hedged borders were filled with a multitude of colourful flowers, the scent of which filled the air. Bees massed on purple lavender, which contrasted with red and yellow wallflowers, queen's gillyflowers and heartsease. Three beehives stood against the gated wall and provided sweet honey and beeswax for the occupants of the house.

At the entrance to the large two-story house, two more guards stood at a great wooden double door, studded with heavy nails. The boy stopped and spoke to the guards, then showed them the note from Lord Newcastle, instructing him to fetch the surgeon back from the camp.

Opening the heavy oak doors, they passed through and entered a hall lit with candles. A refectory table stood in the centre of the area on a tiled floor. The right-hand wall was dominated by a fireplace, with no fire laid. The opposite wall contained three sets of big mullioned windows, which would fill the room with natural light on a sunny day.

Lord Newcastle stood near the centre window. Removing his hat, Mathew bowed low, his heavy surgeon's bag slipping from his shoulder and hitting the tiled floor with a clatter.

'Follow me,' was all Newcastle said before he turned and led them through a door in the far corner of the room and took them into a corridor that seemed to run the length of the building on the ground floor. They soon came to a stairway on the left that quickly turned right and continued to the first floor.

Looking through a small window as they climbed, Mathew could see that they were close to the road that ran under Beverley Bar. Lord Newcastle stopped at a closed door and told them to wait there. Moments later the door opened, and they were allowed to enter a narrow room with mullioned windows on either side: it looked as if they were inside the room above Beverley Bar, the very one they had passed beneath the night before. The boy did not venture past the entrance of the room as Lord Newcastle led Mathew to where two elderly ladies were fussing around someone who was sitting in a cushioned chair.

Turning and taking a step back, Lord Newcastle indicated towards the lady in the chair. 'We were dining with His Majesty when Lady Gee was taken ill,' Newcastle explained. 'She seems to be in some distress, and as the King and I are guests in Lady Gee's house, His Majesty instructed that you should be brought to see her. It would seem that Colonel Duncombe holds you in some regard. The King has retired to his rooms and the other guests have left out of respect for Lady Gee. I will leave you with her and her maids while you examine the lady. If you should need to speak to me, give your message to the boy that brought you here.'

Having said all he was going to, Lord Newcastle left the room immediately, clearly not wanting to risk catching whatever it was that was ailing Lady Gee.

Mathew felt the pulse at her wrist, noticing her paper-white bony hand with brown liver spots, her blue veins clearly visible through her skin. She lay unconscious in her chair, her breathing seemed normal, and her pulse was steady but weak. As he looked at her face the signs were all too obvious: Lady Gee was suffering from an attack of apoplexy. The left half of her face had dropped, her mouth turned downwards, and her cheek drooped, pulling at the skin below her eye.

Turning to the two maids who stood either side of Lady Gee's chair, Mathew suggested that they take their mistress to bed while he made some preparations. He sent the boy who had brought him to the house to the Fletcher family home, with a note for Mary, listing some ingredients he needed, and asking her to give them to the boy. Within half an hour the boy had returned, with the ingredients and Mary.

'I had to come,' she told him. 'The boy said you were here alone. It will be quicker if I help you make up the medicines.' Mary panted, out of breath, clearly having rushed to get there as quickly as possible.

'That's very good of you, Mary,' Mathew said gratefully. 'Make up the ingredients for a sharp *blistering plaster and a julep*. Get the boy to take you to the kitchen to prepare them and then bring you up to Lady Gee's bedchamber when they are ready. I'm going to bleed and vomit her while you are making the preparations.'

Without waiting for confirmation from Mary, Mathew left in the direction the two maids had taken Lady Gee, reckoning that they would have had enough time to prepare and put Lady Gee to bed. The bedchamber wasn't hard to find—it was one of the rooms that led off from the landing at the top of the stairs. He could hear the two maids talking together inside the chamber as they prepared Lady Gee for bed.

He knocked on the door and was told to wait, as her ladyship was not ready. A couple of minutes later the door was opened by one of the maids, who beckoned him inside. The room was small, smaller and more sparsely decorated than he had expected, with just a decent sized bed, a chair, nightstand with candles, and a couple of trunks with clothes laid across them. This was evidently not the room of a lady, Mathew thought, reasoning that she must have given her own room up to the king, and been left to sleep in what looked like a spare bedchamber.

Mathew sent the slightly younger looking of the two middle-aged maids down to the kitchen for a bowl and a glass, leaving the other sitting in the chair acting as a chaperone. The other maid returned with a blue-and-white earthenware bowl decorated with flowers, and a green fluted glass.

'I need to bleed your mistress,' Mathew explained to the pair. 'I want you to sit her up in bed, while I take some blood.' The two women looked at each other, clearly not happy with what was about to happen. They used pillows to bolster Lady Gee into a sitting position and sat either side of her on the bed.

Mathew placed the bowl on the floor close to the bed. Finding a suitable vein in the crook of her arm, he used his lancet to make a small incision into the largest vein and inserted a *silver cannula*. The blood flowed freely through the reed-like tube and splashed into the bowl. After he had taken about twelve ounces of blood, he removed the cannula and placed a couple of *plegits* to the wound, applying a roller bandage to hold them in place.

Pouring a couple of ounces of *crocus metallorum* into the glass, he tipped its contents into Lady Gee's mouth while the two maids held her head back. The lady gagged a little as the bitter liquid made its way to her stomach. Then, almost as soon as Mathew had put the glass down, Lady Gee retched twice, and then vomited the contents of her stomach into the bowl of blood that Mathew held ready. The stench of the vomit and warm blood filled the room. The two maids gagged and looked away while Lady Gee moaned—it was the first sound Mathew had heard her make since he had arrived.

There was a knock on the bedchamber door, and Mary walked in. Her step faltered for a moment, as the smell in the room took her breath away. Fighting to retain the contents of her own stomach, she brought over the prepared blistering plaster and julep, containing *rue-water, harts-horn and sugar*. Mathew applied the plaster to the back of Lady Gee's neck, with instructions to the two maids that when her ladyship opened her eyes, she was to be encouraged to drink the julep, but that the plaster must not be removed until he returned later that evening.

Mathew followed Mary back down to the kitchen, where they cleaned and packed away everything they had brought to the house. Lady Gee's cook watched them as she stirred a pot over the fire. A bead of sweat hung from the tip of her bony nose, threatening to drip into the bubbling vessel. She was a small lean woman with strands of greasy grey hair peeking out from under her coif. She was wearing a brown linen skirt which showed the remains of meals long past, over which she wore a sleeveless brown linen bodice, atop a grey chemise. A younger woman dressed in similar attire, probably the cook's daughter, rolled out pastry on a table against the back wall. Neither of the women spoke to them; they just exchanged looks with each other as though they could read minds. Mathew noted that whatever it was she was cooking smelt very good, and her appearance probably belied her culinary abilities. A cough from the door brought the presence of the boy to their attention.

'Lord Newcastle is waiting to see you both in the hall,' the lad told them. 'Please leave what you are doing and come with me.'

Mathew and Mary shared a concerned look that meant *have we done something wrong?* Before straightening their attire and following the boy back to the hall.

The boy entered the hallway first, bowed to the lord, and stepped aside to allow Mathew and Mary to enter. Lord Newcastle was standing beside the empty fireplace. Mathew bowed first, while Mary stood slightly behind him and curtsied, wanting to hide her plain clothes from the sight of Lord Newcastle, who was dressed in a silver-grey silk suit, trimmed with yellow ribbons with gold cone-shaped aglets. His fine lace collar was lying across his shoulders under a profusion of thick, curled brown hair.

'His Majesty wishes to know the health of Lady Gee,' Newcastle said, his bored tone suggesting that he would rather be somewhere else.

'Her ladyship is gravely ill,' Mathew told him abruptly. 'She is afflicted with apoplexy and is still unconscious. The longer she remains so, the less likely is her survival. If she should awaken, she will be paralysed down the left side of her body. I have left her medicines and given instruction to her maids on how to administer them. There is no more that I can do for her at the moment. I shall return later today to access her progress. With your permission, I will retain the services of Mistress Mary here, as she can be of great assistance to me.'

'If that is what you require, so be it,' Newcastle informed Mathew. 'I will instruct the guards to allow you admittance at any time of day or night as you may require. As a guest of Lady Gee, the King is greatly distressed by her illness. You are to stay away from the king's rooms. This boy will convey any information or requests you may have to me, while you are attending on Lady Gee. The King has given you that purse as payment for your services.' Newcastle nodded towards a leather bag on the hall table. 'Be back here at four of the clock; His Majesty will wish to hear of Lady Gee's progress.'

The boy stepped forward and bowed to Lord Newcastle, then turned and indicated that Mathew and Mary should follow him to the door. They showed their deference to Lord Newcastle, turned and followed the boy into the garden.

'How do we address you?' Mathew asked the skinny boy as they walked back through the garden. He looked to be about ten years of age.

'My name is Johnny Figis, and I work for the king,' he answered proudly. 'I can run miles and miles without stopping, so I carry messages for His Majesty. Some of the houses we stay in are so big that I'm near knackered by day's end, what with all the running from room to room and up and down stairs that I do. But this house of Lady Gee's is tiny compared to the Palace of Westminster in London.' Figis, spoke with ease and confidence as he elucidated about his job which he was so proud of. 'I'll leave you at the gate, but be back before four of the clock. Lord Newcastle hates to be kept waiting.'

Back in the Westwood camp, Mathew needed time to think. He only had a few hours before having to return to Lady Gee's house. He knew the location of the house the King and Lord Newcastle were residing in. This was important news that Captain Overton should know. He decided that after his second visit to the house he would encode a message for Mortimer to take to Overton to let him know about the location of the king. It was also a useful way of getting rid of Mortimer for a while, and would also allow Mathew to have a practice with the secret code.

Mathew and Mary returned to Lady Gee's house at the appointed time, entering through the gate in the back wall, where the guard greeted them. Mathew carried his large linen surgeon's bag, hung from his shoulder, and Mary had her basket of jars and poultices. As they walked up the gravel path towards the house the heat of the day was easing. The scent from the flowers was thick and heady, and bees buzzed busily over the flowers making the most of the fine weather. The medical pair listened to the hum from the bees' wings, the sound rising and falling as they darted from one flower head to another, as the insects made their way across the orderly laid out garden with its multitude of colourful blooms. Mathew and Mary slowed their pace as they enjoyed the vista around them. The boy, Figis, stood at the door waiting to take them inside, a smile on his happy round face.

Figis, took them straight up to Lady Gee saying, 'I will wait for you in the hall,' he smiled, then left, running back down the stairs. As they entered the bedchamber, they saw that Lady Gee's two maids were sitting dutifully on cushioned chairs either side of the bed, a single candle lit on the small table, the shutters closed at the small window.

While Mary set her basket down on top of one of the oak chests, Mathew crossed to the bed to examine Lady Gee. The old lady did not open her eyes as he felt for her pulse. He noticed the blue-grey pallor to her lips and around her eyes, while her sunken cheeks gave her the look of a corpse. But for the slight rise and fall of her chest, at first sight, she could have easily been mistaken for dead already. Her pulse was weaker than earlier, but it was steady.

'Has she awoken at all?' Mathew asked the two maids.

They both shook their heads.

'Have you been able to get her to take any of the *juleps* I left you?'

'No, sir,' the maid on the right-hand side of the bed said feebly, while the other woman sniffled into a handkerchief. 'She has not roused at all,' she continued. 'I tried to get her to take a sip of the julep, but it just dribbled from her lips.'

Had Lady Gee not been so weak, the right course of action would have been to bleed her again, this time taking blood from the jugular vein in her neck. Since it looked to Mathew as if her death was inevitable, he did not want to hasten the process, so he decided to leave her be.

'I would like a small bowl of rose water. Would one of you ladies fetch one up from the kitchen, please?' Mathew asked.

The maid with the handkerchief rose and left the room, leaving the door unlatched. It swung back a few inches, allowing the light from outside to enter the dimly lit bedchamber.

While the maid was away, Mathew informed the remaining helper that he didn't expect Lady Gee to recover and that she would probably pass over within a day or so. As the room fell silent again, voices could be heard coming up the stairs from a room below. Lord Newcastle was speaking with someone else, a person with a much softer voice that had a slight stammer. This voice, which belonged to the king, went on.

'The Queen is in H-H-Holland; she h-h-has taken her own jewels to pawn them to raise the much-needed funds and weapons we need to continue this c-campaign. Colonel Duncombe is to inform his officers tonight, that we are moving the army. Hull has been such a vexation to us,' lamented the king. 'We will remove our person from this h-h-house to H-H-Halls-Garth House, where we may be better accommodated, until the time of our d-departure.'

'Your Majesty, I have started preparations for your departure to the Midlands. An advance party has left already—' they heard Newcastle say, but the rest of his sentence was lost as the maid returned with a small bowl of rose water. Mathew's attention was brought back to Lady Gee as the maid set the bowl down on the table next to the candle.

'When I leave, I want you to pour the rest of the *julep* into the *rose water*,' Mathew told her. 'You are to apply it, using a cloth, to her ladyship's lips, to prevent them from drying. You are to make her as comfortable as possible. I am going to remove the *blister plaster* and replace it with a balm to ease the irritation on her neck. But there is little more I can do for her. She is in God's hands now. Send for me immediately should her situation change.'

Mary had prepared the balm for Mathew while he had been speaking to the maids. She took the *blister plaster* he had removed and passed him the soothing balm she had applied to an *emplaster*. The scent of lavender filled the room, reminding him of the garden. After ensuring that Lady Gee was resting comfortably, Mathew and Mary gathered their things together and left the two maids with their mistress.

Outside the bedchamber, Mathew found that the voices he had listened to earlier had gone silent. Mathew led Mary down to the hall, to where Figis was dutifully waiting.

'How is she?' Figis asked. 'The King will wish to know.'

'Her fate is with God, but I don't give her long for this world. She is old and frail, and I don't think she has the strength or will to fight the inevitable.' So saying, Mathew took Mary's arm and followed Figis to the door.

'That's a pity,' said the boy. 'I liked her. She always had a smile for me.'

Chapter Twenty-Eight

After saying 'farewell,' Mathew left Mary at the garden gate, for her, it was only a few minutes' walk back to Cuckstool Pit Lane and home. Whereas Mathew headed out onto the Westwood thinking about the conversation he'd overheard. With the advance party already gone and the King to follow shortly, the rest of his army would be leaving Beverley very soon. Meanwhile, the King was relocating to Halls-Garth House, close to the Beverley Minster. With the importance of the news he had overheard, Mathew's step quickened. That night when all his patients had settled, he encoded the new intelligence for Captain Overton.

No sooner had he finished preparing his message than Ethan appeared at his tend door, asking what miracles he had performed today.

'I wouldn't let any of the religious zealots hear you speaking like that—you could be accused of blasphemy,' Mathew retorted playfully.

'Aye, there's little humour to be had from religion these days. Everyone foretelling of the second coming—'Repent ye sinners or thy God will smite you down!'.' He spoke his next words quietly so that only Mathew could hear. 'Tell me, how does anyone know what God really wants of us?'

'He wants us to be sensible and not say things that will result in us being sentenced to a flogging, branding or the piercing of our tongue by a red-hot poker. That's what he wants!' Mathew snapped back, afraid of who might overhear their conversation. 'Now, how about some of that fine ale you keep for yourself and a few scraps of something good, for a hungry friend?' Ethan laughed, 'come on then, I'm sure I've got something to please your belly.'

As they moved to the campfire, the sound of familiar voices encouraged Mortimer to drift over from his wagon.

'May I sit with you a while?' he asked sheepishly.

'If you must,' responded Mathew coldly. Ethan kept quiet and collected another plate and tankard.

'How fares Lady Gee?' asked Ethan, to distract Mathew's attention from Mortimer.

'She'll probably be dead by this time tomorrow. I hate not knowing why these things happen. All I can say is some bad humour has afflicted her brain, but there are no means to determine what it is or how it has happened. It is a disease that afflicts many people as they grow older, but no one can say what the true cause may be. It is one of the mysteries of the body that confounds all physicians.' Mathew's voice rose with the passion of his words.

'I suppose it is God's will,' Mortimer contributed.

Mathew and Ethan stared at Mortimer. Had he heard Ethan's blasphemy earlier on, they wondered? He noticed the looks of surprise on their faces and fell silent for a while.

The three of them ate together making small talk. Ethan couldn't help but notice the coldness that had built up between Mathew and Mortimer and wondered if their acquaintance had been troubled by misunderstandings he was unaware of.

After they had eaten, Mathew excused himself, saying he had some papers to write and gave a parting look towards Mortimer. Ethan detected that some unspoken understanding had passed between them just before Mathew had turned away.

'What's the trouble between you two?' Ethan asked Mortimer bluntly when Mathew was out of earshot.

Mortimer was taken aback by the question and fumbled for a reply: 'Nothing, well, er, nothing really. It's personal, that's all. Things will get better between us in time.' He forced a smile.

Ethan held Mortimer's stare. 'See they do,' he said, sternly, and then offered to top up his tankard with more ale.

'No, thank you, Ethan. That is one of the problems between us. Mathew had to pull me out of the gutter because of drink.' Mortimer's face went red at the half-lie, but the answer seemed to satisfy Ethan. They sat and talked more freely, seeming to have found an understanding, until Mortimer took his leave and went to find Mathew.

Mathew looked up as Mortimer entered the surgeon's tent. 'I have a few things I need from Hull and a message for you to deliver.' There was no warmth or friendship in Mathew's voice, just the coldness of the half command, half request, and the knowledge that Mortimer must obey him.

Mortimer sighed. 'I'll leave in the morning.'

The surgeon folded and sealed the letter in the same way that Overton had done for him. 'You can collect the letter first thing in the morning. I suggest you turn in now so you can get an early start tomorrow.'

Mortimer left the tent and returned to his wagon to bed down for the night. Mathew cursed. He knew he had to make more effort to get along with Mortimer, but he was finding it hard to do so.

Mortimer was determined to correct the wrongs he had done. The roads were free to travel again now the siege of Hull had been given up, so Mortimer took his wagon on the direct route to Hull. As he drove along, he formulated his plan.

Now Sir John Hotham and his son had been imprisoned; he was sure Captain Overton would soon want to rid himself of his troublesome servant.

He had set off for Hull later than he had wanted to and arrived late, the only stabling to be found was near the docks. Leaving his wagon at the inn where he would spend the night, he set off to the offices of Captain Overton. It was dark, and the dockside bustled with sailors and dock labourers heading for the many taverns that frequented the riverfront. The smell of the day's herring catch hung heavily in the air, and discarded bits of fish were being dragged away into dark corners, as the rats came out for their nightly feast.

Mortimer was halfway along Chapel Lane when four sailors entered, blocking his exit to the High Street.

Looking back over his shoulder he saw that another group of men had followed him into the lane, making their way towards him, four abreast, he had no clear way past them and expected the worst. The warehouses either side of Chapel Lane blocked off any kind of escape, so he resigned himself to face one of the groups before they merged and go down fighting.

The scared man decided to continue going forward, to face the group in front of him. They were talking noisily together in a language he didn't understand. His hand went to the knife in his belt, resting it there, ready to withdraw it and use on the first sailor that attacked him.

As he moved forwards, the sailors stopped talking. All of them stared at him as they drew closer. Mortimer slowly began to withdraw his knife in the darkness of the lane. He hoped fervently that they wouldn't see it, at least not until it was too late for the closest one to defend himself against his blade.

The sailors were no more than six feet away from him now; his step faltered for a second as he prepared for the attack. The four men separated into pairs, passing either side of him, giving him a friendly nod as they passed him by. They had been little more than shapes, silhouetted against the light of the lane entrance and he had panicked. He chided himself for his foolishness.

As he emerged from the lane, his hands were still shaking. He needed a drink. Across the lane was the white meat market with the Mermaid Inn on the far side, the light from the windows and open door illuminating the cobbles with a pool of yellow light. Mortimer needed a drink, and a pie after his scare in the lane; this place would do.

He entered the inn, a fug of tobacco smoke billowed around the ceiling as the draught from the door swirled it, like eddies in a pool. The smell of spilt beer and unwashed bodies was even stronger than that of the fish from the dockside, but at least the inn wasn't overcrowded.

He found the landlord and paid for the food and drink, then took a table in the corner of the taproom and sat with his back to the wall on a bench seat. He'd ordered a mutton pie and a jug of beer. The girl who brought him his order came to him with a cheery smile and a swagger. Mortimer was captivated by her beautiful heart shaped face. He watched her as she returned to the serving hatch, entranced by the sway of her hips underneath her skirt. *Umm, not bad,* he thought.

He took a large bite from the pie. The greasy meat flavoured with swede, sage and mint in a plain flour-and-water pastry case, first crumbled in his hand and then fell to his plate, warm gravy running over his fingers. He licked them clean. The action of eating steadied his nerves a little. He took a large swallow of beer to wash down the pie and leaned back against the wall. He watched the girl as she traversed the room from one customer to the next. He felt the tension in his loins, but he didn't have the time to satisfy his longing.

He had been hungrier than he had realised and very quickly the pie was finished. He mopped up the remnants of gravy from his plate with a piece of bread, pushed the plate away, belched and let his eyes scan the room.

At another table sat three men engrossed in conversation, one of whom Mortimer had seen at the Guildhall when he'd gone to meet Sir John Hotham. The one he recognised pushed a folded paper across the table to one of the others, who put it inside his jacket without reading it. He watched the three men for some time as they talked continually, their heads close together, never looking around, or laughing like most of the other people frequenting the inn were doing. It occurred to Mortimer that they were not just three friends sharing a drink. This looked like information that was being shared and passed on.

After a few minutes the party of three split up, one of them going to the door to leave, the others heading for the stairs to the upper floor of the inn. Mortimer could see the one at the door clearly now: he was definitely the man who worked at the Guildhall in Hotham's outer office. Mortimer donned his hat, and slowly rising from his seat; he followed the clerk out into the night. The man he was pursuing didn't look back, but made his way directly across the empty market and onto the High Street, past a couple of warehouses and on towards a large house set back from the road.

At this house, a low garden wall allowed passers-by to view the well laid out garden and the two-storey building's façade, with its columned porch and the large windows. The clerk entered a narrow passage to the side of the garden that led to the rear of the property.

Running to the corner of the passage, Mortimer was in time to see the man enter the rear garden through a gate in a high wall. He could hear the creak of the rusty hinges as the gate swung open. As it closed, Mortimer ran down the passage and passed the gate into the darkness beyond: he needed to see what the clerk was doing and whom he was meeting.

Here, Mortimer could smell the river. The tide had to be low, as the stink from the sewage and rubbish that accumulated daily on the mud had raised an unholy smell during this warm weather.

The branches of a willow tree hung down over the garden wall. Grabbing hold of one, he used it to pull himself up to the top of the wall, where he could see the clerk at the back door of the house talking to a woman in an apron. As he lay across the top of the wall watching and saw the clerk enter the house and the door close. The only light in the garden came from the small kitchen window near the back door.

Mortimer dropped over the wall into what had to be the herb garden, because as he landed, he could smell, sage, mint, thyme and garlic, from the plants he'd crushed under his feet. The garden ran from the back of the house and sloped downwards towards the edge of the river. A small skiff was attached to a post at the river's edge. As the tide was low, the skiff was resting on the mud, but he noted how it would be relatively easy for a couple of men to push it to the water's edge, even when the tide was at its lowest.

Keeping low, he crossed to the window and peered in at its corner, doing his best to keep out of sight. He saw the clerk standing by the table, hat in hand, the woman who had let him in was nowhere to be seen. After a few moments, she returned with a man, presumably the steward to the master of the house, his clothes being too plain and simple to be those of a gentleman: just a brown woollen waistcoat over a linen shirt, with matching brown breeches. He watched them exchange a few brief words. The steward shook his head, then held out his hand and received the paper that the clerk had put inside his jacket at the inn.

The clerk replaced his hat and turned to the door. Mortimer took a couple of steps back out of the light of the window and held his breath. There was nowhere to hide except in the darkness and silence of the night and no time to run. The back door opened and the clerk stepped outside, stopped, and turned back.

'Please, you must remember to give the note to Captain Legge as soon as he returns,' Mortimer heard the man say. 'Sir John Hotham has been taken prisoner by Robert Overton, and only Captain Legge can get word to Lord Newcastle and negotiate for Sir John's release.' He turned toward the garden gate and left the way he came in.

Mortimer heard the kitchen door close and a bolt slide across, to lock it.

He released his breath, leaning back against the wall of the house, taking in great gulps of air. *Quite clearly Hotham still has people working for him*, Mortimer thought. *This could be the information I need to redeem myself in Captain Overton's eyes.*

Once he was sure that the clerk was well ahead of him, Mortimer left the shadows at the back of the house and made his way back to the point in the wall where he'd climbed over. Climbing up again and dropping down into the passage, he found that all was silent, and made his way towards the front of the house.

As he reached the High Street, he could see the clerk crossing the empty marketplace back towards the Mermaid Inn. He let the clerk enter and then watched from the doorway as the clerk paused for a moment in the taproom, looking towards the table where his friends had been sitting before moving off towards the stairs and disappeared.

Mortimer entered the taproom and went back to where he had been seated. There were fewer people in the inn now, it was getting late, but Mortimer was too alert and excited to want to sleep just yet. He ordered a beer from the girl who'd served him before, and resettled in his seat in the corner, to think about what to do next. He surmised that all three men were staying at the inn, so hopefully, he would see them again. He would leave it until tomorrow before finding Captain Overton. If he could learn more about these three men, he would have intelligence of his own to pass on to the captain.

Next morning Mortimer returned early. He'd had a bad night and little sleep. He'd found it hard to get to sleep at first and then he'd been troubled with dreams about being trapped in the garden, remembering its heavy scent of herbs. Then, out of the darkness had come the faces of his family, racing towards him, screaming in fear. He awoke several times, before falling asleep each time to repeat the same dream.

The serving girl came over and placed a plate of buttered bread and a tankard of small beer in front of him. He picked at the bread on his plate and sipped his beer, but it left a bitter taste in his mouth. He looked up at the sound of voices coming down the stairs into the taproom: sure enough, it was the three men he'd seen the night before. They took the table next to his, the serving girl didn't ask what they wanted, but just put a large jug of beer on the table, along with three plates of bread, cold meat and pickled herrings.

'What do we do now that Hotham's been arrested?' asked one of them in a hushed voice.

'I'll let you know after the captain tells me what his plans are,' said the clerk Mortimer had followed.

'I need to know if I still have to find out who the spy is in the Beverley camp,' added the second man. 'With no intelligence from Sir John's office, all I know is it's one of fifteen hundred men the King has got camped on the Westwood common.'

'Just give me a chance to speak to the captain,' answered the clerk. 'In the meantime, we wait. We're still getting paid, so stop complaining. I've been told I have to wait here until the captain sends for me. You two can do as you please for now, but check back here regular, in case things change.'

If I could find out who this Captain Legge was that they were talking about and give his name to Captain Overton, it might go a long way to redeeming my mistakes of the past,

Mortimer thought. *Maybe I learn more by watching the house to see who comes and goes.*

The meat market was getting busy. It was mostly pork that was on sale today, though there was some herring, some vegetables, chickens, eggs, bread and pies for sale from traders around the edge of the market. Mortimer decided to mingle with the crowd; all the while keeping the house in sight.

He wandered from stall to stall looking for a pie to eat. Now that he'd decided what it was he had to do, his appetite had returned, and he wished he'd made more of his breakfast. He bought a pie and ate it slowly as he paced up and down the market.

After about an hour, a woman came out of the passage he'd used the night before. Seeing the apron she wore, he realised that it was probably the women he'd seen in the kitchen. He watched her draw closer, noticing the large basket over her arm. She moved along the meat stalls examining the joints of pork.

Since she was walking ahead of him, Mortimer decided to follow her. He studied the woman, her brown skirt, its hem dragging in the market litter, and now stained black with grime. She was clearly poorly paid, and unable to afford more material with which to make a second skirt to wear while the other was being washed. However, the simple garment showed off her neat little bottom as she leaned over the stalls. The shawl over her shoulders was woven into a checker pattern of various colours made from un-dyed wool. Mortimer kept a few paces behind her, wondering if he could get into a conversation with her. She'd bought a joint of pork and moved on to the vegetables, then purchased some bread. It was when she bought some eggs that the thought occurred to him.

He stopped following her and dodged around the stalls towards the house, where he waited. He'd bought another pie to aid his plan. The woman with the dirty skirt hem came out from between the market stalls and made her way back to the house. Making it look as if he was concentrating on eating, and pretending not to look where he was going, Mortimer barged into the lady from the house, nearly knocking her over. The eggs fell from the top of her basket and shattered on the cobbles.

'You clumsy fool!' she bellowed and burst out crying. 'I have no money left to buy more eggs, and now Alderman Barnard will beat me, and stop the money for the eggs from my wages. You fool! You are an idiot! Just look what you've done!'

This was the first time that Mortimer had managed to get a look at her face. She was a comely lass, though her thin face was ageing before its time, no doubt due to long hours toiling in a sweaty kitchen. Her brown eyes looked tired, and the brown hair was lank beneath her coif. It would probably not take much to make her look pretty, but as a servant, it was unlikely that she'd ever had the chance to improve her looks. Mortimer apologised profusely, throwing the remains of his pie in the gutter.

'Please let me help you,' he begged her. 'If you will follow me back to the egg seller, I will buy you more eggs, and then your master need never know of those that got broken. Please, I beg you, forgive my clumsiness,' he went on, in the most charming manner he could effect. 'Is your master really that cruel, that he would beat you, and make you pay for the broken eggs?'

'Yes, he would,' said the woman after a moment, still staring at the broken eggs on the ground. 'Maybe I should come to the house and explain to him that it was my fault,' volunteered Mortimer.

'No, no, Alderman Barnard would get most upset,' the woman said, beginning to sound panicky. 'Besides, what's the point? You've promised to replace the eggs that got broken.'

'If that is what you wish, Miss, er,' he paused for a moment. 'May I ask your name?' Mortimer gave her a pleasing smile.

'Appleyard, Judith Appleyard. And what might your name be, apart from clumsy fool?' she answered, returning his smile to reveal fine white teeth.

The smile lit up her face. Mortimer looked into her eyes, and his heart missed a beat.

'Well, fool?' she teased, impatient for his reply. 'What's your name?'

'Oh, sorry, it's Charles Mortimer,' he said, regaining his composure. He bought a small knot of pansies from a stall and gave them to Judith. 'Please accept these as an apology.'

Judith blushed and laid them on top of her basket. They arrived at the egg stall, and Mortimer bought a dozen eggs.

'There you are, now all is well again. I would like to walk you back across the market if that would please you, Miss Appleyard.'

She smiled again, and his heart once more skipped a beat.

'That would be welcome,' she replied graciously. 'Thank you, Mr Mortimer.'

They set off at a slow pace, walking side by side.

'Let me carry your basket for you, it must be heavy,' Mortimer offered, and he lifted the basket from Judith's arm. 'This is very heavy. I expect you have a large household to feed.'

'No, not really,' she answered. 'Mr Barnard and his wife live on their own most of the time, but we have a guest at the moment.'

'A relative, I suppose?' Mortimer tried to sound as casual as he could.

'No, Mr Mortimer, he's an army gentleman, a Captain Legge. He doesn't go out much, though he gets visitors from time to time, and he sends lots of letters. Mr Comings, the steward, often has to arrange for letters to be sent out. Mr Comings says he writes to a baron, because lots of the letters go to Baron Belly something, up near Thirsk, wherever that is.' She was obviously enjoying Mortimer's company and attention.

Mortimer escorted her as far as the passageway.

'I very much hope I get the chance to bump into you again someday,' he said, returning her basket before removing his hat in a gesture of farewell.

Judith blushed and curtsied in return before the pair separated.

Mortimer sat on a stool outside Captain Overton's office. He'd been told that the captain was out but would be back shortly, and the man who was so keen to make amends wondered what sort of a reception he would receive when he returned. As he sat waiting he could feel his heart thumping in his chest, his nervousness was making him sweat a little—he could feel the dampness in his armpits and on his top lip. He took a deep breath and exhaled slowly as began to count the number of bricks from floor to ceiling in the wall opposite him, once again.

Eventually, Captain Overton returned. Mortimer stood as the captain came towards him, then removed his hat and gave a short bow. Overton ignored him and walked into his office and closed the door behind him.

Mortimer sat back down and waited. Being ignored was not what he had expected, and it made him feel even worse. His head had started to pound, and his hands began to shake.

Ten minutes later the door opened. The captain didn't come out; he didn't call out Mortimer's name. The door was just left open.

Mortimer waited for a moment, then, nervously got to his feet. Hat in hand, he stood in the doorway.

'Come in, man. What do you want?' said the captain, without raising his head from the note he was writing.

'Sir, I am most humbly sorry for what I have done, but I have news from Surgeon Fletcher and important information I have discovered on my own, that will be of great interest to you.' Mortimer's voice was pleading and pitiful, but deeply sincere.

Overton put down his quill. 'Let me have the surgeon's letter.'

Overton took the letter, broke the seal, and then took his time in deciphering the coded message, leaving Mortimer standing in silence. After he had finished, Overton turned the decoded message over and placed a book on top of it. 'Well? What's this important information you have?'

'Captain, I know I betrayed your trust in me and that I must be punished. But now that you understand why I did what I did, maybe you can understand the power that Sir John Hotham held over me.'

'What is this information you have?' Overton snapped, rapidly losing his patience. 'Tell me, before I have you arrested.'

'Sir, it is this. I arrived in Hull late last night, too late to come and see you, so I took a room at an inn. That was when I saw the clerk from Sir John Hotham's office talking to two other men…' Mortimer went on to tell all that he had learned about the clerk, Captain Legge, the house and the Baron.

Overton's curiosity was aroused by this new intelligence the former traitor had brought him.

'Go back to the Mermaid Inn and find out more about the clerk and these other two men. I want to know why Captain Legge, whom I happen to know is, Master of the Kings Armouries, is in Hull and hasn't announced his presence to anyone in authority. I want to know who his baron friend is. You have done well, Mortimer, I grant you, but you haven't redeemed yourself yet, and it would seem Alderman Barnard has some explaining to do as well.'

Overton removed Mathew's letter and its decoded copy from below the book and locked them in a chest which stood against the wall. He collected a pile of documents from the shelf behind his desk and followed Mortimer out of the building, where they separated.

Mortimer went back to the Mermaid Inn to wait for the three men to return.

Meanwhile, Captain Overton went to visit Alderman Barnard at the Guildhall.

With the bundle of documents under his arm, Overton entered the three-storey red-brick Guildhall on the High

Street. He asked to see Alderman Barnard, who, though ousted as Lord Mayor of Hull by Sir John Hotham, had carried on as the senior council official, doing most of the work that Hotham should have dealt with. Sir John had paid little heed to official council business as Governor of Hull, preferring to take advantage of his status on the council to further his own business dealings and to gain intelligence that would re-ingratiate him with the king.

Captain Overton was asked to wait in the hall. The oak-panelled entrance hall was large, with just one desk set on a platform so that all those who entered would have to look up at the clerk who sat there. It would be this man who, if someone arrived without an appointment, would decide if you would be allowed to meet the council officials. Captain Overton would not be one of those who would be refused attendance: the arrest of Sir John Hotham had seen to that.

The clerk, in his black gown and cap, hurried away to the mayor's office. Clearly, Barnard had not been slow at reclaiming the best office in the Guildhall on the arrest of its previous occupant. The clerk returned, bowing low to the Captain, and requested that he follow him. As they entered the mayor's office, Alderman Barnard crossed the room to greet his visitor.

'To what do I owe the honour of this visit, Captain?' Barnard asked, showing Overton to a chair.

'Duty, Alderman Barnard. I have brought the accounts of the garrison for you to sign.' Overton smiled as he laid the documents on Barnard's desk. 'It is a nice day, so I decided to deliver them myself.'

'May I offer you some refreshment, Captain? It seems that Sir John has left a number of fine bottles of wine in his office when he had to—er—leave prematurely.'

Barnard poured wine from a silver jug into a fine matching silver goblet and proffered it to Overton.

'I must admit, I do have another reason for being here,' Overton continued. 'Now that Sir John Hotham is under arrest, I feel we must nurture an understanding beneficial to us both. I would deem it a great compliment if you would be my guest of honour at a banquet with the East Yorkshire Trained Band Officers tomorrow evening.' Overton smiled as he baited the trap.

Somewhat surprised at the invitation, Barnard was taken aback. 'Why thank you, Captain, I would be pleased to attend. I suppose it is only fitting that I should meet the officers of the garrison. Yes, thank you, Captain, I would be delighted to attend.'

Mortimer entered the taproom in the Mermaid Inn. The inn was getting busy as midday approached. It wasn't an official market day in the town, but many traders had set up to sell their wares and the daily necessities of life. He found a table and ordered a beer, and a mutton pie, and settled down to wait for the three men he had observed earlier.

They arrived not long after three of the clock, and, as Mortimer had hoped, they sat at the table they had used previously. *People are creatures of habit,* he observed to himself, being Captain Overton's steward for over a year had taught him that. He stared into his tankard of beer, trying not to look interested in the three men who were sitting at the adjacent table, as he all the while concentrated hard to overhear their conversation.

'Now I don't have Hotham to watch, I can't see the point in us staying here,' said the greasy-haired clerk from the Guildhall.

'We're staying here 'cos we're getting well paid for an easy job, and I for one don't care if there's nowt to report, so long as I get paid,' said one of the other two men, with a remarkably large nose.

'Well, I've still got Barnard to keep an eye on, but we know he's for the king. Come on Potter, get your cards out, let's have a game of All Fours,' said the third man, who had blond hair.

'Aye,' said Big Nose.

'Well, I should be out looking for the spy in the Beverley camp,' revealed Potter. 'Even if Hotham's been arrested, we still work for Captain Legge,' he hissed in a low voice.

'You can do that tomorrow,' said Big Nose, 'if you're that desperate to please the captain, but you've got no idea of whom you're looking for. All you do know is that the person returned to Beverley because a relative was sick. People are always getting sick; you're wasting your time. There must be hundreds of people in and out of that camp, and you've got to find one, and you say you've got no idea what he looks like!'

'Fine, you win. Only if the captain finds out we're sat here playing cards, I'll tell him it's your fault for not listening to me,' said Potter.

Potter pulled a deck of playing cards from the pouch he carried on his belt. He licked his fingers, gave the cards a quick shuffle and started to deal them out, face down, on the table. 'Walker, you can choose trumps, you're on my left. The first one to get ten points is the winner.'

Mortimer took his chance. He stepped across to the card players' table. 'Excuse me, gentlemen, I wondered if I may impose upon your hospitality?' he asked them. 'I am awaiting the arrival of a couple of wagons with supplies, which are late. I am on my own and was wondering if I might join you in your game and also enjoy your company to help me pass the time until my good arrive? My name is Charles Mortimer; I am a Lead Merchant.'

The three men looked at one another. Potter nodded, saying, 'Take a seat, Mr Mortimer. My name is Thomas Potter, and this is Henry Walker and Joseph Fox.' All four men exchange polite nods. 'We're playing All Fours,' Potter added as he gathered in the cards, to re-deal them, this time for four players.

'Thank you, gentlemen, this is most kind. Let me order us fresh drinks.' Mortimer called over the serving girl and ordered a large jug of beer. He had now learnt the names of all three men. He had overheard the mention of Captain Legge, Hotham and Barnard. Could he find out any more, he wondered?

As the afternoon started to turn to early evening, Mortimer ordered a meal of ham and pea soup with bread and more beer. He was losing most of the hands he was dealt, failing to capitalise on the suit tricks that were called. They were not playing for money, just for the shared company and Mortimer's free beer and food. The evening drew on, and Mortimer bought yet more beer. Fox dealt a hand of cards to everyone.

'My men won't arrive tonight by the look of it,' announced Mortimer. 'I see from your dress that two of you are clerks. Are you in the legal profession, may I ask?'

'Certainly not,' said Walker with a slur. The beer had the desired effect. 'We are clerks of the council,' he spluttered proudly. '*We* run this town, not all those aldermen and councillors who buy their seats on the town council and use their positions to feather their own nests. *We* are the ones who keep the town running.'

Mortimer's gentle manner, free beer and genial questioning persuaded them to talk about their work at the Guildhall.

The day after Barnard's verbal invitation to dine, Overton sent an official request for him to attend the officers' feast at seven of the clock. The opportunity for Barnard to join the officers at dinner had been a fortuitous one that Overton took advantage of, as the feast had already been planned for the officers of the garrison in appreciation of their work during the siege. The siege of Hull had failed, and patrols had reported that all the king's forces had fallen back to Beverley. With the intelligence from Mathew Fletcher, confirming the king's intention to leave Beverley, Captain Overton had suggested the celebration as a reward to the officers.

Alderman Barnard arrived fifteen minutes before seven with an escort of four armed men carrying heavy cudgels with iron bands around the head of the clubs. The men's presence served as a status symbol for the alderman, in addition to protecting him from street thieves. Alderman Barnard had insisted on having them since he was the leader of the Kingston upon Hull Council.

As Barnard was greeted by the officer of the guard, Lieutenant John Northend, Barnard dismissed his men for the evening, being assured he would receive a military escort home. Northend ushered Barnard through to the large, oak-panelled dining hall, with its grand fireplace set in one wall, under a marble mantel. The room was lit by dozens of beeswax candles, which gave out a soft yellow glow and emphasised the colours of the five Trained Bands Company flags that hung on the walls.

The centre of the room was dominated by a great dining table; each place setting laid with an officer's dining set of cutlery. Around the room, officers of all ranks stood in their finery and talked, while soldiers acting as servants carried trays of goblets filled with wine from person to person. Northend took Barnard across to Captain Overton.

'Ah, Alderman Barnard, how good of you to join us, Colonel Leggard has not arrived yet.' Overton removed his hat and gave a curt bow to the alderman.

'I appreciate the invitation, Captain. It is important that the civilian authority and the military garrison gain a better understanding of each other's workings.'   'My sentiments entirely,' responded Overton. He called over a servant carrying drinks for Barnard to help himself.

Colonel Leggard entered the room accompanied by Captain William Goodricke. The two moved to the centre of the room, attracting fellow officers like bees around a flower. Overton hung back, avoiding the crush of younger officers fawning over their commander.

'Are you not going to introduce me to the colonel, Captain?' Barnard looked at the throng around the colonel jealously.

'I'm sorry, Alderman, I was sure that you had met the colonel in your duties as leader of the council.' Overton knew they had met before, both men having sympathies of a royal leaning. 'You will have plenty of time to converse with the colonel later, as we will be seated close to the head of the table, where we will not need to vie for his attention with the junior officers.'

The colonel, at a signal from a junior officer standing at a side door, moved to take his seat at the table. The rest of the officers and guests took his lead and took up their positions at the giant dining board. The colonel took his seat first, and then the rest sat down. Instantly a train of servants carrying platters and serving dishes of food emerged from the side door.

First came the joints of meat: roasted beef, ham with honey glaze, peacock and chicken. Then there was a grand salad and a chicken lemon salad, followed by Salmon Calvert, roasted pike, haddock with black butter and capers, pigeon pie, veal and ham pie, creamy lemon pie, gingerbread with syllabub, jumballs and prince biscuits. The dishes filled the centre of the table, interspaced with boards of white bread and dishes of butter. Servants were on hand to offer various dishes to the colonel and the senior officers. The junior officers helped themselves to what they could reach or would suggest a dish they wanted to a neighbour, if it was too far away to reach, saying it 'Looked very appetising' to a person sitting close by, and then waiting for the dish to be passed down the table to them. One never asked for a dish directly: that would be bad manners.

Overton and Barnard filled their plates with the fine food, making small talk and listening to the colonel's exploits of bravery in the wars on the continent. Overton held up his glass for it to be filled with the strong Spanish wine of sherris-sack and then pointed out to Barnard that his glass was empty and that he should do the same.

'If I hadn't needed to arrest Sir John Hotham, it would have been him sitting here instead of you,' Overton said in a low voice. 'It's such a pity corruption in high places leads men onto the path to their own downfall, don't you think, Alderman?'

'I was under the impression that he had been arrested for his Royalist dealings,' Barnard said, taken aback at Overton's indiscreet statement.

'No, no, Alderman, not at all. That was just a ruse. He had been abusing his position so he could arrange his business affairs in a way to avoid paying duty on goods he imported through the quays of Hull. He got greedy. I am just a soldier; I have no head for politics. I was ordered to arrest him. As an officer I swore my allegiance to the king,' Overton confided.

'Then why did you hold Hotham at sword point and not allow the King admittance to the town?' Barnard asked in surprise.

'Because I am a captain, and not a colonel or a general, I take my orders and follow them.'

'So then, you are truly a supporter of the king, Captain?' Barnard set his goblet down on the table and looked Overton full in the face.

'I took an officer's oath to be loyal to the army and my commanding officer. As I told you, I don't involve myself in politics.' Overton put his goblet to his lips, feigning taking a drink. 'My duty is to do as I am told, by those who have the best interests of the country at heart.'

Barnard toyed with Overton's cryptic comment and took it as Overton had hoped he would. 'I have a man staying at my house,' Barnard volunteered, 'a man loyal to the king, by the name of Captain Legge. I will introduce you to him if you wish. To appreciate who is loyal to the King is an important thing in these troubled times.' Barnard took another drink from his goblet and held it aloft to be refilled.

'You will be a great man, Alderman, and I will be forever in your debt. Let us enjoy the rest of our evening. There will be dancing later, and as some of the officers have brought their wives, we may be able to find you a pretty one to dance with.' Overton spoke with mock drunkenness, slurring his words.

Mortimer's card game with his new companions had developed into gambling at sixpence a game, the winner being the first person to accrue thirty points. He had lost heavily during the evening, making little attempt to try and win, and his generosity in buying beer was proving popular with the other card players. The pace of the games had slowed as the drink affected the quickness of their thinking. Mortimer told them how he had met this nice girl from a house opposite the inn and that in passing she had confided in him that the master of the house had connections to a baron, of all people.

'What was his name? I can't quite remember it, Belly something, was it?' Mortimer looked up at the ceiling, putting his elbows on the table, as though deep in thought. As he pulled his elbows back, he managed to drag his cards and drink from the table onto the floor.

'Oh, shit!' he exclaimed loudly and bent to pick the cards and tankard from the floor. While his head was under the table, he heard Fox exclaim, 'He's talking about Baron Belasyse.'

'Shhh,' hissed Potter. Mortimer repositioned himself in his chair, wiping the cards on his sleeve to remove spilt beer and the dirt from the floor.

'Whose turn is it to lay a card?' Mortimer asked, dropping the subject of the girl he had met and the baron.

Potter complained of feeling tired and suggested they tot up the points to find who had won the most and that they would be the winner of the pot. It turned out to be Walker, who happily scooped the coins into his purse. All three men thanked Mortimer for his hospitality and wished him goodnight. On any other occasion Mortimer would have been offended by their abrupt departure and lack of manners in not finishing the game as arranged, but tonight he had got the information he needed.

He was not only happy to have gained the information, but he was also glad to see the three men leave. Even though he had been drinking slower than they had, he could feel the effects of the beer making his head swim.

Mathew did another a check of his medicine chest. He was getting through more medicines than he expected to with soldiers demanding every penny's worth of treatment they could get, for their two-pence worth of deductions each month. It meant he was spending as much time doing menial tasks that an assistant could do, as he was doing his real job of healing people.

Hearing a noise behind him, he turned abruptly. He couldn't hide the shock on his face when he saw who was standing there: it was Peter Martins.

'Sorry, Surgeon, I didn't mean to startle you,' the killer apologised. 'It's just that my arm is giving me some trouble. It hurts like hell sometimes, and the rest of the time it feels like flies are crawling all over it.'

Martins held out his arm as a child would do to his mother, the irony being that Martins would have cut Mathew down in an instant, had he known how he longed to kill him.

'Sit next to the table,' Mathew instructed, 'and I'll have a look at it.'

Mathew turned back to his medicine chest, gripping the sides of the open box with both hands and taking a slow breath to regain control of his nerves. Now composed again, he placed a pair of scissors, tweezers, squares of linen and a fresh roller in a large blue-and-white earthenware dish and went to join Martins.

'Is it giving you much pain?' enquired Mathew.

'Yes. At times I want to cut the damned thing off.' He looked up at the surgeon for some words of comfort that didn't come.

Mathew cut through the arm's covering and took delight in pulling away a large scab that had stuck to the lint dressing, making Martins wince, and swear out loud.

'The wound appears to be healing well, there is no sign of infection, and the tissue that was burnt off is beginning to regenerate. The pain comes from the lint dressing dragging on the scab, and the itching sensation is caused by the re-growing skin. Next time don't leave it so long before you come to see me. I'll change the covering every day now to prevent it drying out and sticking to the new skin.'

Mathew spread a greasy balm over the arm and covered the wound with the squares of linen. Starting just below Matins' elbow, Mathew placed the centre of the roller bandage and, coming down the arm to the wrist; he crisscrossed the two ends of the roller until the arm was covered, tying a knot in the two ends to finish off the dressing.

Feeling the relief of the new covering and balm, Martins thanked Mathew and left the tent.

Mathew cursed himself for not having the courage to take revenge on the man. The frustration put him in a very dark mood as he racked his brain trying to work out how to get away with killing the creature he had just helped. He needed time to think, but he was too busy now, he would have to do it later.

Chapter Twenty-Nine

Mathew drove the wagon loaded with the half dozen wounded men into Beverley; all of them had broken legs. They were the only soldiers deemed not fit enough to travel with the rest of the army on its journey to Doncaster. He'd found homes for them with various families within the town, with the promise that the town council would pay all reasonable expenses for their keep. The job was going to take him all day, as each man needed to be settled into his temporary home and instructions given on how to look after the live-in patient. The consolation at the end of the day would be his ability to visit his home in Cuckstool Pit Lane and talk with his family.

The day dragged on, and the men in the wagon were getting restless because as each soldier was removed from the uncomfortable wagon, the remainder would complain at being left behind. The problem was that it was the homeowner who decided which patient they took. The smaller men went first; as it was thought they would eat less and not be as troublesome as the larger soldiers. To make things worse, periodically throughout the day, there would be a short summer shower, and the men on the back of the wagon would have to try and hide under a blanket to protect themselves from the downpours. All Mathew had to feed the men was bread and cheese and a keg of small beer, to which they helped themselves each time his back was turned. By mid-afternoon, there was no food or drink left, and that gave the men something else to complain about. With the delays caused by breaks for the men to relieve themselves and the slow selection of patients by their new carers, it was a very tired and disgruntled Mathew Fletcher that finally arrived at his father's house. He wasn't happy about it, but he needed to talk to Mary about the work she had been doing in the camp and with the nurses.

Once home, Mathew found a moment to approached Mary when they could talk alone together. 'I know how unhappy you have become living here without Charles; I guess you feel like an outsider. There really is no need; my father loves you like a daughter. You've also been a real help to me at the camp: you keep the men calm when I have to clean their wounds, you are gentle with them and listen to their problems, and they appreciate it. I would need to speak to father to get his agreement but, if you really are unhappy here, I would like you to come with me when I leave Beverley with the army. Maybe this would be a way we could help each other.'

Mary listened patiently to what Mathew was saying.

'I can arrange for you to be my assistant, nurse and apothecary,' he explained. 'Life with the army is very different from how it is here—you will have very little privacy and you will see many horrors that a woman shouldn't see, but you will also learn a lot about medicine and surgery.'

Mathew had grave doubts about whether he was doing the right thing in asking Mary to join him, but having an apothecary with him would be useful, and they worked well together, but he couldn't shake the nagging doubt that he was making the wrong decision. He just couldn't see what was making him second thoughts; after all, she wouldn't be the only female camp-follower.

Mary didn't hesitate in her reply.

Mortimer was up early, not wanting to meet his fellow card players from the night before. His head ached, and his limbs were tired from his lack of sleep caused by his mind feverishly planning what he was going to do today. With a simple breakfast of bread and butter, washed down with sweet cider to take away the sour taste of last night's beer, he stepped out of the inn door into the Market Square. There were few people about, the sky was blue, and a breeze blew in from the northeast, bringing with it the scent of the North Sea. This was his chance to finally prove himself to Captain Overton and redeem his lost reputation when he communicated the new intelligence he had to give him. Even the day had dawned brightly to greet him, today, he thought, was going to be a good day. He marched with confidence across the market square, heading towards the soldiers' blockhouses.

He asked the guard for the whereabouts of Captain Overton and was told that he hadn't reported in yet. Mortimer decided to wait; he had all the time in the world now. At some point, the captain would arrive, and he would be able to share his latest discovery with him.

In due course, Overton arrived, and upon seeing Mortimer at his office door, gave him a quizzical look, but said nothing. He entered his office, leaving the door open. A few seconds later Mortimer heard one word: 'Well?'

Mortimer entered the office to find Overton sitting at his desk, a firm expression on his face, his arms crossed and his eyes boring into those of his visitor. Mortimer explained about the friendship he had developed with Judith Appleyard and the card game the evening before. At the mention of Baron Belasyse, Overton sat bolt upright in his chair.

'You have done well, Mortimer, you have done very well.' These were the first encouraging words he had received from his master for some time. He felt the tension drop from his muscles, as though a great weight had been lifted from him.

'May I ask, sir, does this mean you have forgiven my error in judgement from before?' Mortimer's voice was pleading and subservient, but ever hopeful.

'The information you have brought is of the greatest importance. So yes, I will forgive your previous treachery, but only because no unrecoverable damage was caused by the information you betrayed me with. But I will never trust you with duties in my direct service again. You will, however, continue in your current duties as a courier between Surgeon Fletcher and me. Someday in the future, I may change my mind, but for now, I have you in my control. I can leave your family where they are, on the Hotham estate, or I can bring them to safety. While I have that power over them, I can control you.' Overton spoke the words with controlled suppressed anger. He didn't want to forgive this man who had let him down so badly, but he had to acknowledge the efforts he had gone to, to repay his debt.

'I need a little time to make plans if I am to capture Legge and his confederates,' Overton went on. 'I want you to stay close by, Mortimer, for you will be needed.' The captain ordered Mortimer to sit outside his office and await his return.

The penitent traitor clutched at the straw of redemption that Overton had given him; it was called 'Hope'. After an hour or so Overton returned with Lieutenant Maynard, the two officers entered Overton's office, and this time Mortimer followed them in. Overton took his seat behind the desk, while Maynard stood at his side.

Overton looked up at Mortimer, saying, 'We have a plan to capture Legge and his men, and you are going to set the trap. We'll go over the details, but it's fairly straightforward, so long as you play your part.'

Mortimer stood outside the door of the Mermaid Inn observing the people walking in the street who were browsing and buying from the market traders. Many of the latter called to the passers-by, trying to sell their goods, and one or two would leave their pitches to take a potential customer by the arm and lead them back to their stall in order to show off their wares. The market was a hive of activity and congested with people.

Captain Overton's newest agent scanned the marketplace, wishing there were fewer people about. His mind rushed ahead, with troublesome thoughts, such as: *What if Judith didn't come to the market today? Would she do as he asked? Would she betray him to her master? What would happen if things don't go to plan?*

No matter how hard he tried to think of other things, the questions repeated over and over in his mind. *Surely Judith should have been here by now? Maybe she wasn't coming at all.* He leaned against the wall of the inn, the tension in his legs making the muscles ache. His senses were acutely aware of his surroundings as he scanned the market area once again looking for the woman in the worn brown dress.

The sky was now slate grey, and flat low cloud had blown in, threatening rain. Mortimer could smell the stench of fish from the fish market, a wind from that direction always meant rain. He shuddered and pulled his woollen jacket close about him.

Judith Appleyard finally appeared at the end of a row of market stalls, basket over her arm, and a shawl over her head. She was in no hurry as she passed by the stalls, curious to see what was being sold, taking to the traders and passers-by that she recognised.

Mortimer stood up straight, relief coursing through his body at the sight of her. He stepped forward, still feeling nervous. He pushed his way past a group of people blocking his passage, ignoring the calls from the traders, his eyes fixed on Judith.

'Good day to you, Mistress Judith,' he called in a friendly greeting, using a manner of address that was above her social station. 'It is good to see you again; I was hoping we might meet. May I take your basket?'

She wore the same brown dress as before—he recognised its dirty hem—but the apron she was wearing was freshly laundered and clean.

Judith looked up at him, startled at first by his sudden appearance. However, recognition soon brought a smile to her face as she responded to his friendliness and unaccustomed attention. They perused the market stalls and chatted innocently, Judith feeling flattered by the attention she was receiving. Mortimer knew that he wouldn't have long to speak to her before she had to return to the house with the groceries she had bought, and he was determined to find a way to get her to help him.

'Is there any way we might spend a day together when you are not working?' Mortimer casually asked as they passed between two stalls, in search of onions. Judith stopped abruptly and turned to face him, her face and neck red with embarrassment.

'Do you mean it, sir?' she asked in delight. 'Would you really like to see me again?' Her eyes sparkled, and her mouth widened into a broad smile, showing her white, even teeth. As a kitchen maid she had had little attention from men apart from the unwelcome advances of gardeners and stable lads, who had rough manners and hands, dried suntanned faces and often smelt of horse dung. She had always wanted a handsome man of her own, but coming from a poor home, she had gone into service as a kitchen maid at the age of eight and stayed in that occupation ever since. Long hours over an open fire and steaming pots had aged her skin so that she looked older than her years.

When she had been younger, her youthfulness had attracted men for the wrong reasons. She had run away from one house when the master had tried to take advantage of her one night when he was far gone in his cups. Now the years had passed, and she wanted the companionship that marriage would bring, but her youth had gone, and she was close to being classed as an old maid.

'I have a half day tomorrow, in the morning,' she said eagerly. 'We could meet here in the market.' Her eyes looked longingly up at Mortimer.

'I shall look forward to spending the morning with you. Come early, and we can breakfast together at the inn, you can let someone cook for you for a change.' Mortimer was growing fond of Judith. Even though she was probably a little older than he was, she had a pleasing manner and a smile that warmed and lifted his heart. As they walked around her basket grew heavier.

'You have a lot of shopping today, the basket is full,' Mortimer commented. 'How do you manage to carry a basket that is so heavy?'

'I'm stronger than I look, though I have noticed that sometimes I can't carry the basket all the way home without putting it down once or twice on the way back.' She enjoyed his concern and interest in the hard work she had to do every day; no one had asked to carry her basket before. As they moved around the market, Mortimer spied Walker, Fox and Potter heading towards the Mermaid Inn for their midday refreshment.

'Judith, would you do something for me?' he asked. 'Would you take this note to those men entering the Mermaid Inn? I'll hold this heavy basket. They are people I promised to help.' With the basket over one arm, he withdrew the note from inside his jacket. Judith hesitated a moment, then quickly walked the short distance to the Mermaid Inn, returning moments later.

'They were a little surprised when I gave them the note,' she said. 'Those men sometimes come to the house to talk to the captain. Do you know the captain?' Judith looked puzzled, wondering why Mortimer had sent her on such a mission.

'It's just something I promised to do the next time I saw them; it's of no consequence. What's the matter, Mistress Judith? Did you not want to help me?' Mortimer put on a pained expression.

'No. No, of course, I wanted to help you, it's just me being silly. Come, my strong man, you can carry the basket back to the gate for me.' Judith gave Mortimer another endearing smile, and the couple made their way across the market back to the house. They talked about the enjoyable stroll they would share the following morning. Mortimer waved goodbye as she returned through the gate to the rear of the house.

Walker read aloud the note he had been given by Judith Appleyard to his companions, Fox and Potter.

'What do you think the problem is?' asked Potter. 'Why would the captain want to see us all at the house on urgent matters?'

'I don't know,' Walker replied, frustrated at Potter's questioning. 'He may have a job for us, or he may want to beat you for being an idiot and not finding that spy who was in the camp at Anlaby and Beverley.'

Potter sat back, put out at Walker bringing up his failed mission. 'I had nothing to work on, very little information at all,' Potter protested. 'If the King hadn't decided to move on I would have had more time to investigate.'

'Oh, so it's the king's fault is it?' Walker retaliated.

'That's enough, you two!' Fox interceded. 'If anyone overhears us they'll want to know why we know so much about the king's business. Let's go and find out why the captain wants us.'

Walker folded the note and slipped it inside his jacket. Fox led the way as the three left the Mermaid Inn and stepped out into the marketplace. It took the three men a few minutes to worm their way through the crowd towards the house.

The High Street was busy with wagons as they carried goods to and from ships which had newly arrived on the high tide. Entering the passage at the side of the house, Walker, Fox and Potter made their way through the garden gate to the back door of the building. It was opened by Judith, and Walker explained that the note had instructed them to come and see Captain Legge. Judith allowed them into the kitchen and went to find Mr Comings, the steward.

Judith and the steward returned moments later, and Walker showed Comings the note. The steward was confused at first, for it would normally have been him who would deliver such a message. He would speak to Judith later to discover how she had been given the job; in the meantime, he took the three men to a small room that Captain Legge was using as an office.

No sooner had they entered the chamber than there came a loud banging on the front door. All five men looked from one to the other. Comings went to the front window. 'Soldiers,' was his only word. For a couple of seconds no one moved, then, taking their lead from Captain Legge, they made a bolt for the door, escaping from the back of the house through the kitchen.

'Don't go through the gate—they will have the passage guarded,' shouted Comings. 'Take the skiff at the bottom of the garden and cross the river.' Legge and his three spies ran down the garden to the boat.

Comings turned towards Judith Appleyard, who was cowering in the corner of the kitchen with the cook.

'It was you who betrayed the captain!' Comings told her. His eyes were wild, and spittle flew from his lips, like venom from a snake that was about to strike.

Judith fled from the kitchen with the steward in pursuit, heading for the garden gate. Meanwhile, the front door burst open, and Captain Overton and ten soldiers with drawn swords rushed into the house.

Earlier on, waiting in Chapel Lane, Captain Overton had watched Mortimer standing outside the Mermaid Inn. He was getting bored as the time passed and his thoughts started to drift. Why hadn't he thought to set a watch on more key people on the town council, he wondered? If Hotham had proved to be a traitor, others members of the council could also be untrustworthy? If he had been diligent, he might have been able to capture Captain Legge sooner. As it was, Henry Barnard was going to have a lot of explaining to do, not least telling him why he was harbouring a loyal supporter of the King without informing the council or himself as parliament's representative in Hull.

Finally, there came some movement as Overton saw Mortimer go to greet a woman with a basket. He watched as they took their time wandering between the market stalls. He looked on enviously. One day he would find himself a good woman and have a family life, but for now, he was a soldier, and his career must come first. He saw the woman go into the Mermaid Inn shortly after three men had entered, and then return to Mortimer. The couple crossed the marketplace back to Barnard's house, where Mortimer left the woman and returned to the edge of the market.

Three men left the Mermaid Inn and made their way to Barnard's house. They passed within a few feet of Mortimer, but they didn't notice him standing there looking at the building. There were too many people now passing to and fro from the market and along the High Street.

Overton brought his men to readiness. He watched the three men enter the passage at the side of the house. As soon as they were out of sight, he marched his men from their hiding place in the lane. Civilians in the street made way for the small column of soldiers, the sound of their studded shoes crunching on the cobbled street as they marched in step, with the occasional clink of metal as swords rattled in their scabbards. Overton left two men at the entrance to the small passage at the side of the house, while the rest followed him to the front door, where he stood aside as a sergeant banged on the door with the pommel of his sword.

The captain caught a momentary sight of a face at the window and ordered the door to be forced and immediately. Two soldiers took the place of their sergeant and proceeded to kick at the door. For a while, the solid oak refused to move but eventually the small day-lock burst from its mounting, and the door flew open, crashing back against the wall. Overton entered first, followed by his sergeant and the soldiers.

'Search the house!' Overton ordered. 'Bring everyone you find to the hall. Harm no one.'

Judith Appleyard fled from the kitchen with Comings hot on her heels. She had never seen him in such a rage before. Hitching up her skirt and apron, it was her fleetness of foot and her lithe figure that allowed her to avoid the steward's grasp. She headed for the gate, flinging it open and running down the passage. The two guards let her pass: their orders were to stop Captain Legge and his three accomplices from escaping, not to capture a hysterical kitchen maid.

From across the High Street, Mortimer caught sight of Judith making her escape as she came into sight where the passage opened up alongside the front garden. He stepped forward, clear of the people who were thronging to the market.

'Judith! Judith! I'm over here!' he shouted to her.

She paused a moment at hearing his distant voice, then caught the sound of the steward coming up the lane following her. Without a second thought, she ran towards Mortimer.

She didn't notice the wagon. One of the horses pulling the heavy wagon caught her in mid-stride. She tumbled over in front of it. The suddenness of her movement and her scream startled the horse, it rose up, its forelegs flaying at the air before they came crashing down to the street. Its sharp metal shoes sliced through Judith's cheap clothing. The horse danced around, startled at finding the woman in its path, and the other animal responded to its alarm. The driver pulled hard on the reins, trying to steady his pair of draught horses, but with their combined strength and panicked movements, they dragged the cart, loaded with lead from the Peak District, forward to escape the hazard under their hooves. The front wheel of the wagon ran across the hips of the woman lying in the road. She never felt the pain caused by the wheel as she was already unconscious, struck on the head by the horses' hooves.

The wagon driver heard the snap of her hip bones breaking as he finally drew the horses to a stop. He leapt down from his seat as Mortimer rounded the front of the horses. While the driver stood in shocked silence, Mortimer dragged Judith from beneath the wagon. Her coif had come off, and her brown hair hung free and matted with dirt from the street, lay across her face. Her clothes were ripped, torn and trampled by the horses' hooves, but from the waist down, what was left of her apron was bright red. Her life-giving fluid stained the skirt and ran down her exposed legs and onto the street. It was more blood than Mortimer had ever seen. He sat in the filth of the street cradling her limp body as her life ebbed away. A crowd from the market soon gathered, but Mortimer didn't notice. The two guards who had been set at the passage entrance did their best to hold back the onlookers, but there were too many of them. Comings, seeing what had happened and while the guards were distracted, fled up the High Street.

Captain Legge, Walker, Potter and Fox found the skiff afloat at the river's edge. Fox cut the mooring line, and the four men jumped into the boat.

'Head for the far side of the river,' Fox commanded. 'If they want to follow us, they'll have to go all the way around and cross the bridge outside the North Gate. Once we reach the other side of the river we'll buy or steal some horses and make our way across country, heading north.'

Barnard and his wife were the only people of note that Overton's soldiers found in the house. A quick questioning of the cook explained how Captain Legge and his men had escaped. Overton's only hope now was to arrest Barnard and persuade him to talk. As Barnard was unceremoniously escorted from his house, the crowd that had gathered around Judith's corpse and grieving Mortimer turned their attention to the soldiers escorting their prisoner out of the front garden and along the High Street towards the blockhouses.

413

Overton was the last to exit the house, leaving a distraught Mrs Barnard on the doorstep. Pushing his way through the crowd, the captain ordered the two soldiers he had left at the passage entrance to assist Mortimer in taking Judith's body into Barnard's house. The pair gave Overton a quizzical look.

'The woman worked for Barnard, she lived there,' the senior man said. 'Take her inside and if Mrs Barnard complains, tell her I ordered it. She can also foot the bill for Judith Appleyard's funeral. After all, it was her husband's steward who drove her in front of those horses.'

On the Westwood Common, Mathew waited for news from Captain Overton on how to proceed with Martins. He had expected Mortimer back before now and the thought that he had simply deserted both him and Overton, began to nag at the back of his mind. The soldiers in the Westwood camp were becoming restless, for it was common knowledge that the King would leave Beverley for Doncaster any day now and they were eager to be on their way.

From Beverley, more and more reports were reaching Colonel Duncombe of soldiers stealing from the residents, women being raped, and of drunkenness and fighting on the streets. Two soldiers had been hanged for raping a young girl as a deterrent to others, but still, the unrest continued. If the colonel hanged any more soldiers, he risked a mutiny. He secretly cursed his King and commander for procrastinating about breaking camp. The soldiers were bored and disheartened at their failure to capture Hull. Accounts of desertions were being reported by all company commanders. The king needed to get his men moving.

The skiff struck the quay on the eastern side of the River Hull, the fear within John Walker's muscles giving him strength he was unaware he had, as he rowed the boat against the changing tide and across the fifty yards of the river to the far bank. Bringing the boat to a halt at the base of an iron ladder, which led up to the top of the quay, he dropped the oars and grasped the rungs, while Potter tied the boat's line around one of the quays piles. His arms shook from the strain of pulling on the oars, for he had put every ounce of energy he had into rowing them all across.

Fox made it up the ladder first, looking back over the river to the garden at the back of Barnard's house. He watched the soldiers exiting the kitchen door, searching the garden and running down to the river's edge at shouting at them as he scaled the ladder.

Captain Overton stepped through the kitchen door, his eyes automatically running down the garden and across the river to the skiff and its passengers. The captain didn't run: he knew he was too late—his birds had flown. He watched as the four climbed from the skiff onto the quay. The tallest of the group looked back at him, removing his hat and giving Overton a sweeping bow, then turned back to his companions and fled with them to the southern end of the town wall, where it met the River Humber. Then they ran around the base of the turret, across some open land and towards the Hedon Road.

After buying four horses from a trader just outside the town walls, they set out into the Holderness countryside towards Hedon. Not stopping at this village, they turned north-east and made their way to the village of Sproatley, where they spent the night like thieves, hiding in a poor farmer's barn, with no food except some raw chicken eggs found below a hedge and drinking water from a trough.

They left the barn the following morning as the first hints of the day started to lift the dark curtain of the night from the land. The fugitives made it to Skirlaugh village within a couple of hours and banging on an innkeeper's door; they roused him from his sleep to make them breakfast, paying him well for his trouble.

Late in the day, they reached the outskirts of Beverley after an easy ride, keeping to small wooded lanes between fields; this time they spent the night at the Wheatsheaf Inn. The beds felt good after sleeping rough in a barn, and they slept late into the next day. Legge had told them that Overton would not pursue them after the first day: having lost his quarry, he would not waste his time and resources on a fruitless search. With instructions from Captain Legge, Potter, Fox and Walker stayed close by the inn. There was nowhere for them to go. The inn was on the very fringes of the town and overlooked flat arable farmland. Small farms dotted across the rich Holderness countryside, a land ideal for growing wheat, barley and oats, spread out before them.

'I'm going into Beverley,' Legge told his men. 'There is business I need to discuss with the army commander. You will be safe here until I return, then we will continue to Newburgh Priory tomorrow.' He left them enough money for food and drink, but not enough to give them ideas of leaving.

Within an hour Legge was tying his horse to the hitching rail outside the Push Inn on Saturday Market. He gave his name to the guard on the door and was quickly admitted to Colonel Duncombe, who greeted him warmly.

'To what do I owe the honour of a visit from the Master of the King's Armouries and Ordnance?' the colonel asked, leading the captain to a comfortable seat in his office on the first floor. A servant poured the two men glasses of Madeira wine and left the room at the instruction of the colonel.

'I have other duties besides the ones you mention,' Legge told him, 'and it is those that bring me here. There are three of my men camped on the Westwood with your army; I need them back. I would be grateful, Colonel, if you would issue them with a pass to draw supplies and horses and allow them to leave with me immediately.' Legge paused to sip his wine, its warm, smooth taste and scented aroma most welcome after his two nights on the run from Hull.

'Are you at liberty to share with me why you need these men?' The colonel asked as though it was of no real importance to him.

Just as casually Legge responded with a simple 'no' and waited for the colonel's next question. Colonel Duncombe refreshed Legge's glass.

Colonel Duncombe asked another: 'What news of Hull? I'm sure the King would be interested as to how you escaped when he found it so hard to get in.'

'The walls of Hull are designed to keep armies out, colonel, not people in; I believe that would be the job of a prison,' Legge said patiently, knowing the colonel was fishing for news to pass onto the king.

'I will be sure to instruct the King on your escape from Hull the next time we dine,' rebutted Duncombe, becoming frustrated at Legge's refusal to divulge his plans.

'The King will no doubt enjoy you pointing out his failure at Hull. I wish you well,' Legge retorted angrily. He was getting tired of this farmer colonel, with his little brain.

Changing the subject, Duncombe called his servant back into the room and requested his clerk to be sent in with pen and paper. While Legge sat and enjoyed the rest of his glass of Madeira, the colonel instructed his clerk to write a letter giving leave from the army, passage and supplies to Wilkes, Martins and Franks. With everything he needed, Legge set the glass down on the small writing table the clerk had used and picked up the note of authority for his men.

'Thank you, Colonel, that was a most excellent Madeira.' Leaving Duncombe sitting in his chair, Legge left without another word.

At the Westwood camp, Legge showed his letter of authority to the sergeant of the guard and ordered Wilkes, Martins and Franks to be found and brought to him at the officers' pavilion.

As Legge entered the pavilion, he found six other officers inside, three of who were studying papers on a long table at one end of the tent. The other three were at their ease, sitting together talking.

Legge paused at the entrance, taking in the layout of the interior. Selecting a chair away from the other occupants of the large tent, he eased himself into the seat, removed his hat and laid it on the small table at his elbow. Silence fell on the pavilion as all eyes turned towards the stranger. A muffled exchange of words passed between the three officers who were sitting together. In the end, the youngest looking of them got to his feet and slowly made his way across to Legge.

'Err, excuse me, sir,......' he asked without confidence. 'I was wondering—'

'—Beer would be fine, wine would be better.' Legge interrupted the young officer before he could finish the sentence. He paused to look him in the eye, holding his attention.

'Yes, sir.' The junior man, still in his teens, took a step back, looked at his comrades momentarily, then turned and went to a side table and poured a glass of wine. Legge stretched his arms and legs and allowed his head to fall back, closing his eyes for a moment as a wave of tiredness passed over him. When his eyes opened the young officer had returned to his seat, and a glass of wine was on the table next to Legge's hat. Legge smiled, took the glass, raised it in a salute to the other man then took a sip of the sweet red liquid.

His mind slipped back to his hasty departure from Hull. It was a setback having to leave prematurely. Had he had more time he might have been able to develop a situation where the King could have taken the town, but the time had passed, and now there was no point in dwelling on what might have been. All Captain Legge could do now was adapt, change and move on.

He viewed the other occupants of the pavilion. The three at the far end had gone back to reading their papers. The three, which included the young officer, sat huddled together talking in low voices, giving him the occasional glance. For the first time, Legge looked down at his clothes. He was a mess. His boots were muddy, his breeches were dusty and splattered with dirt, his jacket was crumpled with buttons missing, and the feather in his once pristine hat was broken. He broke into a smile. *What a mess you are, William*, he thought to himself. *Tut. Tut; we shall let them wonder who we are.* He was enjoying the upset he was causing. He finished his wine just as the sergeant returned.

'The men you wanted are outside, sir.' the sergeant reported, then turned and left. Legge left his empty glass on the table, picked up his hat, gave a polite mocking bow to the three who were sitting talking, then stepped outside. Franks, Wilkes and Martins were waiting for him. All three removed their hats as Legge emerged from the pavilion.

'It would seem that Hull was unlucky for all of us,' Legge said as he viewed Matins' bandaged arm.

'I can explain, sir,' Martins started to say.

'Be quiet,' interjected Wilkes.

'We are leaving, and going north,' Legge said.

Wilkes nodded, understanding what Legge was implying.

'Sir,' Martins said before Legge led them away, 'I would like to stay awhile. My arm is being treated by the surgeon. It's healing well under his care. Can I join you later, when it has recovered? You could leave a note with them at the house, telling me where to find you.'

'Very well,' Legge agreed. 'You two, get ready, we will leave as soon as we can.' Legge was anxious to get back to the Wheatsheaf before dark.

The following day they rode to York, the busy capital of Yorkshire. They decided to rest the horses and enjoy the delights of the town for the day, before carrying on to their destination and Legge finding more work for them to do. They would make Newburgh Priory the following day, where they would receive instructions on what they were to do next.

Captain Overton ordered twenty men and a wagon to go north to Scorborough, their instructions being to remove

420

Mortimer's family from the estate of Sir John Hotham and to take them to the Overton estate at Easington, where they would be safe. Overton's father had agreed to take them and offer them work. The captain now had full control over Charles Mortimer.

Mortimer arrived back in the Westwood camp in the middle of the afternoon on the day after Judith's funeral. He sat down on a box in the surgeon's tent, removed the letter Overton had given him from inside his jacket and handed it to Mathew.

'You're late,' Mathew sneered churlishly. He read Overton's letter, occasionally stopping to look at the other man. 'I'm sorry, I didn't know. Overton writes favourably about you,' he went on sympathetically. 'It seems we now have something in common: the loss of someone we cared about.'

Mortimer stood up. 'Do you need me for anything?'

Mathew didn't reply.

'Good. You know where you can find me?' He left the tent without giving Mathew a chance to answer.

In Overton's letter, it explained how Mortimer had uncovered the whereabouts of Captain Legge and his spies, about the death of Judith Appleyard, and that Mortimer had gone a long way towards regaining Overton's trust, if not his respect. He had instructed Mathew not to act in haste with Martins, as Overton couldn't help him while they were in the camp at Beverley. He warned Mathew of the escape of Captain Legge and to be on the lookout for him arriving in Beverley. The last sentence of the letter asked Mathew to meet Overton at the Crippled Cock in Cottingham; he would be there for three nights only but had to see Mathew before the army left Beverley.

Mathew crumpled the letter into a tight ball and wandered outside, his mind mulling over everything he had read. Ethan was stirring a pot over the fire as Mathew dropped the ball of paper into the flames.

'Bad news?' enquired Ethan.

'I don't know,' Mathew answered cryptically, Ethan's enquiry breaking his thoughtful trance. 'Be kind to Mortimer for me; I'll be back late.'

Ethan's look of surprise made Mathew smile.

He turned and went to find a horse. He could be in Cottingham in just over an hour, and the sooner he knew what Overton wanted, the better. Besides, there was little for him to do now the wounded soldiers in his care had gone.

The ride to Cottingham was a pleasant one, and Mathew enjoyed being away from the hubbub of the camp. The late afternoon was still warm, the hedgerows busy with the buzz of bees. He passed fields of wheat and barley, their long stalks reaching for the sun, not yet ready for harvesting. He could smell the grass and wildflowers that grew along the roadside, all a far cry from the stink of the army camp and Beverley. He saw Skidby Mill sitting atop a hill, its sails turning slowly as the great mill wheels turned sacks of grain into sacks of flour.

All too soon he was entering Cottingham, the stench of the cesspits greeting him first. The Crippled Cock was easy to find on the High Street of the small village. He tied his horse to a hitching post and, ducking under the low lintel over the front door; he entered the inn. The local farmers who had been sat drinking stopped talking as the stranger entered. Travellers rarely stayed very long in the village, as Hull was only a few short miles away.

The scruffy little inn had two rooms at the front of the building. In one there were no tables or chairs, just a shelf running around the walls at elbow height, and a large beer barrel in the corner from which the contents could be tapped by a wiry youth sitting on a stool next to the barrel. This was where Mathew had found the farmers.

However, the other room had places to sit and eat; the evidence still lying on un-cleared tables which crawled with flies. A cold hearth sat at the back of the room, the weather being too warm to light a fire. The sunlight losing its fight to gain access through the dirty leaded windows made the room dull and shadowy. Overton was sat in the back corner facing the door. He was dressed in plain travellers' clothes which failed to disguise the fact that he was a man of breeding. The manner in which he sat straight-backed, his keen educated eyes taking in everything in the room, meant that his presence dominated the gloomy place, even from the far corner where he sat.

Mathew went across to join him as the landlord appeared from a door in the right-hand wall with a large pie on a plate in one hand and two tankards of ale in the other. Mathew greeted his friend and waited until the landlord had deposited their meals and left them alone.

'I wasn't sure if you would be hungry so I asked him to bring a pie as well as the ale when you arrived,' said Overton, before taking a long draw of his ale, Mathew did the same—the ride had made him thirsty.

'It's a strange place to meet, why here?' enquired Mathew.

'It's quiet now, but you wait till later when it fills with farm labourers, then it can be as rough as any whores' tavern on the quays in Hull. It's not a place non-locals frequent for long, but for now, we are alone.'

Leaning forward and lowering his voice, the captain explained his plan. When the King led his army to Doncaster, Overton was going to follow, staying a few miles back, but within easy reach by horse. He wanted Mathew and Mortimer to stay with the army and report on anything of interest, that the officers let slip. Mortimer could then report the news back to him. Overton explained that he would wait for Mortimer in the nearest church to the army's location every morning until nine of the clock. He gave Mathew a ring, which was engraved like a ring with the Rod of Asclepius and Caduceus as its crest.

'You are to seal all correspondence with this symbol,' Overton explained. 'If the symbol is missing or upside down, I will know you are not writing the letter of your own free will. I needed to give you these instructions myself; they are to be our secret. Lord Fairfax will be taking my place in Hull. I am instructed by Parliament, to aid you in discovering the king's plans for the future, and which men of wealth are supporting him. We are to follow the King wherever he may lead us. I feel there is a war coming, Mathew, not just between men, but between Parliament and King, between good and bad; between God and that Satan's spawn, the Popish Devil in Rome.'

Mathew saw the zealot in Overton for the first time. This was a man driven by principle and God—a dangerous combination. The two men talked about their common goal in finding the murderers from Hull. Overton spoke with such fervour about his belief in God, and that all men were created equal, that Mathew found himself caught up in Overton's zeal and belief that he too, one day, could become more than a simple town surgeon.

Chapter Thirty

Sir John Belasyse was not pleased to see Captain Legge and his five dirty and dishevelled companions at his door. He took Captain Legge into the house and left his son, Thomas, and the servants to deal with Legge's companions. Potter, Fox, Walker, Wilkes and Franks were taken to the servants' quarters in the left wing of the house, above where the stables and workshops were housed, forcing some of Sir John's servants to double up to make room for the unexpected newcomers. They were instructed not to enter the house or to leave the grounds unless they were asked to.

Standing in the hall, Sir John looked Captain Legge up and down with disdain.

'Before we speak you need to clean yourself, Captain,' the baron said scornfully. 'You are a disgrace and not fit to be seen in decent company.'

Unable to disagree with Sir John, he would have to put up with his abrupt manner, but at least he was getting the opportunity to change his clothes. He was taken to a guest room by Hibbot, Sir John's steward, where he was provided with hot water, a fresh suit of clothes and shirt belonging to Sir John's son, so that his own clothes could be taken away and cleaned. The captain stood naked in front of the sideboard on which the bowl of hot water stood and sponged the dirt and sweat from his body. The war in Europe had honed his muscles and trimmed his waist, but the scars still remained to remind him of his narrow escapes. He clipped his beard and moustache, combed his hair and put on the clean shirt. He was sitting on the bed feeling refreshed when there was a knock on the bedchamber door. Hibbot entered, carrying a pair of plain latchet shoes.

'Sir John apologises for the shoes, Captain, but they are the only ones he could find that might fit you. I will have your own boots and clothes ready by tomorrow.' He placed the shoes on the floor and took away Legge's dirty clothes and boots.

Legge lay back on the bed and wondered what the Earl of Newcastle would do once he was informed that he'd been driven from Hull by Overton. For now, he had to deal with his upset host and the loss of the vital intelligence he'd left behind in Hull. *I could always blame Hotham. If he'd secured Hull for the King as he had promised, everything would be different.*

He finished dressing and went in search of Sir John. Hibbot was waiting for him in the hall. 'Sir John is this way, sir.' The steward took Legge to a large room at the front of the house. The servant knocked gently on the door, opened it and stood aside for the captain to enter; closing the door after the officer had passed through.

In the centre of the room stood a fine table, which in turn, stood on a new Persian carpet. Set around the room against the walls was an arrangement of comfortable chairs interspersed with tables covered in books and documents. Sir John sat studying some papers at the table in the centre of the room. Behind his back was a small cold fireplace, with screwed up pieces of paper littering the hearth, clearly waiting to be burned. Sir John sat in the only chair at the table, so that Legge had to stand in front of him as if he was an errant schoolboy in front of his headmaster.

'Well, explain yourself, man.' Sir John spoke coldly, setting down his pen and staring up at Legge. 'What went wrong?'

'All was going well until the three men I had watching the town garrison were discovered, then soon after Sir John Hotham and his son were arrested. After which, Overton turned up at the house where I was staying, and I had to escape.' Legge kept his tale simple, implying that Hotham or his son was to blame for his discovery.

'So it had nothing to do with your three murderers killing the apothecary and his daughter, those three drunken clerks not being able to keep their mouths shut and Judith Appleyard, a kitchen maid at the house where you were staying, making friends with Overton's servant? Don't treat me like an idiot, Legge; I have people everywhere. You were a fool and a careless fool at that. Leave me now while I decide what to do next; I will speak to you again when we dine later.'

Sir John had cut the captain down as efficiently as a skilled swordsman. He hadn't raised his voice, he hadn't insulted him, but he had put Legge in his place and reinforced the message that HE was the master of spies and that Captain Legge had been proved to be woefully deficient to the task set him.

Dismissed from Sir John's presence, Legge went in search of his own spy network. They were sitting outside the servants' quarters eating cold meat, cheese and bread, and drinking cider. Being absolutely outraged and humiliated by Sir John's dressing down, Captain Legge was ready to take his frustrations out on the only people he could.

'You fucking useless dog turds!' he screamed at them. 'If you lot had done your jobs properly we would all be rich beyond our wildest dreams now. Instead, I'm stuck with the bunch of incompetent, useless amateurs I see before me now!'

Walker, Potter and Fox hung their heads and let the tirade wash over them. Franks jumped to his feet about to draw his sword, but Wilkes held his arm.

'The main reason our mission failed, is back in Beverley, Martins was too jumpy,' Wilkes snapped. 'He doesn't think before he pulls his sword. And if you had not sat on your arse, being waited on hand and foot, wanting us to spoon-feed you the information you needed, instead of managing the job properly, we wouldn't have failed.' Wilkes was facing Legge, inches from his nose, almost daring the captain to make a fight of it.

Legge could smell Wilkes's rotten breath and feel his spittle on his face. Twice now, in less than an hour, Legge had been dressed down for his failings. It was more than he could take. He knew he couldn't best Wilkes in a fight, so he did the only thing left to him and stormed off, cursing under his breath.

At the sound of urgent banging on his office door, Captain Overton allowed his sergeant to enter and disturb the paperwork that he had been working on and was late in finishing. The flustered sergeant stood to attention after handing his captain the letter that carried the seal of John Pym, the leader of the Parliamentary cause. Overton smiled as the sergeant held himself to attention in front of his desk. This wasn't an overt sign of respect the captain insisted on from his sergeant. He could only assume it was the importance of the official letter from London.

The instructions in the letter were plain. Sir John Hotham and his son, Captain John Hotham, were to be delivered to the Tower of London, where they would be held until their trial for treason against Parliament. They were to be sent by ship, under armed escort, but treated with respect. Captain Overton was to report to the office of John Pym for new orders, and Sir Peregrine Pelham would take over as Mayor of Hull.

After depositing Sir John Hotham and his son in the White Tower goal at the Tower of London, Captain Overton left the prisoner escort with the tower garrison until it was time to return to Hull. Leaving the tower, he headed down to the River Thames to find a water-boatman who would take him upriver to Westminster.

Wherry's waited in turn at the bottom of the steps, next to the tower, collecting passengers to travel up and down the river. He shared a boat with two well-dressed gentlemen who also wanted to be let off at the Westminster steps. Overton sat at the front of the boat facing the stern. It was from this position, low down on the river that the Tower of London appeared at its most impressive and formidable.

The pale grey crenulated walls stood out of the river, with a semi-circular entrance for boats to deliver supplies at its base. Behind the walls, reaching for the sky stood the White Tower, where Overton had left John Hotham and his son in its deep, dark and damp cells. He wondered how it would feel to be in their shoes, not knowing if they would be there a few days, weeks, years or indeed if they would ever see the sun again.

A chill ran through his body, whether it was from thinking about the fate of the Hotham's or a sudden gust of wind from the river, he could not tell. The wherry man pulled on his oars, fighting the outgoing tide, and slowly the image of the Tower grew smaller. The man at the oars kept his boat out of the centre of the river where the tide pulled its strongest, and it wasn't too long before all sight of the Tower was lost in the mass of ships moored at the quays along the Thames.

The other two passengers had chosen to sit together at the back of the boat, so as he was sitting in front of the oarsman, it left him nothing to do except stare at the rowers' backs or at the other craft on the water. Most of the river's activity came from little wherry's like the one he was riding in, or from single-masted, wide-beamed barges taking their cargos to or bringing goods from warehouses ready for shipment to other places. Ships of all sizes were moored at the quays, displaying flags from Holland, France, Norway, Sweden, Spain, Denmark and places he didn't recognise, and between all these ran the wherry's, like oversized water beetles scurrying over the water of the Thames.

His boat pulled in at the Westminster. He stepped onto the wooden jetty, its boards covered in damp weed and mud, before those waiting to board clambered in to take his place in the boat. He made his way up the slippery steps to the street above. Parliament House, Westminster Hall and the Abbey dominated the skyline above the wooden houses; shops and taverns which lined the narrow streets. He had often thought that the streets of Hull were dirty, but they were not as bad as those he found in London. Everyone walked under the eaves of the houses in order to avoid the contents of night pots being emptied from the windows above. Filth and litter accumulated down the centre of the street, in doorways and in alleys. Children in rags ran barefooted through the refuse and could be seen relieving themselves in the alleys between buildings. At least in Hull, the corporation arranged for the streets to be cleaned three times a week.

Kicking off the worst of the dirt from his boots, Overton entered Parliament House, his footsteps echoing off the tiled floor and around the great entrance hall, as he was escorted to the office of John Pym. He received a warm welcome from Mr Pym, a man with intelligent eyes, who spoke with a soft West Country accent. In his late fifties, his fair hair was turning grey. He was wearing a black coat over which lay a white plain collar. Pym questioned Overton at some length over the events that had taken place in Hull during the time of the king's siege. They discussed the betrayal by Sir John Hotham and his son. Hotham had not only betrayed many members of parliament in his attempt to secure Hull for the king, but he had also betrayed many friendships for the sake of self-enhancement. Pym was most interested in the way Overton had befriended the young surgeon and used him to infiltrate the King's Army and helping him embed himself as a spy. Overton quickly warmed to the man and gave him a full account of everything, including his failure to capture Captain Legge.

'I have been in discussion with John Hampdon and others of the Committee of Safety, and it has been decided to promote you to the rank of Major,' said Pym. 'It is our wish for you to continue working with Mathew Fletcher and for you to learn as much about the king's plans as possible, which you will report them back to the committee.' Pym leaned forward, looking Overton straight in the eye. 'You will have full authority to travel wherever you may need to, and Parliament will pay your expenses. *We* need men like you in these troubled times, Robert. Will you help us?'

Overton took a minute or two before answering, thinking of his own career. 'My wish, sir, was someday to have a military command of my own, not to become a commander of spies.'

'All in good time, Robert, for now, what we need is military intelligence. If war is to come, we need to be prepared for it. If that time should come, then we will be looking for military commanders.' Pym let the carrot dangle.

'Then, in that case, I would be willing to help Parliament teach this King a lesson.'

Overton had been drawn in.

Chapter Thirty-One

Mary entered the surgeon's tent just as Mathew was finishing tying off the new bandage on Matins' arm. At the sight of Martins she dropped the jar she was carrying and let out a half-stifled cry of alarm, at the same time stepping back in terror.

Mathew and Martins both froze momentarily turning simultaneously to look in her direction, Martins with an expression of shock on his face as he recognised Mary, and Mathew with a look of annoyance at being startled while treating a man he already knew to be dangerous. The jar crashed to the ground, shards of broken pot exploding across the floor of the tent, its contents soaking into the grass, giving off an aroma of *aniseed and alcohol*. Martins stood and stared at Mary, recognising the woman who had helped him from before. 'You!' was all he said.

Mary's hysterical voice filled the tent as she cried out, 'He's one of the men that killed Charles!'

Instinct kicked in immediately; the unarmed Martins made to dash for the tent door behind Mary, to try and escape. As he barged past her, she took hold of his injured arm, spinning him around. Martins recoiled away from the pain, falling backwards against a small table covered with pots and bowls. The table overbalanced, sending its contents crashing to the ground, the heavy earthenware shattering and filling the tent with more noise. Martins stumbled to regain his balance.

Mathew hadn't moved. He was still confused by Mary's outburst. He'd believed Martins to be involved in Elizabeth's killing, back in Hull, and had no idea of his other crimes.

'He's one of the men that killed Charles!' Mary called out again in a strained terrified voice.

Martins had got to his feet by the time Mathew had taken in the developing situation. Mathew leapt forward to grab hold of Martins, but even with only one good arm, Martins was still very strong, and his instinct for survival had not been dulled by his injury. The two men fell back against the table on which Mathew had his surgical instruments, sending them scattering across the interior of the tent. Matins' one good hand found the amputation knife as they both fell to the floor in a heap, with its curved, razor-sharp blade. He lashed out at Mathew, missing his face by a whisker. Mathew rolled to the side to avoid the back sweep from Matins' wild swing with the knife.

Quickly changing direction, Martins brought the amputation knife back and down. Mary screamed as the knife sliced through Mathew's shirtsleeve and into his forearm. The wound was long, but not too deep—it had caught Mathew as he jumped back to avoid the returning strike. Mary could see that Mathew was at a disadvantage and jumped onto their enemy's back. Grabbing hold of his hair in both hands, she yanked on it furiously. Instantly Martins swung around, trying to catch Mary with the knife. As she fell to the ground, her dress sliced open by a cut across the bodice, it was only the dress's whalebone stays that saved her from injury.

Martins once again found himself with his back to the entrance to the tent. Sensing his escape route to be close-by, he turned to flee and began to run. He arrived at the tent door at the same time a shadow appeared across the tent's entrance. Martins was brought to an abrupt and shuddering halt. Mathew and Mary watched him fall to his knees, then fall back into the tent, the handle of a large knife sticking upwards from his body.

Ethan stepped over the body and into the tent. 'What the hell's going on in here? It sounded like you were having your own personal war!'

Mary retreated to the furthest corner of the tent, sobbing uncontrollably, the realisation of what she had said in her outburst at seeing Martins ringing in her ears. In her original explanation of the death of Charles, she had said they had been stopped by one robber. She had now declared that there was more than one, but, in all the confusion, had Mathew noticed the contradiction in her story. Her mind a muddle from what had just happened, all she could hope for was that in the shock and confusion of the fight, Mathew would not remember the details of her cry of recognising Martins. Mathew looked down at Martins, the large meat knife protruding from just below his sternum, his mouth still open and an expression of shock on his face. While Ethan and Mathew looked on, Martins gave a sigh as his body relaxed and gave up its fight for life.

A bell rang out in the distance as he looked towards the tower. *It was time for Captain John Hotham to be led from his cell in the Tower of London by two soldiers carrying polearms, a chaplain repeating the Lord's Prayer, and*

walking ahead of him. The prisoner would probably have nothing to say. It was too late now anyway; there was no one around who would listen to him. He would not have slept at all; he would be making his peace with his God before it was too late.

The walk to the execution block isn't far from the tower; the chaplain will know that the prisoner will be able to see Tower Hill, the place of his execution, from the White Tower door as he is led down the steps to the parade yard and hope he retains his dignity in his last moments. The prisoner will take one last look around him as he was led slowly across the cobbled parade ground.

He will look at the buildings, and the soldiers going about their business, and they, in turn, will cast fleeting glances at him as they go by, not wanting to look into the face of a man who was about to die. He'll probably look at the sky they often do and offer up one last prayer as he watches the clouds scurrying across the firmament. Then he'll look at the ground, and watch his feet passing one in front of the other, over the smooth cobbles. He'll notice how the stones have been smoothed by years of wear from soldiers marching over them. The constant rubbing of their boots rounding off all the rough edges of stone, while the lines of mortar hold one to the other, each stone in its place. He'll walk past the Bloody Tower and along the narrow street to the Bell Tower, and then out across the moat, turning right, passing the Middle Tower and looking up Tower Hill to me, where his last moments of life will end.

As the small group walked past the Bell Tower, they picked up an escort of six more guards carrying halberds, not to stop the prisoner from escaping, but to keep the crowds and onlookers back. Their job was to ensure the prisoner and his escort safe passage through the crowds that gathered on such occasions.

He'll have a vision of his blood spilling across the scaffold, running between the boards and staining the grass beneath a bright red. A shiver will probably rake through his body, his knees will feel weak and unsteady, and a guard may need to steady him. Will he make it to the block without fainting or trying to run, he wondered?

The executioner watched his victim getting nearer, his heart beating faster and faster as the time drew closer for the execution. He had done this many times before, but it always made him anxious. He had become hardened to the work; it was not for him to pass judgement on the man's past deeds which had led him to this time and place, or to feel for the men he killed. He couldn't allow himself to become involved with them. After he had done his job, he would go to a tavern and get drunk, drunk enough to forget the face of the man who had given him a generous tip to make it a clean kill, and who had forgiven him for what he was about to do. But there was always tomorrow. Tomorrow he would have to do it all again, only this time, his victim was to be the father of today's condemned man. He allowed himself a moment's thought of the wife and mother at home and her distress at losing a husband and son. Then he pushed it from his mind.

After each execution day, he returned to his normal job as a waterman, ferrying passengers across the Thames, fighting the tide's pull on his little boat, feeling the pain in his hands, arms and back as he pulled on the oars. Was the physical pain his penance for the secret work he did in the Tower, he wondered? Through the pain, he would silently pray for forgiveness and hope that when it was his turn to stand in front of the Lord, He, would have sympathy on a poor man doing what he had to, in order to support his family.

'I've killed him,' Ethan Goodman said in disbelief, staring at the corpse of Martins lying on the ground.

'Thank God, you did,' Mathew said with relief. 'He nearly killed me.' The surgeon showed Ethan the knife wound to his arm. Mary had her hands wrapped up in her apron as she held it over her face and sobbed in the corner.

'What made him go mad like that?' asked Ethan.

'Mary recognised him as one of the robbers that attacked her and killed her husband. He tried to make a run for it, Mary made a grab for him, then it all got confused until you came to the door and he ran onto your knife,' explained Mathew.

'He's dead!' wailed Mary.

'What are we going to do with him?' asked Ethan. 'We'll have to tell Captain Hewitt. There's going to be hell to pay for this.'

'No,' responded Mathew. 'I need time to think.'

He moved across to Mary, guiding her to a stool. 'Mary. Mary, listen. It's going to be all right.' Mathew picked up a linen cloth from the floor and dried her tears. Kneeling in front of her, he gave her a hug of reassurance. Mary responded by laying her head on his shoulder, her sobs fading at the feeling of security he instilled in her.

Mathew stood and turned to face Ethan. The normally jolly cook with an answer for everything was looking shocked and pale, his hands shaking. Mathew put the stool

Martins had been using upright and sat the pale-looking Ethan on it. He found his bottle of smelling salts, (crystals of dried *ammonia*,) and passed it under Ethan's nose. The large man recoiled from the smell instantly, his head clearing.

'Mary,' Mathew ordered, 'go and find Mortimer and bring him here. Don't tell him why it'll take too long. Just tell him I need him.'

Mary looked from Mathew to Ethan, then side-stepping Martins' body, fled from the surgeon's tent.

'Ethan, listen to me,' Mathew told his friend. 'I can't have the body found here. I would have too much explaining to do. I need to get rid of him quietly, for Mary's sake as much as mine. All you really need to know is that he is, or was a murderer. Will you take my word of honour on it?' Mathew rested his hands on Ethan's shoulders. 'Please,' he added, 'trust me.'

'I suppose it would be hard to explain how my knife found its way into Matins' chest,' Ethan said, not convinced he was doing the right thing. 'But what'll we do with him?'

Mary returned with Mortimer. As the latter took in the scene inside the surgeon's tent, a look of amazement appeared on his face.

'What the fuck happened here?' Mortimer blurted out in his rough East Yorkshire voice. 'Begging your pardon Mary, I forgot myself.'

'We need to hide him somewhere, 'till we can get rid of him.' Mathew looked to Mortimer for inspiration.

'You can hide him in the back of my wagon tonight,' Mortimer suggested. 'There's plenty of room. I can cover him with some old sacks, behind my toolbox.'

'But, he'll start to stink soon, and his body will begin to seep fluids when his muscles relax. He'll be found by the soldiers,' Matthew interjected, not liking the idea.

'Not if we wrap him in an oilskin and put some sweet-smelling stuff in with him to cover the smell,' suggested Mortimer.

The four of them were quiet for a moment.

Mathew was the first to speak: 'I've got plenty of linen, and I could get some linseed oil from my father's wheelwright shop. If Mary could make a shroud to wrap him in, while I fetch the linseed oil. I could soak the shroud in the linseed to make it waterproof, sew Martins into the shroud adding some sweet-smelling herbs to disguise the smell. Hopefully, that should do until we break camp in a couple of days. If we do our best to ensure we are amongst the last to leave, we can hang back from the others in the baggage-train, then stop, and bury him in the corner of a field, once we are on our way to Doncaster.'

Ethan Goodman was still in shock and not thinking coherently. For the moment he was conceding to Mathew's will, but when he came to his senses, Mathew knew that he was going to have to find a better explanation for his friend to explain his reluctance to report the accidental killing of Martins to the officers.

Mathew sat in a tavern on Silver Street with Major Overton. He had told him all that had happened and all that he had learnt about the king's plans to move to Doncaster.

'Well my friend I owe you a great deal,' the newly promoted officer told him. 'You have probably saved the lives of many people in this town, but I must ask you an important question: would you do it again? Will you go back and continue to work as a surgeon in the King's Army, sending reports back to me on their movements? You will be paid well by Parliament; the money could be sent to your family for safekeeping if you wish.'

Mathew took a big swallow of his beer. 'Me? Be an agent for Parliament again? It's hard to imagine really. I suppose as I've still got the other two murderers to catch up with before I leave the army, I may as well carry on helping you. I now know by some strange twist of fate that the same men that killed Elizabeth and her father also killed my brother Charles. God has already entwined my life with theirs for reasons of his own choosing. So it may be God's will that I am your agent, but my priority is to find Wilkes and Franks. Mary has already told me how she recognised Martins—that he was one the robbers that attacked them on the Westwood while she was out walking with Charles.'

Overton nodded as he listened to Mathew, understanding his motivation for continuing his work as a spy, but pleased and unashamed of the way he was using him for his own ends. Mathew needed to get back to Beverley. He needed to say goodbye to his father and Henry before he followed the army to Doncaster. He took his leave of Overton and left him at the door of the tavern. Major Overton watched him go, his mind racing ahead with plans for what was to come. The major had no pangs of conscience about using Mathew and the others. It was all for the sake of the greater good as far as he was concerned.

Back at the camp on the Westwood, the final touches were being made to the wagons to prepare them for their journey.

Mathew and Mary had told Ethan enough of how Martins and his friends had killed Elizabeth and Charles to justify why they didn't want to involve anyone else in the circumstances of how Martins had died. Mary had continued the lie and changed her story; now saying that more than one robber had confronted her and Charles, during that fateful day on the Westwood. Had it not been Ethan who had actually struck the killing blow, the genial cook may not have been convinced to keep quiet, but he had agreed, and now the four of them: Mathew, Mary, Mortimer and Ethan were truly bound together by the secrets they carried.

With everything packed into their wagon, Mathew and Mary set off to follow the wagons of Ethan Goodman and Charles Mortimer. 'Walk on,' Mathew called to the horses drawing his wagon. The wagon creaked forward out of the ruts the wheels had created while it stood on the soft earth. Once on the road, Mathew turned to Mary, 'Have no fear. I will track down these killers no matter where they try and hide.

Newburg Priory

Newburgh Priory had initially been an Augustinian Priory dating back to 1145. It had provided priests to the surrounding churches in return for gifts of land and money from the wealthy local landowners. Following the Dissolution of the Monasteries, the property was acquired by Anthony Belasyse, one of Henry VIII's chaplains.

The Rod of Asclepius and Caduceus

The Rod of Asclepius is an ancient Greek symbol associated with medicine, consisting of two serpents coiled around the rod of knowledge, with two wings on the top. The snakes symbolise the keeping of secrets (Medical knowledge, diligence and prudence. The wings represent Hermes taking that knowledge to help others.) In Greek religion and mythology, Asclepius was the god of medicine and healing.

The Real historical characters depicted in this story.

Captain Robert Overton   1609-1678
Educated at St John's College Cambridge and served in the
East Yorkshire Trained Bands at the start of the English
Civil War. Given the rank of Colonel with the New Model
Army by Sir Thomas Fairfax in 1645, he rose to the rank of
Major General.

Earl of Newcastle   1592-1676
William Cavendish, polymath, swordsman, politician,
diplomat and soldier. A loyal supporter of the King, but
after defeat at Marston Moor, he and his family left
England for Europe. Was Made Duke by Charles II for the
support he gave to Charles's father during the war.

Sir John Hotham   1589-1645
1st Baronet of Scorborough and Member of Parliament for
Beverley, he became Military Governor of Hull for
Parliament. Was accused of treachery and executed.

Capt John Hotham   1610-1645
A captain in the Hull Trained Bands at the start of the Civil
War, he was the son of Sir John Hotham. Was accused of
treachery and executed with his father in the Tower of
London.

Charles I   1600-1649
King of England 1626-1649, second son of James VI of Scotland. Charles's elder brother Henry, Prince of Wales died in 1612. Charles, frequently quarrelled with his Parliament, believing he ruled by divine right.

Michael Warton   1623-1688
The Warton's were rich Hull merchants who became the wealthiest family in Beverley in the seventeenth century. By 1657 they had a house built into the North Bar opposite that of Lady Gee.

Lt Col Sir Edward Duncombe
Royalist officer in the regiment of The Kings Guard of Dragoons, Duncombe changed sides in 1644 when the Scots entered Yorkshire.

Sir John Meldrum   d.1645
A soldier of Scottish origin who spent 36 years in the service of the Stuart kings of Scotland and England. In 1642, he found himself opposed to the policies of Charles' government and supported the Parliamentarian cause in the Civil War. A captain in the Hull Trained Bands, he was killed at the siege of Scarborough Castle.

Captain William Legge   1608-1670
On 7 August 1638 Legge was commissioned to inspect the fortifications of Newcastle and Hull and to put both in a state of defence. He was appointed Master of the Kings Armoury and Lieutenant of the Ordinance for the first Bishops' War.

Capt John Goodricke   1617 - 1670

During the Civil Wars, he supported the King and suffered in the Royal cause. He was imprisoned at Manchester and later in the Tower of London and was fined £1,508, (or £1,200, with £40 a year) on 23 November 1646.

Sir Peregrine Pelham   1602-1650

A prosperous merchant of Hull, Peregrine Pelham was appointed town sheriff in 1636 and elected to the Long Parliament as MP for Hull in January 1641. He supported Sir John Hotham in his refusal to allow King Charles to enter the city in April 1642, thus securing the northern arsenal for Parliament. A quarrel broke out between Pelham and Hotham. Pelham was obliged to answer before Parliament Hotham's accusation that he had tried to subvert the town. He had his revenge two years later when Hotham and his son were arrested for plotting to betray Hull to the Royalists.

John Belasyse   1615-1689

MP and the King's intelligence officer in the North of England.

Thomas Belasyse   1627-1700

Military commander, he rose to the rank of Major General in the Kings army.

Lady Gee

Wife to William Gee, Alderman of Hull, gave residence to King Charles in her home next to Beverley Bar in 1642 during the first siege of Hull.

Mr James Nelthorp
Mayor of Beverley in 1642

Thomas Beckwith
In 1642, attempted to bribe two garrison officers into
betraying Beverley

Henry Barnard   **d.1661**
Royalist, Alderman and ex-Mayor of Hull

About the Author

Steven Turner-Bone was born in Hull. It was at school that he gained a love of history and science. After leaving school, he trained to be a chef, working as a Commis Chef at the Savoy Hotel, London. He has retained a love of cooking, especially recipes from historical cookbooks. His interest in science supported his research into historical medicine, and it is a combination of history, cooking and medicine that feature in his books that make them so different from other historical novels.

In 1974 he made the huge leap from catering into the computer industry, where he met his wife, Sue. Later as their children grew up, they all joined a historical re-enactment group, where Steven started to learn about the history of medicine and surgery, buy historical medical textbooks and learn all he could on the subject. Steven has toured the country with his historical re-enactment group for many years, giving talks on medicine and surgery from the seventeenth century.

Writing has come late in life to Steven, but with two books published and more in the pipeline. It is proving to be the start of a promising new career.

Bibliography

Atlas of the English Civil War
By P R Newman

Edgehill 1642
By Peter Young

The English Civil War Day By Day
By Wilfred Emberton

Coventry
By David McGrory

The Diary of John Jackson Sometime Macebearer of
Beverley
By Pamela Hopkins

Thorne Local History Society
Supported by Thorne Moorends Regeneration Partnership
2014

*Office for National Statistics: Census 2001: Parish
Headcounts: Doncaster*
Retrieved 26 August 2009

Historic England. 'Church of St Nicholas, Thorne
(334693)'

Alan Macfarlane 2002 paper on BODILY HYGIENE
Colour Atlas of Infectious Diseases

By Ronald T D Edmond, H A K Rowland and Philip D Welsby

A Compendium of the Theory and Practice of Chirurgery in seven books
By William Salmon M.D. original 1698 edition.

Poque card game
Source: Oxford Guide to Card Games

Disease, The Extraordinary stories behind Histories Deadliest Killers.
By Mary Dobson

Dr Sydenham's Compleat Method of Curing almost all Diseases.
By Thomas Sydenham, original 1695 Edition

Alan Salt, at The Old Harington Cheese Shop, Derbyshire.

The Furie of the Ordnance
By Stephen Bull

Three and Fifty Instruments of Chirurgery, London 1631.
By Ambrose Pare. reprinted in 1975 by Theatrum Orbis Terrarum Ltd
Enchiridion Medicum, Manual of Physick
By Prof Robert Johnson MD, London. original1684edition

The Medieval Cookbook
By Maggie Black
The Shakespeare Cookbook
By Andrew and Maureen Dalby

Food and Cooking in 17th Century Britain.
By Peter Brears

Pepys at Table
Christopher Driver and Michelle Berriedale-Johnson

http://www.nottshistory.org.uk/gill1904/charlesi.htm
description of Charles I standard raised at Nottingham 1642

Now you can buy any of these books direct from the publisher.

Friends and Enemies

The Enemy Within

Farewell to a friend

To order simply call this number

07564640442

OR

Facebook: Steven Turner-Bone

OR

Email: steventurnerbone@aol.com

Prices and availability subject to change without notice.